THIS is the world of the celebrities, of the fashion king and drag queen, of orgiastic hedonism in moments stolen from the serious business of Self and Status, of big money and no lives to spend it on.

THIS is the story of the game—The Fame Game—in which celebrities feed on celebrities, in which everything from a lunch to a love affair is a calculated move, the game that's played day and night (quit for a breather and you lose!) by today's packaged people.

ᘖᘗᘖᘗᘖᘗᘖᘗᘖᘗᘖᘗᘖᘗᘖᘗᘖᘗᘖᘗᘖᘗᘖᘗᘖᘗᘖᘗᘖ

The
Fame Game

ଽଽଽଽଽଽଽଽଽଽଽଽଽଽଽଽଽଽଽଽଽଽଽଽ

RONA JAFFE

A FAWCETT CREST BOOK
Fawcett Publications, Inc., Greenwich, Conn.

THE FAME GAME

THIS BOOK CONTAINS THE COMPLETE TEXT OF THE
ORIGINAL HARDCOVER EDITION.

A Fawcett Crest Book reprinted by arrangement with
Random House, Inc.

Library of Congress Catalog Card Number: 76-85553

Published by Fawcett World Library
67 West 44th Street, New York, N.Y. 10036
Printed in the United States of America
September 1970

For Jack Doroshow

CHAPTER

ONE

THIS is the last time, I swear, the last time I'll ever ride the subway, Gerry Thompson thought, feeling like Scarlett O'Hara when she dug out the turnip from the burned ruins of Atlanta. But this was New York, no burned ruin; it was life, excitement, the maddening, indifferent lover, her town even though she had not been born here, even though she had run away and returned. New York was a new job, new love, the smell of new paint in a new apartment. New York was promise even though all around you you saw failure. She gouged her way through the nine a.m. rush hour crowd, being gouged in return, stepped over a drunk left over from the night before, and emerged in the shriek of life that was Fifty-seventh Street.

The Plaza Hotel stood like an oasis in the wasteland of ugly progress. Whenever she saw it she imagined a wealthy septuagenarian peering out of one of its high windows, refusing to come out ever again into the tasteless mess below. That tasteless mess was where it was all happening. Even the Plaza was not immune; there was an office in there now, operating out of a suite, and that was where Gerry was going to work as Girl Friday to the super-publicist—personal manager Sam Leo Libra.

She had never met him. She had been hired by an employment agency in New York because Sam Leo Libra had been

in California where he kept his main office. He was in New
York now to open a permanent East Coast office, which
would eventually be in one of those new office buildings. The
employment agency woman had looked her over carefully as
if she were casting her: a medium-sized twenty-six-year-old
girl with shiny auburn hair, guileless green eyes, and freckles,
who smiled a lot, who looked intelligent, friendly, and not
easily ruffled; the sort of girl you would not hesitate to ask
for directions in the street.

"Five years doing publicity for motion pictures here and in
Paris and Rome," the woman said thoughtfully. "Why did
you leave?"

"Because I never saw Paris and Rome—all I ever saw was
the inside of the office there from nine in the morning until
eight thirty at night and then I was too tired to go anywhere."

"Is money important to you?"

"I'm too old to work for nothing just because the job is
interesting."

"And too experienced." The woman smiled. "You won't be
working for nothing, but you'll be around a great deal of
money, people making what seems like a ridiculous fortune
for what they seem to be contributing to the world, and you
may begin to think you're underpaid."

"I don't expect to be paid as a star," Gerry said.

"You'll be getting two hundred a week."

"My God."

"Don't be so delighted," the woman said. "A year from
now you won't think it's so much. You'll still be working
from nine in the morning until eight thirty at night, sometimes longer. You'll have to be able to keep secrets, defend
the wicked, lie beautifully, and never lose that look of
wholesome happiness. Can you do that?"

"I've been doing it for years," Gerry lied beautifully.

"I trust you have your own apartment."

"What difference does that make?"

"The telephone. Mr. Libra doesn't like roommates tying up
the phone. You may have to get another line in any case, but
if you do, he'll pay for it."

"I live alone," Gerry said.

"And get an answering service."

"Who pays for that?"

The woman looked at her shrewdly. "I should think you'd
need one for your social life—you'll be working many nights,

you know. You can deduct it from your taxes."

I suppose those people like to take over everybody's life, Gerry thought, wondering what this Libra was like. But on two hundred a week, who was she to complain? She'd always wanted an answering service anyway, not that she knew anyone she wanted to call her. New York had changed in the two years she had been in Europe: all the exciting single men had vanished, or perhaps she had changed.

"Oh, yes," the woman said, not looking at her for the first time since the interview had started. "And he wants to know how often you bathe."

"What?"

"Don't look at me. He wants to know."

"Am I supposed to be a Girl Friday or a call girl?"

"I guess he had a dirty secretary once."

"Well, every day, naturally," Gerry said indignantly.

"Only once a day?"

She stared at the woman. She didn't look any cleaner than anyone else Gerry had seen. "Once a day," Gerry said. "And I wash my hair twice a week and brush my teeth after every meal. How often does he bathe?"

"My dear, he's always damp," the woman said.

That had been last Thursday, and on Friday Gerry had gone out and rented a new apartment on the third floor of a reconditioned brownstone in the East Seventies: three rooms with a working fireplace and a view of trees, for two hundred and fifty dollars a month. It was a steal, and she couldn't afford it. But next week she would be out of her Greenwich Village rat-trap, and there would be the smell of new paint. There would be a green phone in the bedroom, a white phone in the living room, and a pink phone on the bathroom wall. With the last of her salary from Europe, except what she would need for food and subway fare, she bought a seventeen-dollar bottle of pink Vita-bath. *Now let him fire me!* she thought.

So here she was on a Monday morning in March, in air that was neither chill nor warm but a heady combination of both, bathed and shampooed and perfumed, neatly made up (her hand had been shaking so much from nervousness that morning that it had taken half an hour to put on her false eyelashes), immaculately dressed, looking more like a girl on a date than a Girl Friday—but wasn't that what Girl Fridays were supposed to look like today? It occurred to her that she was already deeply involved in her job, if only because she had involved herself in debt and could not afford to lose it. But she had always known that she would settle in New York, on her own terms; with an interesting, challenging job, a good apartment of her own, and enough money to feel she was a grown-up at last. This new job *had* to work out; even if it was horrible she loved it already.

The door to Sam Leo Libra's suite was open, propped open by a metal cart holding a stack of matched Vuitton luggage six feet high. Two bellboys were busy unloading it and adding the suitcases to the assortment, also matched, that lined the walls of the foyer. A small, thin, blond girl with her hair in two ponytails sticking out at each side, in a plaid mini-suit, a schoolboy's tie, and textured white stockings, was standing inside the foyer with a clipboard in her hands and a pair of huge tortoise-rimmed glasses balanced on her little nose.

"There are seventy-two pieces!" the girl was repeating crossly. "Seventy-two pieces, and don't you dare let one get in here before I've counted it! Where are the coats? Where are the coats?"

"They're on the elevator," one of the bellboys said.

"You left my mink coat on the *elevator?*"

"The elevator operator will watch it, madam."

"Excuse me," Gerry said, "I'm Geraldine Thompson, Mr. Libra's new assistant. Is he here?"

"I don't know; I didn't count him," the girl said. She pushed the enormous glasses up on her nose and looked at Gerry pleasantly. "I'm his wife, Lizzie Libra."

She wasn't a little girl at all —she was forty years old. It was a shock: the tininess, the blond ponytails, the little-girl clothes, and then suddenly the wicked little face, the eyes circled by crow's feet magnified by the lenses of the glasses. It wasn't an unpleasant shock but rather interesting.

"What do they call you? Gerry?"

"Yes."

"Well, you can call Room Service and tell them to get that trash out of here, and then have them bring some more coffee and some Danish—there'll be people coming in all morning. Get cigarettes too, one pack of each brand and six packs of Gauloise for me. Have you met my husband?"

"No. I was hired here while he was on the Coast."

"You'll find him in there," Lizzie Libra said, waving at the suite, and went back to her list.

Gerry went down the carpeted foyer into the large living

room. Tall windows gave a view of Central Park, the fountain on the Plaza, and the tiny hansom cabs waiting across the street. It was absolutely still except for a soft sound that sounded like breathing. She realized that all the windows were closed and the sound came from an air conditioner and a humidifier that had been newly installed, their warranty tags still attached. There were crystal vases of fresh flowers everywhere. God, it was hot and humid, like a greenhouse. The smell of the flowers rose up in the artificially humid air and on an empty stomach this early in the morning it was a little sickening. She went over to the window but discovered all the windows had been sealed shut. Not a breath of street air or a particle of grit could enter. She lit a cigarette and watched the smoke vanish like magic.

The customary painting above the fireplace had been replaced by a life-sized oil painting of Sylvia Polydor, one of the great ladies of the screen, who had been Sam Leo Libra's first really famous client. People always said: "Oh, Sam Leo Libra, that's Sylvia Polydor's manager." Her portrait was elaborately framed and lit from below by one of those oil painting lights. It was like someone in business framing his first dollar bill.

On the desk there was an office telephone the size of a baby switchboard, bristling with push buttons. Next to it was the hotel telephone. Gerry called Room Service and then located the rest of the office equipment: the typewriter, the address books, the steno pads and pencils, the appointment book. Now there was nothing to do but wait. The breathing of the humidifier felt like a monster in the room with her. She wandered into the bedroom.

The bedroom was immaculate although more Vuitton suitcases of various sizes and shapes were arranged about the wall space. There were two double beds separated by a night table with a push-button phone on it. The windows in here had been sealed shut too, and there was a new air conditioner and humidifier breathing away. There were no flowers. She remembered her mother, who was a terrified woman, often saying that you should never sleep with flowers in the room because they breathed your air and there was not enough for you.

"Mr. Libra?" she said timidly.

There was no answer. No one was there. The bathroom door was ajar, with the light on.

"Mr. Libra?"

Maybe there *was* no Mr. Libra. Maybe he was like the Wizard of Oz, just an amplified voice and a lot of machines. She felt so nervous she had to go to the bathroom immediately. She opened the door and went in.

The floor of the bathroom was partially covered by clean white towels. At the far end, kneeling on the tile and completely engrossed in his task, was a man with maroon-colored hair in a maroon silk bathrobe, painstakingly scrubbing the marble floor with Lysol.

Gerry let out what must have sounded like a startled squeak and backed out of the bathroom, but not fast enough, for the man looked up. An expression of terror crossed his face, then anger. She knew then who it was: the Wizard of Oz himself, behind his own battery of machines and protection.

"Who are you and what do you want?" he said sharply.

"I'm Mr. Libra's Girl Friday and I'll use the bathroom when you're finished, sir. I'm sorry to have bothered you, I didn't see you," she said, smiling weakly and waving her hands like a duck. What an impression she was making! He'd probably either fire her right now or make her finish cleaning the already clean floor, and she couldn't decide which would be worse.

Sam Leo Libra stood up and walked carefully across the clean towels. He looked calm now. She noticed that his hairline was very low, and his hair was indeed damp, glistening as if he had just washed it. Reddish-brown hair sprouted from the neck of the immaculate white T-shirt he wore beneath the maroon silk robe and crawled down his wrists and the backs of his white hands. That hair, too, glistened with health. He looked like a very clean, newly washed ape.

"You're Miss Thompson," he said.

"Yes, sir."

"I'll call you Gerry, you call me Mr. Libra, not sir. I'm not that old."

"Yes, Mr. Libra." She guessed him to be about forty, the same age as his wife.

"You can't trust a new place," he said, gesturing at the immaculate bathroom. "They clean it, but you never know what kind of slobs were there before. Don't you agree?"

"Of course."

"Why don't you go down in the lobby to the Ladies' Room. I'll be through here in about fifteen minutes."

The power play, she thought, beginning to wonder if she

was going to be able to like him. *Make the employees know their place. The public Ladies' Room is good enough for her. Okay, if he wants to play, I can play too.*

"I'll be right back," she said sweetly.

She took her time coming back, stopping at the magazine stand to buy a newspaper. The papers were full of second-page obituaries devoted to the recent death and funeral of Douglas Henry, one of the old-time movie stars with two first names. She read about it coming up in the elevator: one of the pallbearers had been Douglas Henry's personal manager and publicist, Sam Leo Libra. It was well known, the newspaper said, that Libra kept only twelve clients, no more, no less, and there was speculation in Hollywood and New York about who would be chosen to take Douglas Henry's place in the Libra stable.

In the hall just outside the suite there was a commotion. The floor policeman was there, chasing away three teen-aged girls. Two of the girls looked about fourteen, although who could tell, the way they were dressed. The thing that gave them away was their pimples, carefully disguised under layers of beige make-up. They were dressed as if they were going to a discothèque, with false eyelashes and day glo plastic mini-dresses. The third girl was weird: she was about four feet eleven, with a scared little face and enormous eyes, and must have weighed seventy-five pounds. She looked like the Poor Pitiful Pearl doll. She had tears in her eyes. The other two girls only looked aggressive and annoyed.

"Please," said Poor Pitiful Pearl. "Oh, please! We've been waiting here since six o'clock this morning. We just want to *look* at him."

"And we want to give him this Mad Daddy beanbag we made," said Aggressive Number One.

"You can't hang around here," the cop said. "You're disturbing the guests."

"We won't say a word," said Aggressive Number Two.

"You'll just have to wait in the street. Go on, scoot!" The cop raised his hand meanacingly. The little scared one cringed, the other two giggled.

"Can we leave the beanbag?" asked Number One.

"Oh, don't *leave* it, Donna," squealed Number Two. "Then we'll *never* see him."

"This Mad Daddy person is not a guest here," said the cop. "I told you that but you won't believe me."

"We believe you," said Donna, "but we know he's coming here because his press agent lives here."

Press agent, Gerry thought, amused. How Libra would cringe.

"*She* works there!" Number Two screamed, making a rush for Gerry. "Is Mad Daddy coming? Is he?"

"I don't know who Mad Daddy *is,*" Gerry said.

"You don't?" the three girls chorused in amazement.

"No."

"He's darling!"

"Well, if you like, I can see that he gets his present if and when he comes."

"What do you think, Michelle?" asked Donna.

"I don't know. What do you think, Barrie?"

Poor Pitiful Pearl was wringing her hands. "I just think we should wait in the street," she said softly.

Michelle looked at her oversized wristwatch. "I can't, I'll be late for English class again."

"You have to be prepared to make sacrifices . . ." Barrie murmured.

"Yeah, well I don't want to get *flunked.*"

"Discuss it on the street," the cop said, and herded the girls into the elevator.

Gerry watched the cage descend and smiled at the security cop. She remembered very well when she had been like that, and she felt sorry for the kids.

"This is nothing," the cop said. "You should have seen with the Beatles. We caught a kid in the air shaft. She almost suffocated."

In the suite Lizzie Libra had disposed of the last of the seventy-two pieces of luggage and Room Service had cleared away the breakfast dishes and delivered an enormous order of coffee and Danish pastries. Sam Leo Libra, now dressed in a silver-gray silk suit and a thin silver-gray knitted tie, was arranging the packs of cigarettes in a large Baccarat crystal bowl on the coffee table in front of the couch. The smell of disinfectant floated lightly in the air, mingling with the sweeter smell of the flowers.

"You get your ass out of here now, Lizzie," he said pleasantly. "Do you have plans for the day?"

"I'm going to lunch with Elaine Fellin and then I'm going

to my shrink. Then I'll probably go shopping to recover from the shrink."

"That's good."

"Elaine is picking me up here at twelve."

"Well, what are you going to do until then?"

"Would you believe get dressed?" Lizzie Libra marched into the bedroom and shut the door. Then she opened it again and stuck her head out. "My husband," she said to Gerry sarcastically, "he's so concerned about me." She shut the door.

"I'm not concerned about you," Libra yelled. "I just want to be sure you get your ass out of here while I'm working." He turned to Gerry pleasantly. "My wife always works up a mad at me just before she goes to her analyst so she'll have something to tell him to make him think he's worth all that money I pay him."

"Who's Mad Daddy?" Gerry asked.

"If you don't know now you'll know soon," Libra said. "He's got this afternoon kids' show on television that the teen-agers have picked up on. He's turned into their love idol. I'm getting the show changed to a night-time slot, probably midnight, next month. I'll know for sure in a day or two. Then everybody in the country will know him."

"A kiddie show at midnight?"

"Why not? Did you ever hear of one before?"

"No, I hadn't," Gerry said, embarrassed. There was something about this man that made her feel defensive, as if the idea of a children's television show at midnight was perfectly plausible, if not a stroke of genius, and it was only her stupidity that prevented her from realizing it.

Libra looked at his Cartier wristwatch. "Before the people start coming in I'll fill you in a little about what I do. You can't expect to learn it all at once, but you can try to keep up or you'll be no use to me. Do you want some coffee?"

"Thanks."

To her surprise, he rushed over to the table and poured the coffee for her. "Cream and sugar?"

"Black, please."

"Danish?"

She was starving, but she was afraid it would stick in her throat. "Maybe later, thanks."

He handed her the coffee and a napkin. "Sit down. Now, at three thirty we'll watch the Mad Daddy Show and you'll see what he's all about. His wife Elaine will be here to pick up Lizzie for lunch. Mad Daddy's Christian name, would you believe Jewish, is Moishe—Moishe Fellin. When you meet him in a day or two, call him Daddy. If you call him Moishe he'll have a coronary occlusion on the spot and I'll lose a client. I already lost one that way three days ago."

"I know. I read it in the papers."

"Damn shame," Libra said. "He was a grand old man and a great talent. You don't see many like him these days. Today they're mostly schmucks, which is where I come in, trying to find the few good ones and see that they get the success they deserve. You may not realize it, but you soon will—I perform a public service. With all the talent in the world, many of them would never get there at all if it weren't for me. Now, as I'm sure you know, I always have twelve clients, no more, no less. I like to think of them as my Dirty Dozen." He smiled. "I give each of them a one-year contract, which keeps them insecure. It's very important in this business to keep the talent insecure. Otherwise they begin to believe the lies I tell about them and they think they're too good for the man who created them in the first place through his toil and sweat—that's me. If they're good and it works out, I renew the contract."

"May I ask you a question?" Gerry said.

"Please do. As many as you want."

"Well, if they do get big, as you say, then what's to prevent them from going to someone else after the contract is up?"

Libra smiled like the Cheshire Cat. "Insecurity. That's why I tear them down. You'll see. You may sometimes think I'm cruel, but it's good for them, because I'm the best person for them and this is where they should stay no matter who else woos them once they make it. There are always managers and publicists waiting to woo clients who are already famous, but who takes the chances I do on semi-unknowns? Why should somebody else with less imagination and talent than I have reap the rewards of what I planted and cared for, huh?"

"You're right," Gerry said.

"Of course I'm right. There's something else you ought to know. A celebrity, no matter how big he gets, thinks it's all going to be taken away from him tomorrow. Even when he's gotten up to the top of Mount Everest he thinks he's going to fall right off. And I never let them forget that. Because do you know something? They're right."

"I'm not sure I agree with you," Gerry said. "I mean, a Judy Garland, for example; everybody loves her even when she comes out on the stage hoarse."

His eyes narrowed with genuine anger. "Listen, you, I can send you right back to that employment agency where I found you and that'll be the end of you."

"I'm sorry."

"You can be replaced in five minutes. I only have to pick up this phone. Then you can go right back to your schlock publicity job with some jerk movie company. Do you want to do that?"

"No, sir."

"Then what do you say?"

"I'm sorry. I guess I'll just have to learn." She felt like a fool. She should never have mentioned Judy Garland; he was probably jealous because he didn't have her for a client. She didn't even know this man and he was yelling at her as if she was a cretin. She knew her face was getting red.

"I only took you on because I like to give young people a chance. You're really too young for this job. And I wanted someone less attractive. You don't look serious."

"I am serious!"

"Then what do you say?"

"I'm sorry. I said I was sorry."

"Say: 'Please let me stay, I'll be good.' " His eyes stared into hers like that game she used to play when she was a kid: Whoever blinks first loses. She could feel tears of rage and frustration beginning to spill over and she blinked. She put down the coffee cup, carefully so not to break it because what she really wanted to do was hurl it across the room, and went for her coat.

Libra didn't say anything, he just watched her. She took her coat out of the closet and put it on. "Good-bye, Mr. Libra," she said pleasantly.

Her hand was on the doorknob when she heard him laughing. "Red hair and a temper," he said. "How trite."

"You should know," she said with revolting sweetness.

"Take off your coat, you asshole, and sit down."

"I wouldn't dream of it."

"You're not fired."

"I know, I'm quitting."

He strode over to her and took her by the shoulders. "Sit down . . . come on, I love you. Sit down. I wouldn't have an ugly girl around here. They depress me. Come on."

"You're like somebody in brainwashing school," Gerry said. To her horror she realized she was beginning to cry in earnest. She was glad she had not eaten any breakfast or she might have thrown up.

"That's the whole point," Libra said sweetly. He helped her off with her coat and handed her his monogrammed handkerchief. "I just wanted to show you how I treat my clients to keep them insecure. You see now how well it works. The only reason you were ready to leave is that this job isn't your whole life like their success is theirs. But I want you to know what I do because you're going to be very important to me. Your job will be to be sweet and cuddly and pick up the pieces I break. It's a perfect balance and everybody will be happy. Now sit down."

"I have one stipulation," Gerry said.

He looked at her with the pleasant superiority of a teacher humoring a first-grader who has just thrown a tantrum. "All right."

"You are never, never, repeat, never, to call me asshole again, or any name remotely like it."

"All right," he said, amused.

Oh my God, he's won, she thought. *He's won, and I never hated anybody so much in my life. He's made it seem as if I was ridiculous to mind what he called me. He's managed to make me feel humorless and square and I don't even know how it happened.* But in a funny way, she admired him. He obviously had many insecurities of his own—that was an understatement—look at him, Lady Macbeth, scrubbing everything and calling his clients the Dirty Dozen: if that wasn't Freudian, what was? He probably hated everything about himself. She felt almost sorry for him. He seemed to need something in her that she had to give; perhaps her clarity as an outsider. At any rate he was certainly the most interesting man she had ever met. Perhaps she could win him over . . . perhaps they could even become friends.

The doorbell rang. Libra looked at her. She fought back a smile and went to the door and opened it.

There stood a six-foot vision in white suede. He was smiling with capped white Chiclets, and his dark hair was neatly cut in a Prince Valiant fringe above navy blue eyes. He was wearing an immaculate white suede suit with a Mao collar, and white alligator loafers. He had a white attaché case in his hand.

"I'm here to see the vicious Libran," the white-suede vision said. "Tell him Mr. Nelson is here, as in Rockefeller."

"Hello, Nelson," Libra said. "Come on in. This is my new baby sitter, Gerry Thompson. She'll take care of all your needs when I'm not here. Gerry, this is Mr. Nelson, the society hairdresser, my client."

"My, she's pretty," Nelson said, as if she were not there. "Where's Lizzie?"

"In the bedroom," Libra said.

"I came to see you, of course, but as long as she's here I'll do her hair. I want to welcome you to New York. We're all so glad you'll be among the living again."

"Not all the time," Libra said. "I'm keeping the old office too."

Nelson clucked. "The Sam Leo Libra Doll—you wind it up and it flies back and forth to California."

"Nelson is my personal creation," Sam Leo Libra said. "You don't mind if I tell Gerry, do you?"

"I don't mind. I owe everything to you."

"When Nelson came to me he was just struggling along, with a lot of talent but no way to sell it. He used to wear a black leather jacket with a fur lining with fleas in it."

"I never had *fleas* . . . !"

"And he rode around on a big black motorcycle. He was burning hair in a dump in the Village where they played rock 'n' roll all day and the clients danced when they weren't having their hair set. I took one look at him in that black leather and I told him: 'Nelson, you'll never get anywhere like this. You look like the gutter, and the gutter is where you'll stay. I want you all in white. White is clean, it's respectable, it inspires trust like a doctor.' At first he whined."

"You wanted me in white suede," Nelson said. "Hair sticks to suede."

"So I decided that for work he would wear a white kid suit, something soft and clean and slippery. And whenever he wasn't at work he would wear white suede, to keep up the image. Notice the haircut. He looks like the White Knight. Then I turned him on to several of my more glamorous clients, he did their hair, I sent them to parties and got them and their hair into the columns. Mr. Nelson is now a superstar."

"Speaking of clients," Nelson said, "I'm now doing *both* of the B.P.'s. I do them both at home. Her *and* him. He won't let anybody else touch his hair now."

"The B.P.'s," Libra said to Gerry, "Peter and Penny Potter. The Beautiful People. You've read about them."

She certainly had. You couldn't avoid reading about them, *ad nauseam;* what they wore, where they went, how their apartment was decorated, what they served at dinner parties, what their guests wore, who they knew, how beautiful they were. They lived and entertained like forty-year-old people and she was nineteen and he was twenty-one. He was in his last year at college, but of course they lived in a ten-room duplex, paid for by their parents, and when they had a dinner party there was a liveried footman behind each guest's chair and afterward all the Beautiful People's beautiful young friends danced like crazy to the new hit rock group, the King James Version, also one of Libra's clients. It certainly was turning out to be an incestuous little world.

"How did you like her in the Dynel braids with the lollipops entwined in them?" Nelson asked.

"Very good," said Libra.

"I thought so too," Nelson said. "Especially for her, as she's so young. I don't like her in just hair, it's so dull." He gave Gerry a professional look. "I'd like to do your eyes someday."

"What's wrong with them?" she said.

"I don't know, just fool around and see what I come up with. Who cuts your hair?"

"I have it cut in the neighborhood."

"Oh, my dear child, you can't do that. Look at those ends! You're working for Sam Leo Libra you know; you have to have an image."

"If she's good I'll let her go to you," Libra said. "Why don't you go see Lizzie?"

Nelson went to the bedroom door. "Lizzie! Oh, Lizzie, Central Casting is here!"

Lizzie opened the bedroom door. She was wearing a white frilly eyelet bathrobe that stopped four inches above her knees, and pink ballet slippers. Her hair was loose.

"I'm looking for a short, skinny woman, about forty-five," Nelson said. "To play the part of a little girl."

"I have the perfect one," Lizzie said. "Her name is Nelly Nelson."

"Up yours!" Nelson squealed in delight. *"Sideways*—you shouldn't be without a sensation."

They flew into each other's arms and embraced and kissed warmly.

"Oh, Nelson, I missed you so much! I'm so glad you're here. I have lots of things to tell you." She patted him all over, the shoulders, the sleeves, touching him and smoothing the nap of the white suede suit. She patted his face, but when her hand strayed to his hair he cringed and pulled away. "Isn't he heaven?" Lizzie said. "Nelson, why aren't you straight?"

"If I were, you wouldn't have a pet fruit to play with, *miss*."

"Up yours!"

"Let me go fix your hair now, Lizzie. I hope you're going someplace really elegant for lunch."

He shoved her affectionately into the bedroom and they shut the door.

"He makes a fortune for me," Libra said drily.

"My," Gerry said.

Libra looked up at the framed painting of Sylvia Polydor over the fireplace. "We're living in strange times," he said, rather sadly. "You won't see anybody like Sylvia any more. She was, and still is, the greatest, larger than life. The kids just don't have that today; they're just electrically amplified midgets. Sylvia was a publicist's dream come true. All I had to do was follow her and cover up the more sensational things she did so they didn't get into the papers. She even married right—every time." He looked at his watch. "Let me fill you in for a few more minutes and then you can call the operator and tell her to take the stop off the calls and collect my messages. Let's see ... you met Nelson ... the B.P.'s, who you'll have the chance to meet later in the week, are perhaps the two dullest people who were ever born. I like to refer to them as Clients Number Eleven and Eleven-and-a-Half. I handle two musical groups: the King James Version, a rock group that's coming up very fast, and a singing group called Silky and the Satins, five colored girls from Philadelphia. The main reason I'm interested in them is because of the lead singer, Silky Morgan. The other four are nothing special, they just sing background. They're two sets of sisters, actually, and Silky is a kid they found in school. They're all from eighteen to twenty years old. The four of them hate Silky's guts and she hates theirs. Eventually I'm going to take her out as a single; I think she could get to Broadway. They suspect it, of course, so there's no love lost. But we present

them as full of love, practically a family. I hope you're free
tonight."

"Yes, I could be."

"Good. We're going over to the Asthma Relief telethon.
Silky and the Satins are going to be singing, and I handle the
TV director, too, a new young guy who's making quite a
name for himself with visual effects. His name is Dick Devere, better known to those who know and love him as Dick
Devoid. You'll probably fall in love with him. Are you
married?"

"No."

"Do you have a guy?"

"Nobody special," Gerry said. "I've been away for two
years."

"And they all got married while you were gone, huh?"

"No," Gerry said. "It's a funny thing, but none of the men
I was ever seriously involved with have ever married anybody. They wouldn't marry me, either, so it's not such a
compliment."

"Who gets married today anyway?" Libra said. "I love
Lizzie, but I'll tell you the truth: if I wasn't married to her I
wouldn't marry anybody, including her. I met her in college—
we've been married almost twenty years. Twenty years ago I
was an insecure, homely kid who wanted to get laid and
couldn't make out; all the girls were either professional
virgins or went for the handsome guys. Lizzie had a million
boyfriends and she liked *me*. She liked my mind or something. So I grabbed her. It's been okay, you know, ups and
downs, but we never had any kids and I think, what's it all
for? Now I can get any girl to lay; they all want me because
I'm older, I know how to talk to a girl, and most of them
think I can make them famous. And wouldn't you know—
now I'm married. It doesn't stop me any, but it makes it
uncomfortable."

She wondered how he reconciled jumping into bed with all
those girls with his love of cleanliness, but she supposed he
washed them first with Lysol, too. He certainly didn't appeal
to her as a possible lover, and his personal revelations so
soon in their relationship (or whatever it was) made her
uncomfortable.

"I don't think Lizzie knows," he went on. "She must guess,
but she's not quite sure. She doesn't want to know, so she
doesn't let herself wonder about it. Anyway, I'm just telling
you this because you're going to become friends with her and

I want you to know that anything you see and hear in this office is *your* business, not hers, or anyone else's."

"Naturally," Gerry said.

"And I won't tell anybody what you do," he teased.

"There's no one to tell," she said, smiling.

"No family?"

"They live in Bucks County, and they'll come to my wedding. If I ever get married."

"Oh, you'll get married," he said. "Tell them to put the calls through now, and get my messages. And put in a call for me to Arnie Gurney in Las Vegas, at the Caesar's Palace. He's a client I really like: he works all year round, I never see him. You've heard of him—Mr. Las Vegas?"

"Sure," Gerry said. "I've heard of most of your clients—who hasn't?"

He looked pleased. "Maybe I'll take you to Vegas with me one time if I can't get out of going. Arnie Gurney, believe me, you can live without . . . in fact, I think I'll get pneumonia and stay home. He's just the same offstage as he is on: he says hello and tells you five jokes."

"Mr. Libra . . ." Gerry said timidly, "you don't really like them much, do you? The clients."

"Does an advertising man love soap?"

She called down for his telephone messages, of which there were over a dozen already, and put through the call to Las Vegas. While Libra was on the telephone Lizzie came out of the bedroom wearing a blond Shirley Temple wig, all in ringlets, and a Little Orphan Annie mini-dress: red wool with a big white collar and cuffs. She had on white stockings and black patent Mary Janes. From far away she looked about ten. Mr. Nelson followed her out of the bedroom, preceded by a cloud of hair spray which he was aiming at the wig.

"Stop that!" Libra screamed. "Get that stuff out of here! Don't you know it gives you lung cancer?"

"Oh, for heaven's sake," Mr. Nelson said. "Where did you ever hear that?"

"Out! Out!" Libra was beginning to choke, whether from rage, fear, or the hair spray, it was hard to tell. Mr. Nelson hurriedly capped the aerosol can and shoved it into his white attaché case.

"Doesn't this look just like hair?" Lizzie asked Gerry.

"Exactly," Gerry lied.

"Well, it's Dynel," Nelson said smugly. "Dynel is going to replace hair completely. Soon we'll just shave all the ladies' heads and fit them with a wardrobe of wigs. It's easier, chicer, cleaner, and you'll just send your hair out to be washed. No more dandruff."

And all the fruits will keep their nice natural hair, Gerry thought, *and then they'll get* all *the men.*

"Will this fall off in bed?" Lizzie asked.

"Depends on what you're doing, darling," Nelson purred.

"What do you think?" Lizzie asked.

"I'm sure *you'll* have no trouble," Nelson said nastily.

"Oh? Well, Nelly, someday if you're really-really good I'll tell you what *real* women do."

"Oh, I may *throw up!*" Nelson cried in mock horror. He noticed Gerry looking at him and he gave her a wooden smile. "Don't mind us, dear, we're old friends."

The doorbell rang and Gerry opened the door to the suite. A tall, leggy, very pretty blonde girl of about twenty-five was standing there, wearing a fluffy beige fox coat. She looked terribly clean and sparkly, with taut, glowing skin and earnest gray eyes, like a Miss America contestant about to say that the man she admired most in the world, next to her Daddy of course, was Bob Hope.

"Elaine!" Lizzie Libra said.

"Oh, hi," said Elaine Fellin. The voice was a shock: it seemed to have nothing whatsoever to do with the rest of her—it was dead, beaten. She entered with a leggy stride and dropped her fox coat on the nearest chair.

"This is Gerry Thompson, who'll be working for Sam," Lizzie said. "Elaine Fellin, Mad Daddy's wife and my best friend."

"I'm very glad to meet you," Gerry said.

"Hello," said Elaine Fellin and nearly broke Gerry's hand. She was not like a Miss America contestant at all; she was like some great, drugged lion cub. Perhaps she had once been a beauty queen and had never gotten over it.

"Do you have anything to drink?" Elaine said. "I was up all night—I took three Seconals and they didn't do a damn thing. Daddy's away in Atlantic City doing a Charity. The show's taped today, but you can't tell. I feel terrible." She dropped into the chair on top of her fox coat.

"May I hang up your coat?" Gerry asked.

"No, forget it. Can you make me a martini?"

"I'll have a Scotch," Lizzie said.

Sam Leo Libra hung up the telephone. "You can all go

drink at Sardi's," he said. "Go on, scram. Get out. Charge it
to me."

"Nelson, you're coming with us," Lizzie said.

"I can't—I've got to get back to work," said Nelson.

"You have to eat, don't you?" said Lizzie.

"You can eat a sandwich at the salon," Libra said to
Nelson. "Do you want someone else to get your clients?"

"They wouldn't go to anyone else," Nelson protested.

"You want to bet? In five seconds. Five *seconds*. All they
have to be told is that you're out sick for the day and they
have to go to whatever dinner party they're going to with
yesterday's hair and they'll go right to somebody else."

"Oh my God!" Nelson said.

Lizzie, Elaine, and Nelson hurried out of the suite with a
flurry of waving arms getting into coat sleeves and making
farewell gestures. The telephone rang. The second line rang.
The third line rang. The doorbell rang. Gerry was glad for
the pressure. It meant she didn't have time to think about
those people who had just left and the life they represented,
or her own life, which didn't look as if it was going to be
much better. It was all too depressing. She'd rather be an
automaton. And please, God, she prayed, let the next client
be a nice, sweet *normal* person I can *stand*.

But this one wasn't a client; it was a middle-aged messenger carrying a script. He rushed into the room like the
nearsighted Mr. Magoo and fell over the coffee table. It
didn't appear to faze him at all, for he picked himself right
up and ran into the bedroom. Gerry ran after him, turned
him in the direction of the living room, and let him run back
in. Libra was laughing. Gerry plucked the script out of the
messenger's hand, signed the paper he held out to her, and
pointed him to the door that led to the hall. He disappeared
at a dead run.

"Messengers are getting worse all the time," Libra said. He
read the letter attached to the script. "Another horror story
for Sylvia Polydor," he said. "That's what happens to them
when they've had their last possible face lift and won't play
nice mothers—they have to play hatchet murderesses.
They're all doing it now; Crawford, Davis—all of them.
When they're young they castrate with their beauty, when
they're old they have to do it with an axe. I hate the idea of
Sylvia, my beautiful Sylvia, doing it, but there's money in
blood . . . so what the hell." He put the script on his desk. "I
have to read every damn one of them," he said. "I send on

some of the dogs to the clients, along with the good ones—
otherwise they wouldn't know a good one when they saw it.
Clients have infallible bad taste in scripts. Gerry, let me give
you a word of advice in case you ever want to produce a
play or a movie: if the client loves the script it means the
script stinks and he has a big part where you have to see him
every single minute."

Gerry smiled. The doorbell rang again and she went to the
door. There was a tall woman in her late thirties, with
mouse-colored hair neatly pulled back in a bun, wearing a
black mink coat and white space shoes. She was carrying a
doctor's black bag.

"Come in, Ingrid," Libra called happily. His expression had
changed completely the moment he saw her: he looked like a
small boy greeting his beloved governess who is bringing
toys.

"How are you, my dear Sam?" Ingrid asked in a slight
accent.

"Ready for you," Libra said. "This is my new assistant,
Gerry Thompson—Ingrid the Lady Barber, my doctor."

Gerry shook hands with the woman. Doctor or barber? It
was sometimes difficult to keep track of what Libra was
talking about—but on the other hand, before this morning
she would never have believed there was such a person as
Nelson the Society Hairdresser either.

"I am not a barber," Ingrid said, reading Gerry's bewil-
dered look. "I give scalp massage, body massage, and, of
course, vitamin injections."

"They're fantastic," Libra said. "Completely fantastic. I
can be exhausted, ready to drop, and Ingrid fills me up with
B-12 and Ingrid-only-knows-what-else, and in five minutes
I'm a new man. I can go for two days without sleep or food
on one of Ingrid's shots."

Ingrid took off her black mink coat and handed it to
Gerry. She was wearing an immaculate white nurse's uniform
under the coat. "Now I wash my hands," she said. "And you
come in the bedroom, please, Sam. Excuse us, please."

The two of them went into the bedroom and closed the
door while Gerry hung up the coat and poured herself
another cup of coffee. She was beginning to feel starved. The
telephone had stopped ringing, and she realized it was the
sacred lunch hour. Libra had said nothing about *her* lunch
hour—perhaps she should just ask him. The coffee had grown
cold. Having signed the bill she knew the breakfast snack for

the visitors had cost thirty-one dollars, and she also knew instinctively that none of the nervous, keyed-up people who came into the suite would touch it, and it would all go back in an hour or two, wasted. She wrapped up four of the Danish pastries in a clean napkin and put them into her tote bag. She couldn't stand to waste food, and besides, she was poor today.

Libra and Ingrid came back into the living room. It was miraculous: Libra was bouncing with energy already. Gerry wondered if it was psychological.

"Coffee, Ingrid?" he asked.

"You always ask me for coffee, and I always tell you no," Ingrid said disapprovingly. "Coffee has acid."

"Well, it's just a figure of speech," he said. "To be polite. Would you like a glass of water?"

"Water I would like," Ingrid said. She poured herself a glass of ice water and drank it down in one long draught. "Look at that cake," she said with distaste. "Who eats that cake? Cake is nothing but starch and artificial preservatives."

"You run your store and I'll run mine," Libra said.

"I eat all the time yogurt," Ingrid said to Gerry. "When I was pregnant last year I ate four cups of yogurt every day. Do you know, my son was born with two teeth and all his hair?"

"My," Gerry said.

"You should see him; a big monster! He walks already." She patted her flat stomach. "Do you know I have four children?"

"Guess how old she is," Libra said.

"Thirty-five?" Gerry said kindly.

"Forty-five!" Libra crowed. "Look at her! I'm going to make you a movie star, Ingrid."

"It is not necessary ever to have the menopause," Ingrid said irrelevantly. "With the new hormones women can function normally until they're eighty." She turned to Gerry. "How old are you?"

"Twenty-six," Gerry said.

"You should be taking hormones already. After twenty-five one should start on hormones. Do you take hormones?"

"No."

"Do you take birth-control pills?"

Gerry looked at Libra, embarrassed. She wished everybody in this office would stop treating her like an object.

"Tell her, for heaven's sake," Libra said, annoyed. "Don't be so coy—she's a doctor."

Gerry nodded yes.

"Well, that's good," Ingrid said. "The Pill has hormones in it. But that's not enough after twenty-five. I can give you some hormone shots if you'd like."

"No thank you," Gerry said.

"You don't know what's good for you," Ingrid said. She snapped her doctor's bag shut with a disapproving look on her face. "I come back tomorrow for your massage, Sam. What time is good for you?"

"Eight in the morning," Libra said.

"Very good. How do you feel now?"

"Fantastic. You're a genius, Ingrid."

He bounced to the closet, took out Ingrid's coat, and helped her into it. Then he walked her to the door with his arm around her and kissed her on the cheek. She was as tall as he was.

"Very nice to have met you," Gerry said politely.

"Good luck with your job," Ingrid said, and left.

Libra looked at his wristwatch. "I'm going to the gym," he said. "You can go to lunch if you want, or call Room Service and have it sent up here."

"I'd like to go out, if that's all right."

"That's all right with me, I'll save money."

"Thank you, anyway. And speaking of money, do you think I could have my first week's salary in advance? I'm kind of broke."

He went immediately to the desk and wrote out a check. He tore the check out of the checkbook carefully, as if he was having a little trouble functioning. He inhaled deeply and patted his chest with both hands. He really did look like an ape. "Go to work off that excess energy," he said cheerfully. He handed her the check. "I'll be back at three."

When he had gone Gerry looked at the check. It was for four hundred dollars: two weeks' salary in advance. She could hardly believe it. He really wasn't so bad—he was generous with money, he wanted to help her learn the job, he was a little peculiar, but after all, he had a right to be peculiar if he wanted to be. She called down to the operator to hold the calls, took the extra key for the suite, and rushed downstairs to find the nearest branch of her bank.

She deposited the check, withdrew fifty dollars for spending money, stopped for a hamburger and a glass of skimmed milk, and took a taxi to her new apartment. The painters were there, and the smell of new paint was intoxicating. She found a hardware store a block away and bought a supply of light bulbs. Her new apartment! It was going to be beautiful! On the way back she made a mental note of the liquor store, the grocery, and the cleaners. The neighborhood was so clean and quiet. No hippies standing around; only a few old people walking dogs. Everyone else was at work, or if they were young mothers they had taken their children to the park. She had a pang of regret, wondering what it would be like to be married to someone she loved, taking their own beautiful baby to the park. She wondered if anybody would ever marry her. At college she had thought that she would be very brave and wait until she was an ancient twenty-four before she settled down. But twenty-four had come and gone, and she had found no one she wanted to settle down with, or if she had wanted him, he was too happy being single—or married to someone he claimed he couldn't stand— to give it all up. Maybe Libra was right and nobody got married any more. She thought of her married friends: Were they really as happy as they claimed to be? Did the husbands play around already? Did the couples take as much delight in making love, still, or was it only Saturday night, get drunk and get laid because you can sleep late tomorrow? Were the wives bored staying home alone all day? She knew she would be bored; she would have to keep her job, or one like it with easier hours. What had happened to the few guys she had thought she really loved? Were they lonely, tired of dating new, exciting girls every night, tired of telling the same life stories to impress the new stranger, tired of the game to make the girl love them but not *too much*? How wonderful it would be to love someone too much, and to know he felt the same way ... that had to exist somewhere. She felt it really had to. Maybe when she was fifty, if no one wanted her, she could settle for less than love, but right now the thought horrified her. *Well,* she thought, remembering her favorite heroine, Scarlett O'Hara, *I'll think about it tomorrow.*

She came back to the office at three o'clock. Libra was already there, wearing a fresh, clean navy-blue silk suit and a reddish silk tie that clashed with his maroon hair. His hair was damp again as if he had just washed it. After the comparatively fresh air of the streets outside the suite blasted her with its hothouse smell, but she guessed she would eventually get used to it. Libra turned on the television set.

"You're just in time to watch the Mad Daddy Show," he said. "Sit right down in front there and pay attention."

The show opened with Mad Daddy, who was an innocu-
ous-looking fellow, a little square and out of step in a
Beethoven sweatshirt and tight chino pants, vacuuming the
rug of what was supposed to be his apartment. He was
followed and heckled by Dennison of the Deep, an enormous
fish which evidently had a man inside its rubber body. Dennison of the Deep kept getting water on the rug which Mad
Daddy was trying to vacuum. Mad Daddy told the fish to get
back in his bowl but the fish refused. It said that it was going
to hold a protest demonstration at the Museum of Natural
History because it had auditioned for a Western television
series and had been turned down. There was proof, Dennison
of the Deep said, that there had been fish in the old West,
but the discriminatory policies of the television authorities
refused to cast a fish as a hero in a Western.

Mad Daddy agreed seriously. He seemed a pleasant
enough fellow, but although he had a humorous, innocent
face and what appeared to be quite a sexy body, Gerry
couldn't understand the secret of his charm. And she wished
the fish wouldn't yell so loud. It had probably gotten rejected
for the Western just on the quality of its voice. She realized
then that in the first five minutes the show had already
achieved suspension of disbelief, which was quite something.

A little girl entered, named Little Angela. She was actually
a hand puppet. Mad Daddy was not a ventriloquist; an
actress did the voice. Little Angela looked about five years
old, but she had the aggravating logic of a teen-ager. She
kept heckling Mad Daddy and he kept trying to defend
himself. She told him the way he was dressed was ridiculous
for an old man, and he answered that he thought he looked
pretty nifty. She told him nobody said 'nifty' any more, the
word was 'groovy.' Then she hit him on the head with her
giant lollipop.

Dennison of the Deep exited to begin organizing his protest demonstration. Another hand puppet entered, named
Stud Mouse. He was a mouse in a turtleneck sweater and a
bow tie, who averred that he was a great success with the
ladies and proceeded to recount a story of his latest amorous
exploit and then told several very corny dirty jokes. Stud
Mouse tried to kiss Little Angela, and Mad Daddy tried to
defend her. Little Angela told Mad Daddy to mind his own
business. There was a lot of yelling and screaming and
running around, and finally Little Angela hit both of them on
the head with her lollipop and ran out of the apartment.

Stud Mouse tried to explain to Mad Daddy how to be a success with the ladies, but Mad Daddy said he was always a failure because he was so shy. Dennison of the Deep returned to tell a long story about his protest demonstration, as if it had already happened: how enthusiastic the demonstrators had been, what their signs said, what they wore, and how the cops had broken up the demonstration with their clubs. He went back into his fishbowl (offscreen) to sulk.

Stud Mouse sang a very silly song, off key. He and Mad Daddy exchanged some more corny jokes. Mad Daddy brought out some ridiculous props to enable Dennison of the Deep to disguise himself for the next protest demonstration in case he was arrested. The two of them tried to cajole Dennison of the Deep out of his bowl and finally succeeded. Dennison decided to start another protest demonstration the next day, and the hour was over.

Gerry thought the show was idiotic: a combination of old-fashioned burlesque and modern satire, but she was surprised that the time had gone by so quickly, and in a way she had become rather fond of Mad Daddy, who was a gentle, well-meaning nebbish with the secret soul of a hippie. He was a sort of grown-up flower child without the flowers. The show itself was not much, but he had charisma. She could see why the kids liked it. There was fantasy, harmless violence, and above all a childlike quality about the living toys and the way Mad Daddy accepted them as if they were real people with rights like anyone else. She supposed teenagers, especially the young ones, identified with them: Dennison of the Deep, who was a socially conscious, put-down member of a minority; Little Angela, who was a nymphet pretending to be more sophisticated than she really was; and Stud Mouse, who was a braggart and a liar who knew no one really believed his wild stories but wanted everyone to pretend they did.

"What do you think?" Libra asked.

"I hated it at first but he finally got to me," Gerry said. "I like it. I especially like him. Who writes the show?"

"He does, every word. Mostly he doesn't write it, he just improvises. He writes a sort of script, but then he generally doesn't use it."

"It's funny, but I think he's sexy," Gerry said.

"Everybody does," said Libra. "Everybody loves a loser—he's modern man. I think the show is going to go very big in its new slot at midnight."

"There were some kids in the hall this morning. A fan club, I guess."

"I could run that guy for president," Libra said. "The only reason he wouldn't win is that his fans aren't old enough to vote."

"I think I'd vote for Dennison of the Deep," Gerry said, smiling.

The rest of the day went quickly; a normal publicity day with correspondence and press releases, things Gerry was used to handling by now. Libra wrote all his own press releases, the jokes for the columns, the earnest letters saying how exciting something ordinary was. But she much preferred it to her motion-picture publicity work because at least this man had a wild imagination. When Libra made up a joke or a clever line, it was worth printing. She had grown used to typing up "witticisms" that embarrassed her by their stupidity, but she laughed at the ones Libra invented. She knew he was watching her and that he was pleased at her approval.

At five o'clock Libra went out to a cocktail appointment and told her she could go home for dinner but to be back at the suite promptly at seven because they were going to the Asthma Relief telethon. It had been going on for almost twenty-four hours, and would wind up at midnight. She decided she would change her dress and her make-up so he would think she had taken a second bath, and the little deception pleased her. She found herself giggling. That Mad Daddy Show had really gotten to her—it had cheered her up for the rest of the day.

The telethon was being held in a West Side television studio. When Gerry and Libra arrived the backstage area looked like the floor of Grand Central Station at rush hour. Celebrities were stacked up like commuters, waiting for their turn to go on, disgruntled because the show, as usual, was running behind and they had still not been called to appear on stage. There were several monitors arranged about the room, and at the far end there was a table with a coffee urn, cups, and a vast mound of garbage that had once been sandwiches. There were not enough bridge chairs, and performers and their agents, managers, and entourages were standing in hostile groups or sitting on the long table amidst the garbage. Some were watching the monitors, but most were watching themselves or other stars in person. Some were friendly, chatting to new friends whose work they admired or to old friends they had not seen in a long time because of busy schedules. In a corner four young black girls who looked like sisters, dressed in identical velveteen little-boy knicker suits with frilly white blouses peeking out of the jackets and identical wigs of banana curls cascading around their faces, were playing cards.

"The Satins," Libra said. He went over to them with a quick, determined stride. "Get up! What do you think you're doing?"

"We're playin' Old Maid," one of them said, looking up with a giggle. "Honey's the Old Maid . . . as *usual*." The three of them laughed, except for the one who was evidently Honey, who shook her head with a wry smile. She looked a little older than the others.

"You look like bums," Libra said. He took the cards away from them. "Didn't you bring any books?"

"We didn't think we'd have to sit here so long," one of them complained.

"You managed to bring your cards, all right," Libra said nastily. "I'm surprised you aren't shooting craps. You're supposed to be young ladies, even if you aren't."

"We were just playin' *Old Maid*," Honey said.

"How is anybody going to know that?" snapped Libra. "Are you going to hold up a sign? Just sit here and talk, or shut up."

The four girls sulked.

"Where's Silky?" Libra snapped.

"We don't know."

"You're supposed to take care of her!"

"Silky can take care of herself," one of them murmured cattily.

"Yeah," said another.

"*Yes*, not *yeah*, you dumb bitch!"

The girl's eyes filled with tears.

"This is my new assistant, Gerry Thompson," Libra said. "This is Honey, this is Tamara, and these two are Cheryl and Beryl. Honey and Tamara are sisters and Cheryl and Beryl are twins."

Gerry shook hands with all of them and gave them a sympathetic look. She thought Libra was overdoing his contrived nastiness; after all, they were all only about eighteen years old and they seemed like nice, quiet girls.

"Your hair looks terrible," Libra said. "Where's Nelson?"

"He went home," Cheryl said.

"What gave you the idea to use those banana curls?" Libra asked in a fury. "You look forty years old! I wanted you in the plain, straight wigs with the bangs."

"*Silky* said she didn't like the bangs," Beryl said, sounding quite pleased that Silky was going to get it this time.

"*She* said we should look more dressy," Cheryl agreed.

"I think their hair looks very nice," Gerry said timidly. She regretted it instantly; now Libra would turn on *her,* and she was frightened. But to her surprise he did nothing of the sort.

"You think it looks all right, huh?" he said, as if she were his equal.

"Well, I haven't seen the other wigs, but I think these are really what's in style right this minute for formal wear."

Libra pursed his lips. The four black girls looked back at him like four startled kittens. "There's nothing I can do about it now in any case," he said. "Nelson is going to hear from me in the morning. I don't want you girls ever—I mean *ever*—to tell Nelson what to do, do you hear me? Never again!"

"We won't," they chorused, relieved.

"What are you going to sing?"

" 'You Left Me' and 'Take Me Back,' " Honey said.

Gerry remembered hearing both those songs on the radio; they had been rather successful. She placed Silky and the Satins in her mind now, if vaguely. They were that group who was always singing of unrequited love.

"I want you to sing 'Lemme Live Now,' " Libra said. "It's late at night, I don't want you to put the people to sleep."

"You better tell Silky," Tamara said.

"Don't you worry. I'll tell Silky," Libra snapped. He took Gerry by the arm and led her away.

"See you later," Gerry called over her shoulder to the girls. They smiled and waved. Good ... they seemed to like her. She didn't want them to get the idea she was Libra's surrogate tyrant just because she was his assistant and he chose to be nice to her this time.

They pushed their way through the crowd, Libra greeting and being greeted by many of the celebrities and their managers, until they caught sight of another velveteen knicker suit in a corner by one of the TV monitors. Silky was hunched up in a folding chair, chewing her fingernails, about a foot away from the set like a child, watching the show intently.

"Silky!" Libra said.

"Oh, hello Mr. Libra," Silky said, and stood up reluctantly, flashing him a big smile that never reached her eyes. She was a small, curvy, perfectly built girl, everything about her delicate and flowing. She had enormous eyes, made larger by the triple-thick theatrical eyelashes she was wearing, dimples, and a pouty mouth with very white teeth, a little buck, which instead of being unattractive were rather charming. They gave her face a piquant look. Even in the heavy television make-up and sophisticated wig she looked very young, barely eighteen. She had incredibly silky-looking, soft walnut skin.

"Silky Morgan, Gerry Thompson, my new assistant," Libra said.

"How do you do," Silky said.

"I'm glad to meet you at last," said Gerry. Silky's hand was tiny and delicate in her own, weighted down by three huge rhinestone rings.

"What's that trash you're wearing?" Libra snapped.

"What? What?" Silky's hand flew to her face.

"Those rings. Take them off. Have you been shopping in the five-and-ten again?"

"I bought them at Bonwit's," Silky protested. She put her hands behind her back like a child.

Libra held out his paw. "Give them to me."

Silky wrestled off the rings behind her back and dropped them into Libra's outstretched palm.

"You can have them back after the show," Libra said. "You can wear them at home with your basic leopard-skin lounging outfit with the ostrich trimming and the rhinestone belt." His voice was poisonous.

"Mr. Libra, you know I wouldn't wear anything like that."

"Really?"

"He likes to kid around," Silky said nervously to Gerry.

"Tell me the whole story about Mr. Nelson and the bangs," Libra said sternly.

"I just thought it would be nice for a change ..." Her voice trailed off and she looked down.

"Since when have you become an authority on chic?"

Silky shook her head and bit her lip.

"Mr. Nelson works for me, do you understand? Not for you. For me. You do what he tells you, you *don't tell him what to do*. Do you understand that?"

"Yes, Mr. Libra."

There was a long, embarrassed silence. Gerry felt very sorry for the girl. "I guess I know why they call you Silky," Gerry said. "You're the silkiest-looking girl I ever saw."

"It's not how I look—it's ma' voice," Silky said softly. She did have a silky voice; it rippled over you like waves of the softest silk in the world.

"Wait till you hear her sing," Libra said, kind now. Silky smiled gratefully. "I've made a change—you're going to sing 'Lemme Live Now' instead of 'Take Me Back.' "

"Do the girls know?"

"They know."

"I'll have to tell the musical director."

"So tell him."

"Yes, Mr. Libra."

About fifteen minutes later Silky and the Satins finally went onstage. The four Satins positioned themselves behind Silky, at one microphone, and Silky stood in front of a detachable floor mike. The Satins harmonized in a soft background with a rock beat, while Silky belted out the lyrics in a voice that still rippled and flowed but had a surprising power and range. When she sang "You Left Me" it really sounded as if she meant it, and the simple, corny lyrics became poignant, even sad. Silky took the mike off its base and held it to her mouth, singing into it almost as if it were only an extension of her hand and not a mechanical instrument at all. She moved beautifully. Her large, sad eyes focused somewhere out in the darkness behind the lighted stage.

The audience applauded wildly. Silky and the Satins went into the upbeat song "Lemme Live Now." Now Silky was smiling, moving to the beat, but her large eyes under the heavy lashes were still sad. *Yeah, yeah, life is a ball, that's all, Gonna stand tall, No more cryin', Lemme Live Now. . . . Now, now, Lemme Live Now. . . .*

Gerry felt the hair at the base of her skull begin to prickle with excitement. Silky's marvelous voice filled her with a sweet, sad nostalgia; it was pure, distilled memory of every young girl's hope and heartbreak. A dozen pictures flashed through her mind: a man she had been in love with when she thought it was good and going to work out, being held in arms that would never leave her, the flash of sun on snow piled up outside an open window while she lay safe and secure in those arms . . . a sunrise on the river . . . a night full of stars . . . Silky's brave, knowing voice again made the

inane lyrics emotional and meaningful. She seemed to be
saying: I've been hurt, but I won't give up—I know there's
always another chance.

The audience applauded as if they would never stop.
"Wow!" Gerry said.

"You like her?"

"My God, she's fantastic."

"She's a bright girl," Libra said. "Eighteen years old. I've
had the group for seven months now. I don't think she knows
how good she really is."

"Did she ever study singing?"

"Never," Libra said. "None of them did. I doubt if they
can even read music. I know Silky can't. She just listens to a
song and she gets it right down. Spades have natural talent."

"Oh, Mr. Libra, you don't believe that!"

"What do you mean I don't believe that?"

The five girls came off the stage. Tamara, Honey, Cheryl,
and Beryl got their coats—identical white bunny-fur polo
coats—and said they were going home. Silky said she wanted
to stay and see the rest of the telethon.

"Don't stay up all night," Libra said. "And no drinking."

"No, Mr. Libra. No, sir."

"If you go to a nightclub and fall down on your ass, I'll
hear about it," he threatened.

"We're goin' right back to the hotel, Mr. Libra."

"And you're not to break your diets. I want a list tomorrow of everything you ate today. Dance class at ten o'clock,
remember."

"Yes, Mr. Libra."

"You're not to sleep in your make-up. *You*, you hear what
I said?"

"Yes, Mr. Libra," said Honey.

"All right," Libra said, dismissing them. The Satins ran
away, giggling and chattering among themselves. None of
them had bothered to say good night to Silky, and she had
not even looked at them.

Gerry felt tired. It was late, and it had been a long day,
full of tension. Silky took her place again on the chair in
front of the monitor, nibbling her nails. Libra took a chair
away from a man and gave it to Gerry. She sat down next to
Silky and watched the show.

"He's wonderful, isn't he?" Silky said.

"Who, Mr. Libra?"

Silky looked around to make sure Libra was not listening.

"No—Mr. Devere, the director. Look at that shot. You never see a shot like that on a telethon; it looks like something on an expensive special. Mr. Devere is really a genius."

The director was doing something with three cameras that made the images melt into each other. Over them were superimposed shifting eerie blobs like oil on water. Now there was a taped section that looked like a kaleidoscope, with the dancers spinning around in the center of it. Vaguely, through this, could be seen a blowup of the Statue of Liberty.

"He took that from a show of theirs he did," Silky said. "You should have seen it in color, it was so beautiful."

Gerry was surprised she was so knowledgeable. "Have you done much television?" she asked.

"No, this is only the third time. We were on two teen-age shows before, with the songs pre-recorded. I hate to work pre-recorded because sometimes I change the lyrics a little when I get carried away emotionally, and when I'm supposed to be lip-synching to the record it looks terrible." Silky flashed Gerry a shy smile. "I know I shouldn't improvise—it makes it difficult for the girls. But sometimes I just get carried away. Mr. Devere says I'm the Sandy Dennis of singers."

"Do you know him well?" Gerry asked idly.

"I met him six months ago on one of those teen-age shows. He directed that, too. He's done some wonderful things. He's a client of Mr. Libra's," she added hastily. "I think it's important to watch the work of the other clients."

"Yes, I guess you can learn a lot," said Gerry.

They stayed on until the end at midnight, because Libra said he wanted to talk to Dick Devere. Gerry alternately watched the show and Silky watching the show. She really was so pretty, and such an endearing combination of shyness and enthusiasm, but she was a nervous wreck. When she finished devouring the mini-nails of one hand, Silky promptly started on the other. There didn't seem to be anything left to bite, but Silky found it. Libra had disappeared, but then he returned when the telethon was over, leading a tall, not very attractive young man with wispy, receding brown hair, a hawklike nose, and hollow cheeks. He was wearing a well-cut, expensive-looking plaid suit and a black turtleneck sweater.

"This is Dick Devere," Sam Leo Libra said.

So this was the infamous Dick Devoid, with whom she was

going to fall in love, according to Mr. Libra. Well, well.
Gerry was not impressed. They shook hands and Dick began
discussing the show with Libra. He did have a wonderful
voice, low and deep and cultivated—the unlikely sort of sexy
voice Gerry had often heard from these undernourished
specimens who looked as if their mothers had starved them
in childhood. She'd made blind dates with quite a few by
telephone in her youth, and had always been disappointed
when she saw them in person. Silky was hanging on every
word, not bothering to pretend she wasn't listening. Her big
eyes were shining—the first time Gerry had seen them look
anything but sad. She wondered if Silky was in love with
Dick Devoid.

Finally Dick said to Libra, "Why don't we all go and get
some coffee?" but he was looking at Gerry.

Libra looked at his watch. "Not me. I have to meet some
people at Reuben's. You take the girls."

"Gerry?" Dick said. He gave her a charming smile.

She looked at Silky. Silky's eyes had gone flat again. My
God, the girl was jealous! "I have to get up early tomorrow,"
Gerry said. "Some other time, if that's all right."

"Maybe we'll have lunch together this week," Dick said.

"Whatever Mr. Libra says," said Gerry.

"I don't care who either of you have lunch with," said
Libra. He looked almost too pleased. *Well, now, isn't this a
bitch,* Gerry thought in dismay. *Either I antagonize Dick, and
Libra, or I antagonize Silky, and eventually Libra. And what
about me? I have a headache and I want to go home to bed.*

"I'll call you one morning at the office," Dick said.

Gerry smiled politely.

"Good night," Silky said. She gave Gerry an apologetic
smile, as if to say it wasn't her fault about Dick and the
lunch, or Dick and anything.

"I'll just drop the kid home," Dick said casually, taking
Silky's arm. "Where's your rabbit?"

"My *lapin* is in the dressing room upstairs," Silky said. She
grinned and stuck her tongue out at him.

They went off, and Libra took Gerry outside to a cab.
"What do you think of him?" Libra asked.

"He's all right."

"I hear he has a cock like an elk."

"I really couldn't care less, Mr. Libra."

"Well, a lot of other people care," said Libra cheerfully.
"Silky?"

"What about her?"

"Are she and Dick going together or anything?"

"Why do you ask?"

"I just wondered," she said.

"*No,*" Libra said coldly. "They're just friends."

"This is off the record," Gerry said. "I just want to know so I won't make any *faux pas* with the clients."

"There is nothing between them," Libra said firmly. "If there is, let Silky tell you for herself."

"I see."

"What do you see?"

"I hope she doesn't get hurt," Gerry said.

"That's her business, isn't it?" Libra said. "You can't change anybody's nature. Why don't you just enjoy yourself? Nobody's going to get our friend Dick Devoid. Not for long, anyway. He only wants to have a good time. What's wrong with that? Why do girls always make such a big emotional crisis out of everything?"

"Do you mean me?"

"I mean all girls. What a nuisance you all are! Thank God I'm a happily married man!"

Gerry looked at him as her cab pulled away. She wondered if he really was going to Reuben's on business, and she wondered what Lizzie Libra had done with herself this evening and the many other evenings like this one. At least Dick Devere was single.

CHAPTER
TWO

WHEN Silky Morgan was ten years old her mother died of tuberculosis in the hospital. They were living on South Street then, the famous street of the song, in South Philadelphia, an area composed of Negroes and some Italians. Her mother had been sick at home for a long time, and after she went away to the hospital Silky's father came back home for a while to take care of the kids. They lived in a red-brick row house, three stories high, with about twelve people in each small apartment, although in Silky's family there were only eight, counting her father when he was home. When they came back from the funeral someone had marked up their front door with big splashes of white paint: a skull and crossbones, and the letters TB three feet high. It was the first time her father had cried after her mother's death; he cried and cursed and pounded on the door with his fist until his knuckles bled. Then he made Arthur, her older brother, get some water and yellow soap and try to scrub off the white paint. They didn't have enough money to buy paint to cover it up. Her father said it was the goddam Eyetalians who done it—a Brother would never do a low thing like that.

But they couldn't get the paint off, not Arthur, not her father, and it stayed there, finally peeling, while the seasons changed and the memory of her mother's soft face gradually became as blurred in her mind as the paint on their door. She dreamed of her mother almost every night. Nobody ever came near them during that time; the neighbors avoided them in the halls and backed away from them on the stairs. Arthur told her TB was catching. She wanted to catch it so she could go to heaven where her mother was. Her father didn't even wait for the paint to disappear; he disappeared first, telling the woman next door to look after them. She was the only one who didn't avoid them, although for several weeks she wouldn't let them play with her kids. Then she relented. And the day Silky knew her father had gone away again, this time for good, although she didn't know that at the time, the woman next door took her on her lap and hugged her, and said: "I'll be your Auntie Grace now. I'll take care of you the best I can, so you come to me when you need a mama."

Silky didn't think anybody had ever had a father as handsome and wonderful as hers had been. He was like Santa Claus, disappearing and then coming back, and almost always leaving a little brother or sister behind. Younger than she was Cornelius, then William, then La Jean, then the baby, Cynthia. Her own Christian name was Sarah, although her father had nicknamed her Silky when she was just a baby. Her mother told her she looked exactly like her father. He was tall and strong, with hair black as night; even when he was older, it never had a speck of gray in it. To her he was a sort of celebrity. When he came around everybody was happy. But then after a while he would begin to sit around the apartment doing nothing all day, just looking out the window, and then one morning he would be gone.

Auntie Grace had ten children of her own. Two of them, the twins Cheryl and Beryl, were Silky's age, and as long as she could remember the three of them had been best friends. They did everything together. And when they were fourteen they all decided that they were going to become famous singers. They were in junior high, and there was a girl in their class named Tamara who wanted to be a singer too. She brought along her older sister, Honey, and the whole bunch of them would meet every day after school to practice popular songs. They learned them off the radio, or hanging around the Record Shack. Honey, who was sixteen, was going around with a boy named Rudolph, who had stolen a phonograph. He stole a whole bunch of new records too, and after school they would hang around his apartment and play the phonograph and try to copy the singers on them until

Rudolph got bored and took Honey into the bedroom and threw the rest of them out.

Sex was something Silky took for granted at a very early age. She knew how not to catch a baby long before she was old enough to have to worry about it, but even though she started doing what her friends were doing when she was about fourteen, she didn't think sex was much. She hated school, but she liked reading, and in one of the books she took out of the library she read that all famous people had to make sacrifices for their goal. She couldn't give up food, because there was never enough and she was always hungry. Usually she got through the day with a sweet-potato pie from the grocery and two or three nickel Cokes. When her mother had been alive she remembered having lunch money to take to school, but after her mother died and her father went away she never had any. Her older brother, Arthur, who worked in the filling station, gave her money once a week, and the rest of her brothers and sisters ate at Auntie Grace's. She didn't like to eat there; Auntie Grace wasn't her family, and she felt uncomfortable. Many evenings Auntie Grace or Cheryl or Beryl would catch her hanging around down on the street and make her come upstairs to their apartment to eat dinner. Sometimes she was so hungry she had to forget her pride and come along. No, giving up food was out of the question, but she wanted to sacrifice something. She didn't smoke or drink. She thought of giving up Cokes, but that didn't seem significant, so finally she decided to give up sex.

That was when she was sixteen. So even though she flirted with the boys at school, hoping one of them would buy her a hamburger or even take her to the Soul Kitchen for a real meal, she managed to stay out of bed with them, knowing in her heart it wasn't such a sacrifice as she pretended it was because sex meant nothing to her.

Cheryl and Beryl didn't know who their father was. They pretended that their mother's boyfriend was their real father, and all their friends went along with the pretense. Their mother's boyfriend was a nice guy, although once he went after Silky. That was when she was seventeen, and it was one of the things that made her decide to run away to New York. She couldn't hang around Auntie Grace's knowing that guy was always looking at her and trying to cop a feel. She thought it was disgusting for an old man like that to go after a kid like her.

She still thought of herself as a kid, even though she

plastered her face with make-up she shoplifted from the
five-and-ten with Cheryl and Beryl, and teased her hair up
high. They were always running around with their hair in
rollers in those days, either that or teasing it up to look
sophisticated. She had a big bust, and she wore tight Orlon
sweaters, mostly hand-me-downs from Auntie Grace's older
daughters; Marie, who worked in a beauty salon and made a
lot of money, and Ardra, who worked in a five-and-ten, not
the one they stole from. They would never steal from Ardra's
five-and-ten; she might lose her job.

The five girls decided to drop out of school that spring and
hitchhike to New York. Auntie Grace didn't care. She had
just lost a baby in the sixth month, and she was always
complaining how much work she had taking care of the kids
she had already. The five of them were just dying to get out
of school. Honey could barely read. It was a big secret about
Honey not being able to read—if you really wanted to make
her mad at you, you would ask her, "What does that sign
say?" Or, "What's playing at the movies?" She'd either make
something up or give you a hell of a smack. Tamara couldn't
read so good herself. She and Honey had had about ten
different fathers and nobody ever made them do their homework. Silky remembered when she was only about six, how
her mother had watched over her every night to be sure she
did her homework, busy as she was with all the rest of the
family. She was glad she could read so well now, because
with reading you didn't need school, you could get a whole
education by yourself as long as books were free. She swore
to herself that after she dropped out of school she would
read a whole library book every week, and she did.

One morning Silky and her friends packed everything they
owned, which wasn't much, into shopping bags, and hitched a
ride to New York with two guys in a white Cadillac. Honey
and Tamara and Cheryl and Beryl drank a lot of beer on the
way down and took turns screwing each one of the two guys
in the back seat while the other one drove, but Silky told
them she had syphilis and they'd catch it. They wanted to
take her to the clinic when they reached Manhattan, but she
told them she was too embarrassed, and cried, so they let her
alone. She had been scared to death that one of the guys
might say: "Oh, that's okay—I have syph too," but they
didn't. They kept far away from her. She was still keeping to
her vow; no sex until she was famous.

Honey and Tamara had an aunt in Harlem, so they all

stayed with her for a while, hitching rides downtown all the time so they could hang around music publishers whose names they had found in the phone book. Honey got a job waiting table, but she got fired the next day because she was trying to remember all the orders on account of not being able to write, and she couldn't read either. Then Silky went to work there and supported the rest of them. Cheryl had a lot of boyfriends who laid bread on her, and Beryl was going steady with a guy who they all suspected pushed dope. He gave them all free pot, and both the twins turned into big heads. Tamara had found herself a white boy named Marvin, who had pimples and lived in the Village. He'd run away from his rich Jewish family in Lefrak City, and he thought it was really a gas to be screwing a black chick. Tamara privately called him the Village Idiot, but he couldn't do enough for her. So in a way they were all doing their bit to keep the group eating until they got their break.

Summer turned into fall, then winter, and it was cold. They still hadn't been able to get an audition for anybody, but they practiced every day. Silky was working nights, and the others were dating. Then one night Silky met a guy in the place she was waiting table who knew a lot of people in the music publishing business, and he got the girls an audition. They had named themselves the Satins, but after they auditioned the man at the music company told them they would do better if they made one of them the lead singer, and he made them each try out separately. It was a toss-up between Honey and Silky. Silky *said* Honey should get the lead singer bit because she was the oldest, but secretly she knew that if anyone got it but her she would just die. Then the man said it should be Silky because she had such an interesting voice. He named the group Silky and the Satins.

The other girls didn't seem to mind so much at first, because what was a lead singer when they weren't working anyway? But about a month later the man had them come back to audition again, and then he let them cut a record. It never got anywhere, and that winter they really thought they were going to starve for sure. Honey got pregnant and had an abortion in New Jersey. It cost them every cent they made on the record, and then some, but they had vowed to stick together and this was part of it. After that Honey broke out in a rash from the penicillin she'd had to get in the clinic after the abortion, and they were all afraid she was going to die. The doctor at the clinic said she could never have any more kids, but two months after she got out of the clinic she was knocked up again—from Tamara's Marvin. Tamara said she was going to kill that little Jew bastard, but the other girls talked sense into her and rich Marvin paid for Honey's abortion, at a Village doctor who was much better than the one in New Jersey, and after that he really couldn't do enough for Tamara because he was so upset. Tamara said she was thinking of marrying him to give his family a heart attack, so then she could inherit all that money.

Silky didn't like to see the girls getting hard this way. They had all had such fun when they were kids together on South Street, but being alone in New York had changed them. Sometimes at night, alone in her corner of the crowded apartment, she cried, pulling her coat over her head so none of the others would hear her. Maybe they should just all go home and get married. But even when she was crying she couldn't believe that was what would make them happy. No, they had to make it, they just had to. Otherwise she'd end up like her mother and die young, she was sure of it.

She became obsessed with death. A rat could come and bite her in the night and she would die. She could get TB. Maybe TB ran in families. Maybe she would get malnutrition and her teeth would fall out. She bought vitamins at the drugstore and ate everything that looked healthy at the restaurant where she worked. She began to fill out, and even though she had never felt more miserable she had never looked prettier. She was really getting curvy. She looked at her body in the cracked mirror on the bathroom door and thought how really good she would look in a slinky evening gown when she got to be a big singing star and could perform at the Apollo.

Then they cut another record, but this time it got a little attention and they made some money. The next song they cut was "You Left Me." Silky thought of her father when she sang it, and the way she loved him and felt about him leaving her made her voice come out in a new way she had never dreamed possible. Listening to the record she thought: *My God! That girl has really lived and suffered! Who would dream it was only me?*

The song became a hit. They even played it in the restaurant where she worked, and while she was slinging dishes she hummed along with it, but nobody ever knew it was her. Then she quit her job.

They cut "Take Me Back," and it was a hit, too. Everybody who was anybody in the business had heard of Sam Leo Libra, who made people into stars, so Silky and the Satins took their two records to the Libra office listed in the phone book and found only a secretary there. The secretary mailed the records to Sam Leo Libra in California.

Then one day, in late winter, almost a year from the time the girls had hitched to New York, they were in a big hotel suite talking to this terrifying, marvelous man himself, and he had one of their two records spinning on his stereo set, and he was looking at them with distaste as if they were bugs.

"That make-up has to go," he said. "Mr. Nelson will tell you how to make up. Your hair is ridiculous. He'll fit you with some wigs. I'll lay out the money and you can pay me back. I'm going to handle all your money; you obviously don't look competent. You'll get enough to live on. I want you out of Harlem and into a downtown hotel. You can all stay in the same room; I'm sure you're used to it. If anybody asks you, you'll say you each have your own room. You are never, do you hear me, *never* to invite men up to your room. Do you hear me?"

"Yes, Mr. Libra," they chorused.

"None of you finished high school, I suppose?"

"No, sir," Honey said.

"I trust you can read and write?"

"Oh, yes, sir." None of them looked at Honey.

"Well, then, look at this contract, sign all of the copies, and return them to me. This contract says I'll be your manager and publicist for a period of one year. If you're good and it works out, we can renew it. If you're bad and it doesn't work out, you're all out on your asses."

"Yes, sir."

"I'm going to present you as sweet, clean-cut, wholesome American girls. That means no night clubs, no drinking in public, no pot, no dope, and no swearing. Do you know what swearing is?"

The girls nodded.

"It is fuck, damn, shit, and screw," Mr. Libra enumerated. "It is also cunt, cock, balls and hell and anything else your evil little minds can think up. You are never to refer to white people as honkys. Every time you curse or swear I will dock ten dollars from your allowances. I want you to get used to even *thinking* clean. You are never to say anything controversial, and if anyone asks you about civil rights you say you are all for it of course and then shut up. You are never to discuss Black Power. I doubt if you can carry on an intelligent conversation about the subject anyway."

Silky looked at Honey and Tamara nervously. They were the two with tempers, and she was afraid Honey might blow it and tell this man to go shove it up his ass and rotate. She fixed them with a desperate stare. They were seething, but they kept still. She hated him as much as the other girls did, but she knew he was the only man who could make them become famous. They would have to listen to him. Maybe he knew more about how ladies acted than they did. After all, they had almost raised themselves. It would be nice to be a lady.

Mr. Libra thrust a pile of contracts at them. "Take them home and read them and sign them. And wash that filthy hair. Tomorrow I want you here at nine sharp for styling, make-up, and gown fittings. I'm going to put you on television."

"Television!" The girls looked at each other wonderstruck.

"Shee-it!" Honey said in delight.

"That's ten dollars," said Mr. Libra.

"Oh, f . . . fudge!" Honey stammered. Ten dollars was a lot of bread.

"Very good," said Mr. Libra. He handed them some money. "Here's fifty dollars for carfare and shampoo for all of you. Be back tomorrow. Good-bye."

They left the suite, counting their money, and took a taxi, the first taxi they had been in since they got to New York.

"That Whitey sure is one ugly-lookin' motherfucker, ain't he?" Honey said in the cab.

"He sure is," Tamara agreed. "When he was born I bet they threw out the baby and saved the afterbirth."

The girls laughed. "That motherfucker talked to us like we was his *maids*," Beryl said.

"Carfare!" Honey stormed. "Up his syphilitic ass!"

"Cocksucker!" said Cheryl.

Silky decided the present was none too soon to start thinking clean, so she said nothing.

The next morning they showed up promptly at Mr. Libra's hotel suite, and for five hours they were terrorized by a nitty faggot hairdresser named Mr. Nelson, who was wearing a really sharp white leather suit. He fitted all the girls with Buster Brown wigs and a couple of extra hairpieces to change off. Then the dress designer arrived—Franco, who was very young but completely bald—and he and Mr. Libra consulted on what the girls were to wear. No one asked them for their opinion on anything, so the five of them kept a sullen silence. They had been through a lot in life, but they had never met anyone like Mr. Libra or Mr. Nelson or that Franco, so the truth was they were rather awed.

"I'm going to dress them all alike," Franco said.

"But no sequins," said Mr. Libra. "I'm sick and tired of sequins—you see them on every singing group in the business. The Supremes *invented* sequins. I don't know how anyone else gets a chance; there isn't a sequin left on Seventh Avenue after those three get through. I want Silky and the Satins to be unique. And no fishtail mermaid dresses, either. I want them to look young."

Franco suggested baby dresses, but Mr. Libra said his wife and all her friends wore baby dresses and they were a hundred years old. Young, he kept saying, young, young. Silky privately thought that she would like nothing better than to look like Diana Ross of the Supremes, who was her idol, except Diana Ross *was* awfully old—twenty-four or something. Finally Mr. Libra and Franco decided to dress them all in knicker suits like little boys.

"We're going to look like a bunch of dikes!" Tamara protested.

"I know you'd rather look like whores," Libra said, "but I'm managing you now, and you'll do what I say."

"Couldn't we wear tuxedos?" asked Honey.

"Oh?" said Libra. "So you want to look like *elderly* dikes?" That shut them all up for good, and Franco said he would make them knicker suits in black velveteen, burgundy velveteen, and white brocade to start off, with maybe one in a nice plaid wool for the daytime teen-age show Libra had booked them on.

It was the first the girls had heard of their booking. "What teenage show?" they chorused. "What show? What show?"

"The Let It All Hang Out Show," Libra said triumphantly. "You'll be on next month."

The girls squealed with delight. The Let It All Hang Out Show was the top afternoon teen-age song and dance show on television, and everyone they knew at home who had a TV set always watched it.

The next morning Mr. Libra installed the girls in the Chelsea Hotel, and after that there was a round of more fittings, more experiments with make-up with Mr. Nelson until all the girls could do their own make-up properly, both for street wear and public appearances, and then there were their dance lessons, which they all loathed. Mr. Libra even put them all on a diet to clear up their skins and keep them trim. He constantly corrected their grammar, and gradually they were all becoming conscious that there was a world they knew nothing about.

Silky got a card to the Public Library, and faithfully read her book a week, carrying it with her all the time because there was so little free time to read now. The other girls kidded her about it, and said she was carrying a book so she could meet an intellectual fellow and that she never actually read it.

Their first album was making it big, and the new single, "Lemme Live Now," was in the top ten. The money was pouring in, but they never saw any of it, except their allowances and living expenses. It didn't matter, though, because they had more money now than they had ever seen before. They haunted the five-and-ten, as purchasers now, and were thrilled to flaunt a ten-dollar bill to pay for a lipstick.

Meanwhile, Mr. Libra booked them on every free benefit in town. All those shows needed free talent to fill up the bill, and were glad Silky and the Satins were so available. Mr. Libra said the exposure was invaluable, because eventually they would be invited on the Tonight Show. Silky was amazed that there were so many free benefits. You could work your whole life away and never make a cent. But it was thrilling to see all those other *real* stars in person, and the dresses and jewels on the rich ladies in the audience fascinated her. She made it a point to study them carefully so that when she got to handle her own money she would know how to dress.

Their room in the Chelsea was a shambles, with clothes and empty boxes, bags, and tissue paper flung everywhere. The twins' cousin, Lester, arrived from Philadelphia with his girl friend and moved in with them, sleeping on the floor, because with the five beds the sofa had been removed. The girls decided that family was not considered men, and Mr. Libra could not possibly object, but anyway they did not tell him. Then the twins' sister, Ardra, arrived, and after her, Silky's brother, Cornelius. The girls sent down for more pillows and blankets, and all their guests settled comfortably on the floor. Rich Marvin wanted Tamara to live with him in the Village, but she thought the Chelsea was more fun. The boys bought beer and Bourbon with money the girls gave them, and there were parties every night. Sometimes they would buy big bags of fish and chips and break their diets, drink and stuff themselves, and dance and sing to the stereo the girls had chipped in to buy. They bought about a hundred and fifty records, and then they bought a color television set, and nobody ever got much sleep except Silky, who was terrified that she would lose her voice if she didn't take care of herself, and who had long ago learned how to fall asleep through any kind of racket.

The Chelsea was really a groovy place, full of nuts like themselves, and they made a few new friends. One of them was a good-looking black boy named Hatcher Wilson, who was a singer, too, and played the electric guitar. He was twenty-four, and he liked Silky. She liked him, too, but she remembered her vow, and she told him she wanted him for a friend, not a boyfriend. He hung around anyway, mainly because she didn't pay much attention to him and he wasn't used to that. Hatcher was a real ladies' man, and terribly vain about his looks and his clothes. The other girls thought Silky was crazy not to get some use out of a fine-looking stud like him, and they flirted with him and made him feel right at home.

"If you don't grab that Hatcher Wilson," Tamara kept threatening, "I'm goin' to grab him and *marry* him." Tamara was going to marry everybody; if it wasn't rich Marvin to get his money, it was her own cousin Lester to raise halfwits.

"I ain't goin' to marry *anybody*," Honey said. "Not me. I been married a hundred times."

They all wondered about Mrs. Libra, how she ever could have married an ugly freak like Mr. Libra. "What do they ever do in bed?" Honey would ask, and they would all howl with laughter trying to imagine that ape in bed with his wife.

"She jus' throws him a banana and says: 'Come git it, King Kong!'" Beryl screeched, rolling on the bed with laughter.

They all agreed Lizzie Libra was a good-looking woman. "I bet she's got somebody else," Cheryl said wisely.

"You think so?"

"Yeah," Cheryl said. "Wouldn't you, married to *that?*"

"She looks kind of dried up," Honey said.

"Don't you kid yourself," Cheryl said. "Did you ever look at her eyes? That woman got *real* man-hungry eyes."

They all decided to take a good look at Mrs. Libra's eyes the next time they saw her.

It was a good time, that month before their first television show. It was a real good time. Later Silky was to look back on it and remember it as the last good time of her life.

The girls rehearsed the Let It All Hang Out Show for two days. Silky was so nervous she couldn't eat a thing the entire time, except for many cups of tea laced with honey for her throat. She kept feeling her throat close up, as if she would never be able to get a note out of it, and although she was not a religious person she prayed almost constantly that everything would be all right. The only thing that kept her going was the young director, Dick Devere. He was a tall, skinny, distinguished-looking man, with a calm, professional attitude that set her at ease whenever he spoke to her. It was only when she was not actually the focus of his attention that the panic began again. This show wasn't just one of those free benefits; it was the big time.

From the moment Dick Devere first spoke to her, or actually to all the girls, Silky admired him. He had this real *cultural* way of speaking, the way he pronounced words. And he dressed in a way that wasn't at all sharp but certainly was hip. She knew his clothes were expensive. And she liked the way he moved, sort of relaxed but quick. She would watch him moving about the set, directing the other acts, and she thought he was kind of sexy. That surprised her, because it had been such a long time since she had thought of any man as sexy, or even as anything. Then, after she sang for the first time, she had the idea maybe he was noticing her too.

She didn't at all hold it against him that he was white. Silky had never been prejudiced. In fact, she kind of liked it. He was nothing like pimply Marvin, or that ape Mr. Libra, or the cruddy Eyetalian boys in her old neighborhood. He was real classy. She wondered if he had a wife or a girl friend.

They did the show in their new plaid knicker suits, with little red ascot ties and their Buster Brown wigs. They looked groovy. And they had never sounded better, since they were only lip synching to their records, so it was crazy of her to worry about losing her voice, although logic had nothing to do with it. After all, someday soon they would be doing their singing live, on an even bigger TV show than this, and it would be a heck of a mess if she couldn't sing *now*, just because there were millions of people watching what was coming over the camera at their end. All the girls were aware of the unseen audience, and the thing was, you had to sing out loud anyway, or it didn't look real. When they did "You Left Me," as usual Silky got carried away and changed some of the words without even knowing it. The girls knew it, though, and they were furious.

"Can't you even remember that old song?" Honey said, mad.

"I'm sorry."

"You certainly had enough practice," Honey said. "*I* know the words."

"I know the words," Silky said.

"That girl sure is dumb," Honey said to the others.

Dick Devere just laughed. After the show he asked Silky to come have a drink with him. The girls raised their eyebrows when they saw her go off with him, but Silky didn't care. She was floating on air. All the way to the bar she was wondering whether she dared order a real drink even though Mr. Libra had told them they must never drink in public.

They went to a little bar down the street from the television studio. There were a lot of television people there. Silky had changed into her own clothes; a navy-blue wool sailor suit with a white blouse, and she was still wearing her wig and her television make-up. She glanced at herself in the mirror over the bar when they walked in and she thought she looked real good. They sat in a booth near the back, and Dick Devere ordered a Scotch on the rocks.

"Bourbon and Coke," she said recklessly.

"Cigarette?"

"Thank you, I don't smoke."

"Good girl."

She chewed on a nail.

"How did you ever get the name Silky?"

"On account of ma' voice," she said, because it was what Mr. Libra had told her to say.

"You're going to be very famous one day," Dick Devere said.

"You think so?"

"There's no doubt about it. I can always tell. I see hundreds of singers, but none of them have what you do." He smiled at her. "What's that book you're reading?"

Silky showed him. It was *The Death of a President*.

"I'm glad you're not reading *Valley of the Dolls*," he said.

"Oh, I read that too."

"You read a lot," he said, sounding surprised.

"I read a book a week. I really read them too; I don't just carry them around like the girls say."

"You don't get along too well with the other girls, do you," he said. It was a statement, not a question.

"Oh, sure I do!" Silky protested. "We get along just fine. They're great girls."

"I think they're jealous of you," he said.

"Oh, no, they're not. We all get equal money."

"That doesn't make any difference. They know you're going to be a star someday and leave them far behind, and what's worse, they know you deserve it and they don't. Don't you notice they're jealous?"

"I'm just too busy singing," Silky said. The drinks came and she gulped down half of hers. It made her feel warm and more relaxed. "I'm trying to figure out where you're from by the way you talk," she said, "but I can't."

"I'm from the Middle West. What you're listening to is the accent I learned in a short stint at radio-announcer school. I did that for a while after college, while I was trying to break into directing. Where are you from?"

"South Philadelphia."

"Then why do you have a Southern accent?"

"I don't," Silky said.

"Sometimes you do."

"My parents were from Georgia," she said, remembering.

"Are they still alive?"

"No," she lied. "They're both dead." Well, maybe her father *was* dead; she hadn't heard from him in years.

"I think you should take acting lessons," he said thoughtfully. "Has Libra talked to you about that?"

"No. We're taking dancing lessons now."

"Well, you should ask him about an acting class. Eventually you're going to do a Broadway musical, and you should know how to act."

She had forgotten about the rest of her drink. The things he was saying to her were making her dizzy. "What Broadway musical? Me? What are we going to play, a black *Little Women?*"

"Not *we*," he corrected. *"You."*

"I'll never leave the girls," she said.

"You left them to come out with me," he said. She realized he was teasing her.

"That's different," she said.

"Not so different. People are going to seek you out, want to see you on your own. You're going to have a life of your own. I'm just telling you this because I want you to know it isn't going to be so easy for you to get along with the girls after a while, and I don't want it to be a shock for you. It's always better to be prepared."

"I don't go out with anybody, and I never minded who they went out with," Silky said. She finished her drink.

He ordered two more. "Don't you know anybody in New York?"

She thought about telling him about her vow and decided against it. Telling anybody might break the magic. "Oh, I know a few boys," she said.

"But you don't like any of them?"

"I'm too busy to date," she said. Then she realized what a dumb thing that was to say—he might think she didn't want to see him ever again. "I mean, I guess I don't like *them* much."

He smiled. He seemed to know a lot of things she didn't have to bother to tell him. She couldn't decide if he made her nervous or not. He certainly was sexy. She had decided that, anyway. He was as sexy as hell.

"Have you always read a lot?" he asked.

"No, just since I quit school. I didn't think quitting school was any reason why I should stop my education."

"Have you ever read *The Wind in the Willows?*"

"I never heard of it," she said.

"It's a children's book, but like all good children's books it's really for grown-ups. You should read it. And read *Mary Poppins.*"

"I saw the movie," she said.

"It's much better than the movie. Movies of children's books are terrible. The great thing about a children's book is you have to use your imagination. Once you see the people in front of your eyes on the screen you have to go by the director's idea of what they should be like instead of your own." He took a little leather-covered note pad out of his pocket, and a slim gold ballpoint pen and began to write. "I'm writing down a couple of books you've probably missed that I think you'll enjoy."

Well, get her! She was sitting here in this bar with all the television people and a big director twice her age was talking to her about books and movies as if she was an educated person! Shee-it ... I mean, wow! She sipped the new drink.

Somebody had put money in the jukebox and it was playing
"Lemme Live Now." It was like a dream come true. She
would have *paid* somebody to put her record on now! That
was her voice there, and here was her body here, having a
drink or two with this groovy guy, and oh, wow, who had
ever heard of a gold ballpoint pen! She made up her mind to
buy one just like it tomorrow, and a leather-covered notebook too, and write down little things in it.

He tore out the page and gave it to her. "Where are you
staying?"

"The Chelsea Hotel."

He nodded approvingly. Then he wrote that down in the
little notebook, and put it away in his pocket. "I'm not going
to do television forever," he said. He sipped his Scotch.
"Eventually I'm going to do a new kind of musical, using
techniques of film and the total environment of the discothèques. Have you been to Schwartz's Lobotomy?"

She shook her head no. It sounded like a delicatessen.

He looked at his watch. "Known to the regulars as the
Lobe. We have time to get something to eat before it opens,
if you're not doing anything."

"I have nothing to do for the rest of my life," Silky said
cheerfully. At that moment it seemed as if she didn't.

He took her to a French restaurant where she didn't know
what she was eating, which didn't matter much as she hardly
ate a thing. She had half a glass of wine. Then they took a
cab to the Village, to an ugly-looking warehouse with a lot of
trash piled up outside. Inside it was like another world. There
was a big room with a round balcony hanging in the center
of it, suspended by big things that went right through the
ceiling and led to by a catwalk. The balcony, suspended by
the foundations, was the only thing in the room that was not
shaking. The walls, ceiling and floor were covered with moving patterns of psychedelic colors and flashing lights, and the
whole room was shaking like a bowlful of Jell-O: the floor
they were trying to stand on, the walls, the ceiling. The tables
were just tiny silver boxes, and they were shaking too, so the
drinks were anchored to them with rubber plungers, but the
liquid kept splashing out anyway on to the customers'
clothes. The music was deafening, and the room was evidently wired to vibrate to the sounds. People were trying to
dance and stand up at the same time, and most of them
looked seasick. Silky could smell pot in the air. She wondered

if pimply Marvin took Tamara here, and she hoped he did so they could see her with Dick Devere.

"The ultimate in masochism," Dick said.

"What?"

"This place. It's my theory that all discothèques are experiences in masochism for the people who go there, and the reason this one is so popular right now is because it's the most sadistic. Look there."

He led her to the side of the room where there was a long line of people waiting to get into a small room with a sign over it: *De-vibration Chamber*. That room wasn't shaking at all. There were chairs to sit on in the room, and admission was a dollar. The room was so small that only six people could go in at a time, which was why there was the line. The people waiting to get in looked sicker by the minute. Silky didn't feel too well herself.

Then he took her back to the center of the room. He refused a table and he didn't want to dance; he just stood there watching professionally, taking it all in. Once in a while he would nod to himself. She didn't see how he could use any of this on his show but she supposed he had to know about everything that was going on. She felt like they were two outsiders, just standing there. It was a funny feeling, but kind of nice. They were out of it, but special. It was like everybody else was out of it and they were in.

"That's the V.I.P. balcony," he said, pointing. "We can sit there if you feel sick, they'll know me. You see, the celebrities can come here and watch and not have to be tortured. It's the only way the management can make them feel like they're celebrities."

There were shades all around the hanging balcony in front of each of the tables, and some of the celebrities had pulled their shades up so they didn't have to watch anything at all, in case *that* made them sick. *What a laugh,* Silky thought. *It costs fifteen dollars a couple to get in here and then they don't even look at it.*

"Okay," Dick said. "Let's split."

It was midnight, and he took her to an ice cream parlor on Third Avenue and bought her a sundae about ten inches tall. She would have rather had an Alka Seltzer, and she just played with the sundae, pretending to eat it. Which was just as well, she thought, because fudge sauce made her break out. The sundae cost three dollars and fifty cents and she was glad he didn't seem to notice that she had hardly touched it.

He must make a lot of money, she thought, or else he's really a gentleman.

She was feeling much better now that they were away from the Lobe, and she tried to remember that groovy thing he'd said there, about discothèques being sadistic or maso-something, and try to get it right so she could say it to somebody sometime and impress them. But he kept talking, saying more groovy things, and she was too busy trying to keep up with what he was saying now to keep her mind on what he'd said an hour ago. Sha—being out with him was like being out with ten people!

And then he took her to the Chelsea and told the cab to wait. Maybe she had bored him, she thought, beginning to feel very depressed. He didn't even hint to come up, he just told the cab to wait. She wondered if he was going to kiss her good night or anything, but he just took her hand and held it a long time and looked at her.

"I had a wonderful time," he said.

"Oh, I did, too," she said. "I really did." She thought for a moment of asking him up, but she realized they had turned the room into a pigsty, and Leroy and his girl friend and Cornelius and Ardra would be sleeping on the floor, and he would probably run out of there in horror. "I'll get those books," she said.

He smiled. "I envy you, reading them for the first time. Good night." And then he went away.

She pretended to be walking to the elevator and then when she saw the cab had pulled away she sat down on a chair in the lobby so she could be alone to think. She didn't know what to make of him. She had thought all evening, until the end, that he really liked her. He certainly wasn't shy. Maybe he thought she was repulsive. Maybe he wouldn't go to bed with a black chick. Maybe he was gay. No, she was sure he wasn't gay. Maybe he had a jealous woman at home. She'd have to get up her courage and worm it out of Mr. Libra in the morning. Boy, she was stupid! She should have asked him something about himself instead of letting him talk about all those arty things at dinner. But she had been so flattered and interested it hadn't mattered at all about his private life at the time. Maybe the way he acted was just the way people on a date acted in New York when they were his age and sophisticated. She thought that was probably it. He respected her. Wasn't that a gas! *He respected her!*

When she got upstairs everybody was having a good time,

playing their records and the television set all at the same time, and nobody even asked her if she had had a good time. The girls pretended she hadn't even been out. Only her own little brother Cornelius finally asked her if she'd had fun, and she was so glad somebody has asked that she almost cried. Honey was in bed, not asleep yet, and Silky noticed that all the girls had taken off their television make-up, except Honey, as usual. She began to cream her face and finally she turned to Honey and said as sweetly as she could: "Hey, do you want some of this?"

"What for?" Honey said, in a very mean voice.

"To take off your make-up."

"Kiss my ass," Honey said, and turned over and pulled the covers over her head.

"What's the matter with *her* tonight?" Silky asked the others. Nobody answered her. She felt her heart go up in her throat. Dick was right; they *were* jealous of her. But they had been her best friends for ever and ever—they couldn't just stop liking her. She turned to Cheryl and Beryl, who had *always* been her best friends.

"What do you say I call down for some fish and chips?"

"Didn't he feed you?" Cheryl said nastily.

"Sure, but I thought ... it might be fun."

"We're not hungry," Beryl said flatly. She turned the volume up on the stereo set.

"I don't know what you're all so mad about," Silky yelled over the noise of the record. "He's never going to call me again."

"Why not? Did he find out how *frigid* you are?" Tamara yelled back.

"It's not always like that," Silky yelled.

"Oh yeah? Did he *pay* you for balling him? Is that why you want to buy all us poor niggers fish and chips?" The other girls laughed.

Something in Silky snapped. "You don't know anything!" she screamed. "You take Marvin for everything you can get. What would you know about going out with a nice guy?"

"I guess you would," Tamara yelled, her face getting purple with rage. "You only go out with big white directors, you asslicker. Why don't you fuck old ape-face Libra?"

"Yeah, yeah," Beryl said. "Climb up a tree with him."

"Silky fucks Libra, Silky fucks Libra," they all began chanting. Her brother Cornelius just stood there looking stupid. Silky ran into the bathroom and slammed the door.

She was shaking. It was like a nightmare. She realized it
wasn't just her date with Dick tonight, although that had
been the last straw because he had so obviously singled her
out to take her out in public with him to a fancy place where
his friends might be. No, it had been coming for a long time,
only she had been too stupid to notice it. It had really
happened at the show today, when the Satins realized Silky
was their star. They had to realize it because everybody else
realized it. But it wasn't her fault. They had *let* her be the
lead singer. She had pretended she hadn't even wanted to be.
She hadn't asked for more money than they were getting, or
a different costume than they were wearing. It hadn't been
her idea to stand in front of them at her own microphone;
the lead singer always did that. She hadn't flirted with Dick
Devere. She hadn't done a damn thing. And that was the shit
and piss of it. She didn't have to *do* a damn thing—it was all
going to happen to her just because God had given her this
voice and she could sing. She wanted to run out into the
street, but she didn't have a place to stay. Was this what being
a star was going to mean? Having Mr. Libra treat her like
trash all day and then having the girls treat her like a hated
enemy every night? *Oh, my God, Dick* ... she thought, and
she realized she missed him. He was the only person who
understood her. She wished she knew his number so she
could call him. She pounded the sink with her fist and looked
at her face, ugly now with rage, and all the make-up off, in
the mirror. Without her wig, with her short, straightened hair
all smashed down, she looked like a boy. If he saw her now
he wouldn't like her any more either. She was nothing to
look at. But he hadn't seemed to care about how she looked.
He thought she was a nice person. He would understand. She
couldn't stay here with them, not after what they had said to
her.

She wiped off the last of the cold cream with astringent
and combed her hair so it didn't look so much like a horrible
crew cut. Then she went out of the bathroom. The girls
continued to ignore her. Cornelius, who had always been a
cry-baby depending on her to settle his fights, was just looking at her trying to figure out what the fuss was all about.
Silky picked up her purse and her jacket and walked out of
the room.

Downstairs in the lobby phone booth she looked up Dick
Devere in the phone book and called him. Her hand was
shaking so much she could hardly get the dime into the little

slot, but she felt icy cold inside. He answered after two rings.
"Yes?"

"It's Silky. I'm sorry to bother you, but you were right."
Then she burst into tears.

"What's the matter?" he asked. "What is it? I can't hear
you. What happened? Oh, the hell with it, have you got a
pencil?"

"Yes," she sobbed.

"Take down my address and come right over here. I'd
come get you but I'm not dressed."

She found an eyebrow pencil in her handbag and scribbled
his address on the wall. She remembered it anyway from the
phone book. Then she got a cab and went to his apartment,
which was not too far away, and by the time she got there
she realized with surprise and triumph that she had done
quite an extraordinary thing, because this was really what she
had wanted to do all along.

Dick Devere lived in an apartment in a brownstone. Silky
pushed the buzzer next to his name, and went upstairs. He
opened the door, dressed in a white terry-cloth bathrobe, and
she could see the apartment was dark. He put his arm around
her and cuddled her head to his chest, casually locking the
door behind her with his other hand.

"There, there," he said.

It was so dark she couldn't see how awful she looked with
all her make-up off and her face swollen from crying. She
could hardly see him either, just a white glimmer in the light
from the street lamp outside the big window. "There, there,"
he kept saying, patting her, and he led her into the bedroom
and right to bed.

She thought briefly about her vow while he was undressing
her, and then she didn't think about it any more because he
was kissing her. It was lovely, and she thought maybe she
loved him. He knew just what to do and it wasn't at all like
those boys when she was a kid who just shoved it in. Oh, my
God, he was divine ... Was *this* what sex was like? If she
had known this was what it was all about, she would never
have been able to give it up. She'd heard plenty of talk about
all these things he was doing, but nobody had ever told her
how groovy and wild and really marvelous feeling it *felt*. So
this was what all the older girls did with their boyfriends!
And it was a good thing he knew what to do, because he was
enormous. She certainly hadn't expected that.

He really knew everything there was to know about loving,

and she was sure sex wasn't always like this, that what was so
fantastic was *him,* what he was all about, what he was
thinking, how he felt about her. He was a real man. She
didn't think there was anybody like him in the whole world. *I
love you,* she thought, *I love you, I love you.* She thought he
was whispering "I love you" too, but she wasn't sure.

When it was over they curled up together with their arms
around each other. Her eyes had become accustomed to the
darkness and she could see him. He looked happy. She knew
she was happy.

"Silky," Dick whispered.

"What?"

"I can't sleep like this, you'll have to get over on the other
side of the bed. Do you feel better now?"

"Yes," she said, and reluctantly inched away from him.

"Good," he said, and a moment later he was asleep.

She couldn't think much about that because she felt too
marvelous. This had been one of the biggest days of her life.
He certainly didn't have a wife or any girl living with him. *I
wonder if I have a boyfriend now,* she thought, looking at
him, and she wished more than anything in the world, more
even than to be a star, that it could be true.

She didn't see the girls until the next day in Mr. Libra's
office, and no one mentioned the fact that she had been out
all night, or asked her where she had slept. Silky hoped the
girls would think she'd had to rent a room at the Y, or go
back uptown to Harlem. She tried to look martyred, but she
was bubbling with happiness. The truth was, she realized
regretfully, the girls really didn't know much about her, how
she thought, what she dreamed. They knew she wanted to
sing and they knew she read books, but actually she had
never had a private conversation with any of them. She'd just
gone along with what they wanted, sharing their jokes, kidding around, trying to be part of the gang. She realized now
that none of the others had tried to be part of the gang at
the expense of their own wants; they'd balled any guy they
wanted and spent their money on their own clothes and
make-up and perfume and gone their own way. *She* was the
one who'd worked in that restaurant while they were out
balling, *she* was the one who sang lead and carried the
group. *She* was the one who'd had to memorize all those
lyrics while they just went "ooh, ooh, ooh" in back of her.

She wondered if they were sorry they had driven her out of their room into the night, and then she began to realize that she would never really know if they were sorry because she was their meal ticket and they had to be nice to her or there would be no Silky and the Satins. She'd always considered herself a cool and tough little chick, but now Silky realized there were depths of toughness she hadn't even reached yet. A year ago, when they started the group, she never would have believed they would be treating each other the way they were now, or that she would be able to accept how important she was and how much they needed her. And who was she? She wasn't even sure she was a good singer. She'd never taken a lesson; people just seemed to like her voice and her delivery. Maybe she was a fake, and she'd conned the girls into believing she was necessary to them.

Mr. Libra was telling them that he'd hired someone to work up an act for them and that they'd begin to do bookings in small clubs out of town. Then they'd come back and do another Let It All Hang Out Show. The reaction to the show they had done the day before had been excellent, and now the clubs were willing to have them. They were going to need more costumes, and he was going to let them have two rooms instead of the one they now had.

Silky breathed a sigh of relief. Two rooms was better than one, but what she really wanted was a room of her own so the girls couldn't pick on her. She'd left Dick in the morning and he said he would call her, but he hadn't said anything about her coming to live with him and she certainly wasn't going to ask. If she did, she might lose him. When their meeting was finished, she asked Mr. Libra if she could have a word with him. The girls gave her a look that could kill and left.

"Well?" Mr. Libra said.

"Mr. Libra, I hate to tell you this, but things have gotten real bad between me and the girls. They seem to hate me. I think they're jealous. They're making me miserable and it's bad for my work. I think I should have a room of my own. I'll pay for part of it out of my allowance."

"You think if you have your own room they'll be *less* jealous?"

"No, I guess they'll be even madder."

"Isn't there even one of them you can get along with?"

"No," Silky said. "They stick together."

"You want me to talk to them?"

"Oh, no!" she said, frightened. "You don't know them! That would fix me for sure."

"I don't care how you girls get along privately," Libra said, "but I don't ever want to see any sign of a feud in front of anyone or I'll get rid of all of you. I don't need that. I'll give you your own room if you'll make it your responsibility to see that everything is sweetness and light in public. After all, you're the one they don't like, according to you. They like each other."

"Could you explain that to them? Tell them that you're giving me my own room to get me out of their sight, not because I'm the star or anything?"

Mr. Libra smiled nastily. "Do you think they'll believe that?"

"Well, they'll *never* believe it if *I* tell them."

"Don't I have enough to do without worrying about your school-girl feuds?" he exploded.

Silky felt herself trembling. That man always scared her to death. But she wasn't going to back down now, because not getting her own room would be worse than anything Mr. Libra could do to her.

"I think this would be the best thing to do," Silky said, trying not to sound frightened.

"Do you think I'm the keeper of a bunch of juvenile delinquents? You girls think you're professionals, but you still act like slum bunnies."

"I'm sorry, sir, but you're the only one I can turn to."

"I suppose if you don't get your own way you'll end up shacking up elsewhere anyway, probably with some guy," Mr. Libra said in disgust.

Silky didn't answer.

"All right," he said, and reached for the phone. "Get out. You'll get your own room. I'll tell the girls. You can move your things this afternoon."

"Thank you, Mr. Libra." But he waved her away, already talking to the desk at the hotel, asking for the manager, and she ran out of the suite.

Now that she had her own room it was much easier to talk to Dick on the phone, when he finally did call that evening, and she could go and come as she pleased. She bought a radio, because after chipping in for the room rent she didn't have enough to pay for her own TV set, but Silky was glad anyway just to have the quiet and privacy. Rehearsals started for their new act, and there were new songs to learn. She

saw the girls at rehearsal, at dance class, and in Mr. Libra's
office, but they never asked her to have meals with them and
she usually picked up something at the delicatessen to take to
her room or forgot to eat at all. Her brother Cornelius
moved in with her for a while, but soon found it boring, and
moved in with some kids he'd met who lived in the Village,
and that was the last of him except when he needed money.

Now Dick was her only friend. She saw him every other
night, and she never asked him what he did when he was not
with her. She thought he might be working, or more likely
with other girls, but she also knew enough not to ask any
questions. He always asked her what she did, and she told
him truthfully that she read, studied her new lyrics, and went
to bed early.

She had no interest in looking for other men. Now that she
had her own room, Hatcher Wilson really thought he was
going to get in at last, but she kept telling him no, and she
told him not to waste his money taking her out to dinner
because she didn't want to be his girl friend. Once in a while
she had a Coke with him in the hotel bar, always a Coke and
always just one, so he wouldn't have to spend much money,
and only because she wanted the girls to see her with him
and forget about Dick Devere. But even that plan backfired,
because by now Hatcher had balled each one of the other
girls, and they were jealous because he still liked Silky the
best.

She wished she could like him more. He was a good-
looking boy and dressed well, and he was talented in her field
so they should have a lot in common. But he had nothing to
talk about. He kidded around, and flattered her, and
bragged, and they talked about their work, but she might
have been anybody. Hatcher had never read a book in his life
and didn't intend to. He thought women were to look at, and
show off with him when he went places, and something to
screw, but that was all. His aspirations were something he
shared with his buddies in his own group; the guys, the boys,
the gang; and he felt it was somehow unmasculine to share
these feelings with Silky. The more she saw Hatcher, the
more she missed Dick.

She was becoming dependent on Dick for everything. He
advised her how to dress, corrected her grammar, enlarged
her vocabulary; but always in a very nice, constructive way—
nothing at all like the way Mr. Libra did it. She told Dick she
was Pygmalion, and he answered that Pygmalion was the

sculptor, not the woman he created, just as Frankenstein was the doctor, not the monster. He'd do that: answer with logic or a correction, but never a real answer.

Silky and the Satins had professional photos taken for publicity, and Silky gave one to Dick. She bought a real silver frame and put the picture in it, figuring even if he didn't think the picture was much at least the frame was worth something. But whenever she went to his apartment she saw her photo there on his dresser. It made her feel wonderful. She asked him for a photo of himself, but he said he never had owned one.

Sometimes they went out, but more often she went over to his apartment after rehearsals and cooked something. She was a fair cook, but he was teaching her that, too. She figured she'd be a great wife someday, after Dick got through improving her, but she didn't want to think about that because she knew that as long as he was alive she'd never marry anybody. She didn't have to bring up the subject; she just knew he would never marry her. She wanted badly to be married before she was dead, because she'd grown up around so many people who'd had children and never married the man that she was determined it would never happen to her. She went to a doctor and got birth-control pills. She was glad her mother was dead and didn't know that she'd ended up going around with a man who would never marry her, but at least she knew her mother would be glad to know there wouldn't be any grandchildren who knew they only belonged to their mother.

They went off on tour then, and did some clubs, and Silky always telephoned Dick after the last show was over, at about two thirty in the morning, and of course sometimes he wasn't there and sometimes he was but she didn't know for sure if he was alone. She knew men were like that, and she knew you could never mention it or there would be a big fight and the woman always lost. She never mentioned him to the girls and they never mentioned him again either, except that if ever a rich-looking white guy from the audience would come backstage after the show they would give Silky mean looks as if she was going to grab him. She was so busy worrying about remembering everything in the act, the jokes, the bits of business, and all the new lyrics, and worrying about not losing her voice from the strain of doing all those shows, that it gave her something to think about and kept her from caring what the girls did to her. She had her own room on the road, too, and she usually did her make-up upstairs in the room so she wouldn't have to spend much time with them in the dressing room. The people who came backstage from the audience always flipped over her and wanted her autograph, but usually if they were guys they ended up liking the other girls just as much as they liked her because the other girls were friendlier.

In small towns people recognized them on the street, and asked them for their autographs, and all the girls had taken to wearing their stage make-up and false eyelashes and wigs when they were offstage too, to keep up their image. Silky was just as aware of that as the other girls were, and she always wore big dark glasses in the morning if she had to go out to eat and didn't have her eye make-up on.

Without Mr. Libra to supervise them every minute, the other girls were gaining weight. Mr. Libra flew to whatever club they were at to beat their opening and supervise them, and he'd hired the twins' older sister Ardra to be their chaperone, but Ardra didn't do much except stay with them and enjoy all the attention they were getting, and Mr. Libra had other clients to attend to in New York, so the girls were pretty much independent. After a few clubs all the girls had to have their costumes let out, except for Silky. Mr. Libra discovered that, and he blew the roof off.

"I'm not spending money on four ugly sows," he screamed. "You see this? This is a list. I want you to write down every single thing you eat and drink, and give me the lists every time I see you. If you lose your looks, you're going right back to that slum I picked you out of, and I'm going to get four other girls who look just like you and call *them* the Satins. You think you can't be replaced? You can be replaced in one minute. One minute! There are hundreds of little black slum bunnies just waiting for me to give them a chance to be the Satins. There are plenty of girls who can go 'Ooh, ooh, ooh' just like you're doing now. Just *watch it*."

He didn't say a word about replacing Silky, and it was so obvious that she was afraid they might take all their anger for Mr. Libra out on her when he was gone; but he had really scared them by yelling at them and when he got finished all the girls were crying and they didn't look at Silky at all. She thought Mr. Libra had really gone too far. You couldn't expect people to work and do their best when you told them they were worthless. The girls had feelings, too.

Silky was really mad at him. She still liked the girls, and she hated Mr. Libra.

"He has no right to talk like that," she told the girls when Mr. Libra had left. "He's the rottenest man in the world. Who does he think he is, Hitler?"

"Hitler? Hitler?" Honey said. "Who the fuck is Hitler? Somebody from one of your books?"

"What did you do, sleep through school?" Silky said. "Hitler was this white cat who went around killing children. He killed only about eight million people, is all. Mostly Jewish people."

"What the fuck has Jews got to do with them?" asked Ardra, who didn't like Silky any more either.

"He killed them because they were a minority and he hated them," Silky said.

"Yeah?" said Tamara. "When was this?"

"Before we were born," said Silky.

"Yeah? Where did he live?"

"In Germany."

"Well, no wonder I never heard of him," said Honey.

"What was his name again?" Tamara asked.

"Hitler."

"Oh, yeah . . ." Beryl said. "I remember him. We had him in history class."

So they began calling Libra Hitler, and it made them feel a little better.

They came back to New York to do the Let It All Hang Out Show, and Silky resumed with Dick. Then Dick was going to direct the Asthma Relief Telethon, and the girls would be on that. At the telethon Hitler-Libra introduced them to his new secretary, Gerry Thompson.

Gerry was a really classy-looking girl, with straight red hair. She knew how to dress, too, Silky noticed at once. And she was pretty, and probably smart. Dick seemed to like her immediately.

The minute Silky saw Dick looking at Gerry she got really sick to her stomach. It was one thing to imagine all the girls he took to his apartment at night when she wasn't there, but it was another thing to see him in action. She thought she was going to choke. This Gerry was probably the kind of white girl he liked to date, and she was going to be trouble. The worst of it was she was nice, and not a bitch at all. It was obvious that Gerry didn't dislike him but she wanted to get rid of him because she knew he belonged to Silky. There

had been a sort of understanding between the two girls
immediately: Silky knew Gerry liked her, and she felt friendly toward Gerry. It wasn't Gerry's fault that Dick liked
her—she was just the kind of girl he would like—and that
made it almost worse. It was as if Silky was powerless to
change anything.

But Silky knew one thing: she'd been fighting for her life
as long as she could remember, and she wasn't going to give
up now. This Gerry looked soft, like a girl who'd always had
things her own way and never had to fight for anything. Silky
could teach her a thing or two about fighting. She wasn't
going to let Dick just drift away. She was going to make it
her business to really make friends with Gerry, so the girl
would feel too guilty to let Dick get anywhere. And she was
going to be so sweet and cool around the house and so much
a woman in bed that Gerry wouldn't stand a chance. Dick
was her whole life. What would Gerry know about a man
who was a woman's whole life? It was just sickening to think
that this pretty, classy-looking girl who'd always had everything could just walk in and take away the one thing that
meant everything to her, a girl who'd never had anything at
all before. Silky knew one thing: if Gerry thought Dick was
going to be just another romance she was going to have to
put up a hell of a fight.

CHAPTER

THREE

THE morning after the telethon *Time* Magazine came out,
and there was great jubilation in the Libra office because
Franco, the dress designer who was one of Libra's clients,
was in it. His new collection had just been shown, and the
highlight of the collection was the bride's dress which cus-
tomarily closed every designer's showing—but Franco's
bride's dress was called "The Empress's New Clothes" and
was a mini-tent made completely of transparent vinyl, worn
with nothing whatsoever underneath it but body make-up and
a G-string covered with stephanotis like a bride's bouquet.
There was a photo in *Time* of Franco with the naked bride,
and a caption which said: "Nobody tells the Empress."

"How do you like the *bird's* bouquet?" Libra asked Gerry,
laughing at his own joke. "A bouquet on the bush is worth
two in the hand. Jesus, I wonder what Ingrid puts in those
shots." He placed the issue of *Time* in the place of honor on
the coffee table. "Franco should be here any minute and
you'll meet him. Damn jerk's real name is Alvin. He calls
himself Franco because he doesn't know it's the name of a
Spanish dictator."

Lizzie came out of the bedroom wearing beige wool over-
alls with wide Mickey Mouse suspenders which attached with
oversized pearl buttons above the bosom. Her hair was in the
two ponytails and she was wearing her horn-rimmed glasses.
She helped herself to a cup of coffee from the breakfast

70

display which Gerry had learned was to be a permanent feature every morning. "Franco made these for me," Lizzie told her. "How do you like them?"

"They're darling," Gerry said. She did not add that they would be more darling on a four-year-old.

"I think we should give him a party," Lizzie said to Libra.

"Who's going to pay for it—you?" he said.

"I'll pay for it," Lizzie said. "From our joint account."

"The B.P.'s are already giving him a party," Libra said. "Let them pay for it. You can go free."

"I certainly will," Lizzie said, and went over to the appointment book on the desk to check.

The doorbell rang. Gerry opened the door. It was Elaine Fellin, in her fox, wearing a pair of very dark glasses.

"When does Franco get here?" Elaine Fellin said, by way of greeting. She dropped off her coat and collapsed into the nearest chair.

"If you two girls think you're going to stay here and learn any secrets, you're sadly mistaken," Libra said. "You can congratulate him and then I want you both out."

"I got up early to see him," Elaine said. "I didn't even sleep off my pill. I won't even let you see my eyes."

"When does Daddy get back?" Lizzie asked her.

"Today, the son of a bitch. I called him last night and the hotel said he wasn't taking any calls. I screamed at them and said I was his wife, but they said that's what all the fans say. He was fast asleep, the stinker, while I had to stay up and worry. He didn't even bother to call me."

"Husbands are rotten," Lizzie said.

"Thank you," said Libra.

"Oh, I don't mean you, darling. You're sweet." She smiled at Gerry. "Sam is a very good husband. Daddy is a lousy husband."

"He used to be nice," Elaine said in her dead voice.

"Would you like some coffee, Mrs. Fellin?" Gerry asked.

"I can't eat in the morning, it makes me sick," Elaine Fellin said. "Do you have any Bloody Marys?"

Gerry went to the bar to make some.

"What do you expect when you marry somebody in show business?" Libra said to Elaine. "They're all children. He was rotten to his first two wives—why should he treat you any differently?"

"*They* were *horrible*," Elaine said.

"*They* were *horrible*," Libra imitated her. "That's what wives always say. *He* was ducky, I suppose?"

"You have no right to criticize Daddy," Elaine said, her dead voice taking on a semblance of expression. "I can say what I want, but *you* keep out of it."

"I love loyalty," Libra said drily.

"Never mind, Elaine," Lizzie said. "He'll be back today and you can punch him in the mouth."

"I'm not going to punch him," Elaine said. "I'm going to buy Franco's whole collection. That'll be a body blow."

The phone rang. Gerry answered it. It was Atlantic City for Libra.

"Yeah, baby," Libra said into the phone. "How's everything? You're going to the Toy Convention? Yeah. Yeah. Well, she's here now; do you want to speak to her?" He waved at Elaine. "It's your husband."

Elaine undulated out of the chair like a lion cub and stalked across the room to take the telephone receiver Libra was holding out to her. "When are you coming home?" she said to Mad Daddy.

There was a long silence. He was evidently explaining. Elaine bit her lip. "Why the fuck didn't you tell me today's show was taped?" she screamed. "You don't tell me anything. I could have gone down there with you; I didn't have to stay here and be bored to death. Why don't you ever tell me anything? Don't you care about me at all?"

Lizzie looked embarrassed and took her coffee into the bedroom.

"Well, I don't care when you come home," Elaine said. "Just have a good time, you bastard. You can come home next Tishah b'ab for all I care." She hung up and snatched the Bloody Mary Gerry had made her off the bar. She took several big gulps and turned on Libra. "You knew it all the time, didn't you? You don't tell me anything either. Why are you men always in cahoots?"

"Maybe because you women are always in cahoots," Libra said calmly.

"Oh, I'd like to throw this drink right in your face!"

"Do it and you won't get another one."

Elaine stamped into the bedroom and slammed the door.

"I'm afraid her days with him are numbered," Libra said to Gerry. "She's too old."

"Too old?"

"She's going on twenty-six. That's too old for him. He

married her when she was sixteen, right after she won the
Miss Bensonhurst crown. She'd told them she was eighteen.
She was disqualified, but she married the judge. His other two
wives were teen-agers too, and he divorced them when they
reached senility, or twenty-one, which is the same thing as
far as he's concerned. Elaine's lasted the longest. But the
handwriting's on the wall."

"How old is *he?*" Gerry asked.

"He'll be forty next week," Libra said. "And it's killing
him."

"Wow!"

"Don't act so surprised. You've been around."

"I know, but I still feel awfully sorry for both of them."

"She knew what she was getting into," Libra said, giving
her a shrewd look. "Don't all you girls know? Huh?"

"I guess so," Gerry said. There was no point in telling him
a sixteen-year-old girl was not exactly rational; she didn't
want another fight with him this early in the day. She
thought of Mad Daddy's fans in the hotel corridor the day
before, who loved him because they thought he was so safely
unapproachable. Wouldn't they be surprised to know one of
them could even be the next Mrs. Mad Daddy if she played
her cards right.

"She'll get a lot of money when he dumps her," Libra said.
"Daddy is going to become a very rich man this year when
he starts that midnight show. One thing he's always been is
generous with alimony. He pays until he's broke, out of guilt,
and as soon as the lady in question remarries and the alimony
stops, he always dumps the next wife so he has to pay
through the nose again. It's either bad timing or his Jewish
sense of guilt. Elaine will take all she can get, too. She's no
fool."

"Do they have any children?"

"They have a beautiful little girl, four years old. She looks
just like Elaine. And he has two kids with wife number one,
and a kid with number two. He thinks if you get married you
have to procreate instantly. Luckily for him both his other
wives married very rich guys. They were still young and
beautiful when he dumped them. Elaine will get along."

"She drinks a lot," Gerry said.

"Oh, as soon as they get divorced she'll go off the sauce so
fast it'll look like it's out of style. She's too smart to let
herself become a drunk and lose her looks. The former Miss
Bensonhurst knows very well how to take care of herself."

Well, Gerry thought, *it's none of my business.* Still, she was feeling depressed. She was relieved when the doorbell rang and she had to let Franco in.

Franco was a slender, pale-looking young man about twenty-five who looked older at first glance because he was completely bald. He had evidently decided that thinning hair was worse than a Yul Brynner haircut, so he had carefully shaved off any vestige of hair that nature had left him. He was wearing an expensive-looking Irish hand-knit turtleneck sweater, rust-colored suede pants, and a fleece-lined suede car coat. *Libra could go into the leather business,* she thought.

"It's cold out today," Franco said.

"If you'd wear some hair you wouldn't be so cold," Libra told him. "This is my new assistant, Gerry Thompson. This is Franco."

They shook hands. Franco gave Gerry his coat and she hung it up in the closet. "One thing I like about your dump, Libra," Franco said, "is that you always keep it so warm. You must know when I'm coming."

"I only have to ask your models," Libra said. He turned to Gerry. "Franco looks like a fruit, but he's really a super-stud."

"Oh, I like boys, too," Franco said. He smiled at Gerry. "You don't mind, do you?"

"No," she murmured politely, giving him a sweet smile because she was going to have to work with this creep, and took out a cigarette.

"Leave her alone," Libra said calmly. "She's a bright girl. I'm going to leave her in charge of the office when I'm out of town."

"Then we certainly must get better acquainted," Franco said to Gerry. He leaned over with a gold lighter and lit her cigarette, smiling at her again.

Lizzie and Elaine came out of the bedroom. "Congratulations, Franco!" they chorused happily, and Lizzie kissed him on the cheek.

"*Time* Magazine!" Franco said triumphantly. "I bought up all the copies on my local newsstand, and then I put half of them back because I didn't want my neighborhood to be deprived of the good news. It's really a dilemma, you know, wanting all the copies for yourself and wanting the world to read them too. I guess I should have bought one copy at each newsstand on the East Side. I think I'm going to make a coffee table top out of the write-up; paste them all together and lacquer them."

"Wait a while," Libra said. "I'll get you the cover of *Time* one day."

"That's what we have to talk about," Franco said. He glanced at the ladies, evidently wanting them out.

"Lizzie and Elaine, scat," Libra said. "The Pope's audience is over. Gerry stays."

Lizzie and Elaine gave him dirty looks. Elaine picked up the pitcher of Bloody Marys and the two women went back into the bedroom.

"That's what I like," Franco said to Libra. "Instant obedience. My models never listen to me until I yell at them."

"That's because you bang them," Libra said. He sat down and Franco and Gerry sat down too. "Now, Franco, what I went to discuss with you is this: a naked model is a brilliant idea, but you can't top it and you can't sell it on the street. Your next collection ... your whole next collection ... has to be completely unusual, new, breath-taking. You've done one mind-bender with your bride's dress, but your new collection has to change the face of fashion all over the country. I don't want your collection to be like any of your others and I don't want it to be like anybody else's. Have you got any ideas?"

"What about the look I gave Silky and the Satins?"

"Out," said Libra. "That's new for a singing group because singing groups copy other singing groups and they never have a new idea. You put them in something that's good for the girl on the street and everybody says 'Wow!' They think that's unusual. No, I want your new collection to stop people in their tracks; I want them to say, 'There goes a Franco.'"

"Yeah," Franco said dispiritedly. He chewed a nail.

Libra looked up at the framed oil painting of Sylvia Polydor, as if for guidance. It was as if he was looking at a painting of the Madonna to see if a divine ray of inspiration would be given to him. Then his face lighted up and he sprang to his feet and began pacing the room. "Shoulder pads!" he cried. "Peplums! Snoods! Platform shoes with ankle straps and nailheads around the platform! Wedgies with hollow lucite heels with goldfish swimming in them!"

"Yeah!" Franco cried, springing to his feet, too. "The Gilda Look! I saw that movie again on television last night. God, Rita Hayworth was the sexiest woman in the world!"

"Nobody was as sexy as Sylvia Polydor," Libra said.

"Do you think she would wear my clothes?"

"Everybody will be wearing your clothes," said Libra. "I'll get Nelson to do the snoods. He can braid them out of that damn Dynel he's so in love with. And you can give them . . . stockings with seams! Oh, my God, Lizzie's going to look terrible—two feet tall with shoulder pads and a peplum. Well, I guess there are some sacrifices even I must make for your career."

"I'll go home and start on the sketches right now," Franco said. He grabbed Libra's hands in his. "Ole, ole, Matador, we're in business!"

"Don't Matador me, you bald freak," Libra said, not entirely unmoved by Franco's show of affectionate gratitude. "You're as Spanish as I am. And don't forget the beads on the peplums for evening."

"Oh, it's beautiful, beautiful," Franco said happily. "Gerry, I can't wait to see you in the Gilda Look."

"I already have long red hair," Gerry said, thinking she'd rather die than wear any of the things he was proposing.

"I have a brilliant idea," Franco said. "Will you be here later this afternoon?"

"Probably," Libra said.

"Well, you be here," Franco said, and grabbed his car coat out of the closet and was gone.

Libra looked triumphant. He gave Gerry his Cheshire Cat grin. "That's how a genius does business," he said. "And don't you forget it. I don't want you to tell anyone, promise me. Fashion secrets are more carefully kept than government secrets. Tell no one a word of this."

"I won't," she promised. She wouldn't have told anyone anyway, because one thing she didn't want them to think was that she worked for a crazy man.

Libra went off to a luncheon appointment, Lizzie and Elaine had lobster and champagne sent up at Libra's expense to soothe their egos, and Gerry went out to Chock Full O'Nuts. She was saving her money for the new furniture she was planning to buy for her new, lovely apartment.

At four o'clock when Lizzie was at her shrink, Elaine had gone home, and Libra was giving Gerry dictation, Franco appeared again. At first Gerry didn't even know who it was. Franco was wearing a flowing auburn paste-on wig, the hair rippling down to his shoulders, with a Gilda wave flopping over one eye.

"Good God!" Libra said. "I think I'm going to be sick."

"What do you think of that?" Franco said proudly. "I have a new image too."

"You'll have to learn not to sweat," Libra said drily. "Your net's popping."

Franco ran his finger around the net. "Oh, my, so it is." He produced a bottle of spirit gum from his coat pocket and reglued the net where it had sprung away from his temple. "Long hair is in for men," Franco said, "and I'm sick and tired of your cracks about my bald head."

"I'd grown rather fond of your bald head," Libra said.

"Well, you'll just have to miss it," Franco said smugly. "No, seriously, this isn't for me—it's the wig I'm going to put on every single one of my models."

The telephone rang. It was Dick Devere.

"Hello, Gerry. What's new in that lunatic asylum?"

"Oh, nothing much," she said. "We have a man here in a brand-new long red wig with a Gilda wave, and a bottle of glue in his hand."

"It sounds like Nelson," Dick said.

"It's Franco."

Franco was still at the mirror, tossing his head to watch the hair ripple in the afternoon sunlight.

"Would you like to speak to Mr. Libra?"

"As a matter of fact," Dick said, "I called to talk to you, Gerry."

"Yes?"

"Don't sound so nervous," he said. "It's nothing bad."

"It's just that it's a little hectic here," she said.

"That's why I think we should have lunch. Are you free tomorrow?"

"No, I'm sorry," Gerry lied.

"Well, I have a rehearsal in the afternoon, so we can't have a drink—how about lunch the day after tomorrow?"

"I don't know ... I might not be able to get out. I just started here and there are a lot of things I have to do."

"One of the things you have to do," said Dick Devere, "is get to know the clients. How about the day after tomorrow?"

He was right, of course. She couldn't fool him by lying; he was obviously too smart for that. All Libra's clients were important to him and therefore they had to be important to her. What was she going to do? She wished Dick would say something about Silky and bring it out into the open—either say he and Silky were just friends or say that Silky was his girl and he wanted to see *her* for purely professional reasons, to be nice or polite or something.

"I'm sure you have a lot more important things to do than spend a couple of hours with the secretary," she said, not at all coyly, trying at the same time not to sound bitchy.

He laughed. "Secretary? Did you just get demoted?"

"Well, you know what I mean."

"I haven't the faintest idea what you mean. Unless you mean that you think I've been rude and you don't like me."

"Oh, no, it's not that," Gerry said quickly. Franco was still in love with his mirror image, but Libra was looking at her and she realized she'd better terminate this discussion in a hurry or Libra would. "Whatever you say would be fine."

"I'll pick you up at the office on Thursday then, at one o'clock. Write it down."

"All right. See you then."

She hung up and gave Libra a weak smile.

"Who was that who preferred you to me?" Libra asked.

"Dick Devere," she said.

"Good. I want everybody to like you."

Oh God, Gerry thought, *in that case I'd better call Silky and take her to lunch. If she'll go . . .*

Franco left to begin his sketches for the Gilda Look, and Libra kept her busy with dictation and typing so there was no time to think. But on the way home that evening Gerry began to realize that what was really bugging her was more a guilty conscience than unselfish guilt. It was flattering to have someone who was not a freak or a fool take a liking to her. She hadn't had a date in two months. Who had she met in this office? So far, freaks and fools. Who was she likely to meet? More freaks and fools? She was too old, sophisticated, shy, and proud to go to singles' bars. She could call up some of her old romances and say: "Hey, I'm back in New York!'" but they were why she had left New York in the first place. Maybe, as her mother would say, this Dick Devere had a nice friend. He probably had plenty of them.

She stopped at the grocery and bought a small barbecued chicken and a cantaloupe. There she was, picking out the smallest chicken in the store and knowing it would still be too big for one. She was too lazy even to cook for herself. At least she wasn't at the stage where she bought one lamb chop like an old maid. A chicken was more dignified; anyone watching her would think she had someone coming to dinner, or perhaps a husband at home to feed. Still, it was

depressing. The chicken felt warm through the paper bag;
something nice and warm to hold, and that was depressing
too. You could make yourself forget about sex and babies
you didn't have, but it was hard to forget about loneliness.
Television was interesting, but there would still be plenty of
television when she was ninety years old. She saw a young
couple running down the street, the girl dressed up, the man
waving at a cab. She hadn't had a date in New York in
years! She didn't want to look forward to having lunch with
Dick Devere on Thursday, but in spite of herself she *was*
looking forward to it, because she knew as well as he did that
it was a date.

Why are you being so noble? she asked herself, as if she
were a stranger. You've gone out with *married* men, and you
believed them when they said they had nothing to say to their
wives. You didn't worry about their wives then either. Sure,
you were younger, and you hadn't learned yet what it felt
like to be hurt, but why are you playing so noble now?
Because Silky's black?

You're taking all the sins of the world on yourself and the
man's only asked you to have lunch with him, she told
herself. She climbed up the three flights of stairs and let
herself into her brand-new, lonely apartment with her brand-
new, one-set-only key. She looked around the living room. It
looked so clean and bare. She would have to buy some paper
flowers, and candles. She wondered if she would ever invite
any man to have dinner there. Sure, being single was lonely,
and dating was tough, and a new apartment didn't feel like it
belonged to her yet, or she to it. She put the chicken in her
immaculate kitchen, feeling like a guest in a hotel. No wonder people had invented lunch dates and dinner dates; it was
awful to eat alone. She might as well be honest with herself
and look forward to her lunch date on Thursday—it was the
only thing she had to look forward to all week. And she
could wear her new green suit that she'd brought back from
Paris, the one that did all the things green was supposed to
do for green eyes. God knows, if she didn't wear it sometime
it would go out of style.

CHAPTER

FOUR

MAD DADDY, formerly Moishe Fellin, was in the bathtub
of his room in the Albermarle Hotel in Atlantic City, accompanied by a floating Dennison of the Deep toy, about a quart
of bubble bath, and a fourteen-year-old girl named Marcie,
who had come backstage to ask for his autograph the night
before. Marcie was a tall, gloriously sun-tanned blond girl
with slender, nymphet limbs covered with the most delicate
frost of platinum hair. Right now those limbs were also
covered with a froth of bubble bath, and with her long
straight hair held up out of the bubbles with a barrette, a few
tendrils damp and escaping, he thought she was one of the
prettiest girls he had ever seen. He pushed the rubber fish toy
to her and she pushed it back, giggling.

The bubble bath, being the new, patented Mad Daddy bubble
bath that came in a plastic replica of the man himself, was
the kind that got you clean by soaking, without soap. It also
smelled good and gave heaps of suds. They had been in the
tub for about forty-five minutes, while the radio in the room
blared rock 'n' roll; frolicking and soaking and having a
snowball fight with the suds. The Dennison of the Deep toy
was just like a friend in there with them. Marcie had a nice
giggle, and very friendly blue eyes. When he had met her the
night before Mad Daddy had been very much attracted to
her. It was only a matter of a few moments before he was
buying her a frozen custard on the Boardwalk and taking her

to see the Ripley's Believe It or Not exhibit, and only a little more time before she invited herself quite coolly up to his room. He'd turned off the phone because he was sure Elaine would call to holler as soon as she found out he had taped today's show too and was going to stay and have a good time.

There were two things that Daddy definitely did not want to think about at this moment: one was Elaine, who had a mean temper, and the other was his birthday next week, when he would be forty years old. He had told Marcie he was thirty-five. He told everybody that. It was an awful thing to get old, especially when you felt just as young as when you were a teen-ager. The things that made him laugh were the things that made the kids laugh, and his grown-up friends bored him. Libra, for example. Libra bored Daddy to death. Libra was always talking about girls in a dirty way, saying that if he was Daddy he'd certainly take advantage of all the little teeny-boppers who were in love with him. Libra had no soul, and no sentimentality at all.

"I think my skin's shriveling up," Marcie said. "Isn't *your* skin shriveling up?"

"What a terrible thing to say!" Daddy exclaimed, and jumped up and out of the tub. He looked at his body. "I'm not shriveled up. Are you shriveled up, Marcie?"

Marcie looked down at her splendid body. She had jumped out of the tub too, and was shaking bubble bath suds on the bathmat like a frisky puppy. "No," she said, giggling. "Everything's here." She scooped the Dennison of the Deep toy out of the bath. "We mustn't let him shrivel up."

"You can have him if you'd like," Mad Daddy said.

"Oh, can I? Oh, he's groovy!" Marcie hugged the rubber fish. "I'd really rather have you, Daddy. I think you're even groovier."

"You can't have *me*," he reproved mildly. "Hey, can you do this?" He had a toy that shot a pingpong ball into the air and caught it in a net. The gadget was hard to work. He played it for a while, deftly, showing off for her. Then he gave it to her to try.

"Oh, I can't do that at *all!*" she cried, giggling.

He led her to the full-length mirror in the bedroom and made her try it, and then he showed her again, but Marcie had no sense of timing and even less manual dexterity and she missed the ball every time. Finally she got annoyed and tossed the pingpong ball at him, hitting him on the ear. He

whooped happily and tossed it back at her, but she ducked.
Then they ran around the room throwing everything at each
other—pillows, magazines, toys, a slipper, her bra.

"Where did you get that beautiful suntan, Marcie?"

"I went to Florida between semesters. There are lots of
boys in Fort Lauderdale. We had lots of fun." She became
serious for a moment. "Daddy, tell me something. Nobody
knows if you're married or not. Are you married?"

"Well, of course I'm married," Daddy said. "I'm a grown-
up. Grown-ups are always married."

"How boring."

"Yes, it's very boring."

"Do you like her? Your wife?"

"Oh, she's a nice girl."

"How old is she?"

"Eighty-seven," Mad Daddy said, shoving Marcie on the
bed.

She giggled and hit him with the pillow. "Is she as old as
you are?"

"Do I look eighty-seven?"

"How old is she?"

"Twenty-six."

Marcie shrugged. The subject bored her. "I'm starving,"
she said.

"Me, too. I'll send down for some breakfast."

He called Room Service and ordered two hamburgers with
chili and two Cokes. As an afterthought he told them to add
some French fries and some ice cream with chocolate sauce.
"That's my very favorite breakfast," Marcie said.

"Mine, too."

"How come you have all these toys?" she asked.

"The people from the Toy Show sent me a lot of sam-
ples."

"Are we going to the Toy Show?"

"Do you want to?"

"Not particularly," she said. She wrinkled her nose. "I'd
rather watch television. Your show should be on soon."

Mad Daddy looked at his watch on the dresser. They had
played the whole morning away, and some of the afternoon.
His show would be on in ten minutes. He turned off the radio
and went across the room and turned on the television set.

"I love your show," Marcie said. "I watch it every day
when I come home from school. I didn't go to school today.
I wonder if they'll tell my parents." She had called her

parents the night before and told them she was sleeping over
with a girl friend.

"Will you get in trouble?"

"Nah."

She wouldn't get in trouble, but he would, he was thinking.
Elaine was going to kill him. To tell the truth, he was rather
afraid of Elaine. She was so big, and when she was drunk,
which was every night now, she became paranoid. She cried,
and a few times she had even slapped him. But the thing that
scared him the most was when she yelled. Elaine was a
champion yeller. She had invented tantrums. Every time
someone cursed she got a royalty. It was hard to believe
Elaine had once been so sweet.

People kept changing. It wasn't like children growing up
and changing, like his children had, which was wonderful to
watch. It was scary the way adults changed. They got neurotic and mean. He'd seen it with his older sister, Ruth, who had
brought him up after their parents died when they were kids
on the Lower East Side of Manhattan. Ruth was beautiful
and loving, but then when she and he were both grown-ups
she became a nagging yenta housewife like all the other
women in the neighborhood. Her husband, Bernie, was in the
tie-pin business, and when Ruth and Bernie moved to Scars-
dale there was no stopping her. She did her whole house in
white wall-to-wall carpet and put plastic on top of it, and you
had to take your shoes off anyway when you walked into the
room. She kept introducing Mad Daddy to terrible replicas
of herself, only unmarried or divorced or widowed, who she
wanted him to take out. She had hated all his wives. And she
and Bernie always called him Moishe. "I only had one
Daddy," Ruth would say, "and it wasn't *you*."

Oh, Ruth would have a fit when she found out his
marriage with Elaine was in trouble. She would say "I told
you so" until it came out of his ears. She only seemed to like
his wives when he was well rid of them and they had married
other people. Then she would look back on them with nostalgia, comparing them to the new one. He hated having dinner
at Ruth's. Her nagging gave him indigestion, and her cooking
was enough to give him indigestion all by itself, even if she
had kept still.

"There he is!" Marcie squealed. She pulled the sheet
around herself like an Indian and sat on the floor cross-
legged in front of the set. "Oh, I just love him! Isn't he a
gas?"

"That's *me*," Mad Daddy corrected her.

There he was, on the screen, taped from the day before yesterday. He looked very good; no one would know he was going to be forty years old next week.

"*Ssh*," Marcie said reprovingly.

"That's *me*," Mad Daddy said again, beginning to feel left out, beaten by his own television image.

Marcie gave him a blank look. "Will you keep quiet? I'll miss all the jokes."

He went to the closet and took out his bathrobe and put it on. He didn't want to see the show; he knew what he'd said. A show was a show, it was a job, and it was finished until the next one. He had never basked in his own glory. Sometimes he watched the show for a minute or two on the occasions when it was taped, but once he had reassured himself that he looked well his interest was finished.

Room Service arrived with their breakfast and Mad Daddy signed for it, keeping the door discreetly ajar and his body between the boy and the sight of Marcie rapt on the floor.

"Can I have your autograph?" the boy asked.

"You have it on the bill."

"I mean for me."

"Why don't you keep the bill?" Daddy asked slyly, and he and the boy both laughed. He signed the piece of paper the boy held out to him.

"Hey, that's you on TV now," the boy said, craning his neck to see into the room. Daddy blocked his view with his body. "Hey, how does it feel, seeing yourself on television?"

"It feels like a piece of glass," Daddy said. The boy laughed.

As soon as the boy turned away Daddy shut and locked the door. "The food's here," he called to Marcie.

"*Ssh*."

He looked at the hamburgers, feeling lonely. He opened a Coke with the opener on the bathroom wall and sipped it, looking at himself on the seventeen-inch screen and wishing the show was over. He nibbled at a French fry. He hated eating alone and he hated cold food. If she wouldn't eat with him, he'd either have to eat alone or eat cold food, and that really depressed him. He unwrapped one of the hamburgers and put it into Marcie's hand. She accepted it without looking at it or at him and transferred it to her mouth like a sleepwalker, her eyes never leaving the screen. She didn't say thank you.

"Wow, I'm hungry," he said, trying to sound cheery. She didn't seem to hear him. "Hey! There's a fishbone in my hamburger!" No response. He put his uneaten hamburger on top of the television set so it would keep warm and retired morosely to a corner of the messed-up bed, nursing on his bottle of Coke, and wondered if he should try to get to the Toy Show before it closed. There would be salesmen there who would sell twice as hard if they met him in person. He was getting a healthy royalty from the dolls: Dennison of the Deep, Little Angela, and Stud Mouse, and from the Mad Daddy Bubble Bath in the lifelike Mad Daddy plastic container. Libra was a good man to have on your team if you wanted to get rich. He thought about the midnight show and wondered if it would be a success. He was planning to use the same kind of material he used in the daytime. Indeed, he didn't know how to write any other kind of a show. He hoped Libra was right and that the midnight hour would draw twice as many people as the daytime slot had. He'd be taping all the shows, with a live audience. He'd probably continue to tape in the afternoon because he was used to it. It was funny to think that he, the clown from the Lower East Side who always did impromptu skits to amuse the neighbors, was going to have all those big sponsors and become a millionaire. Libra said he *would* be a millionaire. Then he could retire to a desert island and run around without clothes all day long, drinking from coconuts, eating bananas, and swimming in the ocean whenever he felt like it. He would have a tree house, the kind he'd always wanted when he was a kid. He'd meet a beautiful girl and give her a shell he'd found, without a word, and she would accept it without a word, just a smile, and lead him by the hand into the lush jungle where they would lie down together. She would have long black hair and she wouldn't be wearing anything either. She wouldn't look anything like Elaine.

He thought about Elaine. Elaine had *grown* after he married her. Not more mature, just taller. And she had turned into a bossy woman. Who had known she was going to grow and fill out? Nobody told him sixteen-year-old girls grew any more. She was two inches taller than he was. And she thought just because she was married to a TV personality she had to acquire culture. She had started studying French. That wasn't so bad, except she talked French all the time when they were out and she was trying to impress people. The last straw, the day he knew their marriage was finished, was the day Elaine insisted on talking to the goddam Puerto Rican waiter in French.

After that everything she did drove him crazy. She bought all those five- and six-hundred-dollar dresses when she knew he couldn't afford them. She put the kid into a French kindergarten. Then she started hanging around with Lizzie Libra, who was old enough to be Elaine's mother, and who was a big whore besides. He ought to know: he'd gone to bed with Lizzie Libra once when he'd had a fight with Elaine at a big, rotten, drunken party. Lizzie wasn't his type, but she was so little and dressed like a kid, and for a moment, feeling unloved and mad as hell, he'd imagined she was a little girl. Lizzie had always been after him. She'd batted those horrible false eyelashes at him and made double entendres—even he knew that word. He hated false eyelashes on older women. It made them look even older. But Lizzie had taken him by the hand and led him into one of the bedrooms at the party, after Elaine had stormed out drunk, and Lizzie had locked the door. "You've always been my idol," she had said to him. She didn't say it sexily, as if she was coming on or anything, but wistfully. He had felt sorry for her. She had this kind of hunger about her, like a woman who never gets any love. He'd felt sorry for her. Poor little Lizzie. She had seemed very sexy at the time. Her blond hair was hanging down loose and she was wearing a little pink dress. She had taken off her glasses and looked at him with those big, hungry, myopic eyes. "You're the greatest thing since sliced bread," she said. So he'd done it with her, there on somebody's bed, and afterwards he had felt so guilty and scared to come back to the big, rotten, drunken party where her husband and all his and Elaine's friends were that he couldn't even look at Lizzie, much less talk to her.

She'd been happy as a lark. She was absolutely bubbling, like seltzer. He'd never seen a woman so happy just because of a little fling. Maybe it was him? He didn't think he was so much, just an ordinary guy. She hadn't even come. How strange she was! He was scared to death afterwards that she would say something to Elaine, because of how close they were, but evidently Lizzie never had, because Elaine was the most jealous woman in the world and she had never said a word to him about Lizzie, even as a prospect.

The doorbell rang again. He glanced at Marcie, still enthralled in front of the set, and realized with relief that the show was almost over. He went to the door.

It was the bellboy. "Telegram, sir."

Mad Daddy signed for the telegram and got some money off the dresser for a tip, first shutting the door in the bellboy's face. The bellboy was delighted to get a dollar tip and did not seem to know who he was, which was a relief.

Safe in the room again he grinned when he saw Marcie turn off the television set. She ran over to him and sat on his lap, putting her cheek against his. "Oh, you are the grooviest!" she breathed.

"Let's see what this telegram says," Mad Daddy said, pretending to be unimpressed with her now that she had ignored him for so long. He opened it.

"Your Kew Gardens Fan Club wishes you the greatest success ever at your benefit in Atlantic City," the telegram read. *"We love you. Michelle, Donna, and Barrie."*

"They know everything," he said.

"I'm so glad I live right here," said Marcie. "Or else I never would have met you."

"Do you want your hamburger now?"

"Oh, yes!" she said, all excited.

"Well, it's hanging out of your hand."

She looked at it. "It's all cold and greasy."

"Your own fault. Here, you can have half of mine."

He shared the warm one with her that had been waiting for them on top of the warm television set. They munched and gobbled and stuffed themselves, smearing the chili inside the hamburger roll and washing the whole mess down with Cokes. The ice cream which he'd stupidly put on top of the TV set in the same bag, was all melted, so they mixed it up with Coke in the water glasses from the bathroom and made sodas.

"I love to cook," Mad Daddy said.

"Yeah? Can you cook?"

"Just stuff like this. Ice-cream sodas."

She giggled. "Oh, you are silly! I really love you."

"Well, I love you, too," Mad Daddy said solemnly.

"Do you really?" She looked ashamed. "You know, I didn't tell you, but I have a boyfriend, Howie, who I go steady with."

"That's okay—I have a wife who I go steady with."

"Howie wouldn't mind," Marcie said. "You're not like cheating. You're not a person ... you're a ... a phenomenon!"

"Well, you'd better not tell him anyway," Mad Daddy said.

"I won't tell him if you won't tell *her*."

"Oh, no, I most solemnly promise I won't tell *her*."

"Will I ever see you again?"

"Let's not talk about that," he said. "We have a whole evening ahead of us."

"When do you have to go back?"

"I should go back tonight."

"Can't you stay longer?"

"I have to do my show."

"If I save up my money and come to New York to see your show during spring vacation, will you speak to me?"

"Of course," Mad Daddy said, kissing her on top of her cornsilk head, "I'll always speak to you. But you'll have to cool it. You know, pretend you're just a fan."

"Oh sure, I know," she said calmly.

Panic gripped him. He hoped she would act as cool as she was acting now. He hoped even more that she would forget all about him by the time spring vacation came. He didn't need any more trouble with Elaine than he already had, not to mention with the police for molesting a fourteen-year-old girl who was really older than he was, but how could you convince them of that?

"Are you sure you're only fourteen?" he asked.

"Wanna see my identification card?"

"No, I believe you."

"Did you ever go out with a fourteen-year-old girl before?"

"No," he lied solemnly. "Never."

"How come you like me then?"

"Because you're so beautiful."

"You think I'm beautiful?"

"I think you're the most beautiful girl I ever saw."

"Wow," Marcie breathed. "Wow . . ."

He put the music on again and took off his bathrobe. Marcie unwound herself from her sheet. "Wow," Mad Daddy breathed, closing his eyes to kiss her, then opening them again because she really was so beautiful he wanted to see her. "Wow . . ."

CHAPTER

FIVE

AS IT turned out, two interesting things happened to Gerry that Thursday: she had lunch with Dick Devere and she received an engraved invitation to the party the B.P.'s were giving for Franco two weeks hence.

The day of her lunch was one of those false spring days New York sometimes has in March, just to keep the inhabitants going until real spring rescues them from their eternal bouts with flu and slush. She recklessly left her coat at the office so the whole world could see her new green suit, and Dick Devere was charming. He reeled off the names of what she already knew from reading about them were three of the seven best restaurants in New York, and she let him make the choice because she'd never been to any of them. At the one he took her to they saw two Kennedy ladies and a movie star, several socialites, and of course Penny Potter, Mrs. B.P., who was lunching with her mother. Although Gerry had never met the client, she nodded at Penny Potter, who gave her a totally nonplused look back and a fake smile just in case she was somebody after all. The girl was smaller than she looked in her photographs, and terribly young.

"Are you going to her party?" Dick asked.

"Yes. I just got the invitation this morning. I guess Mr. Libra forced her into it." She didn't want him to think she traveled with the jet set.

"I'm going too," he said. "If you have no one to escort you, I'd be glad to take you there."

"That would be great." At least she'd know somebody.

He ordered knowledgeably, in perfect French, and Gerry was glad her French was as good as his. The restaurant intimidated her. She was relieved that she was wearing the green suit, and that even though it came from an unknown boutique it was at least an original. The food was marvelous and so was the wine he chose, and he surprised her by making her laugh almost all through the lunch with amusing stories about people he had worked with on his shows. He evidently had a keen eye for satire, and she thought that if he hadn't turned out to be a director he could probably have been a writer.

After lunch he said, "I want to do something extremely corny because it's a nice day." He had his car parked near the restaurant; an unshowy little yellow Mustang convertible, and he took the top down and drove her to the East Village, where he seemed to know a great many people—shopkeepers, old ladies leaning out of windows, whom he waved at, hippies lounging on benches in the sun, whom he said hello to. Everybody seemed to like him. "This is my second home," he told her.

He took her into an antique store, where he had a long chummy talk with the proprietor, priced several things he did not buy, and picked out a string of green glass beads which he bought and hung around Gerry's neck.

"Love beads," Dick said. "So you'll be lucky and loved."

She fingered the beads. She was touched. They were the nicest sixty-cent present anyone had bought her in her whole life. She liked the way Dick seemed to fit in anywhere, and the way people accepted him whether he was in an intimidating restaurant or on Avenue A. He really wasn't as bad looking as she had thought the first time she saw him. A man didn't have to be pretty, or even handsome, if he was bright and had charm. And Dick Devere certainly was bright and had charm.

She realized in panic that it was a quarter to four. Libra would kill her. Dick drove her back to the office and shook her hand.

"It was a pleasure," he said, "and I'll see you the night of the party, if not before. Give me your home phone number and address." She did, and he wrote them down in a small leather-bound note pad, using a gold ballpoint pen. He seemed very neat. She wished she knew how to analyze handwriting. His was tiny and impeccable. Did that mean he was repressed—or just that he had a small notebook?

That evening when she got home from the office a florist's boy delivered a dozen roses with a card saying: 'Thanks again. Dick.'

It was the same tiny handwriting. She put the roses into her one and only vase, pleased and flattered. He didn't have to do a thing like that, but wasn't it marvelous to get flowers from a man, even if he was a client! Somehow she knew there was nothing businesslike about sending those flowers.

She phoned him the next day from the office while Libra was at the gym working off his vitamin shot from Ingrid the Lady Barber, and thanked him.

"I hope they didn't clash with your apartment," he said.

"What could clash with an empty apartment?"

"If you're looking for furniture, I know some very good, cheap antique stores I can take you to. I also know a very cheap, good carpenter who builds things—shelves and shutters and stuff. He's an artist. I can turn you on to him if you'd like."

She wrote down the name of the carpenter and made a date to go looking for antiques with Dick on Saturday afternoon. Then she looked at the schedule of where all the clients were, thinking she would invite Silky to lunch tomorrow, and she discovered Silky and the Satins were doing a club date out of town. The news didn't please her. Now she still didn't know where Dick and Silky stood.

On Saturday they went to several cheap antique shops, where Gerry bought a metal headboard that had formerly been a gate, two glass bottles that had formerly held opium and marijuana, according to the labels, and a miniature chest to use as an end table, which Dick told her was what they used to sell furniture instead of blueprints in the old days. It 'was an exact replica of what the chest would be when the customer ordered it full-sized. He told her the carpenter would install the headboard, and didn't offer to come up and install it himself, so she realized he would never allow himself to be categorized as Good Old Helpful Dick, which in a funny way pleased her. The store said they would deliver that evening, so Dick took her to a dark bar for a three-hour lunch and then drove her home.

"Would you like to come up for a drink?" she asked.

He looked at his watch. "I have to go to a dinner party.

I'm in great demand because I'm single and have a blue suit." He smiled and patted her on the head. "I'll call you."

She couldn't figure him out, but he was nice. He was very cool. She went up to her apartment, glad that the day had been spent so pleasantly, and thinking that a Saturday-afternoon date was as good as a Saturday-night date because at least you didn't have to be depressed that you didn't see a soul all weekend.

There were great plans in the office for the B.P.'s party the following week. Lizzie and Elaine were both going to wear new Franco creations, fortunately not the Gilda Look, which was still on the drawing board, and Nelson was going to do everybody's hair, even Gerry's. The day of the party Gerry went to Nelson's salon on her lunch hour and he trimmed off an inch of her hair and set it in ninety-three pigtails so she looked like a cross between Topsy and Medusa. If Libra hadn't been picking up the bill she would have cried right there. She thanked him profusely, rushed back to the office, and in the lobby Ladies' Room—which she had been using faithfully since Libra's rebuff that first day, although he never seemed to notice it—Gerry brushed out all the pigtails until her hair was normal-looking again, if a little crimped. At least it was shiny, and Nelson gave a very good blunt cut. She hoped the crimps from the pigtails would all straighten out by that night; maybe sitting in a steamy hot bath would help.

"Didn't Nelson do your hair?" Libra asked when she returned upstairs.

"Yes."

"It doesn't look like he did anything," Libra said.

"It's the Gilda Look," Gerry lied beautifully, letting a wave of hair slide over one eye.

"So it is. It's very nice."

"Thank you," she said, and returned to work.

She was allowed to leave at six, and hurried home to fix herself up. Dick was coming for her at seven fifteen. The party wasn't black tie, so she decided to wear the best thing she had: a pink and gold brocade Chanel suit—or copy, rather, from the same little boutique where she bought her other things. It was a hand-made copy, and she figured she would see two or three of the originals in the same room that night, but since nobody was taking off their jackets to show labels it wouldn't matter. Besides, she was a Girl Friday, not the wife of some millionaire, and if she'd owned diamonds to wear everybody would probably assume they were glass.

Dick picked her up and she made martinis, which he liked, to fortify them for the ordeal ahead. He wandered into the bedroom to inspect the new headboard his carpenter had installed for her, and very casually looked at everything as if he were taking inventory so he wouldn't fall over anything on a dark night. He was the kind of man who made her feel glad she had made the bed and cleaned up the place. She had a porcelain hand on the dresser, and the love beads he had given her were entwined around one of the fingers. He noticed that, too. She hated martinis so she gave him hers to finish, and then he put both glasses into the sink. You could certainly take *him* home to mother—the problem would be getting him to go.

The B.P.'s lived in a duplex apartment on Fifth Avenue. There was a doorman, of course, an elevator man, of course, and a line of limousines, both rented and privately owned, along the curb—of course. There was no coat rack in the hall outside the apartment, nor was there a pile of coats on anybody's bed. A uniformed maid whisked Gerry's coat away almost before she could get out of it, and a butler with a silver tray asked her what she wanted to drink.

One room was the bar, decorated exactly like a Third Avenue bar, complete to Tiffany lamps and dark, mirrored walls. A bartender in a red jacket was busily in attendance. Gerry figured there must be almost a hundred people at the party, all of them either Beautiful or rich or famous, or all three. She saw her suit going by on two other ladies, both of whom gave her a smile and then avoided her for the rest of the night. Libra was already there, in the corner of the bar, with Lizzie and the comic Arnie Gurney, who had flown in for this party between engagements, and a woman in silver with badly dyed black hair, who must have been Arnie Gurney's wife.

Libra introduced Gerry and Dick to Arnie Gurney, who said hello and told them five jokes, exactly as Libra had said he would. Lizzie and Arnie Gurney's wife laughed merrily at all the jokes, none of which Gerry could remember two minutes after he finished telling them. Then Gerry and Dick wandered off to inspect the rest of the party.

The living room was huge and done all in pale silks and English antiques. There were many oil paintings, all fairly famous and obviously real, elaborately framed in curly

goldish frames and lit from below. There was a big needle-
point thing on a stand in front of the working fireplace, and
the fireplace looked as if it had either never been used or had
been scrubbed from top to bottom by a maid. Four butlers
and four uniformed maids circulated through the crowd,
passing drinks and hot hors d'oeuvres. There was no place to
put your drink down, however, because every table was
covered with *objects*: a collection of alabaster, porcelain,
gold and silver eggs; a collection of vermeil flowers; and a
collection of photographs of famous people and relatives
(some were both) in identical sterling-silver frames.

"All that stuff is real," Dick said, gesturing at the furniture.

"I figured."

Penny Potter stood in the middle of a circle of admirers,
small and frail, wearing a mauvy-colored watered-silk dress
that was cut on top like a Nehru jacket, and love beads made
of real rubies, diamonds, and pearls. She had at least three
falls on; Nelson's famous Dynel, judging from the hair's
abnormal straightness. Next to her, dressed in a real Nehru
jacket of identical mauvy watered silk, and real love beads,
was her husband, Peter Potter. They made a very pretty
papier-mâché couple.

Mr. Nelson was there, in his white suede suit, and when he
saw Gerry he gave a strangled scream and rushed over to
her.

"What did you do to yourself?" he cried in horror.

Her hand went up to her hair. "Me?"

"Where is your coiffeur?" She thought he might take a fit
and collapse right there, frothing at the mouth. "What's the
matter with you?"

"Mr. Libra thought the Gilda Look you gave me was
divine," Gerry said innocently. "I just adore it."

"Don't give *me* credit for that *mess*," Nelson said indignantly. "You look like you're going to the beach!"

"I think she looks very sexy," Dick said. "I compliment
you, Nelson. Very simple hair does wonderful things for
Gerry's eyes."

"The only reason it hangs right is because she had it
braided all afternoon," Nelson said malevolently. "Gerry has
hair like straw. You can't do anything with it. I think she
should give up and get a decent *wig*."

A tall, beautiful-looking young man wearing a thin coat of
make-up came in accompanied by a short, middle-aged man

who was wearing a thin coat of make-up carefully disguised as a suntan. Nelson rushed over to them, waving greetings.

"I don't know how to thank you," Gerry said to Dick. She started to laugh. "I thought he would die when you pretended you thought he'd done my hair the way it is now."

"Well, I'm peculiar," Dick said. "I like hair that doesn't cut my fingers."

"I'd better go over and introduce myself to the hostess."

Dick led her through the crowd to where the B.P.'s were standing with their admirers. He already knew the B.P.'s and he introduced Gerry to them. Peter B.P. looked rather pleased to see Gerry, his eyes acknowledging that she was an attractive girl, but Penny B.P. looked bored.

"So glad you could come," Penny said, looking over Gerry's shoulder.

"Do you have everything you need?" Peter asked.

"Yes, thank you," Gerry said.

"After dinner the King James Version will play for dancing, and Silky and the Satins are coming to sing," Peter said.

"Oh, good!" She looked at Dick, but he was smiling politely and she couldn't read him.

"Honey, where's the Senator?" Peter said to Penny. "Has anybody seen the Senator?"

"They're coming," Penny said. She turned to resume her conversation with the couple at her left, whom she had introduced to Gerry as Mr. and Mrs. Mumble. Obviously she thought they were so well known that to enunciate their names would be insulting to them. Gerry glanced at Dick and he led her away.

A butler gave them more drinks, and they went into the next room, which was all done in Chinese style, complete to the last detail. Elaine Fellin and Mad Daddy were standing in the corner with some people. Elaine was wearing a twenty-five-hundred-dollar beaded number by Franco, and she looked slightly drunk already. Mad Daddy, in a tuxedo, looked as uncomfortable as a man could get. He didn't seem to have anyone he wanted to talk to. He glanced around the room furtively at all the people, like a child at a grown-ups' party who is afraid he will be caught peeking from the stairs. Elaine waved at Gerry.

"Oh, hello," Elaine said gaily. "Isn't this a lovely party? I was just telling the Ambassador here about Nina's French school. They don't speak a word of English all day. They even do their little arithmetic in French. She's going to be completely bilingual. Isn't this room divine? I love *Chinoiserie*."

Mad Daddy sighed.

"You should see the other room!" Elaine went on. "It's all done in *Turquerie*, just like Lee Bouvier's apartment, or is it Lee Radziwill?"

"I work for Mr. Libra," Gerry told Mad Daddy.

"Oh, yeah?" he said, obviously delighted. "Come on, I'll show you two the Turkey Room."

They made their excuses to the Ambassador and his wife and left them with Elaine chattering on. Mad Daddy took them directly to the bar. "I'm starving," he said morosely.

"There's some caviar," Dick said, pointing at a tray one of the butlers was carrying. The tray held an impressive ice mold which cupped a large dish of real Beluga Malossol caviar. Dick motioned to the butler to come over.

"I hate caviar," Mad Daddy said. "I wish they'd have some of those little hamburgers on toothpicks."

Gerry and Dick helped themselves to caviar. Mad Daddy shook his head.

"I love caviar," Dick said.

"Me too," said Gerry.

"I wish I had some pizza," said Mad Daddy sadly. "What do you think they're having for dinner?"

"Not pizza," Gerry said. There was something about this man that she liked enormously. He was like a big kid. "My name is Gerry Thompson," she said. "And this is Dick Devere, who's a client of Mr. Libra's too."

Mad Daddy's face lighted up and he shook Dick's hand. "I don't know why they invited us to this thing," Mad Daddy said. "I guess because Libra helped with the guest list. I don't know anybody here. There's nobody I even feel like talking to. I wish I was at the movies."

"Yeah," Dick agreed with a charming smile.

"Do you know any of these people?"

"Well, as a matter of fact," Dick said, "I do know a few."

I bet you do, Gerry thought without rancor. *You would.*

Suddenly everybody in the room was applauding. She looked toward the door and saw Franco making his grand entrance as guest of honor. He was bald again, not brave enough to wear the wig of his dreams except as a joke, and he was in black tie and ruffles, topped by a splendid Count Dracula cape of black velvet lined in red. He bowed his head slightly in appreciation of the applause, and solemnly smiled greetings at the people he knew. A step behind Franco, evidently his date, was a tall, thin girl in a tiny little dress that looked like a doily. She had luxuriant tawny hair and a classically beautiful face. Gerry recognized her from the picture in *Time* as the model who had worn the transparent bride's dress in Franco's collection.

Franco and the girl accepted drinks from one of the traveling butlers, and made their way to where Gerry and the others were standing. Mad Daddy looked at the girl with obvious pleasure and no lust. Dick just looked cool. Gerry noticed that most of the women were looking jealous and insecure. The girl really was a knockout, if you liked models.

"This is Fred," Franco said.

The girl, Fred, smiled at all of them. "How do you do," she said in a thin squeak which immediately dispelled the illusion of an inaccessible princess and turned her right into a kid from the Bronx with good bones.

"How do you like my party?" Franco asked, pleased.

"Very impressive," Dick said.

"What do you do, Fred?" Mad Daddy asked.

"Oh, nothing," Fred squeaked. "I'm an heiress."

"She's my favorite model," Franco said. "Did you see her picture in *Time* with me?"

"Yes," Gerry said. "You looked very lovely," she said to the girl. The girl shrugged, bored.

"What do you do?" Fred asked Mad Daddy.

"I have a television show."

"Oh? I never watch television."

"You should watch him," Gerry said. "He's marvelous. The Mad Daddy Show."

"Oh, all right," Fred said pleasantly, as if she was doing them all a favor. Mad Daddy seemed to be cringing. The girl obviously frightened him as much as the socialites at the party.

Libra came plowing his way through the crowd, alone. He patted Franco on the shoulder and gave Fred a look of pure, slavering lust. "Glad you could come," he said to her.

"Mmm," Fred said.

Gerry figured that Fred was window dressing for Franco and had really been brought for Libra. She wondered if Libra was considering replacing the deceased Douglas Henry with a model-turned-starlet, but figured with her voice the girl didn't have a chance. If she could be in a silent movie she could capture the world.

"A very good turn-out of clients," Libra said approvingly to Franco. "You're here, Nelson and the B.P.'s are here, of course, Arnie Gurney, Dick, Daddy, the King James Version and Silky and the Satins are coming, and Zak Maynard's in the other room. You know him," he said to Gerry. "The super-beauty new male star, a male Fred." He winked at Fred. "The only ones who aren't here are Shadrach Bascombe, who's at training camp getting ready for his next fight, and Sylvia Polydor, who wouldn't go across the street to go to a party, especially fly from California. Do you know that Sylvia won't fly? She still hires an entire car of the damn train, just to come here. An entire car! She's wonderful."

"Zak Maynard isn't a male me," Fred said. "I went out with him once. He's a moron."

"Mrs. Einstein ought to know," Libra said sarcastically. "Come on, Gerry, I want to borrow you and introduce you to Zak."

Gerry hoped Dick would follow them, and he did. She was flattered. He had evidently gone out with enough Freds not to be impressed any more. She followed Libra into the living room, which was more mobbed than ever, and was pleased when Dick casually took her hand in preparation for her exposure to Zak the super-beauty.

Zak was in the corner talking to Lizzie Libra. He had thick, sexy, golden-brown hair, broad shoulders, slumberous golden eyes, and a young, sensual mouth. He towered over Lizzie by about a foot. He looked just like his pictures: cinemascope and pure technicolor.

"Zak Maynard, my new assistant, Gerry Thompson. And Dick Devere, who, if you're very lucky, might direct you in a show one day."

Zak enveloped Gerry's hand in his and threw her a few sparks from the golden eyes. "Hell-o," he said, looking her up and down. Finally he released her hand and shook hands with Dick.

"I think he's wonderful," Lizzie said to her husband. "Why haven't you ever brought him around to the office?"

"Because he sleeps all day," Libra said.

"Are you in love with this man?" Zak asked Gerry, indicating Dick.

"I love all the clients," Gerry said sweetly. "And they love me. I formerly worked at the 4-H Club."

"I was in the 4-H Club when I was a kid," Zak said. "I took all the little girls behind the haystack."

"That was before you started to sleep all day," Lizzie said.

"Dinner is served," a butler said discreetly.

They went into the dining room, which was decorated like an arbor, with a roof of leaves lit mysteriously from above and rows of real trees and bushes planted all around the edges of the room. In the center of the dining room was a long table with a flowered Porthault cloth, bearing silver chafing dishes and silver platters artfully decorated with exotic food. The lobster salad was crowned with a whole lobster, there was some sort of fish mousse, salad, rolls, and all the accompaniments for an Indian curry, which was what the chafing dishes contained. The silverware was heavy, bearing the crest of the Potter family, and the napkins were from Porthault too.

After they helped themselves to food a butler directed them into the Turkish Room, where small round tables had been set up, each covered with the same Paisley print that covered every wall of the room and all the chairs, couches, and floor pillows. It was a little dizzying. There were tall, delicate crystal wineglasses on each table, and three of the butlers were busy filling them part way with wine.

Gerry saw Mad Daddy and Elaine sitting at a table which had two empty seats, and she and Dick went there and sat down. Elaine had her drink on the table next to her wineglass, and she really was looking drunk by now. Mad Daddy's plate contained salad and a roll.

"What is that stuff?" he asked, looking at Gerry's plate.

"Curry."

"I hate curry," he said morosely. "And that fish stuff scares me. I wish they'd have hamburgers or something."

"You have no class," Elaine said.

"Maybe I have class," Mad Daddy said, "but my stomach has the same old class I was born with. Waiter!"

"Yes, sir?" the butler said.

"Do you think I could get a Coke?"

"Of course, sir," the butler said, looking as if Mad Daddy had asked for hemlock.

"Oh, for heaven's sake!" Elaine said, taking Mad Daddy's wine and pouring it into her already empty wineglass. "Do you know what he did once? We went to Pavillon, and he asked them for a club sandwich. I was so embarrassed."

"They gave it to me, didn't they?" Mad Daddy said. "They have more class than you do. They aren't snobs."

"Don't you call me a snob in front of those people!" Elaine snapped. Mad Daddy tried to take her wine away but she pulled at it and spilled it on the tablecloth.

"The evening is finally getting interesting," Dick said.

"I'm not going to fight with you, Elaine," Mad Daddy said mildly.

"Just take your hands off me, that's all," Elaine snapped. She beckoned to the butler. "More wine, please. My clumsy husband spilled his."

Gerry felt embarrassed for Mad Daddy. She smiled at him and he smiled back. He cut his roll in half to make a sandwich and filled it with some of the salad.

"Oh my God," Elaine said. The butler appeared with more wine and refilled all their glasses. She drank hers down defiantly. "I hate those people in there," Elaine said. "And those people in here. They're all stinking snobs."

"I think they're pretty nice," Mad Daddy said, just to annoy her.

"You would! The big star, getting all the attention."

"You didn't mind that I was a star when you met me."

"Are you going to start on that again?"

"You brought it up."

"I'm going to bring up my *dinner* if you don't shut up."

"What dinner?" Mad Daddy said.

Elaine gritted her teeth and glared at her husband, evidently trying to decide whether to waste the wine by throwing it in his face. She decided against it, and lapsed into a seething silence. Gerry and Dick ate as fast as they could.

When the dessert was served, chocolate mousse, the sound of a band tuning up was heard from the Chinese Room. It was the King James Version, assaulting the ears with electronically amplified experiments. Then they began to play in earnest and it was not bad at all, especially since they were a room away. It was almost as loud as if they had been right in there with the diners. Gerry hoped the building was soundproof. She looked around the room and saw that Lizzie was still with Zak; Franco was with Libra, the B.P.'s, Fred, and a man whom she recognized as the Senator. Libra must really like Fred if he had maneuvered to have her at the same table with the brass, since most of the couples had split up. Penny B.P.'s mother was sitting with the Senator's wife, the Ambas-

sador, and the Ambassador's wife. Arnie Gurney was with
some people she did not know, regaling them with jokes, and
Arnie Gurney's wife was across the room looking uncomfortable with Nelson and the two fruits and a terribly jet-set
looking girl who was wearing a wedding ring and a diamond
engagement ring the size of a pigeon's egg. There was demi-
tasse after the mousse, and an assortment of fine brandies,
and then the B.P.'s led the people at their table into the room
where the music was pounding. Almost everyone followed
them. Dick and Gerry jumped up instantly, said good-bye to
Mad Daddy and Elaine, and hurried to the Chinese Room as
fast as they could.

The King James Version had established themselves on a
large square of something that looked like lucite, and they
were all dressed in biblical robes with long, thick, clean hair.
They all looked like young studs, but even though some of
the women were as close as they could get to the band,
disregarding their eardrums in favor of sex, the five boys had
their eyes closed, grooving to their own beat. The lead singer
was standing, with his eyes shut and his hands over his ears,
screaming into the microphone. There was something almost
insulting about the way he had closed himself into his private
world; it was not so much as if he were trying to concentrate
as that he seemed disgusted by the people who were admiring
him. The women who stood in front of him gazing at him
raptly seemed charmed by his arrogance, and some of them
were even touching him, pretending it was accidental, in
order to wake him up.

The B.P.'s were dancing wildly, showing off the new
dances which they knew perfectly. Gerry noticed two gossip
columnists in the crowd. She felt like dancing, but Dick was
just standing there, looking at the group, and he was not even
tapping to the beat.

"Don't you dance?" she asked.

"Only if I have to. Do you want to?"

"Maybe later. I'm going to find the ladies' room." She left
the room and looked around. A maid came by and Gerry
was directed downstairs.

The lower floor of the duplex was lovely, bathed in lam-
bent golden light. The hallway and one room, which was
evidently a library, were done in old Spanish style. This
apartment was turning into a house of all nations. There
were several doors leading into other rooms. One was half
open, and she saw that it was done like a child's room,

except that there was a huge king-sized bed in the center of it. Everywhere there were tiny flowers printed on walls and material, and there was a lot of white wicker. There were various dolls and toys lined up on the dresser, and there was a dressing table covered with bottles of perfume and make-up. Since the B.P.'s had no children, she realized *they* were the children. Their bedroom was the only young thing about them except for their dancing; the party, their friends, and the apartment looked as if they belonged to people at least twice their age. She headed for the bathroom, but realized Fred and Nelson were already in there, Nelson recombing Fred's hair.

Gerry was just going out into the hall again when she saw Lizzie Libra leading Zak Maynard by the hand. "Oh, Zak," Lizzie whispered, "you're the greatest thing since sliced bread." They opened one of the doors and looked in, then, reassured that the room was empty, they entered it and Gerry distinctly heard the sound of the old-fashioned key turning in the lock. *Well, well,* she thought. *It would be nice if that room were decorated with haystacks.*

So *Lizzie fools around with clients.* Well, why not? Libra fooled around with clients. Still, she would have thought Lizzie was above being impressed by these vapid people her own husband had created. Of all people, Lizzie Libra should know what a sham and a fake most of these people were. Lizzie had been around all of them from the beginning of their transformation. But Zak *was* beautiful and sexy, and probably the question would be more apt if she had asked herself what a young man like him saw in Lizzie.

She finally found that one of the doors led to a bathroom, deceptively done like an office, with brown marble, armoires, a petit-point toilet-seat cover, and a large, upholstered arm-chair with a TV set in front of it. The walls were paneled in dark wood, and you had to call a committee meeting to find the toilet paper.

She couldn't stop thinking about Lizzie and Zak, even though she had seen things like that ever since she started working around movie people. But he was twenty-five years old, and Lizzie was at least forty. Yet Lizzie had gotten him just like that—zap! It had been rumored around the Industry that Zak Maynard would screw a snake, and that he'd probably be the first person to find out how, too. Yet there were plenty of younger, prettier girls than Lizzie Libra at this party. And it wasn't that Zak had to be nice to Lizzie to get to Libra, for if Libra found out he would hardly consider the client going to bed with his wife *nice*. Libra seemed a strict double-standard man, so much so that he wouldn't even allow himself to suspect that Lizzie was cheating, because it would upset him too much and take his mind off business.

I wonder what Lizzie has ... Gerry thought. Obviously what a man found desirable wasn't what she as a woman thought he would prefer. It certainly was a mystery. She thought about Dick. Did he think she, Gerry, was desirable? He hadn't indicated anything, but a woman could tell there was interest there. Dick seemed like the sort of man who wanted the woman to make the first move. Or did he only act that way because he was taken?

"Hello." The soft voice was unmistakable; it was Silky. Gerry turned around.

"Hi!"

"You're staring at the mirror like Alice Through the Looking Glass," Silky said with a giggle. "Are you goin' to jump right through it?"

"I'd like to," Gerry said. "This party is a drag." She wondered if Silky knew she had come with Dick. "Are you going to sing soon?"

"Soon as I see how I look." Silky peered into the mirror with obvious distaste, and wrinkled up her nose. She was wearing the group's costume: a white brocade knicker suit this time, and the Buster Brown wig. "Ugh!"

"You look great," Gerry said.

"From a hundred feet away maybe. I called you earlier, but you weren't home."

"I was here. I wanted to call you, too, but you were out of town. How did it go?"

"Great," Silky said. "Lots of people. Good reviews. Did you see the reviews?"

"I've been keeping a scrapbook of them for the office. We're all thrilled."

"Did you come with Mr. and Mrs. Libra?" Silky asked, too casually.

"No." Oh, well, why make it seem more important than it was? "Dick Devere brought me because I didn't know anybody."

"Oh," Silky said, almost too kindly. "That was nice."

"Look ..." Gerry said. "I hope you don't think I'm being too personal, but if you and Dick are dating or anything I wish you'd tell me and I won't see him. He doesn't mean anything to me except as a friend and a client. I'm new here, and if you don't tell me I can't help it if I tread on your property by accident, can I?"

"Property?" Silky said thoughtfully. "No man is any woman's property unless they're living together. Dick and I aren't living together. He's just a very dear friend. I don't know what you've heard, but it isn't true."

"I haven't heard anything," Gerry said.

"Well, then, there's nothing to hear."

She saw Silky's hand was shaking as she tried to put on her lipstick. What a lot of pride that girl had! She must have been kicked around a lot. Silky's sweetness upset Gerry more than if she had made a scene.

"I hope we can be friends," Gerry said. "I like you . . . a lot."

Silky turned around and looked at her. "It takes a long time to make a friend," she said. Then she smiled quickly, that smile that never reached her eyes, and said: "Oh, I didn't mean that personally. I like you very much. I'm sure we can be friends."

"Could we have lunch next week?"

"If you don't mind a coffee shop," Silky said. "I can't stand to get dressed up during the day."

"That would be great. I'm saving money to buy furniture."

"Furniture?"

"I just got a new apartment."

"I wish I had an apartment," Silky said. "Mr. Libra makes us live in that hotel. Not that I don't like the hotel, it's a groovy hotel, but I'd like to own something of my own. But we travel so much I guess an apartment would be silly."

"Yeah, I guess so."

"Well, I have to go to work now," Silky said. "Are you coming?" She led the way out of the bathroom. In the hall Gerry saw the four Satins emerging from another bathroom, and Silky joined them without a word. Gerry hurried upstairs to find Dick. She wondered if she shouldn't try to meet another man here. After all, this was a party; there had to be someone here who wasn't married or a snob. Now that Silky had arrived, Gerry wondered which of the two of them Dick would decide to take home. No matter what her mother had warned her about New York at night, she was perfectly well prepared to take a taxi home alone. She was sure she wouldn't be mugged. After all, it was just a party. She hadn't expected to meet her future husband here. Where she *would*

meet him was a mystery she didn't seem to be able to shed
any light on.

Silky and the Satins had brought their own musicians—this
party was going to cost the B.P.'s a bundle. Gerry found a
place on the floor between Dick and Mad Daddy. Elaine was
off in the corner with Arnie Gurney's wife; they were both
drunk and grouchy and looked like the two Furies, or was it
the two Fates? Gerry glanced around the room and saw that
the faces of all the women were sparkling with tension and
false gaiety. The men didn't look any happier. Yet this was
one of the New York parties they would all sell their souls to
get invited to, and if they were left out they considered it a
major tragedy. Mad Daddy was looking at Silky and the
Satins with respect. At least he seemed, at last, to be having
a good time.

When the girls began to sing Gerry glanced at Dick. He
was watching Silky with great pleasure, both for her performance and for her, that she was so good. But there was
nothing really personal about it. Then Gerry stopped looking
at him because whenever Silky sang it gave her such an
emotional experience that she didn't really care what else was
going on. For Gerry, at least, whatever Silky sang became
very personal. *That girl is going to be a star,* Gerry thought.
Now she was sure of it.

When the singing was over the guests applauded for a long
time and seemed genuinely impressed. A few of them went
over and told Silky they liked her. The King James Version
started blasting away again. Dick grabbed Gerry's hand.

"Come on, let's get out of here," he said.

She saw that Libra had trapped Silky in a conversation and
the Satins had disappeared. Libra was probably giving her
notes about what they had done tonight, and catching up on
what had happened out of town. It was just like him to talk
business right here and now without even giving her a chance
to say hello to Dick.

"Come on," Dick said again.

"All right."

They got their coats at the door and left, without bothering to say anything to their host and hostess, who were
dancing wildly and couldn't care less. The air outside was
fresh and very cold. The doorman got them a cab.

"That was a New York party," Dick said. "The way I
know it was a party is that I'll read it was tomorrow in the
newspaper. Otherwise I wouldn't know what it was. I knew it

wasn't a wake because at a wake there's only one dead body, but here there were about a hundred."

Gerry laughed. She was glad he wasn't impressed with the B.P.'s and their friends. For a while she thought he was.

He told the cab to wait when they got to her building and he walked her to the door. He gave her a look she couldn't read—was it affection, amusement, affectionate amusement?

"Good night," he said. "Sleep well. I'll call you tomorrow." And then he was gone. She went upstairs. It was two o'clock and she was tired. She set the alarm for eight. Dick was nice, and she felt at ease with him. She liked him. He probably liked her. You couldn't tell, really, what he was thinking about at any given time. He seemed so cool and self-sufficient, he had good manners, he knew exactly what he was doing. Did he act the way he did because he was so smart, or didn't he really need anybody? She decided that she intended to find out.

CHAPTER

SIX

THERE is a limit to the amount of loneliness a person can take, and spring is the silly season. Loneliness makes you live in fantasies until you are ready to fall in love with the phantom lover. When he appears, whoever he is, you are ready for him. If he appears in spring, so much the better, for you are that much more ready for him. So when Gerry asked Dick to dinner at her apartment a week after the B.P.'s party—her first dinner guest—and when after dinner he took her to bed as naturally as if they both belonged in each other's lives, her reaction was excitement, tenderness, and even hope.

She had always been a guarded person, very much aware of what was a fling or a one-night stand and what was more, and afterward, with Dick, she tried to keep rational but it was difficult. She had always suspected that she would never be able to feel the real happiness of love if she was not ready to risk the pain of a mistake, and this time, lying in Dick's arms feeling elated and protected, she decided to try to take the chance.

Libra had called him Dick Devoid. Libra was full of slogans and nicknames. Whatever Dick was devoid in, it certainly wasn't charm or masculinity. Perhaps it was character. But if he was, he certainly hadn't shown it with her. She could tell Dick really liked her. Perhaps whatever he had done to other people's lives, if indeed he had done anything destructive, which she doubted, had only been done because he was looking for more than he had found.

During their lovemaking she had thought he'd said he loved her. She was too wise to question him about it after their passion was over—for all she knew, she had told him she loved him, too. If he loved her, or grew to love her, he would say so when he was ready. It was sad, she thought, to be so self-protective as she was, but she couldn't act any other way. She had learned that love was something you could really believe you felt for a moment or an hour, but it was not a promise. During the moment it was felt, it was real.

But the next morning when he left and she had to go to the office, she found herself daydreaming, looking out the window of the suite at the green spring trees in the park, and she was full of bittersweet joy and yearning for him. She liked the way the hair grew on the back of his neck—had she ever thought he had thin, ridiculous hair? Oh, but it was baby-fine and soft. And she liked his mouth. He wasn't cuddly to sleep with; he liked to stay on the far side of the bed, and that made her feel lonely; but in the morning when he woke up he looked so glad to see her that she was reassured. And he had almost made her late for work. It obviously wasn't just a jump in the hay the night before because she was *there;* they had wanted each other again in the morning—or was that just because she was there? No, she wouldn't allow herself to be cynical about him. She wouldn't allow herself to spoil what they had.

When he called her that afternoon she was so overjoyed she almost said something silly and sentimental. She had thought about him all day. He said he had to work that night but would see her the following night. He hadn't had to say anything. But he had, and he had put himself in the position of responsibility toward her. He had set the relationship, he had steered it, and she was going to try to trust him. Even while thinking she would try to trust him she knew she was already hooked. It didn't make any sense, but she was hooked.

After that she saw him every other night. It seemed an intelligent pattern, for if they had spent all their time together they might have grown tired of each other. Gerry had learned that sex made a relationship advance in a lopsided way; the sex made two people seem much closer than they really were emotionally. It took a long time to feel close emotionally. What had Silky said that night at the party? "It takes a long time to make a friend." It took only a night to make a lover. A lover wasn't a friend. Still, she could tell Dick everything. He was a sounding board, a fellow cynic, an ally. He laughed at the things she laughed at, no one impressed or deceived him. If she looked the slightest bit unhappy he was so quick to notice and ask her why that she took to trying to look happy all the time.

He sent her flowers, and he bought her silly presents. Sometimes he telephoned her at midnight and told her he had just come from a boring business meeting and he needed her. Then she would get dressed and go to his apartment, where he would cook spaghetti—although there were a lot of gourmet things in the cupboards and lying around in the refrigerator—and they would stay up until four o'clock. She began to leave her make-up on until midnight every night when he was not with her, hoping he would call. Sometimes he would call late and come to her apartment. He didn't like to go out. But he did seem to keep going out to those dinners where he was invited as the extra man, and although it began to annoy her Gerry realized that was one of the advantages of being an attractive bachelor in New York, and she couldn't ask him to give it up until he was ready. She wished someone would invite her somewhere so she could be popular and unavailable, too, but no one did. She hadn't run around looking for men before and she couldn't change her pattern now. She had always been a one-man woman; all or nothing. She was twenty-six, and she'd been dating—how long? Fourteen years! That was a long time and she was bored with dating. If she couldn't be married, at least she could have the next best thing—someone she cared about whom she spent all her time with. Sometimes Libra made her work late, and she was irritated and nervous about it, although she knew it was a good thing because she wasn't always on call for Dick. Work wasn't as romantic as a party she had been invited to, but if there were no parties for unattached, attractive girls because there were too many of them already, at least work was better than sitting home waiting for him to call.

The stove and pots and pans in Dick's apartment looked well used, and Gerry thought he must have had someone living with him quite recently who had been domestic. But there was no other sign of a girl, no old make-up, no left-over clothes. He had a maid who came in every day and he himself was personally immaculate. He was too neat and too secure to leave any clues of previous love affairs. Since she wasn't very domestic herself she didn't try to change him. Spaghetti was fine. Once in a while she brought him a bottle of good wine, which they shared in bed, but it was only a personal gesture because he had enough cases of wine and liquor to open a bar. He really didn't seem to need anything, not even company. She knew if he wanted her there it was because she really meant something to him.

At the end of the month she handed Libra a bill for all the quarters she had spent as tips in the Ladies' Room in the hotel lobby.

"What the hell is this?" Libra asked her, waving the bill at her.

"You told me the first day, remember?"

"Told you what?"

"To use the Ladies' Room in the lobby, Mr. Libra," she said sweetly.

Libra exploded with laughter. "I like you," he said. "You're a lunatic." But she knew what he meant was that she was a smart girl and not one to be pushed around. "Would you be insulted if I asked you to do me the favor of using the facilities this office provides from now on? I can't afford tips."

"All right."

He didn't reimburse her for the tips, which, after all, had not amounted to much except another blow to her ego, but that night when she got home there was a case of champagne from Libra with a card that said: "Drink this at home so you won't pee on my time."

She and Dick both laughed about it, and Dick bought caviar, which they both loved, to go with the champagne. It gave them many happy evenings at home. Oh, things were really going well—Libra liked and respected her, Dick was a part of her life and she cared about him more every day. She had been right to come back to New York and start her life again. If only Dick could become a part of her life forever she would be the happiest woman in the world.

She didn't want to think about marrying him, but the thought still entered her mind when she was not guarded against it, and it eventually became an unavoidable wish. They had so much in common, their interests, their work, the things that gave them pleasure, their sense of humor, their observations about life—and he was a perfect lover. She wanted him more all the time. She knew she would be good for him because she understood him and she was intelligent and attractive enough for him. He was certainly good for her. She looked forward to every day now that she was with him. How many months did it take for a man to decide he really needed a girl? She usually thought of herself as a woman, but sometimes she realized she was a girl. She had always dreaded being one of those ladies from the Helen Hokinson cartoons who called themselves "girls" when they were middle-aged. But when did you stop being a girl? When you were married, certainly. She knew Dick had never been married. He never said anything bad about marriage the way most men did, nor did he say he wanted to be married. They really had never discussed it, except as a passing comment, but most of the men she had known had made it very clear that they thought marriage was a trap. A man like Dick who was too secure to protest was probably the hardest kind of man to trap. Wasn't marriage a trap? What did he have to gain? She was the one with everything to gain. He wouldn't go to any more dinners as the extra man, she would see him all the time. They could live together and have children. Dick had managed to keep their romance on the dating level even though it was an affair; he didn't suggest she leave any little things in his apartment or that she stay even for an entire weekend. She had too much pride to deposit extra clothes and make-up at his place to get a hold on him. It was much too easy to make a little package of an unwanted girl's things and leave it with the doorman. That was a humiliation she was determined would never happen to her.

But she really did trust him. It was just that she knew he was the one who always had to call the shots, and to tell the truth she found it easier that way. He would lead and she would follow. Anywhere . . .

CHAPTER

SEVEN

LIZZIE LIBRA, née Elizabeth Bentley Marchman, had been in the top third of her class at college and editor of the Senior Yearbook. When she married Sam Leo Libra she had not ceased to have a creative function and had never allowed herself to dwindle into a mere wife. Never mind your ticker-tape parades—Lizzie Libra was a one-woman congratulatory committee in bed. She had slept with Dick Devoid the night the Let It All Hang Out Show had won the Emmy Award, she had slept with Mad Daddy the week his picture was on the cover of *TV Guide,* and she had slept with Franco (who swung both ways) when he had his picture in *Time* Magazine. She had slept with each and every member of the King James Version (the drummer was her favorite) and Shadrach Bascombe had broken training for her when he was getting all that publicity as the hottest new future contender. He had broken training for her, and she had crossed the color line for him, she later told her analyst in delight. That Shadrach had been really frustrated in training camp: six times in one night ... whew! No wonder they called him Shack-Up Bascombe, one nickname that hadn't been created by Sam.

She had slept with Arnie Gurney, of course, long ago, on one of the trips to Las Vegas where Lizzie was allowed to accompany her husband. She had slept with poor, dear, dead

Douglas Henry, and she'd had a crack at two of Sylvia Polydor's ex-husbands, while they were still married to Sylvia, of course, or they wouldn't have been anybody. She had slept with adorable Zak Maynard the night of the B.P.'s party, and a few days after the party she had also slept with Mr. B.P. himself, Peter Potter, who may have been beautiful but certainly had a lot to learn in bed.

Except for Shadrach, who was a darling beast, and Dick, who was sweet and romantic, Lizzie did not really bother to rate any one of her famous lovers as any better than the others in the kip, since the feeling that overwhelmed her when she saw each famous face above hers in the feathers was something akin to a heady drunkenness. She had even been happy with Peter Potter, even though he was a premature ejaculator, because after all, he *was* a B.P. and he *was* with her. If she had been asked to describe any of her sexual encounters—and Dr. Picker, her analyst, always wanted her to describe them—she would have been at a loss, almost an amnesiac. It was great. She had been happy, overjoyed, ecstatic.

"Did you come?" Dr. Picker would ask (oh, those old fossils, they really tried to talk so hip!), and she always said "Yes," because it was none of his business. She was not in analysis to discuss her womanliness, although Dr. Picker seemed to consider that an issue.

Why was she in analysis? Well, because she cheated on her husband, she supposed, since that wasn't a well-adjusted thing to do. And because she was bored to death, and talking to Dr. Picker gave her something to think about when she wasn't with him, trying to think of new, lively stories to tell him. She was sure she was Dr. Picker's most interesting client, although he insisted on telling her dull stories about other interesting patients, which Lizzie truly did not think was very ethical. Of course, he never mentioned names, but he gave out enough hints as to background and occupation and marital difficulties that if she had really tried she could have figured out who they were.

Dr. Picker was a shrunken little old man from Germany, fortunately not a Nazi, and besides being at least a hundred years old he sat in his dingy office, laden with Biedermeyer furniture, all day long, so she supposed the juicy stories the patients told him gave him his view of what life outside was really all about. It killed her the way he tried to alter his language to get on the patient's wavelength, the poor old vicarious letch.

DR. PICKER: "It iss not zat ve haf zis problem vit scwewing, as you put it, but zat ve scwew only stars."

LIZZIE: "Dr. Picker, I wish you would stop saying 'we.' "

She supposed he really did think it was the two of them that were busy *scwewing* stars, but she had news for him: while she was doing it she never gave him a thought.

It had all started years ago in Hollywood. Not that she didn't love Sam—she did, she adored him. He was the most brilliant man she had ever met. Why else would she have married him? But Sam had opened up a whole new world to her in Hollywood, and she was proud to think (if it was something to be proud of) that she had *never,* never even *kissed* a beachboy, gigolo, or unknown male starlet, nor any of her friends' husbands, unless, of course, the friends' husbands were famous.

She had never been predatory, and she had never even intended to start. But at one party (she even remembered what she had been wearing) there had been a great circle of people around Douglas Henry, who was young then and terribly attractive. Douglas Henry never cheated on his wife, and he was known to be kind but aloof. Knowing he was no danger whatsoever, Lizzie had been nice to him at the party (the first time she'd ever met him) and had proceeded to do his horoscope. He was a Virgo, and she had told him that Virgos were undersexed. He had raised an eyebrow at her.

"Oh?"

She had glanced at his attractive wife across the room. "Well, I mean that if they do love anybody, they love that person forever and are always faithful."

"Thank you very much," Douglas Henry had said, and the next day he had called her.

She told him Sam was already at the office, but Doug said he wanted to see her. So he had come over, and Lizzie, demurely dressed in a sundress, had tried to hand him a drink. There she was with the drink in her hand, and he had unzipped quick as a flash and laid his cock in her other hand. None of those young stars wore underwear. Well, what was she to do? She just held it, with the drink still in her other hand, and she thought it (his cock) was certainly very large. Then he had picked her up and tossed her on the couch, pulled her clothes off, and proceeded to show her that Virgos weren't undersexed at all.

She wasn't drunk, having had only one drink before he arrived, but sleeping with him absolutely intoxicated her. She felt the room reeling, and knew she was grinning and giggling like an idiot. He thought his masculinity had really flipped her out, and they had an affair for several weeks before he had to go away on location to do another picture. Lizzie did a lot of investigation among the industry gossips and discovered that if Douglas Henry ever had any affairs he had always been so discreet about it that no one knew for sure. Why, she had been the chosen one! She couldn't figure out why. She certainly wasn't sexy or beautiful. Hollywood was full of carefully manufactured sex machines. But he had chosen *her!*

Her success with Doug gave her an aura, perhaps visible to others, of triumph, of knowing she could conquer the whole world. She, a little housewife, had been Douglas Henry's mistress! So when the next star approached her, and the next, she was never really surprised, only more intoxicated, more gloriously happy.

She still slept with Sam once in a while, whenever he thought about it, but he loved his career first and put in a twenty-hour day. She was quiet and discreet about her love life, although she would have loved to have bragged, but she was clever enough to know that none of her friends would trust her any more if they knew she had slept with even one husband. She never felt guilty. With Elaine Fellin, for example, who was her best friend, she only felt pity. Elaine was soon to be dumped because Mad Daddy liked little girls. He had intimated that to her, Lizzie, that is. And he had chosen *her!* She was older than he was, and he had chosen *her!*

Of course Sam didn't know. He didn't have a clue. He didn't cheat on her, poor thing, although he certainly had the chance. But Sam was a nice, old-fashioned boy at heart, and he thought husbands were supposed to be faithful. She didn't know what she would do if Sam cheated; probably laugh and forgive him. After all, he was entitled.

No, she loved Sam and he loved her. Their marriage was forever. It lacked a lot of things, and she felt she could have been of more use to him if he had let her, but it was a good marriage and it satisfied her. They had no children, for which Lizzie was just as glad. Somehow she thought it would have been immoral for a mother to carry on the way she did. They didn't even have a dog.

She had started going to Dr. Picker on one of Sam's and her trips to New York, and she enjoyed it at first. She thought analysis would give her a firmer grasp on what she was all about. And she had a secret dream: to write the greatest dirty book in the world, and she felt analysis would give her the discipline to do it.

Her book was to be called *An Elegant Book*, and it would concern the adventures of a beautiful, innocent young girl who always found herself in extraordinary sexual experiences. Then, right in the middle of the experience, just as things were really getting wild, the girl would cry: "Get out, get out! This is an elegant book!" and would extricate herself and go about her business. The possibilities were limitless, and so was the humor—the girl with a cock in her mouth trying to mumble "Get out!" for example. Pornography was in, and the book could make Lizzie famous in her own right, not just as the wife of Sam Leo Libra.

But except for dinners and cocktail parties, where she regaled all within earshot with the amusing possibilities of her book, and of course her sessions with Dr. Picker, who was an inexhaustible audience, Lizzie had not written a word of it. She just didn't have the energy to start. She knew just what she wanted to say, but when faced with a blank piece of paper she couldn't manage to make even the first sentence come out to her satisfaction. She fervently hoped that her analysis would give her the discipline to start in earnest; perhaps she could retreat to Palm Springs, where she and Sam had friends, and become a recluse. A recluse writer! Wouldn't that be divine?

Meanwhile, of course, all her friends loved to hear about the book. Everybody said Lizzie Libra had a great sense of humor and was really fun to talk to. And her experiences with her famous lovers had given her further grist for her mill. If Sam ever asked her where she learned all those things she would tell him from reading dirty books, of course. Anything went nowadays in fiction. There was a mint in pornography, especially humorous pornography, although she had enough money now. It was fame she wanted. She had everything else. She had a darling, famous husband, she had a glorious past, a glorious future coming up with stars she hadn't even met yet, and she had so many good friends she could hardly count them. She was a happy woman. If only Nelly Nelson wasn't such a fruit. It would be heaven to be

the only woman Nelson had ever slept with, but Lizzie was
wise enough to know that even in the glitter world she lived
in no one could have *everything* he wanted.

Sam Leo Libra, pacing the living room of his suite at the
Plaza, could hardly contain his elation. Fred, that bitch, had
finally called and said she wanted to see him. He had sent
Gerry out on a wild-goose chase so he could be alone with
Fred when she arrived. Not that he didn't trust Gerry completely, but the business he had in mind with Fred would
have to be done in private.

He had been yearning for Fred for two months now, ever
since he had met her. She had that patrician kind of looks he
found so sexy—he had always believed that girls who
looked like icicles were the hottest when you finally thawed
them out. Not that he would pass up someone inferior to
Fred, and he certainly hadn't in the past: a man had to get
his heart started some way. In fact, some of the girls he had
balled were pretty odd—Ingrid, for instance. He'd always
secretly thought she was either a dike or one of those ladies
who took a whip to men—he didn't like the look in her eyes.
But luckily, the affair with Ingrid had been brief and expedi-
ent, and now she was just his doctor, as if nothing had
happened. He knew very little about Ingrid, and she seemed
to prefer it that way, so he had never questioned her about
her life, even during the cozy time in bed after the dirty deed
was done, which he had found was just about the best time to
pry secrets out of anybody. And don't think he hadn't used that
time to best advantage. He remembered that lady agent . . .

He looked at his watch impatiently. Tardiness infuriated
him. Fred had exactly four minutes to be on time, and then
she would be late, putting him at a disadvantage and wasting
his precious time. He had taken his second shower of the day
at the gym and he was fresh and clean as a baby. Ah Fred
. . . beautiful ice maiden! He wouldn't even make her take a
shower before he touched her; he trusted her. She was always
so perfectly groomed. Fred . . . He hoped to God she had
clean underwear. Oh, Fred would, he knew it, and Sam Leo
Libra was a perfect judge of people.

The doorbell rang. He waited a beat, then walked slowly
to the door, his heart pounding. She was exactly on time. Oh,

she was going to get it, the royal screwing of her life! He opened the door, smiling welcome.

The bitch had brought someone with her! A girl. He tried to conceal his look of furious disappointment and ushered them both in. He would have to get rid of that other girl. What did Fred have in mind, anyway, a business meeting?

"Hello, Mr. Libra," Fred said sweetly. "I'd like you to meet my friend, Bonnie Parker."

Bonnie Parker! What was the fool, anyway, a stripper? She didn't look like a stripper. She was as tall as Fred, and as thin, with pale blond hair cut like Twiggy's, and enormous, innocent violet eyes. Her face was all soft curves, with a mouth that curved upward at the corners all the time, even when she was not smiling, and lips that looked very soft. She was probably a model.

"Hello," Bonnie Parker said, in a voice that was so soft and husky that it was almost inaudible. She looked down shyly. She did not shake hands. She was like a terrified little fawn—if he hadn't been crazy about Fred he would have been interested.

"Aren't you going to ask us to sit down?" Fred asked.

"Sit down."

The girls sat, legs crossed, side by side on the couch in their mini-skirts: two of the loveliest girls in New York, he decided.

"Bonnie's new in New York," Fred said. "She wants to be a model. I think she has a great future, more even than me. I'm not being modest ... I know I haven't got a chance with my voice to become anything more than a model, but I think Bonnie could make it in the movies. That's why I brought her to you."

"Who am I? Central Casting?" He glared at Bonnie. She looked down again. "What's your real name?"

"Me?"

"Yes, you."

"Bonnie Parker."

"Now come on," Libra said. "We all saw the movie. What was your name before?"

"Jewel," the girl murmured.

"No wonder you changed it. Have you ever modeled before?"

"No, but she brought pictures," Fred said, taking the model's portfolio away from Bonnie and opening it. "Look at these, just look!"

Grudgingly, because Fred was standing so close to him that he could smell the scent of Ivory soap that drove him wild, he looked at the girl's pictures. They were superb. Even he could tell that. The girl definitely had something—an air of . . . sexless sex. A look of innocent amoral giving. And the clothes hung on her perfectly because she was built like a slat. She was not so thin or small-boned as Twiggy, and her face, although young, was not so much the face of a child as that of a young girl.

"How old are you?" he asked.

"Eighteen."

"Speak up. How do you expect to get in the movies if you mutter like that?"

"I thought they used microphones," the girl said.

He laughed. It wasn't so much that what she said was funny, although the kid seemed sharp, but that she had a sort of deadpan delivery that made the line seem hilarious. She'd be great on interviews . . .

"Why don't you just let your modeling agency handle you?" he said.

"Because I think she should do more," Fred said. "Come on, Mr. Libra, be a sport. You wanted me, and you and I both know I can go only so *far* and no *further*. I'm doing you a *favor*."

Oh, so that was it. Fred was pulling out gracefully, handing him a lay. He should have known. That Fred was diabolical. The gift of Bonnie was her way of saying he could never have *her*. Well, then, the hell with her. He'd lay Bonnie.

Libra stood up. "Well, Fred, I think I'll give the matter some thought. If you'll leave me alone with Bonnie now to discuss it further . . ."

Fred gave Bonnie a quick, triumphant smile and stood up. She held out her cool hand and gave him a firm handshake. "You're a peach, Mr. Libra."

Some peach! They all knew what was going on. At least, he hoped Bonnie did, too. "You'll be sorry," he said, ushering Fred to the door. "I could have done a lot for you."

"You'll do it for Bonnie," she said, smiling. And she was gone.

"Would you like a drink?" he asked Bonnie.

"Do you have a Coke?"

"Of course."

He opened a bottle and poured it into a glass over some ice. Then he held it, standing there by the bar, so she had to get up and come over to him to get it. She walked in a very delicate way, taking little steps, like a geisha. He'd have to teach her how to walk, that way was too affected. When she stood close to him he caught the whiff of Ivory he loved. He wondered if Fred had coached her. He looked carefully at the roots of her hair to see if it was dyed, but it wasn't, and he looked at her ears and the back of her neck, and they were as clean and soft as his own. Her little white vinyl dress looked squeaky clean, and the heels of her high white vinyl boots were as neat as if she had just come from the shoe-maker's. She had painted a tiny black beauty spot on one cheek, but other than that her face was as clear as porcelain, if artfully made up. She wore no lipstick; he liked that, too. She was really a lovely thing. He could feel his heart getting started, his heart being an area somewhat below his belt. He wanted very much to touch her. He took her hand in his. Her hand felt surprisingly rough, but her nails, he noticed with satisfaction, were immaculate.

"You should use hand lotion," he said. "Better yet, sleep in gloves with emollient cream on your hands."

"I will," she said softly.

"So you want to be a star."

"I never dreamed it was possible."

"Somebody must have convinced you."

"Fred encouraged me. She's a good friend."

"There's nothing between you and Fred, is there?" he asked, looking at her shrewdly.

The girl looked genuinely shocked. "Oh no! I'm not a Lesbian, thank God!"

"Just checking."

Bonnie sipped her Coke, looking up at him from half-lowered lids in a flirtatious way. Oh, she really looked ready for it, the hot little thing! He'd give her twenty minutes, maybe fifteen, and he'd have her in bed. Fortunately Lizzie was at a matinee with Elaine and they'd probably get soused somewhere after, so the bedroom was his, even though it was risky. Hereafter he'd have to make the kid take him to her apartment. He hoped she didn't live with her parents.

"You'll have to have a modeling agency, anyway, you know," he said. "They'll get you your bookings and I'll handle your career."

"I have one. Fred's."

"That was fast work."

"Fred has done so much for me."

"Amazing," Libra said. "Amazing that she's not jealous."

"Oh, we're completely different types," Bonnie said. "I think Fred is the most beautiful girl in the world."

"You're not so bad."

She smiled, enticingly. He let his finger stray to the nape of her neck, and seeing that she did not move away he let his hand move until it cupped her cheek. She smiled at him and quickly transferred her glass to her mouth. He took the glass away from her and put it on the bar. She moved away from him in a very quick, practiced motion, and stood smiling shyly at him from three feet away. He strode over to her, but she was already at the window.

"What a lovely view," she said.

"Isn't it?"

He got her at the window then, where there was no escape but down a long way, and put his hands on her waist. She was wearing one of those goddam waist-cinch things; those skinny models were so paranoid they always thought they were too fat. He hoped it did not have a million hooks in the back.

"What are you wearing that thing for?" he asked.

She looked startled, as if he'd said something obscene. Her eyes opened wide and she didn't answer. He let his fingers stray up until he was just touching her tits. She pulled away and almost ran to the bar, picked up her Coke, and drank it, looking at him over the rim of her glass with those great violet eyes. She was really a morsel. So juicy and tender, like white meat of chicken. He wanted to bite that soft, curvy mouth.

"Cigarette?" he asked.

"I don't smoke, thanks."

"Pot?"

"Oh no."

"I was just kidding about the pot. We don't have that here."

She shrugged. "I don't mind."

"You don't mind that I don't have it, or you don't mind if I do have it?"

"Either way."

"Do you have a boyfriend?"

She shrugged. "Nobody special."

"Would you like to have a boyfriend?"

She looked down, smiling.

"Have you ever been to California?"

"No, but I'd like to go."

"Maybe I'll take you with me."

"Really?"

"Why not? If we get along. How do you look in a bikini?"

She smiled and did not answer. He took a few casual steps toward her. She watched him but did not move. He was right up to her then when she slipped away from him and was across the room. This was unseemly and undignified! He was not going to chase her! But then he saw that she was giggling. He raced toward her and grabbed her shoulders, kissing her on the mouth.

That mouth! It was softer than he had ever dreamed. He mauled that mouth, sinking into it, until she gasped. His heart was really started now, he couldn't breathe. Oh, that tender mouth! With one hand firmly around her waist so she could not get away, he let his other hand race to the hem of her mini-skirt, pushing aside her frantic hands that were trying to keep his hand away, and his passionate fingers probed the dark wonder that was between those thighs.

Holy shit, it was a boy!

CHAPTER

EIGHT

WHEN Vincent Abruzzi was a little boy he liked to play with dolls, but since his parents did not want him to play with dolls he called them his "puppets." "I'm going upstairs to play with my puppets now," he would say, and his mother would smile and go on with her work around the house. Then he would go into his room and for hours he would design and sew little dresses for his dolls, creating a fantasy life about them. They were always girl dolls.

Vincent was a shy and beautiful child, very well behaved, and since his parents were already middle-aged—he had been a menopause baby, born long after his parents had resigned themselves to being childless—they were glad that he was so good and did not trouble themselves to find out what he was thinking. He liked to play with girls, because they played games he liked. The girls loved him, because he was so gentle, and adults who noticed how much time he spent with girls laughed and said that he was already quite a ladies' man. Because he was always so sweet and so pretty, none of the boys taunted him for being a sissy until he was in high school, and even then it was only a few who were already insecure about their own masculinity. For the rest he was a sort of mascot. Because he had a heart murmur he didn't have to go to gym, but he hung around anyway to watch and

123

attended all the school baseball, basketball, and football games, always with a gang of friends. People liked him.

Vincent lived in Irvington, New Jersey, in a run-down neighborhood that might even be called a slum. His parents had one of the nicest houses on the block, if it could be called nice, and he was never conscious of being impoverished. He never had anything much of his own, so he simply did not have any conception of ownership about anything. If something took his fancy he would usually manage to get it, and if a friend liked something of his, he would give it to the friend. His mentality was a curious cross between a slum mentality and that of a resident of the Garden of Eden.

By the time Vincent was in high school all the boys who were going to be homosexuals knew who they were and were already well versed in homosexual practices, but Vincent did not yet know what he was. He was sure he was straight, even though girls terrified him. The girls who had been his playmates were now his dates, but all the kids went out in groups, and the only time he started to shake with fear was during the car ride home when all the other couples were necking. He knew everyone was looking at him, wondering if he was going to kiss his girl. When he took her to her door he knew they were watching from the car, and he would start to plead a headache long before the car reached his girl's house. At her door he would give her a quick handshake, say: "Well, it was nice seeing you," and think: *Her make-up looks the worst.*

Three of the boys on the block he'd grown up with liked him, and after all of them had deposited their girls home the three of them would each phone Vincent, to ask him how he was and if he wanted to go out for a late cup of coffee. He often did, but he did not have sex with them. He'd already had the customary sexual experimentation with them when they were all thirteen or fourteen, but he didn't see anything queer in that. At this age, though, it seemed different.

He thought he was just slower to develop socially than the other boys. Some of the boys had lovers, but at the time Vincent thought they were only good friends. There were a few flagrantly nitty fags at school, who minced through the halls trying to attract attention, and some of the boys beat them up periodically. But Vincent was so timid and likable that some of the boys used to form a flying wedge around him in the school halls when the fag-beaters were around, and say: "Don't worry, Vincent, we won't let them beat you

up for being queer." Vincent would think: *Me, queer?* He
knew he was effeminate, and supposed that was why everyone thought he was gay. When the fag-beaters yelled after
him in a taunting way: "Oh, Vincent, you great big A-
BRUTE-ZI!" that hurt. He cried easily. But he had never confid-
ed in anyone, so when he was lonely or confused or hurt,
which was often, he went somewhere where he could be
alone and cried for a while.

As he grew older he became more of a recluse, preferring
to stay home and play canasta with his mother to hanging
around with the kids. He never went to school dances,
although he prided himself on being a good dancer, and
whenever he was invited to a party he spent the evening
dancing with girls, embarrassed and confused, because some
of the boys kept staring at him. At one party, a boy he didn't
know stared at him so much it began to annoy him. But after
the boy left, Vincent found himself missing him. He could
not figure out why he missed that boy so much. But he
always asked his friends when the boy would be around
again. His friends nodded knowingly, and Vincent couldn't
figure out what they knew that he didn't.

His parents, who were religious Catholics, saw nothing
strange in Vincent's mental and physical purity; to them he
was a good boy. They thought perhaps he might become a
priest. To be a priest was the farthest thing from his mind.

He was very blond, and although he grew to normal size
and had quite a large penis, from what he observed of other
boys' organs in the school locker room, he never had to
shave. There was a pale blond peach-fuzz on his jaws, much
like what you would see on a girl's face, but that was all. He
naturally assumed that was because he was so fair-haired. He
always wore his hair cut short and combed back neatly, and
he wore jeans every day except Sunday, when he wore his
one good suit. He knew he was a rather pretty boy, but he
did not consider himself handsome, and he wondered if
anyone would ever find him attractive enough to fall in love
with. He never let himself wonder whether that someone was
to be a boy or a girl.

There was one boy in gym class whom Vincent particularly
admired. That boy was a star athlete, well built, tall, and
blond; an older, more masculine version of Vincent himself.
His name was Buzz. And then one day, after basketball
practice, Buzz asked Vincent out for coffee. Vincent was
seventeen, Buzz was eighteen.

Vincent fell in love like a girl. He and Buzz took long walks holding hands, went to the beach that summer, and talked and talked. It was very romantic. From Buzz, Vincent learned all about how to have sex with a boy, and he liked it very much. It never occurred to him to be unfaithful to Buzz, or to cruise faggots in the streets, or even to date anyone else. It was bad enough that they were two boys, Vincent thought, but at least they were in love. Buzz told him he looked like a girl, but treated him like a boy. After all, Vincent *was* a boy, and he knew what he was himself better than anyone else seemed to.

Then Buzz went away to college. Vincent mourned his lost romance, the feeling of belonging, the affection. He began to date other boys, but for him it was always a romantic relationship, never just a number. He acquired quite a few fraternity pins and wedding rings.

At seventeen he still wasn't shaving, and he was quite sure that he was pretty because so many people had told him so. One of his closest friends was a boy named Flash, who was a hairdresser who spent his time making shellacked confections of hairdos for the married women in the neighborhood who had their hair done on Friday and didn't even put a comb to it until the following Friday, when they had it washed and set again. Flash despised his clientele, and longed to create really fashionable hairdos because he knew what was what—except that those horrors didn't want to be chic. So Flash exercised his talent for creating chic women on himself, painting his face and wearing a wig and a dress, as a weekend drag queen. It was the first Vincent had heard of drag, being quite out of everything, but Flash took him to his first drag ball and Vincent was fascinated. He thought they were going to a masquerade; then they got there and he thought it was an ordinary dance ... then Flash told him all those beautiful girls were really men.

"Could *I* do it?" he asked Flash, almost in tears at the thought of how wonderful it would be to have an image at last.

"Sure. You'd look great. I'll put you in drag myself."

So Flash did. He got Vincent a blond wig, showed him how to paint, told him what cosmetics to buy, how to care for his skin, and even took him to buy a dress. One night he and Flash went to a gay bar in drag and Vincent was the star of the evening. All the men thought he was a girl. He was so happy he burst into tears.

He let his hair grow a little and Flash styled it like Twiggy's. He began to paint all the time, copying everything he saw on the models in *Vogue* and *Harper's Bazaar*. He needed a name for drag, so he named himself Jewel because he thought it sounded classy. Vincent was not hip and he did not like to poke fun at himself. To him, drag was serious business. He felt much more at home as a girl than as a boy, and he knew he looked better. He knew he was a strikingly pretty girl. On the other hand, he was still quite aware— much more so than the other queens he met in the bars were about themselves—that he was a boy. He did not, for instance, ever carry a handbag; that was ridiculous. He kept his carfare in his underpants. He did not bother to wear a padded bra, knowing that flat-chested girls were perfectly acceptable, and because a padded bra made him feel uncomfortable. He never wore lipstick, only a little Vaseline. Although he always wore boys' clothes except when he was in drag on weekend nights or for parties, he gaffed, tucking his cock back so it did not show, and often when he was in the street wearing no more paint than a little mascara, people would say within his hearing: "Is it a boy or a girl? It's a girl, of course, silly." He was a natural beauty wonder.

Often straight men came up to him in bars and asked him to dance, thinking he was a girl. He always told them that he was a boy, not believing in the fantasy enough to deceive himself, but they always wanted to dance with him anyway. Sometimes college boys invited him to their college dances, in drag, and passed him off as their date. Vincent liked that very much. He knew he was the prettiest girl in the room, and he looked *real*.

Vincent met a lot of queens in the bars, and he spent many weekend evenings dishing with the girls, dancing, flirting, until the sun came up, but he always went home alone. For one thing, drag queens like him did not appeal to many fruits, and for another, Vincent still had his girl's mentality— he believed in love, or at least someone he could have a relationship with. If someone approached him who was just a number he did not even bother to talk at all. He knew the difference between a number and a real date, and he never deceived himself about that either.

At first when his parents found him going around wearing make-up they were shocked and saddened. He never put his dress on at home at first, carrying it in a bag and putting it on at the home of one or another of the queens he had

become friendly with, but after a while when he realized his
parents weren't going to throw him out of the house for
painting, he became bolder and pranced right out of the
house in front of their noses in high drag. After a while he
really believed they were beginning to accept him as their
daughter, although of course they refused to call him Jewel
and he never even asked them to. He thought of himself as
"Jewel . . . she" when he was in drag, and as "Vincent . . .
he'" when he was out of drag. Out of drag, for Vincent,
meant not in a dress.

When he wasn't painted he spent hours with complexion
creams and moisturizers on his face, taking better care of his
skin than almost any girl. Luckily, he was never troubled
with adolescent acne. He graduated from high school with
excellent grades, but then he just stayed around the house all
day, watching television, napping, or just thinking. Sometimes
he played records. He never read a book or a newspaper,
which was not surprising because there were no books in the
house. The only magazines he read were fashion magazines,
and sometimes drag-queen magazines, if anyone he knew had
her picture in it. He refused to get a job. What kind of a job
could he get? He refused to look for work as a boy, and he
was too shy to look for work passing as a girl. Sometimes a
boy who liked him would buy him some article of feminine
clothing, so he managed to keep his wardrobe up, and Flash
had given him the wig. His parents gave him small amounts
of money. But the main reason Vincent stayed in the house
all day was that the life he had chosen to follow was
essentially the life of the night people. All the queens lived on
pills, slept all day, and cruised the bars all night. There were
private gay clubs for after the bars closed. Often they went
into Manhattan, where there were bigger, better private
clubs.

Although Vincent attended every drag ball, he never entered a beauty contest for female impersonators, giving as
the excuse that he was too poor to buy the proper gown and
wig. He knew that you had to look really spectacular to win,
and although his friends assured him he would mop any
contest he entered, he knew you had to know a lot to be a
winning contestant.

He was often depressed. His depression took the form of
inertia. He could sit for hours, curled up on the couch with
his cheek resting on his knees, and think about nothing at all.
The hours would go by, then somehow the days. He took

little naps, like an animal. He hardly ever ate. Sometimes he
cleaned the house for his mother, or cooked dinner. He liked
to be helpful. He would joke to the other queens that he was
going to find a rich man and get married, because he would
be a wonderful wife, but sometimes he wondered what was
going to happen to him. It didn't really matter right now,
though, he was only eighteen. He had a long time to think
seriously about his life.

Then, one night in Manhattan, at a drag ball, he met Fred.
At first he thought Fred was either a drag queen, because she
was so chic and beautiful, or a dike, because she really
looked *real*. If she was a queen he liked her, if she was a dike
she terrified him. He hated dikes. Fred had come to the ball
with a hairdresser named Nelson, an up-tight East Side queen
who wouldn't be caught dead cruising a gay bar because he
was famous, and would go to a drag ball only if he brought
along a girl and pretended he thought it was all a camp.
Nelson, Vincent knew, was probably a tireless cruiser of the
streets, not to mention the bath houses when he got desperate. Vincent couldn't stand phonies: he didn't like Nelson and
Nelson obviously hated him because he was doing what
Nelson really wanted but didn't have the courage to do.
Nelson looked as though he thought if he touched Vincent by
accident he would be contaminated.

But Fred seemed to adore Vincent, fussing over him,
calling him Jewel, saying over and over how beautiful "she"
was, how "she" looked just like a girl, how she could fix
"her" up to look even more real. She told him he should
model. Fred turned out to be perfectly straight, and eventually by the end of the evening Nelson decided Vincent was not
going to contaminate him after all and let Fred persuade him
to restyle Vincent's hair and help him with his new make-up.

After that it was just like a dream. They went to Fred's
apartment where she made coffee and they spent four hours
experimenting with make-up and wigs, while Fred kept up
this chatter about turning Vincent into the greatest model
who ever was because he had "a new face in the modeling
world." Fred let Vincent try on many of her dresses and even
gave him two which she said didn't really suit her. After all that
experimentation Nelson decided the Twiggy hairstyle really
suited Vincent the best, although Vincent's dream was to
have a mane of hair like Fred's. "You have to be a sweet
little girl," Fred told him. She taught him the difference
between painting for drag and making up subtly.

Vincent couldn't wait to try out his new look back home in Irvington. He went into the bars the next night, and socked them beauty *back!* The queens died of envy. Everyone buzzed around him telling him how beautiful he looked. He knew then that it was an improvement.

After a year in the bars Vincent had lost all touch with the straight world, and he had never gone out alone with a girl, so straight people frightened him. Fred took him to stores to buy clothes, lending him the money; encouraged him, took him into restaurants with her for lunch just as if he were another girl, and gradually Vincent grew to love her dearly, although in a purely platonic way. He certainly wasn't a dike! Nelson didn't want to have anything to do with him socially, but Fred even invited him to several straight parties, in drag of course, and everyone there thought he was a girl. He was absolutely unreadable. (Later when she took him to the photographer and he saw the photos, he was sure of it. He looked as much a girl as Fred did, and Fred was certainly quite a woman.)

"Now you have to change your name," Fred told him.

"What's wrong with Jewel?"

"It sounds like a drag queen, that's all. You should get an ordinary girl's name."

He kept protesting, because all his friends knew him as Jewel, and he had come to think of himself as Jewel when he was in drag, but then one day a date took him to see *Bonnie and Clyde* and Vincent knew instantly the name he wanted to have.

"I'm Bonnie Parker now," he told Fred.

"You can't be Bonnie Parker. No one will believe it."

"Why not? Bonnie is a nice name, and I can't be Bonnie Abruzzi—it sounds ridiculous. I like Bonnie Parker. If I can't be Bonnie Parker I'm going to stay Jewel."

"Oh, hell," Fred said. "What am I going to do with you?"

But Fred finally resigned herself to Bonnie Parker, and the queens in the bars thought it was inspired. A lot of them had movie stars' names and the names of real girl models they admired, but none of them had called herself after a character in a movie. It really was a good idea, they all agreed. When the queens in the bars agreed on something Vincent became unshakable, for they were his jury. If they didn't like something, if they thought something wasn't *real*, then he wouldn't do it. Not that he had any illusions about them, for many of them were crazy. In the past year, several of his

friends had committed suicide or o.d.'d on drugs, and he
knew his was a neurotic world, peopled with freaks and
dreamers. But who else could he trust? Straight people, to
him, were like men from Mars. Until he'd found the queens
in the bars to be friends with, he hadn't had anybody he
could communicate with. Neurotic was better than nothing.
He was sure he was pretty neurotic, too, just being a freak
the way he was, trying to look like a girl.

Although many people naturally asked him about it,
Vincent had never for one moment considered the sex
change. He was a boy and he was proud of what he had. He
liked fruits, and fruits didn't want to go to bed with girls. The
few sex changes he knew who still hung around the gay bars
got none, poor sad freaks. They were more *men* after they'd
had it lopped off than they were before. He knew surgery
couldn't make any man a real woman. A sex change was just
a mutilated man who'd thrown away the only thing a fruit
saw in her in the first place. He liked straight men the best,
of course, as what fruit didn't, but he liked the kind of
straight men who liked him because he was a beautiful boy
who looked like a girl. In Vincent's mind, any man who told
him he was straight until he met beautiful Jewel, or Bonnie
Parker, really *was* straight. Fred told him that in the places
he met these "straight" men a straight man shouldn't be
there in the first place. But he knew she was just being
bitchy. Fred couldn't begin to understand. Why, Vincent had
even met a beautiful straight boy in the delicatessen!

Finally, after much coaching and encouragement, Vincent
was ready to meet the famous personal manager-publicist,
Sam Leo Libra. Fred told him that Libra was "this horny
fossil who's been chasing me, and very influential." According
to Fred, Libra would do anything for her, and if he chose to
do anything for Vincent (whom she was now calling Bonnie,
quite naturally), the sky would be the limit. Fred was such a
wonderful person. Vincent really cared for her. He just
couldn't believe that a real girl would do all these nice things
for him and spend all that time with him, and help his career
without for one moment being jealous. But Fred was so
secure in her position as a model, so convinced that the
addition of Vincent to the scene would never cut in on her
own success, that she was all altruism. She must have told
him that a million times, but he still could not believe it. The
world he lived in was so competitive that it was hard to
believe there existed anyone as secure as Fred said she was.

He trusted her, though. He knew she never lied to him and he knew she really liked him.

"I think I'll get the sex change so I can dike it up with you," he told Fred, kidding.

"Well, if you ever go straight you can marry me," Fred kidded back.

"I really would marry you if I was a man," he told her seriously.

She kissed him. They kissed now, quite naturally, on the mouth, like sisters. He was as at ease with her as he was with any of the queens.

Fred planned their assault on Mr. Libra as carefully as if it was D Day. First she took Vincent to her lover, who was "one of the very best photographers in the world," she assured him, and her lover, the photographer, took hours of photographs, lovingly lighted, until he had two dozen perfectly unreadable ones. Vincent was very photogenic, and Fred taught him how to stand and what expressions to make with his face. It was not too difficult to photograph Vincent looking real, the photographer assured him, if you didn't use too harsh a light. The photographer agreed with Fred that Vincent was a natural as a fashion model.

Then Fred took Vincent and his photographs to the woman who ran her agency, and told the woman that it was a big secret but Bonnie was going to become Sam Leo Libra's twelfth client, to replace Douglas Henry, that movie star who'd died. The woman had a fit, the news gave her such a rush. She said she certainly could find room for Bonnie, such a sweet girl, in her roster, and a little publicity was always a nice thing. Vincent was afraid she would call up Mr. Libra right there to check, but she did no such thing. Apparently straight people were as gullible as queens.

Then Fred called Mr. Libra and made an appointment. She coached Vincent carefully.

"He can be very rude, but don't let him scare you. I don't think he'll catch on to your voice, because I've heard women who talk lower than you do, but just to be on the safe side don't say much until he's had a chance to look at you for a while, then he'll believe his eyes, not his ears."

Vincent could have told her that; he'd been keeping quiet for over a year now.

"If you get a chance to be a little sassy," Fred went on, "don't be afraid, sock it to him. He respects that. Besides, you're very funny, and nobody ever gets mad at you."

"You think I'm funny?" Vincent asked suspiciously.

"I mean humorous, darling. You have this great sense of humor. And you're very sweet and everybody adores you. I'm going to clear out as soon as I can and leave you alone with him. He'll make a lunge at you."

"Oh my God!"

"Now, when he does, you escape ... I'm sure you're good at that by now. But flirt and let him think you're not rejecting him altogether. When he gets up a good head of steam, giggle, so he thinks you've just been kidding about trying to evade his clutches. Then let him kiss you."

"What do I have to kiss him for?" Vincent said. "You said he was this terrible old fossil."

"You don't go to *bed* with him, silly. You just let him kiss you, and fight him off when he tries to do anything else. If I know Mr. Libra, he'll have his hand up your skirt before you can say one-two-three, unless you break his arm, and you're not strong enough."

"But if he gets ..."

"Exactly. If he doesn't have a heart attack he'll realize that what we've pulled on him is probably the greatest publicity gimmick ever thought of by anyone but Sam Leo Libra. It's a happening. He loves crazy things. Bonnie, darling, if you were just another model, he wouldn't bother, but the bastard would like nothing better than foisting off a boy on the public and making them all fall in love with him as a girl. *He's* not going to tell anyone you're a boy. He's too smart for that. You'd never get work as a boy; the fashion magazines are too up-tight about that. I've heard for years that there were boys modeling as girls, but nobody's ever been able to find out who they were. It may be just a rumor. But Libra would just love to be the man who pulled it off. It would be his private joke, and he'd love it."

"He sounds sick," Vincent said.

Fred smiled cheerfully. "Aren't we all?"

So, carefully coached, Vincent had met Mr. Libra, and everything went as planned, including Libra's lover's leap. He really did think Libra was going to have a coronary occlusion when he grabbed at Bonnie's enormous clit, and he was afraid Libra would throw him out the window or choke him or something. But Libra, after a minute of stunned silence, had thrown back his head and roared with laughter until tears streamed out of his eyes.

"Fan-tastic!" Libra said. "Fan-tastic!"

Then he made Vincent sit there while he, Libra himself, typed out a paper that said Vincent was never to appear anywhere out of drag, that he was never to tell anyone he was a boy, that all his dates were to be supervised and chaperoned by Libra or his assistant, Geraldine Thompson, that he was not to have sex with anyone for a period of one year, and that during that year he was to be Sam Leo Libra's client under exclusive contract and was never to grant an interview or speak to a columnist, except for exchanging pleasantries unless it was first cleared with Libra and either Libra himself or Geraldine Thompson was present.

Vincent knew perfectly well that he couldn't go without sex for a whole year; that was unnatural. But he wasn't going to tell Libra that. He would sneak out somehow. As for the rest of the contract, he was thrilled, even about giving Libra thirty per cent of everything he made.

"I know I'm going to have to watch you every minute," Libra said to him. "I know you fruits. You'll be down on your knees in an alley the minute I close my eyes to sneeze. But don't think I won't keep tabs on you. First of all, who do you live with?"

"My parents," Vincent said.

"Where do they live?"

"Irvington, New Jersey."

"Well, from now on, you live in New York, with Gerry Thompson. You can sleep on her couch."

Who was this Gerry Thompson? Some hostile woman? He was afraid of her already. He didn't want to live with a stranger. Maybe he could live with Fred. She had a lover, but they might find room for him in the corner or something. He wouldn't even mind sleeping on the floor.

"I could live with Fred," he said. "I know *her*."

"You'll like Gerry too. Fred's too busy to take care of you. Fred doesn't work for me. Gerry has to watch you if I tell her to."

"I'm going to be a prisoner," he mumbled.

"Damn right you are. One infraction, one slip, and *out*. I won't have to throw you out, Miss Bonnie Parker; the public will throw you out. The public will *stone* you out. Today's headlines wrap tomorrow's garbage. Remember that."

Vincent shivered. He could see it now: his face wrapped around a mound of decaying lettuce and eggshells. How horrible! But he was afraid of that Gerry, too. He didn't know any straight girls except Fred. What could he say to her? Maybe she wasn't straight ... maybe she was a dike. That would be worse. If there were as many dikes as fags, she was bound to be a dike, because the world was so full of fags.

"I'll miss my mother," he said.

"You'll see her as often as you want. But I want you to live in New York where I can watch you. Besides, you have to be close to your work. I don't want you getting tired on the subway."

"It's a bus," Vincent said.

"So, the bus, then. Who goes to New Jersey? Here's the contract for your signature, and sign this paper. I'll attach it to the contract. Bonnie, you realize how important this is. This is not a joke. I may laugh at it here, but I know as well as you do it is not a joke. It's your life. Without me and this chance I'm giving you, you're finished. Do you want to be rough trade on Forty-second Street? You'd last just about three minutes. Or do you want to stay in those bars—just another painted freak? Or is your idea of dreams of glory to be in the chorus line at the 82 Club? Believe me, Bonnie, there is a real world outside. The real world is not your friends in the gay bars you live in. The real world is *Hollywood*." He paused significantly to let it sink in. "Do you remember when I asked you if you wanted to go to California?"

Vincent nodded.

"Well, I was kidding then, but I'm not kidding now. I can make you the top model in New York, Bonnie, and that means the top model in America. From there I can get you a motion-picture contract. You'll be rich beyond your wildest dreams. You'll be famous, loved. You'll have a life. You won't be anonymous, you won't be forgotten. You'll be able to choose your friends. You'll travel all over the world. The real world, Bonnie." He held out the contract and the sheet of paper.

Vincent took them gingerly in his hands and scanned them quickly. It was hard to make out the words because his eyes were full of tears of gratitude and happiness. "Which name do you want me to sign?" he asked. "Bonnie Parker or Vincent Abruzzi?"

"Oh my God!" Libra said, beginning to laugh again. "I don't *believe* it!"

"What?" Vincent asked, hurt.

"Vincent Abruzzi! Oh, oh, oh, oh ... Vincent Abruzzi!

You sound like a truck driver. Sign both names, just to make it completely legal. Uh-oh, I just thought of something. Have you been to your draft board yet?"

"They rejected me," Vincent said. "I have a heart murmur."

"Then from now on," Libra said, "there is no Vincent Abruzzi any more. Vincent Abruzzi is dead."

That's what you think, Vincent thought. But Bonnie Parker nodded amenably and signed the papers.

CHAPTER

NINE

ON A beautiful morning in late spring, Dick Devere went to David Webb, his favorite jeweler, and commissioned him to make a pin in the shape of a nightingale, of gold with enamel and diamonds. He was well known at the shop, having patronized them often in the past, and there were a few lifted eyebrows because everyone knew Mr. Devere was ordering another of his famous kiss-off pins. He always presented one to the girl of his choice when their affair was about to be over. The pin was always in a shape representative of the girl's true inner life, and the amount of money he spent was commensurate with his guilt.

That same morning, in an expansive mood, Silky Morgan bought a new refrigerator-freezer for her Auntie Grace in Philadelphia, as a surprise. The Satins, also feeling expansive, went to the spring fur sales and bought their mothers white mink stoles (Cheryl and Beryl did not know that Silky had bought their mother a refrigerator, and even if they had they certainly would not have chipped in on that stuck-up bitch's gift).

Sylvia Polydor, in Hollywood, feeling depressed, checked in for her first day's work on the film that starred her as a hatchet murderess. She brought along a bottle of vodka and a water glass so she could console herself on the set.

Sam Leo Libra spent his morning at the Twenty-first

Precinct station house, with his attorney, springing all the members of the King James Version, who had been caught with forty other revelers at a private marijuana party in someone's penthouse. Because none of the King James Version had any pot on their persons at the time, they were let go, in the custody of Mr. Libra, who promised to take good care of them. He proceeded to dock his attorney's fee from their allowances and gave them one of his famous blistering speeches, which reduced them to nervous laughter.

In Hollywood, Douglas Henry's widow put flowers on her husband's grave and then went to lunch with his doctor.

Arnie Gurney, in Las Vegas, woke up sixty thousand dollars poorer due to an unusually bad streak of luck at the crap table, and resolved never to gamble again. Then he went to his local loan shark and took out a large loan so he could win it all back just in case he changed his mind.

Elaine Fellin, full of ire, bought a new white Cadillac Eldorado with air-conditioning and stereo tapes, paid for it out of their joint account, and put it in her name. She told Mad Daddy it was her Mother's Day present.

Mad Daddy had great respect for mothers, even Elaine, and said it was all right. He bought himself a much less expensive consolation present, for two Tastee Freezes and a box of popcorn—a fifteen-year-old girl named Linda.

Penny Potter had lunch with her mother and told her tearfully that her husband hadn't slept with her for two months. Her mother took her to Gucci and bought her a crocodile handbag.

Mr. Nelson awoke with a frightful rash which his doctor diagnosed as chicken pox. Throughout the city, sixteen young hustlers either had or were going to get chicken pox before the week was through.

At four a.m. the Bottom of My Garden was raided and Franco lost his black Count Dracula cape in the rush to escape. He was sure it had been stolen, and he was right, because Bonnie Parker had it. One of her admirers wrapped it around her shoulders during the stampede through the back door. It looked darling on her, and since she didn't know whose it was, she felt she was justified in accepting it.

Gerry Thompson, who was resigned to playing house mother to Bonnie, who was sleeping on her couch, was furious when she saw the Dracula cape the next morning, and gave Bonnie a lecture on mopping—a word she'd learned from Bonnie herself. Bonnie insisted that a nice man had given it to her so she would not catch cold in the pre-dawn hours. Gerry finally believed her. She knew Libra would kill her if he knew she was letting Bonnie go out at night, but on the other hand, she also knew that Bonnie never picked up anyone and was scrupulous about keeping her new career a secret. As long as no one knew she was modeling, no one would tell. Anyhow, once the photos started coming out in the fashion magazines, Gerry knew that all Bonnie's old friends would recognize her anyway. She also knew that any fruits who realized what a trick Bonnie was playing on the public would be only too glad to keep quiet about it so the ruse could be a complete success. She only hoped none of the lady magazine editors were gay.

At the Cannes Film Festival, Zak Maynard screwed six girls and was done by three fags at an orgy at someone's villa. He had a fine time.

In Chicago, Shadrach Bascombe gave a black eye to a girl who was trying to nail him on a false paternity charge. He had only slapped her, but he was strong. It did not make the papers, and the girl dropped her plan to shake him down. She didn't want him to break her neck.

In New York, Ingrid the Lady Barber stopped off at her favorite supplier to get some more of the miracle ingredient she put in her special vitamin shots. The price had gone up.

Lizzie Libra told her analyst Dr. Picker about a fling she had had with Hatcher Wilson, a young black rock 'n' roll singer who had brought his new hit record to Libra, hoping to change managers and get Libra to handle him. The record was number one that week. Lizzie, who had talked alone to the boy for a while, had sneaked right off with him to his hotel, telling her husband she was off to the analyst. When she returned she discovered that Libra had decided not to handle the boy. She was so aggravated that it almost gave her a trauma, she nervously told Dr. Picker. But still, Libra or no Libra, number one was number one. Wasn't it?

Outside Libra's suite, a fourteen-year-old girl named Barrie Grover, who was the president of the Mad Daddy Fan Club of Kew Gardens, spent a fruitless six hours waiting for Mad Daddy to appear. She had nothing better to do because it was final exam week, and she didn't have an exam until tomorrow. She brought her books with her, but she was too excited to study at all. When it was time to return home for supper she left a passionate and funny note for Mad Daddy, which she slipped under the door. It was the hundred and seventeenth note or letter she had sent him since the day she first fell in love with him. She had received several printed replies from the television studio, the kind they sent to everyone, but she hoped that Mad Daddy would see this one in person and would write to her himself.

All in all, it was not an uneventful day for the inhabitants of Sam Leo Libra's stable, and those who loved them.

IN THIS corner, Silky Morgan, the fighter—featherweight division, Silky thought, looking at herself in the full-length mirror on her bathroom door. She had changed during the past few months, filled out, become almost a little too curvy to be fashionable. She was definitely now more woman than girl. Only her face was still the face of a child, except for her eyes, which hadn't been a child's eyes for as long as she could remember. She scrutinized herself carefully, trying to see if Dick still found her sexy. She had this really big bust—men liked that. Her buns stuck out a little too much, well, men usually liked that too. She had a tiny waist. Her legs had become curvier since she had started the hated dancing lessons, and although they were still long and slim they were dancer's legs now. Men whistled at her on the street when she wore her mini-skirts. Well, she looked okay. But obviously how you looked or the games you played or how cool you were had nothing to do with making a man stay in love if he didn't want to.

She was confused, and often now she felt her throat closing up, not with fear about her singing but with unshed tears. Dick hadn't called her for two weeks. He had given her this really elegant pin: a gold nightingale with diamonds and enamel on it, and she had thought with a rush of pure joy and relief that he really did still love her after all. But after the night he gave her the pin he had simply disappeared.

New York was so big that someone could disappear into it and you could never see him again for the rest of your life. She had called Dick's apartment every day and left her name with the answering service. She didn't want to call the studio and bother him when he was working, although one day when none of the messages she had left with his service had been returned she did finally call the studio and left her name there. He had never called her back. He was not dead. He had never been too busy for her before. What he was doing was getting her off him cold turkey.

It might as well have been cold turkey he was putting her through; she had chills and shivered, she had sweats, her teeth chattered, she couldn't keep food down and finally gave up eating at all except for tea with honey for her throat. Oh Lord, if she could just get over him, then he would know it by telepathy and he would come back. She just knew it. That was how men were. When they were afraid you would throw a fit, they hid. But they came back someday. Her father had kept coming back. He had left, and her mother had cried, and then finally he had come back again just when her mother had begun to hum again a little around the apartment. She remembered those days. Wow, if she could just flip the pages of the calendar ahead the way they did on those old movies on TV, and make it be fall, then he would come back. Maybe he'd even wait till winter. But he had to come back. She'd wait for him forever.

She knew it was Gerry he was seeing, but all along she had hoped that the thing with Gerry would die, and then finally she even hoped that he would keep on with *both* of them. From hoping for something she had begun to accept the tiniest crumbs. She had tried to be so happy with him, but he had seen how nervous she was. It was hard to hide it. The jokes they had shared had disappeared, the fun was gone. It was just smile and fake it. That was no fun for either of them. Why did she have to change and stop being fun? She had tried so hard to stay the same. But if you knew you weren't loved any more, you couldn't find fun in things, even when you tried to fake it. And oh Lord, the day of the pin, she had finally thought it was all going to turn out all right!

Everyone had noticed the pin. She wore it all the time, and when she wore her costumes she pinned it to her bra. The girls had known of course it was from Dick, but Honey had asked anyway: "Who gave you *that?*"

"Oh, it belonged to my Grandmama," Silky had replied airily. Honey knew darn well Silky's grandmama hadn't even had a toilet, much less a gold and diamond nightingale. But Silky had learned to give them back what they gave her, and their relationship was now one of cold politeness, which was at least better than them ignoring or insulting her. Dick had even taught her how to handle the girls.

Oh, Dick had taught her so much! She even *thought* clean now. She used big words, and almost always got them right. She had bought a big dictionary. She read better books. And he had taken her to the theater a few times, and told her about acting and directing.

Gerry had admired the pin, never asked her where it appeared from, and during the hard time when Dick was gone and Silky was feeling so sick, somehow she had felt closer to Gerry even though it was Gerry who had taken him away. She felt in her heart that Dick wouldn't last with Gerry either. She didn't know how she knew, but she knew. But Gerry seemed so content, so secure. Silky wondered if Gerry had thoughts of marrying Dick. Girls liked to kid themselves, and girls like Gerry *did* marry guys like Dick Devere. But he had never given Gerry any jewelry, or if he had, she hid it at home and never showed it off at the office. Silky knew that Gerry would never throw it in her face about Dick.

Mr. Libra did, though. He was the meanest man on earth. He had spotted the nightingale the very first day she had worn it to the office, and had managed to get Silky alone for a moment so he could say: "Oh? Dick Devoid gave you his famous kiss-off pin, eh?" She would have torn it off right there, she was so mad. Libra was cruel, but so was Dick, because if you wanted to get rid of a girl the cruelest thing you could do was to give her something of sentimental value that she'd always have to keep around so she couldn't forget the rat even if she wanted to. She needed the pin. It was something from Dick, something he had chosen specially for her because she sang, because he cared for her. And there it was, so there he was, always with her, him and the pain.

Then finally things happened that helped keep her busy. One was that Silky and the Satins were finally making their debut in a New York club, and there were intensified rehearsals, the act to be added to in places, cut in others, polished everywhere. Silky prayed that Dick would come to the opening, and then prayed that he would stay away. She supposed Mr. Libra would make all the clients show up, to make the opening a really gala affair, but nobody could make Dick do what he didn't want to do.

When they came out on the stage that opening night she saw that Mr. Libra had taken a long table at ringside. Mr. and Mrs. Libra were there; Mad Daddy and Elaine were there; Peter and Penny Potter with several of their friends were at the next table; Franco, the designer, and his favorite model, Fred, were there; Mr. Nelson ran out from backstage after fixing the girls' wigs and made a commotion trying to pull his chair back in the crowded space, there in the dark ... the new client Bonnie Parker, the model, was there with Zak Maynard, the movie star, who kept nuzzling Bonnie's neck all during their songs and never looked at the stage; there were two old men with their wives (Mr. Libra had said two Broadway producers were coming, so that must have been them); and there were two empty seats. Silky knew who the two empty seats were for, and the suspense made her tremble almost more than the fear of the New York opening. The orchestra began to play and she shut her eyes, belting out their opening song. When she looked at the audience again she saw that Gerry had arrived with Dick, the two of them sitting right smack in front of her nose. Her heart turned over. Gerry gave her a big, encouraging smile. Dick smiled and winked. He smiled! His smile was so full of affection and pride in her that Silky almost soared off the floor. Oh Lord, he had come to see her after all. He didn't hate her.

And she was good, she knew she was good. The audience didn't want to let them off the stage. When the lights went up after the last curtain call, the people were still clapping and screaming "More!" Mr. Libra brought the producers backstage to the dressing room, and everyone had drinks and sandwiches. Gerry rushed over to Silky and hugged her. Gerry was alone. Dick hadn't even bothered to come backstage. He was waiting for Gerry outside. The goddam sonofabitch coward!

The party passed in a haze. Silky had two drinks and felt so dizzy she nearly fainted. She had to go lie down on the cot in the other room. Mr. Libra looked furious, for he had let them have liquor because they had been good and he was there watching them and now she had to go look drunk and make a fool of herself. It wasn't the two drinks on an empty stomach that had made her feel sick; it was her anger at Dick for being such a coward. Why couldn't he have just come back to tell her she was good?

Gerry went into the other room with her and brought her a cold, wet washcloth for her head, and then a cup of coffee and a chicken sandwich.

"You have to try to eat something," Gerry said.

"All right. I'll try." Silky put the sandwich under the mattress when Gerry was in the bathroom dampening the washcloth again.

"What beautiful flowers," Gerry said. "Who sent them?"

"Oh, this boy I know—Hatcher Wilson."

"That was nice of him. Oh look, there's the arrangement from Mr. Libra. It's perfect."

"I knew you picked it out," Silky said.

Gerry smiled at her. "I made them put in a lot of baby's breath because that's your favorite."

"That was nice."

"Oh, Silky, please try not to be too unhappy. You have such talent. I know that doesn't sound like much of a consolation, but think of all the people who want to be famous and won't ever get there. Everybody adores you. You're going to be a big, big star. Those two men out there, they're going to do a musical. They loved you. I'm not supposed to tell you this, but they're very seriously considering you for the lead. Mr. Libra is going to send you to acting class. Silky, if you do the lead in a Broadway musical next year, do you realize what that means?"

"I can't believe it," Silky said.

"You'll believe it when it happens," Gerry said. "Please don't let on that I told you. When Mr. Libra tells you, act surprised. That'll be your first acting lesson, free from me."

"I don't think I'm ready for a musical," Silky said. "Especially the lead."

"You have to start in the lead. That's Libra's way—hit 'em right between the eyes—pow! You'll be ready. Don't worry."

"Why didn't Dick come backstage?" Silky said. "He doesn't have to be scared of me. I wouldn't try to get him back or anything."

Gerry looked down. "Dick isn't perfect," she said quietly. "In some ways, sometimes, he's a fool."

"You like him a lot, don't you." It was a statement, not a

question. Somehow, if Gerry really loved him, it would make it easier to bear.

"I guess you have to like him a lot," Gerry said. "He's hard not to like, even when he does things that don't seem right."

"I guess you know I loved him," Silky said. "Now that it's over, I guess I can tell you. When it's over, somehow that's the time you want to tell somebody that it really was real, just to keep on believing it I guess."

"I'm really sorry," Gerry said.

"Did he ... does he ever say anything about me? Never mind, don't answer that."

"He wouldn't discuss anything like that with me," Gerry said. "But he thought you were just brilliant tonight, and he always says you have a great and unique talent. He really respects you."

"I don't know about that," Silky said.

"Believe me," Gerry said, "he does respect you, and he likes you. Men just ... disappear. That's what some men do. But you have to believe that Dick respects you, because you're going to be working with him next fall. He's going to direct the musical you're going to star in."

"Oh my God," Silky whispered. She knew she shouldn't be happy, but she was. She was going to be with him every day. She was going to work with him. At least she'd see him. She knew she should be afraid, and she was afraid, because the worst thing that could happen would be to have Dick in her professional life at a time when she was going to feel so unsure. But Dick had always made her feel sure. "What's going to happen?" she asked.

"He's going to be a big boy and you're going to be a big girl, and you're going to work together to make yourselves and each other big stars," Gerry said. "That's what's going to happen."

"That's what's going to happen," Silky repeated obediently. But she didn't believe it ... she couldn't even imagine it. Life was sure crazy.

And the other big thing that kept Silky busy and helped keep her mind off her troubles, at least about ten per cent of the time, was that as soon as they finished their two-week engagement at the New York club (with rave notices in all the papers) Mr. Libra enrolled her in this acting class, and she found herself in a room full of the weirdest lunatics she'd ever met in her life.

The Simon Budapest School of Theater Work was one of
the best known in the country. To get in you had to be
genuinely talented—or famous. Silky was an oddity: a famous pop singer who was headed for the stage, so she got in
with no trouble. She did not even have to audition. Mr. Libra
gave her a slip of paper with the name and address of the
school on it, and the list of the days and hours of classes. She
had to attend a minimum of twice a week. Classes were held
in a mangy loft with folding chairs set in rows in front of a
small stage. Props were frowned upon; pantomime was preferred. Simon Budapest was a tall, middle-aged man with
thick black eyebrows that made him look like Satan. He
would have been a fine actor except that he stuttered. None
of his students ever laughed when he stuttered because they
were all in love with him. He almost seemed to hypnotize
them, especially the girls. After a scene, which was always
done by two partners, usually a girl and a guy, Simon
Budapest would rise from his chair, circle the actors, look at
them, and then touch one of them. When he touched the girl
she always burst into tears. Then he would go back to his
chair in the front row and make the girl tell him why she was
crying. It usually ended up sounding like that group-therapy
show Silky had seen on television. The girls talked about their
emotional problems and the men talked about their sex lives.
Silky was dreading doing her first scene.

She always sat in the last seat of the last row, trying to be
invisible. This was impossible, as there were only two other
black faces in the room, and both were men. What a creepy
place! What was she supposed to learn there, anyway? She
listened to everything Simon Budapest managed to stammer
out, but she couldn't understand half of it. Evidently you
were supposed to really feel things and not "intellectualize."
She'd been feeling things all her life. It was the way she sang.
She understood that part of it, anyway.

Some of the kids took notes. All of them dressed as if they
were off to a hippie protest parade as soon as class was over.
They looked poor and dirty. Evidently that was the way you
looked serious when you went to school. The only one who
ever dressed well was one girl who was some kind of movie
star, and she always arrived draped in furs, with a ton of
make-up. She always did scenes where she had to take her
clothes off, or where she started out in just bra and pants.
Once she spent the whole twenty minutes—the time that was
allotted to each scene—shaving her legs. Simon Budapest

made her repeat the scene, and she shaved her legs for
twenty minutes again. Silky waited for the blood.

The worst thing that ever happened was the day one of the
girls flipped out. She was a mousy-looking girl who liked to
do scenes where she had to do nineteen minutes of pantomime before she got to her one line. When she spoke you
could hardly hear her. She looked about eighteen, but someone whispered to someone next to Silky that she was forty.
Anyway, she did this scene, and when it was over Simon
Budapest picked up her arm and it just stayed there, stiff, like
she was a movable doll. He sat down and asked her what she
had been trying to do in the scene. The girl just looked at
him.

Everybody waited. He asked her again. Nothing. The girl
opened her mouth to speak and nothing came out. She finally
put her arm down. There was an audible sigh of relief in the
room.

"Well, darling?" Budapest said. "Come on, darling. What
were you working for?"

Silence. The boy who had done the scene with her sat on
the floor, looking annoyed because the girl was getting all the
attention.

"Speak, darling," Budapest said.

Usually just calling a girl "darling" was enough to set her
off into hysterical tears, but he'd called this zombie "darling"
three times and she just looked at him. People started shifting
in their seats. Ten minutes went by. The people who always
rushed out into the hall for a cigarette after a scene were
mesmerized there, waiting to see what would happen next.
Silky looked at her watch. Ten more minutes went by. Simon
Budapest had uncovered a mental case.

The time for the class was up. It was time to go home. No
one left. Simon Budapest started looking nervous, and his
stutter became worse than ever. He was like some party
hypnotist who had put somebody into a trance and now
couldn't get her out. He had to keep the class there until he
got that zombie to say something, or even move, and it
looked like they were going to be there all night—either that
or someone would have to call Bellevue. Some of the kids
were looking bugged because they had shows to get to. But it
was too interesting to leave, and besides, Simon Budapest
looked so nervous that it seemed disloyal to go until the class
was dismissed. They'd been sitting there half an hour now.
Wow!

Then Silky began to look more carefully at the girl and she realized what had happened. She'd seen people like that before, and it was so obvious she wondered why no one else noticed. The zombie was all doped up. She'd obviously been so nervous before the scene that whatever she was on she'd taken too much of it. One thing Silky was prepared to stay for was a nut case, but junkies bored her. She'd seen them all her life on the stoops and street corners of her neighborhood. Evidently these protected, carefully grubby would-be livers-of-life had never seen a head before.

Silky raised her hand. She'd never spoken in class before, and when Simon Budapest noticed her hand up his mouth fell open.

"Yes?" he said, looking rather annoyed. He was probably thinking her royal highness had picked a fine time to decide to join the group.

"Ask her what she took in the ladies' room before the scene," Silky said. She was surprised at how ringing and sure her own voice sounded in this room where she had never before had the temerity to even whisper.

"Darling," Simon Budapest said to the zombie, "did you take anything?"

The girl's throat worked feebly. She opened her mouth.

"Did you take anything? A pill?"

"An . . . an aspirin," the girl whispered.

"An aspirin? That's all?"

"A . . . sleeping pill."

What a lie! Some of the class laughed. Simon Budapest gave an angry gesture for quiet. But he looked relieved. He wasn't the amateur hypnotist any more, he hadn't driven her crazy by his personal appeal. He was acquitted. "Somebody take her home," he said.

Two boys jumped up and said they'd be glad to. They led the zombie away. Everyone rushed for the door, free. They couldn't wait to get away so they could gossip about the whole thing. Silky rose wearily and followed them.

"Darling!" Simon Budapest was standing behind her.

"Me?"

"Yes, you. What's your name?"

"Silky Morgan."

"Why do you always sit in the back row?"

"I'm not really an actress," she said.

"Everyone here is an actress. Why haven't you ever worked in class?"

"I'm scared to," she said.

"Scared? Scared? You're supposed to be scared. That's good. A conceited actor is no actor. From now on I want you to sit in the front row."

Silky gulped.

"And I want you to get a partner and do a scene. Make an appointment with the girl at the door for the time." He turned away without even saying good-bye and walked away.

Silky walked to the elevator. People were looking at her with envy because the great Simon Budapest had singled her out. She felt embarrassed. A tall white boy with long black hair and a tattoo on his forearm came up to her.

"What's your name?" he said.

"Silky Morgan."

"I'm Don. Do you want to do a scene?"

"Okay."

"I have an appointment for next week. I always keep appointments so I can work a lot. You have to make them so far in advance. I have a couple of scenes we can do. Do you want to come have some coffee with me now and talk about it?"

"Okay," she said.

"I have all your records," he said. "You're great."

"Thank you."

"I have just the scene for you," Don said. "It's from *The One Hundred Dollar Misunderstanding*. Have you read it?"

"No."

"We'll stop at the bookstore and you can buy it," he said.

They went to the nearest bookstore and he found the book for her. Then they went to a greasy spoon where they had coffee, exchanged phone numbers, made an appointment for the following day to rehearse, and he borrowed a dollar from her, telling her he owed her eighty cents—deducting fifteen for her coffee and five cents for her share of the tip. She was relieved that he seemed to have no interest whatsoever in dating her.

That night she read the book and was appalled. The girl was a teen-aged black hooker. What kind of a part was that? Was that what he thought of her? And the words! She'd just gotten over saying all those words; she was darned if she was going to get started again saying them in public. If Mr. Libra knew he would kill her. Don had already marked several parts he thought would make good scenes for class. She didn't like any of them. But what the heck, a scene was a

scene. She had to start somewhere. She'd just cut out all the
dirty words.

The next afternoon Don appeared at her hotel room with
his own copy of the book. He was wearing a sleeveless
T-shirt and tight, faded corduroy pants, and he had an old
Army jacket slung over one shoulder. She really hated his
tattoo.

"Okay," Silky said, resigned. "Let's read. Is that what we
do first?"

"No," he said. "First we get to know each other a little."

"Oh? All right. What do you want to know?"

"You're not married, are you?"

"No. Are you?"

"Nope," he said. "Is that Bourbon?"

"Yes."

"Can I have some?"

"Oh, sure," Silky said, bored with him and wishing he'd get
on with the rehearsal. Maybe he was just nervous. She
poured them both drinks. He sat on the bed.

"Hey, sit down," he said. "Why are you so nervous?"

"I'm not nervous."

"Then sit down, for Chrissakes."

Silky sat in the chair.

"Why don't we play some music to relax?" he said.

She turned on the radio. It was Hatcher Wilson's song
again—every time you turned on the radio, there it was. She
was glad that Hatcher was making it.

"Do you want to dance?" he said.

"No."

He drained his glass of Bourbon. "Hey, drink up."

She took a few sips and looked at her watch. "I don't have
much time," she said.

"Yeah," he said. Then he jumped up, pulled her to him,
and kissed her very hard on the mouth. She tried to pull
away but he was very strong. She turned her head from side
to side but he clamped his mouth on hers again so she bit
him, at the same time stamping hard on his instep. He was
wearing sneakers and it hurt. He yelped and let her go.

"What's the matter with you?" he said, furious.

"What's the matter with *you*? I thought we were going to
rehearse."

"We are. But we have to know each other first. How do
you expect to do a scene with me where we have a relationship if we don't relax together first?"

"What is this, a rehearsal or a date?" Silky asked, mad
now.

"What's the difference? Don't you like men?"

"I like *men*, not little boys. If you don't want to work, get
out, please." She opened the door.

"Oh, come on."

"Come on *what?*"

"Did you ever have a good orgasm?" he asked.

"Did you ever have a good punch in the mouth?"

"Oh, wow," he said, laughing. "Wow."

"Get out of here!"

"Oh, come on. I'm not going to force myself on you. If
you don't want to be friends, we can just work. I thought
you'd be warm."

Her eyes filled with tears. She wished she had a knife so
she could kill him. She imagined stabbing him in the heart,
seeing his arrogant, ugly-handsome face contort in surprise
just before he fell down dead. He thought all black women
were whores and nymphomaniacs, that was obvious. Oh, she
would love to kill him.

"All the other actresses I work with like to ball," he said,
all hurt innocence. "That's half the fun of rehearsing."

She wiped her eyes. Maybe she was wrong, maybe he just
thought all actresses were whores and nymphomaniacs. "I'm
not an actress," she said.

"I really wanted to get to know you," he said. "Boy, you
really know how to bring a guy down."

Silky picked up the book. "Shall we start to read now?"
she said.

He shrugged and picked up his copy of the book. "You
have the first line," he said. "We start here."

So this was acting class. Crazy junkies flipping out, creepy
studs with no bread using "rehearsals" as an excuse for sex,
kids playing hippie, talking about things they knew nothing
about, a poor old man with a stutter trying to make every
girl in the room fall in love with him so he could make it up
to himself for never becoming the star he'd always wanted to
be. Some of the kids were working in shows, so they couldn't
all be fakes and failures. But what about all the others? What
was all that crying, all that open discussing of their life
problems, that self-indulgence? Were they all so lonely that
this was the only place they could come to feel loved? Mr.

Libra thought a nuthouse like that acting class was going to teach her how to stand up on a Broadway stage and carry a show, but when had he ever been to the Simon Budapest School of Theater Work? The school of confusion and monkey business was more like it. She had never felt more insecure and depressed in her life. She wished she could talk to Dick, ask his advice, ask him what was really going on in that class, could she ever understand it, could she ever learn to act? She needed Dick so badly, and he was gone. But she'd have him in the fall if she got the show. That, at least, would save her life. Meanwhile she would just work and try as hard as she could to do what was expected of her, if she could ever figure out what that was.

She and Don did the scene in class and Simon Budapest told her she was not bad. He asked her what she had used for the emotions and she said she was remembering things from her old neighborhood. But the truth was more that she was using her contempt for Don, the way he made her feel, because that fit in very well with the mood of the scene and it seemed natural. But she couldn't say that about Don in front of the class, even though he was a jerk.

After class Simon Budapest took her aside. "If you have contempt for that boy, you should use it in the scene," he said.

"I do, and I did," Silky said.

"I thought so. Use it more. Let it all come out. I want you to do the scene again." And then he was gone, no good-bye.

So that was what it was all about! Real feelings, just like life! Wasn't it? It was coming a little clearer now. She felt better. Simon Budapest seemed to understand her, even like her a little. He could have said all that in front of Don and the class, but he had spared her feelings and Don's. He wasn't such a crazy old man after all. Don ran after her in the hall.

"What did he say? What did he say?"

"He said we should do the scene again."

"Well, he could have said that in class. You're lucky he spoke to you. He must think you're good."

"Do you really think so?"

"Yeah. He doesn't say you're good at first, but if he talks to you alone it's a sign he's really interested in your work." Don looked at her with new respect.

My work, she thought. Singing was her work. But now acting was her work, too. She remembered the first night she'd gone out with Dick, when he'd told her she should take acting lessons. Oh, Dick was always so right about everything! She missed him so much it was like a constant ache in her heart. People *could* have an ache in their hearts, because she had one. It wasn't just stuff they wrote about in songs. She was just going to have to work as hard as she could and learn as much as she could so that when she and Dick finally met again he would be proud of her. She wanted him to be proud of her. It meant more than even being a hit in a show. The show seemed such a dream she couldn't believe it was going to happen. But Mr. Libra said she was going to have to read for the part in a few weeks, so she'd have to get used to the idea that it was not a dream. Still, maybe it was better not to realize it was real, because if she ever realized fully that it was going to happen she would be so frightened that she wouldn't be able to read for the part at all, acting lessons or no acting lessons.

Why is it, Silky thought, *that now when everything I ever wanted in my life is coming true I can't believe it, and I'd give it all up in a minute if I could only have Dick back again?* But she was not really sure the last part of that was true. She wanted to be a success. Not just because she had nothing else, either. She wanted to be a success because . . . because . . . why? She didn't know. But she did remember the alternative, and if she could think of no other reason for wanting to be a famous star, thinking of the alternative was enough.

ᘰᘰᘰᘰᘰᘰᘰᘰᘰᘰᘰᘰᘰᘰᘰᘰᘰᘰᘰᘰᘰᘰᘰᘰᘰ

CHAPTER

ELEVEN

ᘰᘰᘰᘰᘰᘰᘰᘰᘰᘰᘰᘰᘰᘰᘰᘰᘰᘰᘰᘰᘰᘰᘰᘰᘰ

VINCENT-SLASH-BONNIE! What was Gerry to do with
her/him? When Libra first passed the edict that the kid was to
live with her, making her sort of a foster matron, Gerry was
appalled. He/she was a beautiful kid, with a cuddly sexual
quality that was quite unnerving. She felt rather dikey in the
presence of Bonnie, feeling that odd attraction, even though
she knew quite well that Bonnie was really Vincent, so it was
all right. And Bonnie/Vincent, or Vincent/Bonnie, played
his/her sexuality up for all it was worth. Gerry couldn't
figure out how much of this was unconscious. Evidently the
kid was at a loss for anything to talk to her about, and they
both watched each other like wary animals at first. Vincent/
Bonnie was waiting to see if Gerry was going to laugh at
him/her, consider him a freak. And Gerry was suspicious of
this silent, watchful kid who locked the bathroom door when
he/she went in to dress or put on make-up, used her things
and then denied he'd used them, who watched her every
move as she watched his. She wondered if the kid was a
kleptomaniac. How could you tell? You could hardly get a
word out of him. She knew Vincent/Bonnie resented having
to stay with her far more than she resented having the kid
dumped on her.

But as spring went into summer and then the hot summer
went on and on, Gerry began to see heartening changes in

Bonnie. (She was finally thinking of him/her as Bonnie now, because when the kid had first come to stay she'd asked him what he wanted to be called, and he'd said: "Bonnie, because if you think of me as Vincent and I get a phone call you might forget and say, 'Vincent, it's for you.'") The first time Bonnie really talked to her was the night Bonnie had taken a pill, one of the little cache of Ups Bonnie got from the queens in the gay bars and which she hid somewhere in the apartment. Bonnie was on her way out to romp in the bars, and Gerry made coffee and they sat in the living room and Bonnie talked and talked, about her life, her childhood, her first love who had gone away.

"I talk a lot on pills, don't I?" Bonnie said.

"I'm glad to hear you talk at last."

"I used to be shy. I felt stupid. I've learned a lot, haven't I? I'm not so dumb now, not so loud."

"You were never loud."

"Well, I felt loud," Bonnie said. "I thought you hated me."

"I thought you hated me."

"You used to stare at me."

"Only because you're so pretty. You used to stare at me, too."

"Well, I never had a sister or anything. Do you like me now?"

"I always liked you. I just didn't think you liked me. But I like you more now that I know you don't hate me. Do you like me now?"

"Yes," Bonnie said. She lowered her eyes. "Very much."

Gerry felt a rush of affection for Bonnie. It really wasn't necessary to treat her as either a girl or a boy; she could just treat her like a very young person. Bonnie had teen-agey interests: clothes, make-up, hairdos, romantic records. And she wasn't nearly as dumb as she looked. (It was a stereotype to think someone as confectionary as Bonnie was stupid, but it was also a stereotype to think that any astute remark that came out of her mouth was a gem just because it was a surprise.) Gerry had learned to accept Bonnie on her own terms and she realized that Bonnie was quite intelligent and extremely shrewd, with a perception that saw right through the defenses people put up, if only because Bonnie was from such a different world that these defenses were never something she had become conditioned to accept the way everyone else did.

"I want to learn as much as I can," Bonnie said. "I'm learning a lot with you."

And she was. Gerry was her image for what real girls did. When Bonnie had first arrived she was extremely sloppy, leaving make-up anywhere in the apartment, losing the tops of all her bottles and jars, leaving her false eyelashes dropped on the bookcase or under the cushion of a chair, wherever she had taken them off. She threw her dresses on the floor as if they were *costumes* that had nothing to do with her. Now she was becoming systematic, everything put in its proper place, even keeping a little notebook for her business appointments and the telephone numbers of new friends. "You're neat because you're a girl," Bonnie said. So Bonnie became neat. Gerry didn't tell her how messy most girls were.

Right from the start Bonnie was working all the time. She had bookings every day and by summer her pictures began to appear in the newspapers and soon they would be in the magazines. Magazines worked three months in advance. Libra didn't let her do fashion shows. She was hailed as "the face of the year," "a sexier Twiggy," "the new androgynous sex goddess," "the essence of unselfconscious femininity," "Marilyn Monroe reincarnated." Nobody seemed quite sure how to describe her; they only knew that they loved her.

There were crises too. One day a photographer called up, furious, to say that Bonnie had walked off with one of the originals in a collection they had photographed: a fifteen-hundred-dollar pants suit. Bonnie denied it innocently. Gerry denied it heatedly. Then later Gerry found the pants suit crumpled up in a far corner of her closet, on the floor, behind a can of moth crystals she'd been looking for. She confronted Bonnie with it.

"Well, I thought they were supposed to give models all the clothes they were photographed in," Bonnie said.

"*Give!*" Gerry said. "*Give,* not let you *take!* That's stealing. They need that pants suit to make copies of."

"He gave it to me," Bonnie said.

"Then how come he called up so furious, looking for it?"

Bonnie shrugged and pouted.

"You'll have to give it back."

"I didn't take it."

"If you didn't take it, how did it get here? It walked here?"

Gerry didn't know what to do. She was afraid for Bonnie's

career, for one incident like this could ruin her as a model forever because no one would ever trust her. She couldn't go to all Bonnie's bookings as a watchdog. But Bonnie had to learn that even though she was living a fantasy life she still lived in the real world where people had real values like not stealing. She finally decided to give the pants suit to Libra and let him take care of it, and for herself, she simply stopped speaking to Bonnie for two weeks.

What Libra did with the pants suit was a mystery. The only thing Gerry knew was that the photographer spread it around the industry that Bonnie was a lousy model, too stiff, and that he would never use her again—and no one else paid much attention because Bonnie was an excellent model and most of them assumed the photographer had simply tried to go to bed with Bonnie and had been rudely rejected. As for Libra, he deducted the fifteen hundred dollars, in installments, from Bonnie's allowance, keeping her virtually trapped in Gerry's apartment with no money except carfare to get to bookings, and Gerry keeping a stony silence.

Bonnie stayed at home, watching television when Gerry turned it on, eating when food was given to her, fasting and sleeping when no food or entertainment was proffered. At the end of two weeks Gerry came home one night from the office to find Bonnie sitting on the floor, wearing boy's jeans and a torn boy's shirt, her hair combed back like a boy, no make-up on her face, and sobbing.

"I can't stand it any more," Bonnie said. "Please talk to me." With her eyes and nose swollen from what must have been hours of crying and her hair skinned back like that, she looked more like Vincent than Bonnie. Gerry felt a rush of pity and tenderness.

"You have to learn to respect other people's property," she said.

"I will."

"Maybe you don't respect a lot of the people you work with, but while you're working with them, you have to respect their rules."

"I do respect them," Bonnie said. "The people, I mean."

"I'm not saying you have to respect all of them. You're entitled to your opinion. But just don't play them for fools, because they're not."

"I know it."

"Okay. What do you want for dinner?"

Bonnie rushed over to her and hugged her. Gerry felt

terrible. She didn't want to have to be a mother to this kid, or a watchdog or a warden. She hated the idea of any adult having so much power over another adult. But she couldn't let Bonnie get into trouble, either. The world saw only the good Bonnie, the lovely face, the graceful, lovable nymphet. They were not even interested in seeing Bonnie as a whole human being. She had to see both faces of Bonnie—you had to do that with someone you cared about. And she had to protect her. Not just because Libra told her to—it was different now. She had grown used to Bonnie and more than a little attached to her. She was impressed with the way Bonnie seemed to have solved her emotional problems by herself, without ever complaining or feeling sorry for herself, and even seemed to be having a better time in life than most of the normal girls and young men she knew. Bonnie had a lot of strength. Gerry respected her.

After that the relationship changed. Gerry began encouraging Bonnie to go out with her, to shop for groceries or clothes, to the movies, for dinner on hot nights when she was too lazy to cook. And Bonnie seemed to enjoy it. She didn't go to the gay bars so much any more. She had more dates. The boys came to the apartment to pick her up, and they always seemed like nice, clean-cut, straight boys. They obviously liked and respected Bonnie. Gerry couldn't see hanging around on Bonnie's dates even though Libra wanted her to, so she stayed home on the nights she wasn't seeing Dick. Sometimes now Bonnie insisted Gerry go out with her on a double date, getting the date for Gerry, so Gerry went. It was pleasant, and she did not feel uncomfortable after the first time. Her date was always straight, at least to the best of her knowledge—probably bisexual she told herself, but how did you ever know who was and who wasn't, anyway? On dates Bonnie was quiet, sitting there looking beautiful and knowing she was beautiful, occasionally saying something unexpectedly witty that made everyone laugh a great deal, partly because her delivery was so well timed. Gerry thought that Bonnie was a natural comedienne and could probably make her debut in a comedy part when Libra found the right film for her.

Libra had already decided that. One day at the office he showed Gerry a script. *"The Marilyn Monroe Story,"* he said. "I'm going to get it for Bonnie."

"Wow!" Gerry breathed. "What a break for her. Can you do it?"

"Are you asking *me* if I can do it?"

"No, I mean you can do it if anyone can."

"They'd probably think it's sacrilegious if they ever find
out," Libra said. "But my theory is that Monroe's unique
appeal was that she really wasn't sexy at all. Women loved
her as much as men did, you remember. They were never jealous. And men really didn't want to sleep with her, they just
wanted to adore her. By being un-sexy she became super-sex.
We're still a nation of prudes. She parodied sex and she knew
she was parodying it. That was her genius. Any actress who
got the part would be more sacrilegious than Bonnie because
they would be second-rate Monroe. Bonnie would be first-
rate Bonnie. I think she's the only one who *can* do the part."

"Are you going to send her to acting class?"

"I'm not sure," Libra said. "I want to send her to Simon
Budapest, but I don't know how well she can handle being
around that bunch of animals all the time. I think I'm going
to get Simon Budapest to take her privately and coach her.
She'll learn faster and we'll have more control over her."

Who was "we"? Libra and Simon Budapest or Libra and
Gerry? Gerry realized he meant himself and her. She felt
herself blushing with surprise and pleasure. Libra had given
her her first real responsibility for a client! She was no longer
just Big Nurse. She felt now that Bonnie was almost a
member of her immediate family. She wondered if under the
veneer of scorn Libra showed for his clients he really felt the
same affection for them that she did for Bonnie, even though
for some he would necessarily have it to a lesser degree. But
didn't he have to care? He spent his whole life on his clients'
lives saving none for himself. His marriage was ridiculous,
he had no one to care about except the procession of girls he
showered off and dumped into bed, and he certainly didn't
care about them. He was a strange man. She wondered if she
would ever understand him.

She told Bonnie about the script that night. Bonnie was
like a little kid, jumping around, saying over and over: "Are
you sure? Do you think I'll get it? Do you think I'll be a
star?"

Then she told Bonnie about the acting lessons.

"Will you come with me?"

"You don't need me."

"Yes I do."

"He'll be your acting coach. I'll just make you both self-
conscious."

"Not any more self-conscious than some strange old fossil will make me. Say you'll come, just the first time at least."

"Okay, I'll come the first time."

"Dick called."

Gerry looked at her, surprised. "Here? When?"

"About half an hour ago."

"Well why didn't he call me at the office, the dumb thing. He knows I never get home that early."

Bonnie shrugged.

"What did he say?"

"He's nice," Bonnie said. "He's coming over."

Dick had heard all about Bonnie from Gerry, of course, but he had never met her. He had once even said that he would never want to meet Bonnie, that he was frightened of freaks. He knew that Bonnie was Vincent because Gerry had told him—she told him everything and she trusted him implicitly. She wondered now why he had decided that he was no longer frightened of "freaks," as he had called her, and she wondered if she was jealous. No need to be jealous—Bonnie *was* a boy. Dick was probably just curious in a friendly way because Bonnie was living with Gerry and he wanted to know who his girl was living with. Still, it annoyed her that he had called at the apartment when he knew he would find Bonnie there and not Gerry. It was an odd thing for him to do. With any other man she would just have thought it was an unthinking thing, but she knew Dick well enough to know that he never did an unthinking thing. She spent more time than usual putting on her make-up and put on an extra pair of false lashes for confidence. Bonnie *was* the most beautiful girl she'd ever seen, even though she *was* a boy, and she'd seen too many men insist that Bonnie was a girl even though they were Bonnie's lovers and obviously had been playing with something in that bed. Well, maybe Dick was thinking that there might be a part in his Broadway show for Bonnie and wanted to get a look at her.

"Did he say we're going out, or what?" she called through the open bathroom door to Bonnie.

"He didn't say."

Gerry came out of the bathroom. "How do I look?"

"Ooh, she's got on her bats! Look at her, wearing those bats! Who are you trying to seduce?"

"You, Vincent. I've decided to make a man of you." Gerry chased Bonnie around the bedroom until she caught her. Bonnie squealed until caught, then she fought back and began tickling Gerry unmercifully. She had the strength of a man. "Let go!"

"Don't you kiss me, you sick freak!" Bonnie giggled.

"Let me go, you truck driver!"

"Truck driver! Truck driver! Look who's calling who a truck driver."

Gerry sensed the rough play changing. Bonnie had never really felt or held a girl before, and now her tickling and teasing was turning into curious touching disguised as mischief. She had her hands on Gerry's breasts and was trying to get her fingers under Gerry's skirt. Was she just trying to see what a girl had that she didn't have, or was she really more of a boy than either of them had thought? Gerry pulled away and ran into the living room.

"I'm not a toy," Gerry said. "If you want to know what a girl looks like I'll draw you a picture."

"Don't. You'll make me sick."

"Do you know anything about girls?"

"How could I?" Bonnie said. She went into the bathroom and began painting her face. "I might as well paint for your friend," she said. "I don't want to scare him to death."

Gerry wondered what Dick would think of Bonnie, while she made a pitcher of martinis which she put into the refrigerator—he drank the awful things winter and summer. She put a stack of records on the turntable and went to the air conditioner to turn it up higher. The air conditioner sputtered and clattered at her like an angry car and stopped dead. It was broken. One of the hottest nights of the summer and the air conditioner had to break. She opened the windows and the hot air felt like a wall. Well, Dick wouldn't linger long over pleasantries now, he'd just meet Bonnie, have a drink, and the two of them could go. She didn't know why she was so nervous. She had been working too hard, that was all, and summer in New York was a nightmare even when you kept moving from one air-conditioned place to another all day.

She made a large penciled note for Bonnie to call the air conditioner repairman in the morning and made herself a vodka and tonic.

"Do you want a drink, Bonnie?"

"No thanks. Oh, well, all right if you're having one."

She made another vodka and tonic and took it to Bonnie in the bathroom. Bonnie hadn't locked the door against her in a long time.

"Are you going out?" she asked Bonnie, who was pasting on *her* bats.

"I don't know. Why is it so hot in here?"

"The thing broke."

"Oh God. Then I will go out."

"Are you going to be here tomorrow so the man can come to fix it?"

"Okay. I don't have a booking until three o'clock."

"I left the number in the kitchen so you can call him."

"Okay."

There was a long silence, Bonnie concentrating on her eyelashes, putting them on, taking them off, putting them on again until she was satisfied. She knocked the drink off the sink by mistake and the glass broke. Gerry went to the kitchen for a dustpan and broom.

"Do you think he'll like me?" Bonnie asked.

"Who?"

"Dick Devoid."

"Not if you call him Dick Devoid."

"Do you think he'll think I'm a freak?"

"Why would he think that?"

"Because I am a freak."

"You are not. Who said you were a freak?"

"Well I am," Bonnie said. "You know it."

"He'll love you. Everybody does."

"I'll sweep that up."

"It's okay."

"If he's going to laugh at me, I don't want to meet him," Bonnie said.

"You're not getting another drink till you get out of the bathroom. You only knock them over."

"He's not going to laugh at me, is he?"

"*No.*" Gerry took the broken glass to the kitchen and threw it away. "I wouldn't walk around in there barefoot, if I were you, until the maid comes Wednesday."

"You think I should wear a dress?"

"Why not?"

"Well, he *knows.*"

"Wear whatever you're comfortable in. You can wear your neuter bell-bottoms."

"I think I will. Then he can't laugh."

How funny Bonnie was—she didn't think it was odd to wear two pairs of false eyelashes and a lot of panstick on her face, but she thought it was odd to wear a dress. Her rules were as confusing to the straight world as the straight world's were to her. No wonder she sometimes made serious mistakes. Gerry hoped Dick would like Bonnie, and that Bonnie would feel at ease with him. Perhaps, since it was so hot and the air conditioner was broken, Dick would think to ask Bonnie to come along to dinner with them. It was silly to be jealous. There was a whole world of girls Dick Devere hadn't had yet—he certainly wasn't jaded enough and God knows not naïve enough to want to try a boy.

When Dick arrived, Bonnie was still lurking in the bathroom. He kissed Gerry hello and looked around.

"What happened to your air conditioning?"

"It just broke."

"It's terrible in here." He wasn't wearing a jacket, just a silk turtleneck sweater and tight jeans. "Where's your friend?"

"Getting ready to meet you. Be nice to her."

"I wouldn't dream of not being nice to the gentleman."

Gentleman! It sounded like he was talking about somebody else. Gerry laughed. "I never heard her called a gentleman before."

"What do you call her then?"

"Well, I called her a lady once, and Bonnie said: 'I'm not a lady, I'm a woman. Unless they've lowered the standards.'"

Dick laughed. "I know I'll like her."

Gerry gave him a martini and made herself another drink. It was becoming unbearably hot. "Bonnie, hurry up."

Bonnie glided out of the bathroom, silent and shy as a cat. She was holding her face in that immobile position she always kept for a few minutes after she'd put her make-up on, so that she would not put laugh lines in the paint. It made her look as if she'd had a shot of novocaine in the jaw.

"Bonnie Parker, Dick Devere."

Dick stood up and shook hands with Bonnie as if she were another man. "Hello," she murmured.

"What's the matter with your face?" he said.

"What do you mean?"

"You look like you're talking through your teeth."

"Oh." Bonnie looked so frightened Gerry thought she might bolt out the front door.

"Do you want a drink, Bonnie?" Gerry asked. She glared at Dick.

"All right."

She put a vodka and tonic into Bonnie's hand and watched over her until she'd had a few swallows.

"You certainly are pretty," Dick said.

"Thank you."

"I was prepared to beat you up, but now would you please hold my hand?"

Bonnie laughed, forgetting about her laugh lines. Gerry breathed a sigh of relief. The Devere charm was working again and she knew everything would be all right.

"Mr. Libra has Bonnie up for *The Marilyn Monroe Story*," Gerry said. "And she's going to start acting lessons."

"You should be in films," Dick said. "You're wasted on modeling. You're even better live."

"Oh, I don't think I have a chance," Bonnie said.

"I'm not saying in that particular film. But in something. It's better that you don't get your hopes up too much about *The Marilyn Monroe Story* because it will be very difficult for you as a newcomer to get that. They'll probably take a girl who's done a hundred television shows but whose face is unfamiliar. Big studios seldom take a gamble on an unknown to star in such an expensive picture. But if you don't get it, don't take it personally. It has nothing to do with your talent or your looks. Just keep plugging and you'll be a star someday, I can tell that. You're going to be a big, big star."

"Wow," Bonnie breathed, and giggled.

"It's very good for you to start acting lessons now, not wait until you're already acting in films and making mistakes. Sam Leo Libra is a very shrewd man. Who are you studying with?"

"Simon Budapest."

"Oh. Well, don't take him too seriously. He's a pompous old jerk in love with himself."

"Dick!" Gerry said.

"I just don't like him," Dick said. "But it doesn't matter—studying with him is better than not studying at all."

"Do you think he's no good?" Bonnie asked, worried.

"No ... no, he'll be all right. Don't worry about it. Just don't let him get an emotional hold on you."

"Nobody gets a hold on Bonnie," Gerry said.

"You know it, Mary," Bonnie said. She was sitting there giving Dick her old eye trick: staring at him, letting him drown in those huge violet eyes. She'd often told Gerry that once she turned her eyes on a man he was through. Gerry was amused to see her doing it to Dick, but at the same time she wished Bonnie would stop.

"Let's get out of this steam bath," Dick said. "Bonnie, can you join us for dinner?"

Bonnie glanced at Gerry, who nodded. "Yes," Bonnie said.

Because Bonnie was wearing pants they went to an informal little restaurant which Gerry knew was the chic In-place for the jet set during the summer despite its unpretentious appearance. When Dick walked into the room with the two girls everyone turned around to stare, especially at Bonnie. Gerry had grown used to this—Bonnie caused a stir wherever she went. For one thing, she was spectacular, for another, she was very tall so you couldn't miss her.

At a table in the corner Gerry noticed Peter and Penny Potter with a group of friends. When Penny Potter saw them her eyes widened and she looked down quickly. Dick pretended not to see them.

Bonnie was overjoyed because the restaurant had spaghetti. She could eat spaghetti three times a day, no matter how chic the restaurant was, and it never made her fat. Gerry and Dick settled for something cold, and he ordered wine. He did most of the talking, to both of them, while Bonnie sat there and stared at him with her eye power.

"You understand, don't you, what I was trying to say about the film?" he went on. "I didn't mean it in any way as a personal put-down. I just want you to be prepared for the rejections in this business, because they come every five minutes. And they don't mean a thing."

"Oh, I don't care if I'm not a star," Bonnie said. "I just want to get married and have a baby. Be a mother or father or whatever. Either one, take your pick."

"I can only see you as a mother," he said seriously.

Little Penny Potter was coming toward them, on her way to the ladies' room. She stopped at the table. It was the first time she had deigned to acknowledge Gerry's existence and Gerry knew she was stopping only because Dick was there. She had her hair done up in a Mr. Nelson Summer Horror, masses of Dynel curls with daisies twined among them. She was wearing a Franco creation, a white see-through mini-dress with comic strip cartoons cut out, laminated to some sort of plastic, and sewn on strategic places.

"Hello, Dick."

"Hello, Penny. Do you know Gerry Thompson, and Bonnie Parker?"

They all said hello. Penny's eyes had not left Dick. "How have you been?"

"Fine, thanks. And you?"

"All right. We've missed you at our parties. It's been too long."

"I've been very busy," Dick said.

"I see." She looked at Gerry and Bonnie, evidently trying to decide which one was keeping him so busy.

Dick glanced over at Penny's husband at the corner table. "Say hello to Peter for me."

"I will. He misses you too. Call us." She was nervously fingering something on her shoulder, and when she took her hand away Gerry saw that it was a gold and diamond teddy bear pin, much like the nightingale Dick had given to Silky.

So that's it! she thought, surprised she hadn't figured it out before. Penny Potter was an old affair of his, and she evidently hadn't gotten over it yet or she wouldn't be wearing Dick's famous kiss-off pin in front of her husband. *I hope to God he never gives me any jewelry,* Gerry thought.

"That's a beautiful pin," Bonnie said.

"Thank you." Penny looked at Dick for an instant and then looked away. "Nice to have met you." And she was gone.

Maybe the pin was just a coincidence, Gerry thought. Her husband could have bought it for her, or she could have picked it out herself. Dick Devoid wasn't the only person who bought jewelry for his loved ones at David Webb. But her woman's intuition told her the pin was from Dick—that and the way Penny had looked at him. She knew there were a lot of things about Dick she was aware of but preferred not to think about, and his track record was one of them.

"Did you see all those falls!" Bonnie was saying. "The worst! And her make-up! All that shading—brown, white, beige, pink, like in stripes, carefully disguised to look like no make-up at all. Old putty face. If she had one more fall on she wouldn't be able to keep her head up. And that dress! The only comic strip character that wasn't pasted on that dress was *her.*"

"Be kind," Dick said.

"Her pin was nice. I loved that pin."

"Well, you be a good girl and maybe someone will give you one," Gerry said. She hadn't meant to be bitchy to Dick, but it just came out. She was tired and the wine wasn't helping her disposition any. It was bad enough to have to work and fight all day at the office, but then to have to come home at night and fight for a man was too much. She wished Dick would just make up his mind, but she had begun to suspect that he never would, and that if she ever so much as hinted at it he would disappear.

Bonnie was pushing her spaghetti around her plate, hardly eating any of it. She seemed mesmerized by Dick. Gerry knew her well enough to know that she was flattered because Dick was straight and paying so much attention to her, but that Bonnie had no more interest in him than in any of the other straight or ambivalent or whatever guys who fall in love with her. All Bonnie wanted, as she told Gerry so many times herself, was to know that they wanted her. After that she had no more interest in them. Her whole romantic life was a quest for acceptance—beyond the conquest there was no story. *What am I going to do—get married and have guppies?* Bonnie had often said to her. *When he and I get married we can go to Woolworth's and pick out our babies.* So each man found himself greeted eventually with icy boredom from Bonnie and went away confused and depressed, wondering what he had done wrong.

When they finished dinner Dick took them to his apartment. It was comfortably cool and he made them after-dinner drinks. Gerry wondered what was going to happen next. If Bonnie stayed, then she and Bonnie would both have to go ... if Bonnie left it might look awkward. What had gotten into Dick anyway? It wasn't necessary to make love every time you went out with your lover, but Dick had established, the precedent that they did, and now she felt a little rejected. There were records playing, Dick was talking, and they seemed dug in for a good long stay. She looked at Bonnie: Bonnie was looking infatuated. She looked at Dick: he was looking as inscrutable as he always did. She wondered how she was looking: nervous? Insecure? Ungracious? It wasn't that she *wanted* to go to bed with him tonight—well, she *did*, because it had been two days and with Dick she thought about it all the time when she had hardly ever thought about it before she met him. She certainly did want to go to bed with him, right now, and instead she had to settle for a nice domestic evening at home with friends.

She got up and went into the bathroom. Damn him anyway, so neat, so sure of himself, all the expensive colognes lined up on the marble shelf above the sink, all his things, no room in his life for anyone else. Look at his damn bathrobe on the

hook on the back of the door, always white terry cloth,
always freshly laundered. He must have a dozen of them.
Look at his damned aquarium on the window sill, all lit up,
bubbling away. If he didn't have that he'd have room for all
of a wife's cosmetics. No wonder he didn't want anyone in
his life; it would just be too damn crowded.

Guppies, she thought, looking at Dick's aquarium, and in
spite of herself she laughed.

She came out of the bathroom to find that Dick was alone.
He was fixing another drink, looking annoyed.

"Where's Bonnie?"

"She split."

"What do you mean—just left without saying good-bye?"

He shrugged. "Just left. She said: 'Good night—good-bye'
gaily and ran out."

"Was she angry?"

"Why should she be angry? She was just being kind."

"What do you mean, *'kind'?*"

"She obviously felt in the way."

"Well, I didn't make her feel in the way," Gerry said.

"You must have. I didn't."

"Maybe she had a date," Gerry said. "She always goes out
late."

"Would you like another drink?"

"No, thanks. I think I'd better go."

"Oh?"

"Thank you for dinner."

"You're welcome. Don't get mugged." He turned away.

Bastard, she thought. She went to the door. Then she
stopped. *Double super bastard.* "Come on, Dick. What is it?"

He looked at her innocently, with a trace of annoyance on
his face. "You were obnoxious all night," he said. "Didn't you
notice it?"

"No. I was too busy noticing how obnoxious you were
being."

"Me? I thought I was more than gracious to your fruity
friend."

"You were lovely. But why are you so angry now because
she left?"

"It broke up the evening," he said.

Gerry looked at her watch. "I wasn't planning to stay up
all night. I have to work tomorrow and so do you."

"I don't know ... I just thought it might be interesting to
see what would happen."

"Like what?"

He glanced at her, then away. "Just like . . . anything."

"Like *what*, Dick?" But she knew. And suddenly she hated him.

"Do you and Bonnie make it together?"

"Of course not!"

"Just wondered. She loves you."

"*He* loves me, and I love *him*, but he's a fruit and he doesn't have anything to do with girls—he's scared to death of them. And I am not a reformer of homosexuals, thank you."

"I never had a boy," he mused thoughtfully.

"Well, if you want Bonnie, you know the number," Gerry said, hating him furiously, and at the same time feeling the pain of losing him as if she had been struck in the stomach with a fist.

"After all," he said, "people can't go on doing the same things forever."

"Are you bored with me?"

"Of course not. Are you bored with me?"

"Not yet," she said maliciously.

"I would never make it with a boy alone," he said. "But the three of us . . . it would be different. Bonnie looks exactly like a girl."

And undressed he looks just like a boy, she thought, but she said nothing and looked carefully at Dick, trying to find him ugly, trying to remember what he looked like the first time she saw him before she stopped looking at him objectively and started to fall in love with him. She hated him but she couldn't bring herself to go.

"I was just kidding," he said. "I wanted to see what you'd say."

"I guess in the world you live in you do scenes," she said. "In the world I live in they don't."

"I'm not going to talk about it any more," he said. "Forget it."

"If I don't talk about it I won't be able to forget it."

"Don't be silly."

"Oh, Dick, why can't you be like other people? Have real feelings . . ."

"I do have real feelings," he said. "I love you."

It was the first time he'd said it. She had waited so long for him to say it, imagined it, dreamed of it, and now that he was saying it it didn't mean a thing.

"If Bonnie had stayed tonight, and we'd balled, I would have married you both," he said seriously.

"She and I can wear matching bride's dresses at the wedding," Gerry said. She wanted to cry, or throw up, or leave, but she just stood there.

"Go to bed," he said tiredly. He went into the bedroom.

She hated him and she loved him. She knew she should leave, and she was quite sure that if she did leave he would send her flowers in the morning and apologize. But she knew that the flowers and the apology wouldn't mean a thing, just as nothing gallant Dick had ever done had meant anything. If she left it wouldn't matter, and if she stayed it wouldn't matter. She went into the bedroom where Dick was already undressed and lying in bed under the covers. Without a word she took her clothes off and got into bed, far away from him. He turned out the light.

In moments of stress she'd always been able to find refuge in sleep, and she was asleep in less than two minutes. When she woke up it was morning. Dick was in the bathroom shaving. She didn't speak to him.

When he was finished in the bathroom she went in and washed. She didn't bother to put on any make-up. When she came out he was dressed. She dressed quickly without looking at him.

"Hurry up," he said. "We'll share a cab."

She wondered if she would ever see him again. She felt numb.

"I don't want to spoil your relationship with Bonnie," he said. "I know you have a good friendship going. That's very important. I don't want to come between you."

That's exactly what you want to do, Gerry thought, but she knew this was no moment for dirty jokes. "Don't worry," she said.

"We'll have dinner tomorrow night," he said.

"All three of us?"

"It doesn't matter. Whatever you want."

"Just the two of us."

"Fine."

She got out of the cab first, he was going on. He didn't kiss her good-bye. She knew she had to start getting over him, but she was still too numb to think. Libra had been right. He *was* Dick Devoid. Devoid of feelings. She had thought she had no feelings, but Dick could outdo her any time in the numbness department. He was really dead. She wondered what had happened to him in his life to hurt him so much that he was so dead now. Had there ever been a time in his life when he was young and idealistic and full of love? Wasn't everybody, sometime? She knew something had clicked in her head and made her stop loving him, just like that. The old self-protective instinct. But at the same time she knew she couldn't just turn it off. She wondered when everything she was feeling and couldn't admit would come rushing in on her. She hoped she wouldn't have hysterics in the office.

CHAPTER

TWELVE

BARRIE GROVER, fourteen, President of the Kew Gardens Mad Daddy Fan Club, found many interesting and important things to do during her summer vacation. For one thing, she finally had time to get her Mad Daddy scrapbook up to date. She had three of them, all bursting. She'd been in love with him ever since the first time she'd ever seen him on television.

He was sex to her. He was the kind of boy (even though she knew he was a man) she had imagined the older girls went out with, the kind of boy they made out with. The idea of actually making out with a real boy made her almost physically sick. She was too shy and too young. She knew there would be time for boys when she got older. She dreamed of it sometimes, imagining the boy to be just like Mad Daddy, and it was a delirious thought. Meanwhile, he was her true love. She had photos of him pasted all over the door to her room, more photos in little ten-cent-store frames on her dresser, and more pinned to the bulletin board on her bedroom wall. Before she went to bed at night she kissed each and every photo on the lips, sending him little mental messages of love and lust.

He had never answered the letter she had slipped under the door at the Plaza Hotel. She figured someone had thrown it out before he saw it. How could he be so near and yet so far? She never missed his program and she felt as if he was talking to her. She'd gone by the television theater sometimes and seen the mobs of kids standing on the sidewalk waiting for him to appear. She knew they waited there for hours and he never showed up. He probably sneaked out a back door somewhere. He wasn't in the phone book or she would have stood outside his apartment house. It never occurred to her that he might be listed in the Manhattan phone book as someone other than Mad Daddy.

Although she was small for her age and despaired of ever having a bust or anything resembling a normal shape, Barrie considered herself a normal teen-ager in every way. She had two boring, normal parents who were easy to deceive, and a boring, normal older brother named Rusty who went steady with a girl who wanted to be a model. She had two divine best friends, Donna and Michelle, who cared about Mad Daddy as much as she did . . . or used to, anyway. Lately they hadn't been paying as much attention to the fan club as they should. Both of them had discovered boys.

Before, they'd had marvelous sleep-over dates where the three of them washed and set their hair and discussed Mad Daddy endlessly, but more and more lately the discussion had centered around boys in school, which girls made out with who, which girls were actually taking birth-control pills, whether you should do it with a boy you loved, whether you could steal your mother's pills and get away with it. Donna and Michelle were a year older than Barrie, fifteen, because she was bright and had skipped second grade. They both had big busts and had been using Tampax for years. They were both still virgins, as of course was Barrie. But they had done a lot of other things. Donna was in love, with a boy she'd met at temple named Herb, and Michelle had met a boy at church named Johnny, whom she was going steady with just to have status although she didn't like him very much. Johnny's main claim to fame was that he looked just like Dustin Hoffman in *The Graduate*. Barrie was an atheist and went neither to church nor temple. She knew Donna and Michelle were atheists, too, or at least agnostics, because they had discussed it, but they went to worship because that was the place you met more boys.

Formerly, on Saturday mornings, the three girls would go to wherever they thought they might find Mad Daddy, usually the Plaza or the studio, or if he was doing a personal appearance they would hang around there, and they would wait for him, knowing that even though they probably wouldn't see him the fact of their presence was an act of love. But now on Saturday mornings Donna was busy with her Temple Youth Group and that Herb, and Michelle was sleeping late and fixing herself up for her Saturday-night date with Johnny. Barrie found herself spending more and more time alone.

Donna and Michelle kept trying to fix her up with blind dates, but Barrie accepted a date only in cases of *extremis*— which was a dance or a party where you couldn't go alone. A boy in her class had asked her out once, but she had told him she was busy. She didn't want to go out with boys yet. There would be lots of time for that later. Secretly she was sure that once she started to date boys she would be trapped into going steady like the other kids did, and then she would be trapped into making out, and the next thing she knew she'd be a child bride—*ugh!* The thought of getting married made her physically sick.

She'd been kissed a couple of times at parties, by her blind dates, and it gave her a strange feeling of revulsion and desire. The stronger the desire was, the stronger the revulsion was. *I'm just a little kid*, she kept telling herself. *I'm only fourteen. I don't have to do that stuff yet. Plenty of time for that when I grow up.*

Her mother was terrified that her brother Rusty was making out with his steady girl friend, Tammi, and that the girl would get pregnant. That's all parents thought about: pregnant, pregnant, pregnant. Barrie knew that sometimes when she was out of the house her mother went through her bureau drawers, because Barrie always kept everything in its special place and sometimes her things looked gone through. Looking for what? A sign that she wasn't a virgin? A sign that she was going to be pregnant, pregnant, pregnant? A bottle of birth-control pills, or whatever they came in? A box of Tampax instead of the Kotex her mother had ordered her to use? Her hymen lying there, discarded at last? It made her so furious that her mother looked through her things that once she had bought a little mousetrap and put it under her underwear, and another time she'd collected a whole lot of disgusting worms in Central Park and put them all squirmy into an aspirin bottle made of dark-green glass, with the label washed off, so her mother would have to open it and pour the worms out into her hand.

"Why do you keep worms in your dresser drawer?" her mother asked that night.

"Worms?"

"You heard me. Worms. I found them. What's the matter with you?"

"Who asked you to go through my things?"

"I was only putting away the clean laundry."

"You don't have to do that. My dresser is my property. I can put away my own laundry."

"A mother can't do anything right," her mother complained. "I try to be nice to my child and you scream at me."

"I put the worms there so you'd keep out of my drawer."

"If you want me to keep out of your drawer then there must be something there you don't want me to find."

"There's nothing."

"What don't you want me to find?"

"Why don't you trust me?" Barrie screamed.

"Stop screaming!"

"Why can't you leave me alone?"

"A mousetrap. I found a mousetrap last week. You certainly are a silly child. Why can't you grow up?"

"Why won't you let me grow up?"

"All those pictures of that actor in your room. It's sickening. You should be going out with boys."

"I'm fourteen years old!"

"You're old enough to grow up."

"I won't grow up till you stop spying on me!"

"I'm your *mother*."

What did that mean? A mother had a right to do anything reprehensible, anything lousy and sneaky and rotten, because she was a mother? Mother meant rat? No wonder the black boys at school called everybody "Mother." A mother was the worst thing you could be.

But she didn't hate her mother, not really. Her mother hardly existed, except when she insisted on intruding. It was just that she kept intruding so much, except when you really wanted her. For instance, you couldn't just sit down and have an intelligent conversation with your mother about politics or the war in Vietnam or the draft or anything. Her mother was an arch-conservative. She thought people who went on protest marches were all hoodlums, even the priests and nuns and rabbis who went. The Hoodlum Priest. Her father was even worse. He liked Nixon.

To tell the truth, Barrie wasn't vitally interested in world affairs, but she did have some opinions on them, and she thought the proper kind of conversation to have with your parents would be a dignified discussion about world affairs, not some silly argument about morals or sex or boys. But parents seemed to think that they were on this earth to instruct and forbid, and you couldn't have an intelligent, cool conversation with them about anything without them taking sides and getting all excited. Which was a shame, Barrie thought, because parents were older and ought to be better informed than kids, and they would be very useful if they weren't so bigoted and emotional. They absolutely refused to get on her level or let her get on theirs. You just had to avoid them whenever possible.

She didn't discuss world affairs with her friends. Friends were to talk about feelings with, because they had the same feelings and they understood. You needed friends to make you feel less afraid and alone about things. She missed Donna and Michelle a lot now that they talked about their steadies all the time.

There was one other thing they talked about a lot, and that was the girl who'd been killed one night right in their neighborhood with a whole lot of neighbors looking on and doing nothing. That story haunted them all, and they went back to it again and again.

"You just can't expect anybody to help you in this world," Michelle said. "You've got to have a boyfriend with you all the time to protect you, because if you go out alone you can get killed. I'm glad I have Johnny."

"A midget like that?" Barrie said.

"Oh yeah? Well, Johnny bought a switchblade knife at some store on Forty-second Street and I want you to know if anybody ever tried to rape me he would use it."

"Yeah?" the other two girls breathed in awe.

"And he's taking karate after school. He's little but he's no fool."

"Herb believes in nonviolence," Donna said. "Next year when he's eighteen he's going to burn his draft card."

The girls were impressed. Burning your draft card was braver than carrying a knife or learning karate.

"What would Herb do if anyone jumped on you in a dark street?" Michelle asked.

Donna was stumped. "Run?"

"That's pretty low," Barrie said.

"I guess he'd fight to protect me," Donna said. "He

wouldn't fight a cop, but he'd fight a murderer or a mugger."

"Mad Daddy would protect me," Barrie said.

"Oh, Mad Daddy, Mad Daddy," Donna said. "Mad Daddy doesn't *exist*. He's just a star. Why don't you get a real boyfriend?"

"I hate walking the two blocks home from the bus," Barrie said to change the subject. She hated it when the girls were unsympathetic. "Those two blocks are just where that girl got killed. I just hate it."

"Get a boyfriend," said Michelle.

"I'd be just as scared of the boyfriend as a real mugger," Barrie admitted.

"Why?" Donna asked. "You don't have to go to bed with him. I don't go to bed with Herb and he doesn't expect me to. I'm going to wait until I'm at least twenty-one."

"Do you think you can?" Michelle asked.

"Sure."

"Well, I don't do anything with Johnny because I don't really love him, but if I loved him as much as you love Herb I don't think I could wait that long."

"I don't really care about making out that much, one way or the other," Donna said. "I like it, but I don't want to sleep with him, I really don't."

The talk turned to one of the girls in their class who had done it with a boy and then told her best friend who was the biggest gossip in the school. Of course everyone found out about it. They all agreed it was embarrassing, especially since the boy wasn't in love with her and she had only done it with him because *she* was in love with *him*. The boy really had to be in love with you if you were going to risk doing it with him. Otherwise you'd make a fool of yourself. And one of the teachers had told the girl's mother that if she didn't watch out her daughter was going to go bad. How sick! Imagine having the teacher talk to your mother as if you were a mental case! How gross!

"A girl can't win," Barrie said. "If you go out with a boy, he wants to make out, and if you're all alone, who's going to protect you coming home from school?"

"Why don't you just get your brother to wait for you at the bus stop?" Donna said.

"Rusty? Are you kidding? He never thinks about anybody but himself and that pig he goes with."

Nobody suggested she ask her father to wait for her. You didn't do something like that. Having your father wait for 'you at the bus stop in front of all your friends was even worse than getting killed by an imaginary rapist.

"Besides, I can't imagine anybody ever trying to rape you," Michelle said, looking at Barrie's underdeveloped form objectively.

The girls started pawing through the latest hairdo magazines, but Barrie's mind was on serious things. The world was so full of violence! People getting killed in the streets, cops beating up kids on peaceful protest marches, the war, babies getting bombed and burned, that nut who set himself on fire outside the UN, kids not much older than they were committing suicide because they were getting bad marks at college, those hippies getting mutilated and murdered in the Village last year, all those assassinations, one after the other, police dogs, Mace, fire hoses, people with blood running down their faces ... everybody was nuts. This was the world everybody was in such a hurry to make her grow up into.

Why didn't everybody just let her alone? What was such a groove about growing up anyway? Who wanted to be a part of that violent, stupid world? If only life could always be like the Mad Daddy Show, with his innocent little creatures and his wonderful, kind, loving, sexy self: the best, most beautiful man in the world. She felt so helpless. Sure, she wanted a boyfriend ... but it would have to be Mad Daddy. She loved and trusted him so much. With him life would be just like it ought to be, peaceful and loving and happy and fun. She'd find some way to meet him someday. Every day she was getting older, and soon she'd be the kind of a girl a man might look at without turning right away as if she wasn't there. She felt so lonely and so sad. All her big talk about defending herself was just bravado. She didn't want to be alone. She was so little. Sometimes she just wanted to spend the rest of her life in front of that screen, living in her fantasy of Mad Daddy forever. And other times, like now, she wanted to grow out of her fantasy, to actually meet him, to face him with her love and her need.

She looked at the slightly gross faces of her two best friends, Donna and Michelle, bent over the hairdo magazine. All that time they spent on their hair and their faces, and they were still only slightly pimply teen-aged girls. They looked like a hundred other girls. Everybody looked alike whom they knew. Only she was different. She was *interesting*-looking. She'd spent hours in front of the mirror and she

knew she was interesting-looking. Maybe if he ever met her,
Mad Daddy would like her. Nobody had ever said he was
married. Oh, maybe all her dreams would come true!

CHAPTER

THIRTEEN

SAM LEO LIBRA detested summer because it was hot and you sweated. You could shower five times a day and still you felt unclean. He rented an air-conditioned chauffeured limousine for the summer months and managed to keep his time in the actual hot, filthy street down to about twelve minutes all told, getting in and out of the car on his various rounds, but still he wished the summer would be over.

Arnie Gurney was in Reno at a new club, and Libra had managed with very little difficulty to talk Lizzie into going there for ten days as his emissary. She liked lying in the sun. Elaine Fellin and the kid were going with her. He suspected that Elaine was going there to case the joint in the event that she decided to stay for six weeks and divorce Mad Daddy. The hostility between Elaine and Daddy was becoming so bad that Libra was afraid it would affect Daddy's work, and so he had put the idea into Lizzie's head that she take her best friend along and stay longer than ten days if she felt like it. He also gave Lizzie five thousand dollars to gamble with. That ought to keep her there for a year. Although Libra hated gambling (except in business), he had a profound respect for Lizzie's gambling ability—she knew just what she was doing and never lost. Lizzie was one of the greatest crap shooters on the East or West Coast.

Good riddance to Lizzie! Good riddance to Elaine! Happy,

peaceful bachelorhood! Now he could work twenty hours a day. The Mad Daddy Show had started the midnight slot as a summer replacement, and if it went, which he knew it would, it would continue in the fall. Since it was being taped in the afternoon as always because Mad Daddy was used to that, Elaine had not felt herself rejected at not being asked to stay around for the première. It really was the same show, except that it was reviewed again as a night show. The reviews, as Libra had expected, were raves. Adults found it winsome and sharply satirical; a perfect balm for the summer doldrums.

Reports from the Coast said that Sylvia Polydor's hatchet-murderess film was going to be a big money-maker. Libra had already lined up a sequel for her, and although he had heard some disturbing reports about her drinking, a few long-distance calls reassured him that she was her same intelligent self and the drinking reports were greatly exaggerated. He didn't blame her for hitting the sauce on the set in a dog like that, but she knew as well as he did that these pictures were the only thing she could do right now and she had as healthy a respect for money as any woman alive.

The Marilyn Monroe Story part had fallen through for Bonnie, which was a disappointment, but those were the breaks. The kid had taken it with surprising equanimity. She was a good kid. Libra had grown rather fond of her. She behaved herself well, with dignity and discretion, and staying with Gerry had done worlds of good for her. He congratulated himself again for his instincts. He was busy reading other scripts that might be right for her, and he knew that before the first of the year he would find a starring vehicle which would really put Bonnie Parker on the map. Bonnie was applying herself to her private acting lessons and had learned how to pitch her voice better. You could never tell it was a guy. Her throaty voice was excellent; it reminded him somewhat of early June Allyson.

Silky Morgan was doing well at acting class, Simon Budapest reported, and she had just signed for the hoped-for musical, *Mavis!*, the story of a black girl from the slums who becomes a congresswoman, running on the Love Ticket. The show was a piece of shit, but Dick Devere would direct it with all the psychedelic know-how he had brought to his television shows and it would be as fresh and new as today.

Silky and the Satins continued to be a real money-maker, so Silky would continue to cut records with the group even though she was in the show. You never knew with a show; it could have everything and still be a flop—and if it was a hit it could only help the group. The Satins had hysterics when they learned Silky had been singled out for the lead in a Broadway show and they had been left behind, but a few well-placed threats from Libra put them back in line and they finally accepted it. They were all rich now. They had brought their relatives in to New York for a vacation, all two million of them, dressed in sequins and feathers and diamond pins on mink stoles—enough to make you fall on the floor laughing. They went to all the night clubs and had a hell of a time. Now that they were running around like oil-rich Indians, there were requests from charities for money, requests which were greeted by blank stares of disbelief.

"What charity?" Tamara had said, as spokesman for the other girls. "We ain't finished sending all our brothers and sisters to school yet. We our *own* charity, man."

"You can't blame them," Silky had told Libra. "We had nothing, and now we're making it up to ourselves. When we get our whole families fixed up decently, *then* we can worry about strangers. Who ever gave *us* charity when we had nothing?"

Franco's Gilda collection had gone into production, and it was even more grotesque and wonderful than anyone had dreamed. It would change the entire face of fashion for the fall, and Franco was ecstatic. Fred, in Gilda wig and shoulder pads, was set for the October cover of *Vogue*, and somehow exquisite Fred managed to make the gag look really almost like something every woman would seriously want for herself. Fred could wear a barrel and make it look like what every woman needed. Libra had never really gotten over not getting his hands on Fred, but at least he owed Bonnie to her and he was not angry, only a bit nostalgic and disappointed.

Damn Fred had married her photographer, and was threatening to get pregnant and retire. That was none of Libra's business, because she wasn't a client, and he wished her well as long as she waited until after the première of the fall Franco collection before she became misshapen. She had promised to wait, only because she and her husband wanted to buy a house in the country and the money would come in handy.

Mr. Nelson was doing all the hairdos for Silky's Broadway show, fifty different wigs, and he had raised his fee for a personal hair styling and cut at the salon to a hundred dollars. Libra considered that tremendous *chutzpah*, but it didn't seem to stop any of the society and show business ladies from making appointments with him weeks in advance.

There was, right on his desk, a film offer for Shadrach Bascombe, should he decide to retire from the ring. Oh, Libra's clients all had the magic touch, all right. The world breathed love on them. Even Zak Maynard, running around Spain with a married heiress, had come up smelling like a rose, and there was an offer for him to play—an actor running around with a married Spanish heiress.

Libra had sent the King James Version to London, where they were an enormous hit. They were in a new bag now— religious revival songs with a rock beat, and their version of "Rock of Ages" *"Let me sock it to ya/Hallelujah/Do the Rock of Ages!"* was number two in England, an extraordinary thing for any American group. Their new album was going to devote one whole side to their version of the Songs of Solomon, the flip side being standards, and Libra knew it would sweep the world. Those lyrics were great.

The only person who worried him a little was Gerry. She seemed quieter, and her face looked drawn. It was Dick, of course. Libra had warned her at the beginning, but she wouldn't listen. Now she was getting it, just like all those other girls had. Libra was annoyed at Dick, because he respected Gerry and he didn't like seeing a girl like her getting the shaft from a scrawny bum like him. In a way, Libra felt fatherly feelings toward Gerry. She had red hair, like the daughter he'd never had, and she had guts, like himself. She was a smart girl, efficient but human. She had a sense of humor and she knew when to shut up. Bonnie was crazy about her, and so was Silky. Even Lizzie was fond of Gerry. Gerry was spending longer hours at the office than was necessary, and although Libra appreciated it he knew she was doing it more to get away from Dick, or Dick's absence, than because she was devoted to her job. He wished she'd just ditch the bum. If he didn't feel so incestuous, he'd go after her himself. Gerry was really wasted on the average guy. Dick was better than the average, but he was still a bum. Somebody should take care of Gerry, take her to the beach on weekends or something.

Let the lame take care of the blind, was Libra's slogan, so he telephoned Mad Daddy one morning, after Ingrid had given him his shot and he felt euphoric, and told Daddy that

now he was a summer bachelor he wanted him to spend a
weekend at Peter and Penny Potter's beach house instead of
hanging around the city chasing under-age jail bait. Daddy
was horrified.

"I'll send Gerry to look after you," Libra reassured him.
"You like Gerry. I'll send you up in my car. You won't even
have to drive. Penny will call you later." He hung up before
Mad Daddy could protest further, and called Penny B.P.,
who was delighted to have any celebrity as a house guest.
Then he told Gerry.

Gerry accepted the assignment with little enthusiasm, but
said she'd go. She couldn't stand the B.P.'s, but she liked Mad
Daddy, and Libra could tell she was relieved to be spared the
decision of whether or not to spend the weekend with Dick—
or waiting for him, whichever was the status of their affair
now.

"Shall I bring Bonnie?" she asked. "She loves the country."

"This is the beach," Libra said. "I don't want her getting
tan, and if she stays in the house she'll do nothing but drink
with that bunch of souses. I think she'd better stay home,
unless you think she can't be trusted."

"No," Gerry said, "I trust her. She'll love knowing we both
trust her alone. This is the first time. I think it'll be good for
her."

"Good," Libra said. "Take over now, I'm going to the
gym."

But he didn't go to the gym. Halfway there he changed his
mind, and still euphoric he told his chauffeur to take him to
Henri Bendel's, a store he knew Lizzie liked. He went in and
bought a sexy bikini, a transparent shirt to cover it, a jazzy
little pants suit, a short-sleeved sweater, and a cute blouse—
for Gerry. He paid in cash and had the store deliver them to
Gerry's apartment because he was embarrassed to give them
to her himself.

"Happy July Fourth" he wrote on the card, although it
was the beginning of August. He wondered if Gerry was
really his daughter if he would still try to start something
between her and Mad Daddy. He had no idea. He didn't
know how a real father was supposed to react. But he liked
liking her. It made him feel warm and rather mushy. Except
for Lizzie, years ago, Gerry Thompson was the first girl
Libra had ever really liked in his life. He didn't know why he
liked her, but it made him feel good. He told the salesgirl to
wrap the package in all the gift wrap she could find.

CHAPTER

FOURTEEN

"OH, BONNIE, you are a *beauty!*" Vincent Abruzzi told himself, looking at his reflection in the new dress in the tiny fitting room mirror of the store downtown in the Village. It still embarrassed him a little to walk into a girls' store and ask for a dress, and it embarrassed him even more to take the dress into the fitting room and try it on. At first he had always taken the dresses home without trying them on, after timidly informing the salesgirl that if his "friend" didn't like the fit someone (he, of course) would bring it back the next day, and was that permitted? He knew no one would ever read him, but still he had to fight his panic every time he went into a fitting room, sure someone would come in, outraged, and yank him out, and take him right to jail.

The dress was adorable, and he bought it. Then he went down the street to a faggot store, feeling much more comfortable there, and asked to see some bell-bottomed pants.

"You can't try them on today," the nitty queen who waited on him said. "Girls aren't allowed in the fitting rooms on Saturday."

"I'll girl you, Mary," Vincent said.

The queen did a double-take. "Ooh, sorry. You *do* look real."

Vincent wanted to say: "Look for me in *Vogue* next month," but he stifled the impulse and minced into the fitting

186

room with the three pairs of pants. They were a perfect fit so he bought them, and two silk scarves to wear as little ties with the girl's shirts he had at home. The pants looked just like girl's pants. He liked the way most of the clothes today were so neuter-looking; it left the decision of whether he was a boy or a girl up to the people who looked at him—if they always thought he was a girl it wasn't as if he was trying to *deceive* them.

"Cologne?" the nitty queen asked, trying to spray him.

"No!" Vincent hated men's cologne—except on a man, of course.

"Here, take it. It's a free sample, because you're so pretty."

Vincent took it. He could keep it for a rainy day. That queen had called him "pretty." Most queens hated him because they were so jealous that he was doing what they didn't have the courage to do. He was happy and flattered that the queen didn't hate him, and he gave her his best Bonnie gaze and a little smile. "Thank you."

"Don't mention it, doll. Good luck."

He rode uptown on the subway because it was cheap and quick. He could afford cabs now, but he still used the subway during the daytime, preferring to spend his cab money on clothes. He wondered when he would ever be able to finish paying off Mr. Libra that fifteen hundred for the pants suit he'd stupidly mopped, and he hoped it wouldn't be when he was too old to look nice in the clothes he was dying to buy. This shopping spree today was the result of weeks and weeks of hoarding, walking, going without lunches. When he had a date, or was with Gerry, he ate as much as he could so that he wouldn't starve the rest of the time. He didn't want to lose weight and get his legs so skinny they didn't look like girl's legs any more.

The subway platform was empty. He waited for the train, walking up and down. On the wall there were various advertising posters with wisecracks scribbled on them by subway poets. Someone had written in large letters: "God is love."

Vincent looked at it, then looked around to make sure no one was near to him. He took his lipstick out of his purse— the purse Gerry had finally convinced him to carry even though he thought it looked the *worst* for a boy to carry a purse—and crossed out the word *God*, replacing it with *Fame*. "Fame is love."

"That's about where it's at," Vincent murmured. The train

came roaring into the station and he got on it, humming a
little tune.

The apartment was lonely. He hung up his new clothes and
filled the bathtub with warm water and bubble bath. Gerry
had gone away to the beach for the weekend with a client of
Mr. Libra's and she had told him being left alone was a
compliment and a great position of trust. He was flattered,
but he missed her and he wished she had invited him, even
though he knew he would have been too self-conscious to go
to that beach house with all those society people, and besides
he hated the sun. He put some records on the phonograph
and got into the tub, where he soaked until the stack of
records was finished. He shaved his legs and let the water run
out. Wrapped in a big towel he went into the living room to
turn the stack of records over, then filled the tub again, got
in and washed his hair.

While his hair was drying he stood in front of the
bathroom mirror and carefully inspected his upper lip for any
sign of hair. Unmistakably, there was a downy fuzz. His first
reaction was horror, then curiosity and a kind of embarrassed pride. He was growing up. A moustache was a
nuisance, but he'd seen lots of girls with much worse
moustaches than his. What was he going to do with it?

There was Gerry's depilatory. He smeared it on and waited
as long as the tube said to wait, and then washed it off. What
kind of stuff did she use anyway? The moustache was still
there, most of it anyway. He looked at the tube again. *Do
not reapply*, it said. All he needed now was a red mark and he
wouldn't be able to go out tonight.

With a sigh for his lost innocence Vincent picked up the
safety razor, inserted a new blade, and daintily slathered on
Gerry's shaving cream. It was a good thing she was a pack
rat; their apartment was as well stocked as any drugstore. He
had never shaved in his life, and he drew the blade down his
upper lip gingerly, afraid he would cut himself. The hair
came off like magic. He was flawless Bonnie Parker again.
Whew! He rubbed cream on his lip to take the soreness away
and put a beauty pack on his face to tighten his pores. Then
he sat in front of the air conditioner, listening to the records,
and brushed out all his false eyelashes, replacing them carefully in their little plastic box when he was finished. The sun
was setting in the window behind him and he felt homesick.
Maybe he'd go home and surprise his mother. His eyes filled

with tears. He missed his mother, and he missed Gerry. He
hated Saturday night.

When the phone rang, Vincent let it ring three times and
then picked up the receiver just before the service could get
at it.

"Hello."

"Bonnie?"

"Yes."

"This is Dick."

Oh, wasn't it! Dick Devoid, old scarecrow, big nose, bald
head, closet queen! Vincent wasn't one bit surprised. "How
are you?" Vincent said.

"Fine, thanks. What are you doing?"

"Nothing," Vincent said. "What are you doing?"

"Having a drink with some friends. Would you like to
come over and join us?"

Dick wanted Vincent to meet his friends! Vincent wondered if there would be any stars there. He loved meeting
famous people.

"Well, I'm not dressed or anything," he said.

"Come as you are, we're all informal," Dick said cheerfully. "Hurry up . . . they want to meet you."

"Why?"

"Why not?" Dick said.

"Give me an hour," said Vincent/Bonnie, and hung up.
He painted very lightly, just his panstick and mascara on his
long lashes; then he decided to put on his bats and started all
over again. He was nervous. He'd never been out with Dick
after that night with Gerry. He'd fled when he realized that
Dick was anticipating a scene for the three of them, because
that was a lousy thing to do to Gerry. Gerry was a nice girl,
and she obviously loved Dick. But what the hell? He'd just go
there tonight and see what happened. Nothing would happen.
He'd just twist Dick's mind a little and cut out. He wondered
whether or not Dick would want to go to bed with him.
Would *he* want to go to bed with Dick? No, not in a million
years. He just wanted to see what would happen.

He decided on one of the new pairs of bell bottoms; white,
with a white shirt of Gerry's he'd long admired, and one of
his new scarves tied around his neck to hide his Adam's
apple. He put on his girl's white patent-leather loafers, with
tights under the pants so he could gaff better. His hair was dry
now, and very blond and shiny. He teased and smoothed it
and gave it a light spray. Then he put perfume behind each

ear, tucked the perfume bottle into his purse for touch-ups, and inspected himself in the mirror for a last time. Unreadable. Beautiful. Bonnie Parker the beauty.

He had Dick's address in his little address book (he'd put it in automatically after that evening at Dick's apartment) and he was on his way.

Dick's guests were a fat young man, not too bad, and a bitchy-looking girl. The girl had dyed blond hair and looked at Bonnie's natural blond hair with undisguised jealousy. She'd obviously been the beauty in this room until Bonnie got here. The fat young man's eyes nearly popped out.

"Bonnie," Dick said. "This is Steve, and Truffle."

Truffle! What kind of a name was that? But Bonnie liked Steve—he had a fat little belly but his face was great, lots of hair and sexy sideburns. *Well, I'll have that,* Bonnie thought. She looked at Dick. *I could have him too if I wanted, I bet.*

Steve jumped up to fix Bonnie a drink, but Dick beat him to it. Bonnie sat down on a chair slightly removed from the rest of them, crossed her legs, and waited. She said nothing. Dick brought her the drink and she murmured "Thank you" without smiling; the paint on her face was still too fresh and felt uncomfortable. It was obvious from the conversation that Dick had not told any of them Bonnie was a boy. Steve was knocking himself out trying to be witty, and Truffle was looking lost. Bonnie continued to sit there saying nothing, sipping her drink, looking at the two men from her flawless huge violet eyes, waiting and enjoying it. Dick came to sit on the arm of her chair. He liked her! Wasn't that nice! Well, he wasn't so ugly. *Maybe I will have him,* Bonnie thought.

She thought of Gerry, but it didn't seem at all disloyal to Gerry to be here with Dick, even if she decided later to go to bed with him. After all, Gerry was a girl, with all the right plumbing and all the advantages. If Dick wanted her, Bonnie, instead of Gerry, or in addition to Gerry, it wasn't like taking a man away from another girl because Bonnie *wasn't* a girl. If Dick wanted her, he wanted a boy. One thing had nothing to do with the other. Bonnie would never be jealous if she lost a man to a real girl, even though she might be sad or feel frustrated about her bad luck in having all the wrong plumbing. She thought about it. No, it definitely wasn't bitchy or underhanded to be here with Dick. If Dick was an old closet queen he might as well find it out now. For even though Bonnie insisted all her dates were straight before they met her, and even though most of them insisted it themselves, she knew in her heart they were fags. *Fags*. Why deceive yourself? If they went to bed with her they were fags. They'd tell themselves: "Well, it looks like a girl so I'll tell myself it's a girl while I'm playing with its cock," and they were fags.

Bonnie looked around Dick's apartment, seen now in twilight. It was tasteful and luxurious, but certainly not a fag's apartment. There was nothing nitty about it, no little touches, none of that self-consciously over-masculine stuff either. It was a great apartment. None of the queens in the bars had ever heard of Dick Devere, so it was more than likely that he *was* straight but just had this little inclination that'd come out when he met Bonnie. Bonnie felt sorry for Gerry, not because *she* was with Dick tonight but because Dick was a shit and Gerry was a wonderful girl who deserved a real man who would love her and marry her and give her babies. Old scarecrow, big nose, bald head! Bonnie would fix him! *Vincent* would fix him! *Oh, yes I will,* Bonnie/Vincent thought, looking at Dick with the most innocent, sexiest possible look in her eyes. *I'll fix you, you old lecher, scarecrow, bald head, big nose! I'll fix you for making Gerry cry every night when she thinks I'm asleep and don't know. And when I'm finished with you maybe I'll have a crack at your friend Steve. I think he's cute.*

It turned out that the girl named Truffle was an actress, and Steve was Dick's attorney. Bonnie had never seen Truffle in anything so she dismissed her immediately. But Steve continued to intrigue her. She'd never been out with an attorney. She reminded herself to keep to the business at hand: the wrecking of Dick Devoid, and she noted with delight that even though she'd stationed herself at a distance from the others in the room they had eventually all grouped around her—first Dick, then Steve, finally Truffle who discovered herself left out.

Truffle and Steve brought out some pot and they all turned on. Dick was acting prissy about it (old queen! probably afraid he'd get nelly when he was high) and took one little poke and then said he'd stick to his martinis. Bonnie pretended disinterest but she enjoyed getting high on the pot, it was so much nicer than drinking. Then, as usual, the pot made her hungry.

"Aren't we going to eat?" she asked.

"Of course, of course!" Dick said, jumping up. They were

out on the street in about two minutes. Bonnie's wish was his command tonight, and Bonnie loved it.

They went back to the place where Dick had taken Bonnie and Gerry. Bonnie ordered her favorite, spaghetti, and then discovered after two bites that she couldn't eat a thing. She was nervous. Dick kept talking, as usual, trying to charm and impress everyone, and Bonnie decided that he had a nice voice and a nice way about him. If she didn't know what a shit he was she'd really like him. He had a lot of charm. He had to have something to make all those girls fall in love with him. She'd already cruised his box but you couldn't tell what he had; he was too secure and well tailored to let the public in on the mystery. She'd find out later, all right. And she'd make *him* blow her. Oh, wouldn't she, though! She'd twist his mind, she'd wreck him.

She remembered one guy she'd dated, a really masculine guy, the butch number to end all butch numbers, and then in bed he'd wanted *her,* the little flitty paint queen, to screw *him!* What a shock! Bonnie had done it, just out of curiosity, but she hadn't liked it at all, and after that she'd used him as an escort and nothing more. Wouldn't everybody be surprised if they knew what he was really like, the big queen! She thought now that it would be fun to warp Dick's mind that way, but she knew it would be impossible to bend his mind that far. No, she'd just get him to fall in love with her, and then she'd make him admit what a big fruit he was, and then she would have another conquest and Gerry would be avenged.

It was fun going out with straight people, here in this straight restaurant, knowing she was the center of attention because she was so pretty, knowing they all accepted her and didn't think she was a freak. She was nervous but happy. Maybe she *would* be a big star someday. Who would ever dream it, the little misfit from Irvington, hiding in the house all day like a mole ... a big movie star! God bless Mr. Libra. God bless Gerry, and all those people who'd been so nice to her/him, poor Vincent. Weren't people kind! Wasn't life good! Wasn't it lucky that if he had to be born a he/she freak at least he'd been born a beauty! God bless Flash for plopping his first wig on his head. God bless his father for never playing baseball with him. God bless his mother for buying him his first nurse kit instead of a doctor kit. God bless God.

Steve and Truffle were going to a midnight movie. Dick

took Bonnie back to his apartment without asking her what she wanted to do next, and Bonnie went with him placidly.

In his apartment Dick turned on the lights and put some records on the turntable. He made drinks for himself and Bonnie and they sat on the couch. Bonnie couldn't think of anything to say, so she drank the drink, knowing that two drinks made her very drunk and this was the first. She needed to be drunk. She was a little afraid of what would happen next.

"I could still never believe in a million years that you're a boy," Dick said. "To me you'll always be a girl. Who could ever believe you're a boy?"

Bonnie smiled.

"I have a present for you," Dick said, and took something out of the desk drawer. It was two amyl nitrates. He popped one and put it into a Benzedrine inhaler, holding his finger over the hole on the top, and handed it to Bonnie.

Bonnie loved amyl nitrate. It was her favorite buzz. She held the inhaler to her nostril and breathed in greedily.

"You're taking the whole thing," Dick protested, amused.

Bonnie waited for the buzz—then it came, and she sat on the floor and giggled uncontrollably. Everything was tingling and she felt goofy and happy.

Dick picked up the empty inhaler from the floor where she'd dropped it. "Good thing I have a whole box of these," he said. "You're a dope fiend."

Since he was being so nice she felt it was only fair to share, so she took two blackbirds from her purse and offered one to Dick. They gulped them down with their drinks and sat there smiling at each other, waiting for that buzz to start.

"Let me pick some records," Bonnie said, walking unsteadily to the record player. She pulled her favorite albums out of the neat row in his bookcase: all the sexy female vocalists she loved. Aretha Franklin, Dionne Warwick—oh, no one could touch them! She saw an album by Silky and the Satins and put that on the stack too.

Dick took it off. "Don't play that."

"Why not?"

"I'm not in the mood for it."

Bonnie knew Dick had had an affair with Silky Morgan. The poor old queen is feeling guilty, she thought, amused. Well, now they'd have a contest of wills. "I like it," Bonnie said. "Please?"

"All right." He put the record back on the stack.

He was putty in her hands. "Can I have another drink?" Bonnie murmured.

Dick made the drinks and took them into the bedroom. He turned down the bedcovers. Bonnie followed him and switched off all the lights except for one dim one in the corner. She didn't want to shock him to death. Dick was taking off his clothes calmly. He acted as if it was the most natural thing in the world to be here in his bedroom with a girl who was really a boy. Dionne Warwick was pouring honey through the bedroom speaker. Bonnie took off her bats and laid them on the dresser. She couldn't stand to have sex with her false eyelashes on because one of the queens had told her once that they could get stuck in your eye and make you go blind. She glanced at Dick to see if he was disillusioned with her, seeing her without her eyelashes, but he seemed oblivious. It was so dim in the room that maybe he hadn't noticed. Thank goodness her own eyelashes were so long.

Dick lay on the bed, naked. Well, look what he had! Wasn't *that* nice. *He'd kill me with that thing,* Bonnie thought. *I'd be screaming in pain.* She took off all her clothes except her underpants and got under the sheet quick as a flash, pulling the sheet up so it covered her lack of tits. No point in disillusioning him now.

Bonnie had become adept at hiding her deficiencies in bed, like the dance of the seven veils, so that all the man usually saw was her lovely face and a glimpse of shoulders. She'd learned how to keep the illusion going until the last possible moment, and besides, she was really very shy about her body. Naked she wasn't much to look at as a boy or a girl. Just a pale, skinny kid. No tits and no muscles. Nothing for anybody. As always, she waited for Dick to make the first move, lying far on her side of the bed.

There was a large mirror above the low dresser opposite from the bed, and Bonnie saw the reflection of herself in the bed lying under the white sheet. The image of Bonnie vanished, and there was only Vincent. Vincent the freak. Vincent didn't have a semblance of a hard on. He didn't care if he stayed or left. His heart was pounding with fear. He reached out a pale, skinny arm and took his drink off the bedside table, spilling some of it on the sheet.

Dick had a big hard on. "Look at it," Dick said tenderly, in love with himself. "Isn't it nice? Do you like it? Don't you want to do something to it?"

"No," Vincent murmured shyly.

"Why are you wearing your pants?" Dick asked. He reached over and tried to pull them off. Vincent held on to them with both hands, struggling to keep his modesty and the last vestige of illusion. "That's so silly," Dick was murmuring. "Take them off. Come on."

"No," Vincent said. "Leave me alone." He waited for Dick to reach out to take him in his arms, to kiss him, neck with him, do what boys always did. Boys loved to kiss him for hours because he had such a beautiful, sexy mouth. Vincent was a champion kisser. He didn't care much about other things, considering them degrading, but he loved to kiss.

Dick took a tendril of Vincent's hair between his fingers and played with it shyly. They looked into each other's eyes.

"Just touch it," Dick said.

Vincent reached over and took it in his hand. How degrading! He certainly wasn't going to service this queen! He leaned over Dick and tried to kiss him on the mouth. Dick turned his head away.

"I just can't kiss you," Dick said apologetically. "I can do anything else ... I'll ball you ... but I just could never kiss a boy because I'm straight."

Oh, the gall! Vincent felt himself blushing with humiliation and fury. All the boys in the world wanted to kiss him and this skinny, ugly old queen thought it wasn't masculine! What a laugh! Waves of hate and rejection poured over him, making him feel faint. *You'll kiss me, Mary, if it's the last thing you do,* he thought with fury.

He got to work on Dick then, doing all the things he hated to do that he knew Dick would love. Dick was going out of his mind. It felt like he was working on Dick for hours and hours. The more Dick liked it, the more Vincent hated him. He was going to get that damned fruit so hot he'd kiss him, yes he would, he would ... Dick was reaching out now, grabbing for a tube of Vaseline he'd carefully put on the bedside table before the evening had started. It was brand new. *Oh, no you don't,* Vincent thought. *You'll kill me.*

Vincent still had his pants on and Dick was trying to pull them off. "Please," Dick was saying, "Please ... please."

"I'm tired," Vincent said. "I want to go to sleep." He slithered over to the far side of the bed and held the pillow in his arms like a child holding a teddy bear and closed his eyes.

"Please," Dick said.

Beg me, Mary, Vincent thought. He smiled a sweet gentle little smile. Through his eyelashes he could see Dick edging closer to him. Dick had the Benzedrine inhaler in his hand now, and held it under Vincent's nose. Vincent inhaled deeply and flew with the buzz. He let go of the pillow. Dick was sniffing the inhaler now, his eyes shut. *Now!* Vincent thought. He floated into Dick's arms softly, making himself as limp and cuddly as any girl in the world, and when Dick opened his eyes there was Vincent's tender Bonnie face, those huge violet eyes open, tender and gentle.

Dick kissed him on the mouth.

Vincent sighed a gentle sigh of triumph, knowing that his world was safe again, a place where he could always be sure and strong. And for Dick, he knew, the world would never again be safe, and Dick would never be sure of anything again.

CHAPTER
FIFTEEN

ON SATURDAY MORNING Gerry Thompson and Mad Daddy sat dutifully in the back seat of Sam Leo Libra's air-conditioned chauffeured limousine and let themselves be whisked off through the heat blaze of an August weekend in New York toward hell. They were both dreading the weekend on Long Island with the B.P.'s. Clean and neat in their proper weekend guest clothes, sadly watching the familiar sights of the city whizz by them, they felt like two kids being banished to a season at a hated summer camp. There was a well-stocked built-in bar in the back seat, and a tape recorder with an ample supply of stereo tapes. Music was playing, and they were drinking a morning refreshant—Gerry, vodka and tonic; Mad Daddy, Scotch on the rocks.

"Funny, I didn't think you drank," she said.

"I don't drink in front of Elaine. I keep thinking I'll set a good example, but she doesn't get the hint." He sighed and lit cigarettes for both of them. "Are you sure you want to go there? Wouldn't you rather go to Playland?"

"Of course I'd rather go to Playland," Gerry said.

Mad Daddy leaned forward and rapped on the window separating them from the chauffeur. "Take us to Rye."

"We're going to Long Island, sir," the chauffeur said. He was a tall, faceless young man, like someone from a spy movie.

"We've been kidnapped," Mad Daddy said. He took a bill from his wallet and pushed it through the opening in the glass partition. "We're secret agents. Turn around and take us to Playland without any questions."

"Yes, sir," the chauffeur said, pocketing the money.

"Obviously a mercenary," Mad Daddy said. "I was afraid he really believed in the cause."

Gerry giggled. She felt light-headed and free. It was a relief not to have to visit the B.P.'s and put up with all those revolting women in their Guccis and Puccis and Francos, with their gym-lithe bodies and whiskey voices, talking about people she didn't know and places she never wanted to visit because she knew those places would be full of more of the same. And their sexless husbands and gigolos and lovers! She was sure none of them had ever been to Playland, unless they'd managed to have it closed for their private use.

Enclosed in the car she felt free of Dick and all her worries about him. She had still seen him a few times, and he phoned more often than that, just to say hello, but both of them knew the magic was gone. She wished he would just disappear and get it over with. She didn't have the courage to tell him to get lost because she kept hoping she would get tired of him and that would make it easier. But she didn't get tired of him. She liked him. She didn't love him any more, she was sure of that, but she liked him, and she probably always would. What was the point of hating someone you'd once liked enough to have an affair with—*and loved enough to dream of marrying?* That was like telling yourself you'd been a fool with bad judgment who would have been ready to marry *anybody.*

"Elaine's in Vegas," Mad Daddy said.

"I know."

"Maybe she'll stay and get a divorce."

"Do you want her to?"

"Oh, I'd love it," he said. "I'd love nothing better. It would make me so happy. I wish she'd find somebody and fall in love with him. We haven't gotten along for years."

"Maybe she will," Gerry said.

"I feel guilty about it, but people aren't meant to be miserable together," he said. "I see people who stay together when they're miserable and they manage, but I can't do it. Don't ever get married, Gerry."

"All right," she said cheerfully.

"Are you in love with Libra?"

"Libra!"

"I just asked, that's all."

"You don't know very much about me, do you?" she said.

He looked at her seriously as if really looking at her for
the first time. "No ... no, I don't. You must be in love with
some guy, though."

"I was. I'm not now."

"But not Libra. Oh ... Dick?"

She nodded.

"Well, he's not so much," Mad Daddy said, dismissing Dick
with a wave of his hand. "I think he's a phony."

"You do?"

"Yeah. He's so slick. I don't trust slick men. They act like
they rehearsed their lives before they even got to you."

Gerry laughed. "How about slick women?"

"All women are slick," Mad Daddy said admiringly. "Even
young ones. I love it."

She knew, of course, about Mad Daddy and the young
girls. If she could believe Libra. She looked at Mad Daddy.
There was something irrepressibly innocent about him, like a
kid with his first crush. She liked him; he was sweet and he
made her feel comfortable. He seemed prepared to admire
her whatever she was or did, and it was a feeling not many
men had given her. And he was so talented! Poor thing, she
hoped he would have a happy life and not get into trouble.

"I wonder why I keep getting married," he said. "Have
you been married?"

"No."

"Women are supposed to be the ones who want to get
married," he said. "But when I fall in love I always want to
get married. It's very expensive. Divorce is, I mean. Not
marriage. I like being married, I like a settled life, but when
they marry me they always seem to think that marriage is
going to be one long Saturday-night date ... only better,
because they don't have to wait for me to pick them up
because I'm *there*. But you get married so you don't *have* to
run around any more, or at least I always do. It just doesn't
work out that way."

"Maybe you should try marrying a grown-up," Gerry said.

"Maybe."

He poured himself another Scotch. "Do you know how old
I am?"

"I think so."

"Forty," he said morosely. "It's a secret, but I'm forty."

"You don't look it."

"I don't feel it either," he said. "I used to think: Forty! That's a mature adult! People who are forty have learned a lot. Well, I don't know much. Do you realize that forty is technically middle-aged?"

"Don't be depressing," Gerry said. "If you were middle-aged you couldn't write your show, or be in it either."

"Yeah, it is depressing, isn't it?" he said. He cheered up, looking out the window and humming to the song on the tape. "Remember the roller coaster?" he said. "Well, now they have these things that look like the endurance tests for astronauts. They have one where they strap you in standing up and then they whirl you around in a circle and upside down. It's wild! Do you get sick on the roller coaster?"

"I never did," Gerry said. "Just scared."

"Me too. I like the Tunnel of Love. It's not really scary, but I love being in a boat. And I like darts. I always win."

"I like cotton candy."

"Oh, I love cotton candy," Mad Daddy said. "We'll get cotton candy first thing. And jelly apples. I'm hungry, are you?"

"Starved. I didn't have breakfast, as usual. I slept too late."

"We're drinking on an empty stomach," he said, pleased. "Don't you like doing things that are supposed to be bad for you? Like drinking on an empty stomach, or eating pickles with ice cream?"

"I don't feel drunk," she said. "Do you?"

"Of course not. See, nobody knows that the things you're not supposed to do aren't bad for you because everybody's too scared to do them."

"Like us not going to the B.P.'s," Gerry said. "Not going was the best idea we ever had."

"I knew I couldn't make it," Mad Daddy said. "I would have liked to go to make Libra happy, but I knew I couldn't go through with it. I work hard enough as it is, I do all these things I have to do that I hate to do, like give interviews and be nice to people who don't care a damn about me ... you know, those people you meet when you're a star, they're just waiting for you to do something wrong so they can hate you for it. When you're nobody they don't care if you act like as big a schmuck as the next guy, and when you're struggling they even feel sorry for you and forgive you for things, but oh boy, when you make it! Then they're just waiting for a chance to knock you down. They watch every little thing you do. You say something that looks different in print than when you said it ... like you were saying something, kidding, you know, and then in print it looks serious, and wow! The hate mail! So when I'm not working, the last thing I want to do is to go to some stuffy place like those Potters and have to answer questions for people who aren't even interested in the answers. They think I'm some kind of ... entertainment for them. Like I'm not really a guest. They don't want me to have a good time. They make me feel so guilty for being there, eating their food, drinking their booze, breathing their air ... they want me to get up and do a *schtick* to pay for it, or better yet, make a fool of myself so afterwards they can tell their friends: 'See, that star is really a jerk!' "

She hadn't thought he was capable of anger, but she liked him better for it. "Oh, the hell with them," she said. "We'll have a groovy day."

He smiled at her. "Yeah. Hey, you're really pretty. I never went out with a girl with freckles before."

They were mildly high and very hungry when the limousine pulled into the Playland parking lot. The place was mobbed; teen-agers on dates and in groups, families with babies and picnic baskets. It must have been nearly ninety degrees outside, but no one seemed to mind. Mad Daddy told the chauffeur to go eat lunch and come back in about an hour, and they set off hand in hand to find the action.

They stopped for pizza at a stand, then hot dogs, then Cokes, then soft ice cream. Then, even though they were feeling a little sick, they had to have cotton candy and jelly apples, because they had been planning for so long to have them. Mad Daddy made a plastic dinosaur at a machine and gave it to Gerry.

"My Dennison of the Deep doll looks better than that," he said. "Let's go see if they have it at the Magic Shop."

The Magic Shop was over by the lake. They dawdled along the midway watching the people screaming on the various new versions of the dreaded roller coaster, glad they were not among them.

"You'll like my doll," Mad Daddy said. "Then we can go in the Tunnel of Love, okay?"

"Okay."

"And the Hall of Mirrors. I always like the Hall of Mirrors."

"Okay."

"You can throw that jelly apple away if you don't want it," he said. They looked at each other and laughed, and tossed their jelly apples into the nearest rubbish basket, feeling greatly relieved. He lit cigarettes for both of them.

Four teen-aged girls came walking by, then stopped and did a double-take when they saw Mad Daddy.

"Hey!" one said. "Aren't you . . . ?"

"No," he said.

"Yes he is! Look, look, it's Mad Daddy!"

The four girls started to scream and giggle. People were turning around. "Mad Daddy! Look, it's Mad Daddy! Can I have your autograph?"

Mad Daddy had started to perspire. He gave a weak smile to the kids and pushed Gerry into the entrance of the Hall of Mirrors, thrusting money at the ticket taker.

"You have to have tickets," the man said.

"How much are they?"

"You get them over there." He pointed at a ticket booth with a long line in front of it. He had never heard of Mad Daddy and couldn't care less.

"Can't I just pay?" Mad Daddy asked plaintively.

"Tickets over there."

The kids were upon them, at least fifteen of them now instead of the original four, and they were screaming and giggling. Mad Daddy grabbed Gerry's hand and pulled her with him along the midway again, toward the lake. He was like the Pied Piper. More kids had joined the group that was following them, attracted by the sport of running with a mob, some of them not sure why they were running or whom they were trying to catch. MAD DADD-EEEE!

"Maybe you should have given them your autograph," Gerry panted.

"Then we would have been there forever," he said.

MAD DADD-EEE! The girls were screaming, shoving each other, their faces red with excitement and the heat, their long hair stringy, their mouths open, their eyes gleaming. Their legs, fat legs in shred-edged Bermuda shorts, skinny legs in mini-skirts, tan legs, white legs, a few pairs of black legs, were pumping furiously to keep up with their fleeing idol. MAD DADD-EEE! Boys who had happened to be their dates were dragged along or ran along forgotten. MAD DADD-EEE! There was a line of people at the lake, waiting to have a turn at the boats. Some adults turned around, disgusted at the display the kids were making. Mad Daddy pulled Gerry back toward the parking lot.

There was the limousine, long, silver-gray, grown-up and reassuring. The chauffeur was sitting behind the wheel in the air conditioning, eating a Good Humor. Mad Daddy opened the rear door and pushed Gerry in, jumped in after her, and slammed the door, carefully locking it and all the others. The kids stood around the car, peering in the windows, gaping at them like fish. Some of them knocked on the windows. Most of them knew who Mad Daddy was, but it was clear that some of them did not and were simply happy to have someone to persecute, trapped in a locked limousine and cowering.

"Get us away from here," Mad Daddy told the chauffeur.

The chauffeur started the car and inched out of the lot. Kids fell off the car like overripe grapes off a bunch.

"I'm sorry," Mad Daddy said to Gerry.

"Sorry for what?"

"Well, we didn't get to do any of the things we wanted to. I should have worn a beard or something. I never thought of it. I didn't think they'd notice me ... you know, out of context."

"This is exactly your context," Gerry said.

"But I never *go* to Playland. I haven't been for years. That's why I wanted to come here today."

"They don't know you don't come here. They think you come here all the time because the character you play on television would come here all the time."

"That's why I can't have any fun any more," he said.

The chauffeur turned around. "Where now, sir?"

Mad Daddy was looking out the window, watching Playland fading in the distance. He tapped nervously on the window with his knuckle, chewing his lip.

"What do you think?" Gerry asked him.

"I think we've been punished," Daddy said. "Go straight to jail and do not pass Go. What's your name?"

"Melvin," the chauffeur said.

"Melvin, go back to that place on Long Island where we were supposed to go in the first place. At least they hate me there."

The chauffeur headed the limousine toward Long Island. Mad Daddy chewed up an ice cube. "Did you ever read *1984*?" he asked Gerry.

"Yes, in school."

"Well, do you remember where it said everybody has his one fear that's his cracking point, like that guy with the rats? Remember he was in love with the girl and then Big Brother locked him in the room with the rats, which were his one big fear thing, and then he said: 'Take away the rats and I won't love the girl any more'?"

"Sort of."

"Well, that's how I am with crowds. Crowds are my rat. I don't mind a crowd in a department store or something, but when it's a crowd of fans, or people who recognize me, I panic."

"But they love you," Gerry said.

"Love me? Is that what you think?" he stared at her. "The hell they do! That love can turn to hate so fast it'd make your milk curdle. Let me tell you something. Somebody recognizes me, and then a whole bunch of people recognize me, and then the rest of the people start crowding around because they think: 'Well, there's something everybody's looking at, so I'll look too.' Already I'm the entertainment. And they *expect* me to be the entertainment. They expect me to *give* them something ... time, love, something. A piece of my coat they've torn off. My finger maybe they broke off. It's not enough I gave them all that time and love on stage, behind the camera, and the time I spent planning my shows so they'd enjoy them ... *that* doesn't count. This is a piece of *me* they want. Do you know why people want autographs?"

"So they can prove they met you?"

"Wrong. They want your autograph because it's a socially acceptable piece of interpersonal relating. You didn't think I knew all those big words, did you? Well, I figured it out myself. What they really want to say is: 'Speak to me, look at me, be my friend, spend time with me.' But they can't, because they're strangers and I'm busy and because there are so many of them. Besides, if some stranger came up to a celebrity and said that, the celebrity would think he was a nut case. So they ask for an autograph. Lots of these autograph hounds get your autograph every time they see you. Some of them even make you give them four autographs, one after another, while you're standing there on the street trying to get away. That's your *time* and your *friendship* they're getting, not your signature. They trade autographs and sell them and stuff; they don't care about the actual autograph. They care about the minute they spoke to you and you paid attention to them. And the scary thing is, if you

ignore them or run away like I just did, they stop loving you
in one second and start hating you. All that love just turns to
hate. Wow!"

"Do you hate *them?*" Gerry asked.

"No . . . I like them. I really like them when I'm doing my
show, when they're an audience. That's the way I really like
to communicate with them. After I finish giving them my
show I haven't anything to say to them. My show is what I
want to say to them. All the other stuff is just bullshit."

"What would have happened if you hadn't run away from
the kids just now?"

"I guess it would have been okay. I'd have been signing
autographs for an hour and we wouldn't have had any fun,
and maybe they would have torn most of my clothes off or
something, but they wouldn't have screamed and chased me.
But I just panicked. I can't help it; they scare me to death.
Do you know, some kid cut off my tie once? Cut it right off.
A girl. *Wow!* I felt castrated. That's why I never wear a tie
any more unless I absolutely have to, in case you noticed."

"Well, I guess fame is a great waste of ties," Gerry said.

He laughed. "You're funny. You're smart too—I like talking to you. I haven't talked to a girl for as long as I can
remember."

"Thank you."

"Thank *you*," Mad Daddy said. Shyly, this time, he took
her hand.

She was surprised at the electricity that passed between
them when they touched, and neither of them wanted to let
go. Gerry was a little embarrassed. They were like two kids
holding hands for the first time. He was such a funny combination of grown man and child; she wanted to reassure him
and at the same time she felt that he could take care of her.
They held hands all the way to Long Island, and he played
with her fingers, and once he looked down at himself playing
with her fingers and he actually blushed.

The landscape turned into beach and beach foliage, and
there was the pink shell driveway and the darling little pink
gingerbread house darling little Penny Porter had picked out
all by herself, according to the society columnists, and by the
time the limousine crunched to a stop Gerry thought if Mad
Daddy didn't kiss her she would die. *I'm turning into a mad
nymphomaniac*, she told herself, *and I'm much too old for
him. He likes only little girls*. But from the way he was

looking at her she could tell that for whatever odd reason, he didn't think she was too old for him at all.

A butler met them at the door of the gingerbread house and took their overnight bags. There was a garden in back of the house, with a swimming pool in it, overlooking the beach. The B.P.'s and their guests were grouped around the pool, drinking and sunning themselves. No one was on the beach. Penny Porter arose languidly from her flowered beach chair and introduced them around, forgetting Gerry's name the first time, as usual. She was wearing a tiny white bikini and had a nice, if underdeveloped, body.

"Didn't you bring bathing suits?" Penny asked.

"They're packed," Mad Daddy said, embarrassed.

"Well, get them, for heaven's sake."

Gerry and Mad Daddy went back to the house. The butler had automatically put them in the same guest bedroom.

"Housing shortage," Gerry said, suddenly shy. "We'll have to do something about that."

"Do we have to stay here the whole weekend?" he said.

"Well, as long as we're here let's have a swim anyhow. I'm hot."

"You can have the bathroom first," he said. He sat on the bed. "This is kind of a nice house."

"Yes." She went into the bathroom and put on the new bikini and cover-up Libra had sent her. She'd been surprised and touched when the clothes arrived. Libra wasn't much for compliments when she'd done good work, but he was always generous, and she was very fond of him. She wished Lizzie was nicer to him. She thought of her own moment of lust in the car with Mad Daddy and she wondered if she was going to turn out like Lizzie, sleeping with the clients. It would be so easy . . . they were so available, and they were the only people she met. It must have been too easy for Lizzie . . .

"Your turn," she told Mad Daddy. He went into the bathroom to change.

The bedroom was pleasant, done in white bamboo and a profusion of Porthault flowered material, with a window that looked out on the sea. There were guest colognes and cosmetics on the dresser, like a public ladies' room in a chic restaurant. She put on some cologne and smelled immediately that it was stale. Penny Potter's old cast-offs. She found her own cologne in her overnight bag and splashed it on to cover the smell.

Mad Daddy came out in black-and-white-checked vinyl bathing trunks, with a towel around his neck. He looked good in a bathing suit, young and in good shape for forty, with a tan.

"Where did you get the great tan?" she asked.

"Sunlamp. Elaine bought it."

He *did* need to be married. He wouldn't even think to buy his own sunlamp. "What meal are we in time for?" she asked.

"Drinking."

They went out to the pool. Everyone ignored them. There were six people, counting the B.P.'s—a middle-aged woman with a recent face lift (Gerry could tell because her face was too perfect), a young man with bleached blond hair and a magnificent tanned body, and a fifty-ish couple who seemed either married or going together. The bleached-haired boy looked at Mad Daddy with interest, then looked away when he decided Daddy was too old and too straight. He glanced at Gerry's outfit with approval, and at her hair and make-up with disapproval. Gerry smiled at him and he immediately looked away.

The butler was at their side. "What would you care to drink?"

Gerry didn't want anything, but she asked for a Bloody Mary and Mad Daddy asked for Scotch. The drinks were there in a moment, served from a silver tray, the glasses heavy expensive crystal.

The guests were discussing a guest list for a future party one of them was going to give. "Aren't you going to ask Dick Devere?" the face-lift lady asked.

The middle-aged man puffed on his cigar. "We'll wait till we see what kind of reviews his show is going to get," he said. The others nodded understandingly. Gerry felt sick.

"Let's shake them up and go swim in the actual ocean," Mad Daddy whispered to her. They got up.

"Oh, you can't take your glasses on the beach," Peter Potter said. It was the first time he had appeared to notice them. "It cost me fifteen hundred dollars last year for glasses people lost on the beach. Those glasses came from Baccarat."

"Vot den?" Mad Daddy said.

They put their glasses down carefully and escaped to the beach. "Crystal glasses for plastic people," Gerry said.

"Do you realize—if my show had gotten bad reviews they wouldn't have let us come here today?" Mad Daddy said.

Gerry realized then who the middle-aged man with the cigar was: a comedian who was known as being lovable and darling. She hadn't recognized him without his toupee. His adoring public should only hear him now, King Snob. She and Mad Daddy walked along the white, clean, deserted beach, kicking up the cold surf. He bent down and picked up an empty beer bottle.

"Do you have a suicide note?" he asked.

"How about just: 'Help!' "

"Let's go pee in their pool," he said. "Then I'll tell Yiddish jokes."

"This is such a beautiful place," Gerry said. "Too bad it's wasted on them."

"Let's go into town and find some black orphans," he said. "I'll bring them back here and tell them it's a free picnic."

"Shall we go down ourselves now, or wait until after dinner?"

They ran into the cold water and splashed around. Neither of them was a very good swimmer, but the almost painfully cold water was a relief because it gave them something to think about besides the frustrations of their day and the long disastrous weekend they were sure was to come. Then they came out with relief and sat on the sand. Neither of them had remembered to bring their towels. It was probably just as well, Gerry thought, because Peter Potter would have told them the towels were from Porthault and he'd already lost fifteen hundred dollars' worth of towels, too.

"Did you ever go to camp?" he asked.

"Yes. I hated it, though."

"I never went. I swam in the hydrant."

"That's a good trick."

"We used to steal ice and stick it in front of the electric fan. Who would ever dream I'd grow up to be a Fresh Air Fund kid?"

They sat in the sun for a while, then went back into the ocean briefly to wash off the sand, and took a long walk along the beach past other houses similar to the B.P.'s house, where similar people were drinking cocktails around similar swimming pools. A few children played on the beach, accompanied by uniformed Nannies with blankets and beach umbrellas.

"Nobody has a dog," Mad Daddy said. "Do you notice none of those kids has a dog?"

"They do have dogs," Gerry said, "But they can't take them to the beach. You can lose a lot of expensive dogs that way."

He laughed. "You're very funny for a lady."

They gathered shells, discarding them when they found prettier ones. Gerry washed them off carefully in the water and wrapped them in her cover-up.

"Don't do that," he said. "You'll get it all wrinkled. I'll hold them for you. We can write people's names on them and sell them in the Village."

They walked back then, their backs to the sun to even their tans, until the pink gingerbread house came upon them too quickly. "I love that gingerbread house," Gerry said. "I'd love to live on the beach someday."

"Me, too. That's my secret dream. But not in that house. The witch is inside."

"Somehow I keep getting the feeling *we're* the witch."

He took one of the shells and scratched in letters two feet high on the beach in front of the B.P.'s house: WASPS ARE OUT.

"Stop it," Gerry giggled. "They'll see you."

"Let them."

"Maybe we should go back and try to be friendlier. Let's really try this time."

"I can't—I'm too shy."

"Well, let's just try. Maybe they think *you're* a snob because you're a star."

"They probably do, and I hate it," Mad Daddy said. "They're going to spend the whole weekend ignoring me just to prove they're not impressed. Then somebody will insult me. I know it; it always happens."

"Well, let's *try*."

"All right, but you'll see."

They went back to the pool. The six people were still lying there on their beach chairs, in the same positions, the recent-face-lift lady carefully under an umbrella. Everybody stopped talking when they came over.

"Hello," Mad Daddy said brightly.

"Did you have a nice swim?" the face-lift lady asked.

"Very nice, thank you," Gerry said.

"Wash off that sand under the tap," Peter Potter said. "You'll track it on the rugs."

Chastened, they went over to the water tap beside the bath house and washed their feet.

"This ocean is too cold for me," the face-lift lady said. "I swim in Acapulco, and in the Bahamas, but not here—brrr."

"Of course, you're from California," the comedian with the cigar said. "So you're used to it."

"I'm not from California," Mad Daddy said.

"But of course you've been there," the comedian's wife or girl friend said. "You do a show, don't you?"

"I do it in New York," Mad Daddy said. "I've always done it in New York."

"Funny," said the comedian, "I thought you'd done movies."

"No, I've never done movies."

"He's on television," Penny Potter said helpfully. "The Mad Daddy Show. My friends' children love it. Of course, now that it's on at midnight they can't watch any more."

"Why is it on at midnight?" the face-lift lady said.

"My manager thought it would be a good idea," Mad Daddy said, looking nervous.

"The ratings are up now," Gerry said quickly.

"Midnight?" said the bleached-hair boy. "But who's ever home at midnight?"

"Oh, I suppose some people watch television at midnight," the comedian's wife or girl friend said.

"They watch old movies," the bleached-hair boy said. "Old movies."

"Johnny Carson," the face-lift lady said. "They watch Johnny Carson."

"Some of them watch Joey Bishop," said Peter Potter.

"That was a silly thing, going on at midnight," the bleached-hair boy said. "You'll never make it with the competition."

"Tell my manager," Mad Daddy said. The butler came out with fresh drinks for them and he took his and drank it quickly.

"You ought to do movies," the comedian with the cigar said. "That's where the money is, movies."

"But what parts could he play?" the bleached-hair boy said. "He's not a type."

"*You* certainly are," Mad Daddy snapped, and went into the house. Gerry followed him. She could hear the people at the pool laughing.

"He certainly told you, didn't he?" the face-lift lady was saying.

Mad Daddy was standing in the carpeted hall, banging his fists against the wall-papered wall.

"Your parole board meets at four o'clock," Gerry said quietly.

He turned to look at her and his face was white with rage under his fresh sunburn. She had never seen him so hurt or angry. His eyes were full of tears. "I told you, didn't I?" he said. "Sons of bitches!"

"That's just their sense of humor," Gerry said, automatically falling into her role of pacify-the-client-at-all-costs. "They really like you."

"*Sense of humor?* I'm *funny*, and that's not *my* sense of humor! Goddam inbred leeches! They don't have to jerk off at my expense. Let's get out of here."

"Okay, I'll pack."

She already felt sticky, but she dressed without bothering to shower off the salt water, and she was ready to go, overnight bag in one hand, wet bathing suit in the other. Mad Daddy didn't even bother to take off his wet bathing suit. He picked up his things and led her out the back door to the driveway where their limousine was waiting. Their chauffeur saw them from the kitchen window and came out, hurriedly buttoning his jacket.

"Take us to New York," Mad Daddy said. He threw the bags and his clothes into the back seat and climbed in after them.

Melvin, being Sam Leo Libra's chauffeur, didn't ask any questions. He maneuvered the car out of the driveway and they were off. Green trees whizzed past their windows, the air conditioning was wafting around them, the stereo tapes were playing the Tijuana Brass. Gerry poured drinks from the built-in bar. She didn't say anything.

"Are you angry?" Mad Daddy asked. "Did you want to stay?"

"Of course not. I wouldn't have stayed for anything."

"I couldn't have stayed."

"We didn't have to stay. You're not supposed to suffer, you know. Libra wanted us to have fun. We have the car for the whole weekend. Where do you want to go?"

"I want to stay in the car," Mad Daddy said. "Forever. It's like a womb in here. Do you think we can stay in the car?"

"Sure."

"We'll get a lot of gas and we'll just drive around. Okay?"

"Okay," Gerry said. She smiled at him and raised her glass. "Cheers."

Mad Daddy raised his glass. "Up theirs."

They drank, and he smiled at her. Soon he was humming to the music and doing a take-off of the newest discothèque dance while sitting down. He was funny, and she laughed.

"Would you care to dance with me?" he said.

"I'd love to."

"Nice place they have here. Not too crowded for this time of year." He opened his overnight bag. Even though he had been nearly in tears and frantic to escape the house he had remembered to bring their shells. He took out a pink, whirly one. "Funny ashtrays they have here, though. I think this fag modern decorating goes a little too far sometimes."

It took two and a half hours to drive back to New York, and then the chauffeur asked them where they wanted to go and Mad Daddy told him to fill her up and just drive around. Central Park was closed to traffic so they drove to the Village, then back up Fifth Avenue, then down Park Avenue. It was six o'clock and Gerry very badly wanted a bath and a change of clothes. Their limousine had stopped being a womb; it was now a trap, the pod of an astronaut who has lost the mother ship and is doomed to orbit forever in lonely space. They had heard all the tapes several times and drunk all the liquor.

"Aren't you hungry?" she asked.

"Yes. Why don't we stop and buy some Chicken Delight and eat it in the car?"

"Now listen," she said. "I think we should go someplace—it'll be good for you. And you shouldn't sit around in that wet bathing suit forever in this air conditioning."

"It's dry," he said.

"I'd like to freshen up, as they say."

He was immediately chagrined. "Oh, I'm sorry! I didn't realize ... you probably have something you want to do tonight. A date or somebody you can call up? I'll take you home."

"No, no, I'm all yours. I just don't want to be all yours with pneumonia."

"I'll take you to a restaurant if you want ... but ... well, if we go to a nice place Elaine's friends will be there and she's so jealous, she'd make something of us being together. And we can't go to the movies on Saturday night. Well, I don't want to take you to a dump, either. What do you want to do?"

"Well ... what would you like to do?"

"I'll tell you what I'd like to do," he said shyly. "I'd like to go to your house and watch television. And I'll cook. I'm really this great cook. Do you have any spaghetti?"

"Single girls always have spaghetti," Gerry said. She wondered if Bonnie was at the apartment, and hoped not.

"Tell Melvin where," Mad Daddy said.

The chauffeur took them to Gerry's apartment and Mad Daddy told him he could go home. When she and Mad Daddy got upstairs Gerry realized with relief that there was no sign of Bonnie, just an upheaval of make-up and discarded clothes, the sure indication that Bonnie was gone for the evening.

"That's the bathroom," she said, "and here are some towels. You may even use them, even though they are expensive."

"I'll just use the corner and fold it," he said. "Don't do a thing while I'm gone; I'll make the whole dinner."

Bonnie, who didn't pay the electric bill, had left the air conditioner on as usual, so the apartment was comfortably cool. Gerry put some records on the turntable while he was showering, and made drinks. She'd been drinking on and off all day, but she wasn't high, just tired. She straightened up Bonnie's mess and made the bed. Then he came out of the bathroom, dressed in clean clothes and smelling of her cologne, and she took him into the kitchen, gave him his drink, and showed him where all the food and pots and pans were.

"Go away," he said.

She took a shower and dressed, and put on fresh make-up. When she went back into the kitchen she found that he had boiled a pot of water.

"Just sit there," he said. "I'm going to cook. Wait till you taste my spaghetti. It's my specialty."

"Can I watch?"

"Sure."

She sat on the kitchen ladder and watched him. He put a package of spaghetti into the boiling water, then he opened a can of spaghetti sauce and put it into a saucepan to heat.

"Do you want any spices or anything?" she said.

"Oh, no, that'll spoil it. Just if you have some grated cheese we can put it on the table."

"What about salad?"

"Oh, let's not bother with that. I don't like salad much, do you?"

"Not particularly." She took out two plates and some forks and spoons. She didn't have any wine in the apartment but there was still some of the champagne Libra had sent her, nicely cold in the refrigerator, so she opened it and put it into the ice bucket with ice and a towel around its neck. It looked very jazzy.

Mad Daddy drained the spaghetti and put it on a meat platter he had found, poured the canned sauce on top of it, and held it out with a flourish as if he was Brillat-Savarin. "Wait till you taste that!" he said.

They had spaghetti and champagne in the living room, while the sky turned black outside and filled with stars. Downstairs in the gardens of the other brownstones there were people sitting in beach chairs to get away from the heat, and some people had set up a grill. The smoke from grilling steak climbed in the still night air. Someone was playing with a poodle, tossing a ball for it to retrieve. It was a perfect city summer evening.

"Isn't that *good?*" Mad Daddy said, helping himself to another heap of the spaghetti he had made.

"I bet you make great Jell-O, too," Gerry said.

"What people don't know about great spaghetti sauce," he said seriously, "is that you mustn't fuss with it. It's perfect just the way it comes from the can. People fuss with food and then they ruin it."

"I love it with champagne," she said. "Why not have it with champagne? I love everything with champagne."

"That's right. All those rules are silly."

She was surprised, but it really was one of the best meals she had ever eaten. She thought of all those marvelous meals Dick had bought her in his favorite restaurants, and she realized that every one of those meals had been marred with tension—*hers.* She really hadn't enjoyed anything she'd eaten with Dick; she'd been too nervous, too much in love. Love was a mess. Who had said love made everything else seem better? That was a lie. Love interfered with every one of life's functions. You lost your appetite or had indigestion, you slept badly, you either couldn't go to the bathroom at all or you went all the time from nerves, you couldn't concentrate on things, your skin broke out. Being in love was a mess. *I'm never going to fall in love again,* Gerry thought. She felt as if she was sailing peacefully on a cloud.

"Television!" Mad Daddy cried happily. He jumped up and turned on the set.

"Coffee?" Gerry asked.

"No, no, look—the Marx Brothers! We don't need coffee, there's champagne left. You can't miss the Marx Brothers!" He took a pillow from the couch and settled himself comfortably on the floor in front of the television set, about two feet away from it like a child. Gerry put the champagne and the glasses on the floor and sat down next to him. He jumped up and got a pillow for her. The program was some sort of special—a mélange of old movies of old comics, the Marx Brothers, W. C. Fields, the Keystone Cops, Harold Lloyd, Buster Keaton. It was far better than the usual Saturday-night fare. Mad Daddy watched it avidly, laughing, looking at her every time there was a bit he particularly admired, to make sure she appreciated it too. "Aren't you glad we stayed home?" he said.

"Yes."

During the commercial she took the dirty dishes into the kitchen and he followed her with the platter and forks, putting everything into the sink. She wondered if he was as helpful in his own home. Married men were usually on their best domestic behavior when they were visiting girls, but on the other hand, he didn't have to do anything, she really didn't expect a man to be helpful around the house.

"Don't wash the dishes," he said.

"I didn't intend to."

"Good." He rushed back to the television set.

After the comedy show they watched a very inferior movie which she remembered halfway through she'd seen before, but she didn't mind because watching a bad movie at home on Saturday night was a peaceful thing to do. There was a rather good English thriller after that, then the news, and then a vampire movie.

"Aren't we lucky?" he said happily. "Vampire movies are my favorite. I think I've seen every one of them. Do you have any popcorn?"

As a matter of fact, she did, the kind you popped yourself. Bonnie always bought popcorn and potato chips when they went to the grocery, eating the potato chips secretly because they were bad for her complexion. Gerry wondered briefly where Bonnie was tonight.

"Making popcorn is another of my specialties," Mad Daddy said, taking over with the same culinary authority he'd had with the spaghetti. He held the wire-handled dish of popcorn over the flame and shook it while the popcorn popped and the foil top of the dish bloomed, giving forth an aromatic scent. "I *knew* you'd have popcorn," he said. "I think I'll marry you."

"Okay. It'd be fun to be married to you."

"Nobody else seemed to think so."

"You need an older woman like myself."

"Old?" he said, staring at her. *"Old?* You're just a kid."

"Ha. Some kid."

"What are you," Mad Daddy asked, "Nineteen? Twenty?"

Here we go, Gerry thought. *He throws up and runs.* "Twenty-six."

He kept staring at her in amazement. "Well, don't tell anybody, because they'll never know."

"You're going to burn the popcorn."

"I never burn popcorn."

He put the popcorn into a bowl she handed him and sprinkled extra salt on it. "Elaine is twenty-six," he said.

"I know."

"I still think you're nineteen."

They turned out the lights and watched the vampire movie in the dark, eating the popcorn and washing it down with the last of the champagne. Then all the television stations were off except one which had a movie from the Thirties about two song writers, one of whom was in love with a girl who was in love with the other one. They watched it, of course. Gerry wasn't concerned that Bonnie wasn't back yet because Bonnie often stayed out until nine in the morning when she didn't have to work the next day.

The sun came up with the test pattern.

"That was a perfect evening," Mad Daddy said. "Didn't you think so?"

"Yes."

He looked at his watch. "Let's go walk in the zoo."

"The zoo?"

"Yeah. There won't be anybody there yet. We can see everything."

"You're not allowed in at five in the morning, are you?"

"Of course not. That's the fun of it. Come on." He jumped to his feet and pulled her up.

She was so tired she was getting numb, but still she didn't want to tell him to go away so she could sleep. She went with him to the street where he found a cab and directed it to an all-night cafeteria, where he bought containers of coffee and huge pieces of artificial-looking Danish pastry wrapped in cellophane. Then the cab took them to the Fifth Avenue entrance to the zoo. The city looked very clean and fresh in the dawn. There was no one in the street and you could look for blocks in either direction and not see any traffic. Early morning sunlight sparkled on windowpanes of the big buildings, and a light breeze stirred the leaves of the trees in the park. There was no one to tell them they could not enter the zoo, just a sign which they ignored, so they went in.

A few animals were awake, looking at them curiously. They strolled from cage to cage, sipping their coffee, eating their Danish pastry, which tasted as artificial as it looked, but wonderful.

"Get up, lion!" Mad Daddy yelled at the lion's cage. "Robert F. O'Brien is coming! Don't let him catch you asleep on the job." The lion yawned at them. "Rehearsing already," he said.

A man in a uniform came out of one of the animal houses and looked at them suspiciously. Mad Daddy nodded and smiled at him. "Good morning," he said pleasantly.

The man's face defrosted slightly.

"You keep a very clean zoo," Mad Daddy said. "We just got married this morning. This is our honeymoon."

The man shrugged. "Congratulations."

"You see, we met in the zoo. So we wanted to come back for sentimental reasons."

"That's nice," the man said without much enthusiasm.

"Isn't it?" Mad Daddy said happily. He steered Gerry away toward the bears' cage. "See, Seymour," he told her. "He didn't even notice you were a man."

"You're a nut."

"So are you. Running around like that, in a dress."

She giggled, and then she remembered Bonnie, and Dick, and she stopped giggling. She wondered if Dick would have liked Bonnie if he had thought she was a girl. No . . . Bonnie wasn't really Dick's type . . . he'd run through all the models of note. Dick had really liked Bonnie because Bonnie *was* a boy. Dick seemed far away now, like a stranger she'd once known. She could look at him objectively and it didn't hurt any more. She wondered if Dick would ever have the courage to go out with Bonnie alone, and she knew at the same time that if he did, neither Bonnie nor Dick would ever tell her, and that *it didn't matter*. Dick could do anything he wanted to now; if he didn't want *her* it didn't matter who he wanted.

"You look sad," Mad Daddy said.

"No . . . just sleepy."

He started walking back toward her apartment building. She wondered if he meant to come up . . . she wondered if Bonnie would be there . . . she wondered if Mad Daddy would like Bonnie . . . She knew she had to go to sleep now because she was so tired she was getting paranoid and sorry for herself.

When they got to her building he went upstairs with her. He didn't look as if he was expecting to go to bed with her; he just looked like he didn't want to go home. She knew he was alone in his apartment and she wondered if he was afraid to be alone, or if he found it a relief. There were a lot of things she was curious to find out about him, but there would be time . . .

Bonnie was in the kitchen, wearing Gerry's bathrobe and making scrambled eggs.

"Out all night, you big tart," Bonnie said cheerfully.

"Same to you. Where were you?"

"Oh, I had a date with some guy I *wrecked*," Bonnie said, and gave Gerry a big smile of triumph.

"Anyone I know?"

"No. You wouldn't want to know him either."

"This is Mad Daddy," Gerry said. "Bonnie Parker."

"Hello, Bonnie," Mad Daddy said. He smiled politely and looked at Bonnie with no interest at all. Gerry felt her heart soar.

"Do you want some eggs?" Bonnie asked. She pouted and simpered at Mad Daddy; she couldn't help it, really, it was as instinctive with her as breathing. When she didn't flirt with a stranger she ran away and hid. It depended on how secure she was feeling at the moment. Since she was usually afraid of strangers it was evident she was feeling very secure right now. She really must have wrecked that guy, whoever he was.

"I'd better go home," Mad Daddy said. "I have to write some shows tomorrow. I always leave it till the last minute. I keep trying to stay ahead, but I never can. Nice meeting you."

Gerry walked him to the door. He put his arms around her.

"Hey," he whispered in her ear, "that roommate of yours—is she a dike?"

"Of course not!"

"Well, she looks like a dike. When I first looked at her, the first second, I thought she was a guy."

"Don't say that!" Gerry whispered, horrified.

"Boy," he said, "Models . . . feh! You're beautiful. I love you. Good night."

"Good night." Then he kissed her. She had known all along he would be a champion kisser. It went with the whole kid thing of him, and she knew he would be a champion necker, too. She wondered about the rest of it. They stood there in the doorway, kissing, while the opened door closed softly again. "I better go," he said. "I'll call you tomorrow. Today, I mean. Go to sleep."

And he was gone. Gerry stood there, touching her lips. She could still feel him. She knew now that it was inevitable; they were going to have a romance. She wondered what it would do to their friendship. He was so perceptive it was scary. If he'd spent five more minutes with Bonnie he would have *known* she was Vincent. Like a child . . . a dress and make-up couldn't fool him, because actors and clowns wore costumes and make-up too. What an incredible man Mad Daddy was! A child and a man . . . a precious person.

She walked slowly back to the kitchen, looking at Bonnie. Had Bonnie changed? They'd been so close, maybe she had changed and Gerry hadn't noticed. No, Bonnie looked the same. Thank God! Gerry remembered her mother saying you should never eat capon because it had male hormones in it. Well, from now on she wouldn't even let Bonnie eat chicken. She smiled appreciatively at Bonnie, lovely even after a long, hard night, and went into the bedroom, stopping only to peel off her false eyelashes before she fell into bed and was asleep.

LIZZIE LIBRA lay in the Las Vegas sun, her body oiled, her eyes closed, listening to the mournful drone of Elaine Fellin's voice. If it had been anyone else she would have been whining, but Elaine's dead voice was incapable of a whine. Her rotten kid was off playing by the pool with some other kids she'd found, sending off shrill yips of pleasure. Eyes still closed, Lizzie adjusted the top of her suit to avoid a strap mark. This was the first year she'd bought a one-piece suit, and it depressed her beyond measure ("I do think bikinis are better for the *young girls*, don't you, madam?" the snotty salesgirl had said. "This power net will hold in the little bulge around the tum-tum.") Wouldn't the bitch faint if she knew the names of some of the famous stars who had enjoyed themselves very much indeed atop that little bulge on the tum-tum! *Her* boyfriend probably worked in a drugstore.

"I never should have married him in the first place," Elaine went on. "If I had it to do all over, I never would. What did I know? I was sixteen years old. Daddy was the first and only man I'd ever slept with. I thought I had to marry him just because I'd been to bed with him—I thought otherwise it was dirty. He never talks to me. He never wants to take me anywhere. Oh, he loves to go out with those stiffs from the station he does business with, but he won't take me. All he ever wants to do at night is watch television. He'll

watch anything. He makes me give him his dinner in front of
the set. He sits there till his eyes are ready to drop out. He
doesn't know if I'm giving him meat loaf or dog food. He
watches vampire movies. Vampire movies! When I try to talk
he goes: *Shhh.* Son of a bitch!"

Across the tiled walk from the swimming pool was the
King Cactus Bar, where Lizzie could hear soft music from
the jukebox. It was all done up very wagon wheels and horse
bits. The afternoon bartender looked exactly like Paul
Newman. It was uncanny. Lizzie had made several trips to
the bar simply because the young man with the blond hair
and stop-traffic blue eyes looked so much like Paul Newman
it made her almost horny. What a shame he was only a
bartender! This place was dead.

"At night when I can't sleep I just wander around the
apartment and cry," Elaine said. "I used to take only one
Seconal; now I take three. He doesn't even know I'm awake—
he's snoring away, the pig. Once in a while he notices I exist
and then he grabs me just as if I'm some tart. He thinks he
can ignore me all the time and then expect me to go to bed
with him. The trouble is, he still makes me so hot. I hate
him, and I'd divorce him in a minute, but the damned
bastard makes me so hot."

Lizzie opened her eyes and sipped the dregs of her piña
colada. It was time to see Paul Newman and get another.
Elaine was half smashed, as usual. She was really a gloriously
pretty animal, with her tawny hair down around her shoulders and that Miss America body. Elaine could still wear a
bikini. Lizzie sighed and tried to hold in her stomach. Elaine
didn't have midriff bulge; Elaine had a double ridge of
muscle from her solar plexus down to her impeccable navel.
Elaine's tits didn't sag when she didn't wear a bra. Elaine
didn't have to get that job with the wire under the cups.
Lizzie sighed again and thought she would have to get to
Kounovsky's more often. What the hell—Garbo was old and
she looked great. What was wrong with *her?* She was only
forty-two years old; that wasn't an old hag. She felt depressed.

"He completely ignores his own child," Elaine said. "He's
doing that damn show every night, playing Daddy Two-
Shoes, and he doesn't care about his own kid. Sometimes I
think he's even forgotten her name. He says she's spoiled. I
tell him, well, *you* never do anything about bringing her up,
so if she's spoiled it's your fault. He says it's my fault because

a girl needs her mother as an example. I tell him, a fine example she's got for a father. She thinks her father is that nice guy she watches on television. She doesn't even *know* that grouch who lives with us."

When they'd first gotten to Vegas, two weeks ago, Lizzie had looked in the paper to see who was playing at each of the hotels. Arnie Gurney, of course, and they'd had to spend several boring evenings with him and that drab he was married to. There was absolutely no one for Lizzie. She'd balled each and every one of the stars years ago, with the exception of Sinatra, and he wouldn't have anything to do with her. There wasn't even an interesting celebrity to talk to anywhere in this crass hotel. There was only the gambling, and as usual she'd done very well, winning more than she'd lost. She and Elaine had decided to stay on for another week or ten days. The trip wasn't costing them anything, and New York in the summer was even worse than here. Elaine sat and complained all the time, but she couldn't decide whether or not to establish residence and divorce Mad Daddy once and for all; she preferred to complain. By midnight every night, Elaine was dead drunk. Elaine attracted a lot of men, but she wouldn't have anything to do with them. It made her feel like more of a martyr to be a faithful wife, and it gave her something else to complain about. Lizzie hadn't had anything either, but she didn't care to drink herself to sleep the way Elaine did. What a shame that Paul Newman look-alike was only a bartender! A middle-aged married woman on vacation away from her husband, having a fling with the hotel bartender, was just too trite. She couldn't lower herself to be trite, no matter what else she did. Why couldn't he really be Paul Newman? He even had that same sexy voice.

"I don't know why I'm still faithful to him," Elaine said. "I know it would serve him right if I wasn't. But I just can't put myself on the level of those whores we know. They're all whores. Oh, not you, Lizzie—you're just a nut."

"This nut is getting another drink," Lizzie said. She looked into her compact, fixed her hair, put on a little more lipstick, and got up.

"Bring me a double vodka on the rocks," Elaine said, handing her the empty glass. "Hundred proof—not the eighty."

God, the tiles were hot! It must be a hundred degrees out. Lizzie hobbled back for her thong sandals and slipped them on. Except for the kids playing, the pool area was deserted.

Everyone was either gambling or sleeping it off. Nobody ever came here to work on their tan or swim. She didn't even know who those two kids Elaine's rotten kid was playing with belonged to. An arm opened the screen door of the cabana apartment to let them in and out. Maybe she should stay indoors, too. Sun aged the skin.

Feeling ancient, Lizzie entered the dim, air-conditioned bar. The bartender saw her and gave her a big, sexy Paul Newman smile. She held in her stomach. Goddam power net anyway; she should have gotten something with a little overblouse.

"How ya doin', Mrs. Libra?" the boy said. He winked.

"Pretty good, Jared." The bar was nearly empty; just two tables with drinkers at them, and a middle-aged bleached blonde with a lot of clanky charm bracelets, playing the one-armed bandit in the corner. Clank, clank went the charm bracelets. Clunk went the steel arm. Clank, clank. Dimes tinkled into the steel well, maybe five or six dimes in all. The woman, whose bracelets by weight alone must have cost five hundred dollars, whooped with joy. Lizzie hoisted herself up to the tall bar stool, wondering if she looked as old and grotesque as that woman.

"You're certainly looking great today, Mrs. L.," the bartender said. "You looked like a little kid standing there in the doorway."

Lizzie smiled. "Yes?"

"Man, your husband is crazy to let you come here alone. Some millionaire is going to carry you off on his yacht." Deftly, he began mixing her another piña colada. "This one is on the house." He winked again.

Lizzie felt her body relaxing. It was crazy to feel old just because Elaine was younger than she was. If there were any men here except creeps and gangsters and husbands and tourists she wouldn't feel so old. She took out a cigarette and Jared was right there with his cigarette lighter aflame for her.

"Hey, I got something to show you," he said. He reached behind him and took out a manila envelope. "Photos. I just had them made. Friend of mine is a photographer."

He spread the photos out on the bar in front of her. He certainly was photogenic, especially with his shirt off. There were the standard arty shots, silhouetted against a desert sunset, on a motorcycle, with a standard-brands pretty girl.

"Your girl?" she asked.

"No, the photographer's wife." He smiled. "I don't have a girl, or a wife."

"Have you ever been married?"

"No, but I have a kid, back home. A boy."

They always said they had an illegitimate kid, and it was always a boy. Lizzie guessed they thought it made them sound more masculine. She figured he was probably a bisexual hustler, but then again, he might not be.

"How old is your son?" she asked.

"Six."

"You don't look old enough."

"I'm twenty-three."

Why were they always twenty-three? They could be nineteen, they could be thirty, but they always said they were twenty-three. She was no fool.

"I haven't seen him in years," he went on. "See, I had these pictures taken because I thought I might be able to do some modeling. I've been doing a little, and they told me to get some good photos. I'm planning to go to L.A. in a couple of weeks."

"You should try New York," Lizzie said, for something to say.

His bright blue eyes lit up. "New York? You're from New York, aren't you? Do you think there's something for me there?"

Lizzie shrugged. "It's the city of broken dreams, baby. That's where it's all happening."

"Do you like my pictures?"

"They're very good. It's too bad you look just like Paul Newman, or you could make it in the movies one-two-three."

"Yeah," he said disgusted. "If someone tells me that one more time . . ." He put the photos back into the envelope. "You know, a day doesn't go by that somebody doesn't ask me for my autograph. Maybe I'll go get my nose broken or something and dye my hair."

"You don't want to be in the movies. That's no life."

"Is your husband in the movie business?"

"He's a publicist and personal manager. Sam Leo Libra."

"Wow," he said. "You're really right in the middle of all that, aren't you? And I thought you were just a little girl."

"I suggest you get tinted contact lenses," Lizzie said. "Prescription."

"Oh, come on. What's the matter with you today? Feeling rotten about something, aren't you?"

"I am feeling rotten about life," Lizzie said. She sipped her drink. It probably had two hundred and fifty calories and she shouldn't have had the first two, either. Well, she wouldn't eat dinner again.

"Hey," he said, "if you ever get really bored around here, I know this groovy bar where they have a live group that's out of sight. They're friends of mine. If you ever wanted to go slumming with a member of the working class, I'd be more than glad to take you there after I get off here."

"You're sweet," Lizzie said.

He lowered his voice. "You like grass?"

She shrugged and smiled.

"I've got something fantastic from Mexico."

"I'm not buying."

"Who said anything about buying?" He sounded hurt. "This is just a present from me to you, as a friend. I'm sorry. It's just that you don't look like those other ladies here."

"How do I look?"

"Alive. Living. You've got this smile that lights up your whole body. I think you're probably a very wild lady when you get going—am I right?"

Lizzie didn't know whether to be flattered or insulted. There it was again, that thing in her that attracted the unlikeliest men. That hunger they smelled out right away, while she was busy trying to look like an asexual teen-ager. She wondered if this boy only wanted her because of what he thought Sam could do for him. He was smiling at her. She tried to read his eyes—nothing. Friendship, sweetness, her face mirrored in their gleam.

"I'm lonely," he said.

"You?"

"Why not? I have no one to talk to here. When I'm not working I just sit in the sun and stay round my room and read and play my guitar. I write songs ... oh, they're not very good, but they amuse me. It can be very lonely here."

"I guess it can," Lizzie said.

"I hate nineteen-year-old girls," he said. "They have nothing to say and they're lousy in bed. They only think about themselves, how they look, do you admire them enough. Nineteen-year-old girls are all alike; nowhere."

"That's a shame."

"What do you want to stay around here for, gambling every night? You never win here, in the end. They take everything away from you."

"I win," Lizzie said.

"Not in the end. Stop when you're ahead. I've been around here a long time; I know."

"There's nothing else to do here," Lizzie said.

"I could take you out on the desert under the stars on my motorcycle."

"You really are a mass of stereotypes, aren't you?"

She expected him to be furious, but he wasn't. "Isn't everybody, till you get to know them?"

"Am I?"

"No ..." he said thoughtfully. "There has always been something a little different, a little mysterious, about you. Like a lost little girl, but secretly wild."

"I bet your songs aren't so bad," Lizzie said.

"I'll sing them for you if we get to know each other better."

I bet you will, she thought. Always auditioning. "I need a doulbe vodka on the rocks for my friend," she said. "Hundred proof."

Later that evening when she was dressing in her room to go downstairs for a late dinner, Lizzie heard a rap on the door. She opened it and was not surprised to see the bartender standing there. He knew her room number from all the bills she had signed. She did not pretend to be surprised and he looked as if he knew she had been expecting him. The night outside was purple velvet and the room was cool. He had not brought his photographs, or his guitar, or the pot he had promised her. He had, however, brought his incredible face, a perfect body to go with it, and a beautiful cock, hard and smooth as marble. She let him do it to her because he was there and it would have seemed hysterical to throw him out, and because she ached with loneliness. She felt nothing. He was nobody. It was strange to feel nothing with a boy that beautiful. She was glad when it was over.

He told her she was wild and wonderful, that he wanted to get a lot more of her, and several other lies, and then he dressed and went away, after making her promise to see him in the bar the next day. Lizzie took another shower, and discovered with surprise when she went to make up her face again that she had seldom looked more radiant. She felt empty and a failure, and she looked beautiful. Sex was a very strange deception. She would have to discuss it at length with

Dr. Picker when she got back. She inwardly cringed at the thought of admitting her failure to the old letch.

When she met Elaine in the bar Elaine said, "Well, you certainly look rested. What did you do, catch a nap?"

"Yes," Lizzie lied. For dinner she had a lettuce salad with lemon juice instead of dressing, and black coffee. She began to feel better. He was twenty-three! If she'd made him sick he wouldn't have been able to do it, no matter what he wanted to get out of the wife of Sam Leo Libra.

"Daddy never helps me around the house when the maid isn't there," Elaine was droning over her seventh martini. "He wouldn't lift a finger to help me if I was dying of cancer. Not once does he ever offer to help in the kitchen. He wouldn't make himself a sandwich if he was starving to death. Other husbands bring their wives breakfast in bed. Lizzie, what do you think I ought to do? Should I stay here and divorce him? What do you think, Lizzie? *Now*, while I'm still young?"

"I think we should go home tomorrow," Lizzie said.

"Home?"

"Yes. New York. I'll get the reservations now."

"Oh. Well, all right . . ."

Lizzie went to the desk and booked two seats on the two-o'clock jet. That would give them time to sleep late and pack. Anything as long as they got out of here before that damned King Cactus Bar beckoned to her again with its message of temptation and defeat. Never, never had she ever done it before with a bartender, beach boy, or gigolo.

What's going to become of me? Lizzie Libra wondered, feeling panic for the first time in her life.

＝＝＝＝＝＝＝＝＝＝＝＝＝＝＝＝＝＝＝＝＝＝＝＝＝＝

CHAPTER

SEVENTEEN

＝＝＝＝＝＝＝＝＝＝＝＝＝＝＝＝＝＝＝＝＝＝＝＝＝＝

LATE that summer, Silky Morgan began rehearsals for *Mavis!*, which was now called (temporarily) *The Love Ticket*. The first time she saw Dick was on the first morning of the first line reading, in a hot, bare room where they all sat around a long table. He gave her a warm smile and shook her hand. She almost choked to death.

"You've lost weight," Dick said.

She nodded.

"It's becoming. Don't lose any more, though." Then he introduced her to the cast, which was mixed, and to the author, a middle-aged white cat who looked as if the only black person he'd ever known was his maid. She figured he was just trying to get on the bandwagon with this musical because black was in, but after a while she discovered he wasn't so bad; he had an impish sense of humor, humility, and he owned every record she'd ever made. Two really old white guys had written the songs, and they weren't even there. Silky had always thought that Broadway was very exciting, but now she began to think it was like the stock market, full of old guys selling blue-chip stocks, with gambling reserved for the wild and the crazy. The only decent thing the show had, it seemed to her, was Dick Devere.

She tried to do everything she had learned from Simon Budapest, and felt very dissatisfied with the first day of readings, but Dick said nothing to criticize her. Afterwards she hung around hoping he would talk to her, but he patted her on the shoulder and told her to run along home as he had to talk to the author about changes. She went into the hot street, feeling lonely and sad, trying to pretend she was in a hurry so no one in the cast would try to be friendly to her and ask her to go for coffee or anything.

Dick had given her the script in a beautiful dark-red leather folder, from one of those fancy leather stores, with her name embossed in gold on the front. That was evidently what a star got. She was a star. It seemed unreal. She stroked the smooth leather and tried to think of herself as a star, but all she felt like was a scared kid who was going to make a disgrace of herself in front of a lot of strangers.

That night she had a cup of tea and studied her lines in her room. She'd been working with the choreographer for a couple of weeks now, and the play made more sense than the first time she'd seen it. She thought the songs were square, but she'd only heard them played on a piano and croaked out by the two ancients who wrote them, so that was no way to judge. She wished she had someone to discuss things with. She couldn't go to Mr. Libra; she was afraid of him. She couldn't go to Mr. Budapest; she was afraid of him, too. She was more afraid of Dick than of anybody. It was ridiculous— here she was, a star, and she had nobody to ask about anything. On impulse she dialed Gerry at home.

Gerry was out, and her roommate Bonnie, who sounded like a scared mouse who'd just been awakened, said she'd give her the message if she saw her. The world seemed deserted.

Silky took a bath and went to bed at nine o'clock. Her muscles hurt from the dance routines—it seemed as if they had always hurt now and would hurt for the rest of her life. Was this what dancers did for a living? They must be insane. Who wanted to be in pain all the time?

The phone rang at midnight and woke her up. It was Hatcher Wilson, in town for a few days. Silky was unaccountably glad to hear from him. He seemed like an old friend. See, just when you thought you had nobody in the world, someone always turned up . . .

"I've got so much to tell you," Silky said.

"Me, too."

"You first."

"I'm getting *married,* baby! How do you like that?"

Married? *Him?* She couldn't believe it. She tried to keep
the surprise and disappointment out of her voice. "Hey, that's
groovy. Who is she?"

"A chick I met on the road. We're getting married this
weekend in Connecticut. She's a dancer and a singer. We're
going to do a single together. I wrote it myself for us. You
want to come to the recording session on Friday?"

"I have to rehearse. I'm going to star in a Broadway
musical."

"I read about it. How's it going?"

"Fine," she lied. "It's exciting and fun. A lot of work, but
you know ..."

"Everything's work, baby. You don't get anything for
nothing in this business."

"I know. Well, I'm sorry I won't be able to go to your
recording session ... and I'd like to have met your fiancée."

"You'll meet her. How about you? You still going with
that director or whatever he is?"

"He's directing my show."

"Mmm *hmm.*" He gave a dirty grunt.

"We're just friends. I haven't time for any of that now."

"When did you ever?" Hatcher said, and laughed.

"Well," Silky said. "It was nice talking to you. I have to go
to sleep now; I get up very early."

"Okay. Catch you later." He hung up. She realized she
hadn't asked him where he was staying, and he hadn't volun-
teered the information. The girl probably wouldn't understand that they'd always been just friends.

Friends ... had they even been friends? Now she realized
they had been, and that all these months when she was eating
her heart out for Dick she should have taken time to look at
Hatcher and see that he wasn't just a bum, that even he
could fall in love and get married. Maybe she could have
married him, if things had been different. But would she have
wanted to? Now she would never know. He was the only guy
she really knew, except for Dick, and now he was in love and
getting married and lost forever. Well, lost for the first year,
anyway. She'd never paid one bit of attention to Hatcher
Wilson, but now she felt rejected. Time went by so fast and
she did nothing. She'd be an old maid for sure, and being a
famous old maid wouldn't help at night when she was all
alone in a hotel like somebody who didn't belong anywhere
... like somebody's old suitcase ... transient ... ready to go
at a moment's notice ... where?

She slept badly, had a piece of gum for breakfast, and was at rehearsal early. She hoped she'd have a chance to see Dick alone, but he arrived when the rest of the cast was already there. He was wearing the same clothes as the day before and needed a shave.

The weeks blended into one another, work and panic. They got into the theater and started blocking the show. Now Dick yelled at her when she did something wrong, screamed as if offended that she'd once been his girl and now was only someone stupid who kept doing things wrong. Gerry came to a couple of rehearsals and told her she was marvelous.

"Dick doesn't think so," Silky said.

"He does so. He told me. The only reason he yells at you is this is his first Broadway show and he's more scared than you are. You're going to be wonderful."

"What do you think of the show?" The show was now called (temporarily) *Movin' On.*

"I think it's pretty good. The songs are good. I can see three right now that are going to be hits. I hate the title, but they'll change that."

"Do you really think I'm okay?"

"You're more than okay."

"Well, I just wish I knew for sure."

"You've been working awfully hard," Gerry said, looking her up and down. "Are you getting enough sleep?"

"Eight hours every night, sometimes more."

"You look kind of skinny. Do you eat?"

"Sure," Silky lied.

"Well, maybe you should take vitamins or something."

"I do." That was true, anyway.

"You really look skinny," Gerry said. "How much do you weigh?"

"I don't know."

"Well, maybe you should drink Tiger's Milk or Gorilla Milk or something. If you get run down you'll catch a cold, God forbid, and that's the worst thing that can happen in rehearsal because you never get rid of it. Eat steak. That gives you energy. Tartar steak, if you can stand it. I don't want to sound like your mother, but if Mr. Libra sees you looking like this he'll yell and scream worse than Dick ever did, and you know it."

"Okay," Silky said. That night after rehearsal she went to Alexander's, which was open late, and bought a padded bra, a padded panty girdle, and a lumpy-looking wool sweater and a thick tweed skirt. They made her look like she'd gained ten pounds.

She wore them to rehearsal the next day, which was a lucky thing because Mr. Libra showed up. He didn't seem to notice anything and he told her that she was coming along fine and if she needed anything to come to him. That was a laugh. She just needed a new heart, one with courage, that didn't have a crack in it that couldn't seem to heal.

Dick had acquired an assortment of interchangeable girls who came to rehearsals at night to pick him up. They all had long hair, big busts, and tight dresses that showed a lot of superior leg. They also had false eyelashes and the same face: vapid, self-consciously pretty, and smug. Since she never did see the same one twice, Silky knew that smug look didn't last for long. This was a funny new scene for Dick—he used to stay with one girl for a while, but now he had turned into Mr. One-Night Stand, like he wanted to make it with every girl in the world. She wondered why.

One evening Gerry came to rehearsal and brought her roommate, Bonnie Parker. Bonnie was a beautiful girl but Dick paid no attention to her after giving her a falsely hearty greeting, and Silky wondered why. She would have thought Bonnie would be just the sort of girl Dick would want to go to bed with. Maybe he already had, and was through with her, just like with that long string of rehearsal girls. Bonnie certainly didn't seem to mind; she looked perfectly pleased with herself and flirted outrageously with the stage manager.

A new girl picked Dick up after rehearsal and Silky went home alone. She was exhausted and she had to get her clothes together to decide what to take to Boston next week when they opened there. It seemed as if she was so exhausted lately that she could hardly move by five o'clock, much less the late hours they finished torturing her. She was tired at night and tired when she got up in the morning. She had missed her period, more than a month ago, and she couldn't understand why, because she hadn't been near a man in *months*. It was probably nerves. She felt more nervous than anyone on earth.

In her room she took off her clothes and padded underwear and looked at herself in the mirror. She looked like a Halloween skeleton! She was drenched in sweat from wearing those hot clothes in the hot theater, and she felt faint. It was September and still hot, and those layers of clothes she padded herself with were just like a sweat suit. She took a

cold shower and forced herself to put on a clean cotton dress
and sandals so she could go downstairs and eat something.
There was a coffee shop on the corner and she went in and
ordered a bowl of soup because it was the only thing she
thought she could get down. As usual, she had two spoonfuls
and felt her throat close. She was hungry, but she couldn't
eat. *I'm going to die,* she thought in terror. *I'm going to die
before we even open.*

She looked at herself in the mirror above the counter and
saw only eyes and mouth, like a caricature. Her cheekbones
stuck out like little knives. She must have lost thirty pounds.
Could you lose ten pounds a month? Why not? And it had
been more than three months since Dick had dumped her; it
had been forever. Forever . . . she was drying up, disappearing . . . vanishing. She ordered a Coke, drank a third of it,
and paid the check.

Silky liked Boston because it was a change from New
York and she'd gotten to miss traveling now that she and the
girls didn't go on the road any more. She was sorry she didn't
have more time to walk around and look at the city, but they
were working day and night. The show was now called
Mavis! again. There wouldn't be any more big script changes
until after the Boston opening, just some cuts. The first time
she played to a real audience, at the first run-through, she
was surprised that she had only one moment of panic; then
suddenly the audience seemed just like the people in her
night-club audience (except she was wearing a body mike)
and she could see the faces in the front row just as if she
were playing a club. When she sang, as always she forgot the
people were even there. Their applause rose up to her like
waves of love. It was *real! She* was *real!*

Then, the night of the next-to-last run-through, during her
second song, she felt herself blacking out. She was freezing
cold and sweat was pouring down her face; she saw black
and green lights in front of her eyes, there was a buzzing in
her ears, and she couldn't feel the stage under her feet. When
she came to she was lying on the cot in her dressing room
and everyone was shouting.

Dick was leaning over her, his face pale and very concerned. Behind him, she saw Mr. Libra, who had come down
to Boston for the week, and who was now fading away and
coming back right in front of her eyes like a surrealistic
movie. She tried to get up.

"I have to go back there . . . what happened?"

"Lie down, you little fool," Dick snapped. He pushed her down on the cot. "The show's over."

Suddenly, Mr. Libra was there, shoving Dick away, suddenly nice, a different Mr. Libra than she had ever known. "You really are a horse's ass," he said to Dick. He put his hand on Silky's forehead. "You don't have any temperature," he said, mildly. "Were you scared?"

"No," she said.

"Maybe you ate a bad clam. I told you not to eat tourist food."

"She doesn't eat anything," the wardrobe mistress said self-righteously. "I told her. She's killing herself."

"What do you mean, 'the show's over'?" Silky said. She started to cry.

"Just for tonight," Mr. Libra said. "You'll be fine tomorrow. I've sent for Ingrid, the Lady Doctor, she's flying down. She'll be here in less than an hour. She'll fix you right up. Don't you worry, we're not going to lose our star, or our show either."

"Look . . . I didn't mean to yell at you," Dick said.

She held out her hand for a Kleenex and Mr. Libra gave her the box.

"Do you think you can make it to a cab now, or should I get an ambulance?"

"No ambulance!" She blew her nose. "What did you do with all the people?"

"They went home," said Mr. Libra, "where they're probably screwing for the first time in years. I will hold you personally responsible for the population explosion in this town. Here, put your arm around Dick's shoulders; he's stronger than he looks."

Dick was carrying her in his arms, she had her head on his shoulder just as if she was a little girl again and he was her papa. She hadn't thought the name "Papa" in years. It was always: *her father*, as if he were somebody abstract. Dick even had a bony shoulder like her papa. His arms were strong and gentle. She had loved him once, so much, so long ago . . . Dick . . . but this wasn't Dick, it was just somebody named Dick, who was directing her show. He was holding her at last, the way she'd dreamed for so long, and he wasn't the man Dick she'd loved, he was just something kind and strong and gentle she needed. She was more afraid of being sick or maybe dying than she was of losing Dick. She came first. She had to get well. They had sent those people away who had come to see her show and maybe they would come back and try again, or maybe other people would come, and she had to be ready for them. They were waiting to try to love her and she had to make them love her. Imagine—they had sent all those people away! Just because she was sick, they had sent away a whole theater full of people! Oh, how she loved those people ... how she loved Dick's arms around her ... strong arms she knew at last she was strong enough to go on without.

They took her to her hotel, which was a block from the theater, and put her to bed. They left one lamp on, on the dresser, and the door open a crack, while Dick and Mr. Libra waited in the living room for Ingrid.

". . . house doctor," Dick was saying. "I don't see why we can't send for the hotel physician, who is perfectly capable . . ."

They were trying to talk softly, but she could hear them. She heard someone pacing the floor: Mr. Libra? Dick?

"I don't want someone perfectly capable, I want the best," Libra said angrily. "You're a son of a bitch lately, do you know that? I knew you whored around, but this is getting ridiculous. And you're a grouch. I think I'm going to have Ingrid give you a shot, too, give everyone a shot. God knows, I need another one. Jesus, did anybody remember to call Lizzie?"

"I thought you'd remember *that*," Dick said.

"I need Gerry," Libra said. "Where the hell is Gerry? I can't get along without Gerry."

The doorbell rang.

"Thank God, Room Service," Dick said.

"I need Ingrid, not Room Service," said Libra.

The door closed.

"Have some Scotch," Dick said. "You'll feel better."

"Watch Nero tipple while Rome burns."

"Christ, they brought the wrong kind of gin."

"I hope you don't think Silky's paying for that booze," Libra said. "I hope you had the decency to charge it to your room."

"Of course I did." Dick sounded insulted.

The doorbell rang.

"Dear Sam! I came as fast as I could."

"Ingrid, thank God. The kid collapsed on stage. She's asleep now, I think. In there."

"I just wash my hands first, please."

A large woman in a black coat came clumping into the

room on her way to the bathroom. Silky pretended to be asleep. The woman put a black doctor's bag on the chair and went into the bathroom and shut the door. The doorbell rang again.

"Gerry!" Libra cried.

"I registered us both for the night," Gerry said. "I thought you might need me, too."

"I don't need you, but as long as you're here I'm glad to see you," Libra said calmly.

"Hello, Dick," Gerry said. Her voice was very cool.

"Hello, Gerry."

"I thought you two were over that foolishness," Libra said.

"It's nothing personal," Gerry said. "I just don't like seeing this selfish, egotistical, insecure, hostile turd driving a friend of mine to suicide."

"What suicide?" Libra said.

"Silky," said Gerry. "I saw it coming, I should have done something, but I didn't know what to do. It's my fault too. The poor kid was so scared and miserable she tried to starve herself to death."

"Suicide?"—Libra, unbelieving.

"I don't know what else you'd call it."—Gerry, cold.

"What suicide?"—Libra. "Spades don't commit suicide. Statistics show they have the lowest suicide rate in the country."

Silence.

"All right."—Libra, conciliatory. "If you want to think Silky tried to starve herself to death, I guess you know more about young girls than I do."

"I just don't understand how you could sit there and let her do it, Dick."—Gerry. "I watched you in rehearsals. You drove that girl up the wall. She's still in love with you. You could have gone easier on her. She took everything you said personally."

"Would it have been better if I had told her she was wonderful and then let her wake up to lousy reviews?"—Dick. "I did it for her—I *wanted* her to be a success. Maybe I did it the wrong way, but it's the only way I know how."

"What do you think, Dick? Seriously."—Libra, dead earnest.

"I think she's going to be a smash. I think she's going to be a star. I didn't think so at first, but I knew she had a chance if she worked her ass off. Now I know it."—Dick.

Oh, Dick, Dick said it! And it was clear he meant it. He knew she was going to be a smash, a star!

The woman, Ingrid, came out of the bathroom, wearing a white nylon nurse's uniform and snapped on the overhead light.

"Wake up, my dear."

Silky pretended to wake up, and Gerry and Mr. Libra came peering around the doorway. Gerry smiled hello, and Silky smiled back. She was really glad to see Gerry. Ingrid took a small glass vial out of the doctor's bag, and then a paper strip of disposable hypodermic needles. Silky didn't like the look of the bottle or the needles.

"What's that?" she said.

"Just vitamins and some other things to make you feel better and stronger right away," Ingrid said in a foreign accent.

"I don't want it."

"Don't be silly," Mr. Libra said.

"Tell me what it is."

"I told you," the woman said.

Silky didn't like that the bottle didn't have any label on it, and she didn't like the look of the woman, either. The woman grabbed her arm and swabbed it off with a piece of cotton dipped in alcohol.

"Why doesn't that bottle say anything?" she demanded.

"Because Ingrid makes it herself," Mr. Libra said triumphantly. "It's her secret love potion. I have one every day. You'll feel wonderful in a few minutes, never know you were sick."

"Vitamins don't make you feel wonderful in a few minutes," Silky said. "What else is in it?"

The woman had her arm in fingers like steel. Silky tried to pull away.

"You'll have to hold her, Sam, she's hysterical."

Then Silky really did get hysterical. She didn't know why she knew, but she knew it was dope. She had always suspected, without really thinking about it, that Libra was on something, but she had always thought it was his business and none of hers. But now it *was* her business. "Stop it!" she screamed, struggling to cover her arm with her other hand, to get away. "Stop it! Gerry, don't let her give me dope, don't let her, *I'll get hooked like him!*"

Ingrid stuck her with the needle. Apeface Libra was holding her arm, and he looked sorry for her, as if she was just having a paranoid fit. Gerry's eyes were wide open in shock. Silky could see from her face that she knew, too. The only one who didn't know was Libra. The junkie fake doctor's eyes were like tiny, black holes. She knew, all right. Her mouth looked as if it had been basted together with stitches.

"There, there," Libra said kindly. He let go of her arm.

"What a display," Ingrid said. "It is childish to be afraid of needles."

Silky had never taken speed, but she knew what to expect because a lot of her friends back home had tried it, and some were hooked; she knew more about that scene than she wanted to . . . so, when the trip started she was not surprised, just frightened and desperate under the up that made her feel so strong and happy. Funny how a cat who had the bread could be a junkie all his life and nobody ever had to know about it. He didn't have to steal, he didn't have to hustle, he didn't have to go through the bad times when he needed a fix because he never had to need a fix. Libra had the bread and Ingrid was ready. And the damn fool didn't even know he was hooked.

"There, don't you feel better already?" Libra said. "You look better. A few more of those before the show opens in New York and there'll be no stopping you."

"Can I please talk to Gerry?" Silky said.

"No talking," Ingrid snapped. "Rest." She tossed the hypodermic and bottle into her doctor's bag and snapped it shut.

"Why don't you throw the needle away?" Gerry asked, too sweetly. "It's disposable, isn't it?"

"The maid probably has a bad enough impression of show business people as it is," Ingrid said.

Libra laughed. "Come on, Ingrid, I'll show you to your room. Did you have dinner?"

"I brought some organic vegetables with me," Ingrid said. She went into the living room with Libra.

"Come on, Gerry," Libra called.

"Just a sec . . . I'm helping Silky change into a nightgown," Gerry called. She shut the door fast and locked it. Then she sat on the bed. She didn't say anything.

"It's speed," Silky said.

"Amphetamine?"

"Yeah. I can feel it. I'm really up there with the little birds. They ought to put that whore in jail and throw away the key."

"I always thought Libra acted funny," Gerry said. "What do you think is going to happen now?"

"Nothing, if I ever take it again. Gerry, you got to stop them. I don't want her to give me any more."

"I'll tell him."

"He won't listen."

"I know."

"He's hooked," Silky said. "And if she keeps giving it to me I'll get hooked. I didn't fight all my life to get where I am to turn into a junkie, man. Shee-it, what the fuck am I going to do?" She knew she was stoned because she was talking like the old Silky. She was going to fight like the old Silky, too. But she couldn't think; her mind was going in fifteen directions at once and none of them made any sense.

"How many times do you have to take it before you get hooked?" Gerry asked.

"Four, five, maybe."

"Not less?"

"Sometimes less. Depends on the person and how much you want it."

"We can't start accusing people," Gerry said. "You don't need that kind of publicity, not right now, not you, a pop singer. Nobody will understand. And it'll wreck Mr. Libra's career, too. It's just too chancey right before a show opens, and you can't take the time ... you have to spend every minute getting well and getting strong so you can take care of your own life."

"You're a real company girl, aren't you? And I thought you were my friend."

"I am your friend. Do you want to open in that show or do you want to be out of work forever just because people think you're taking dope?"

"It's not fair, dammit!"

"I know it's not fair, but we just don't have time. I'll call off that Ingrid somehow ... I don't know how, but I will. I want you to promise me to eat like a horse and stop acting silly. I'll get you a real doctor tomorrow and he'll give you some real vitamins."

"The funny thing is ..." Silky said. "Right now I feel as if I could get right up and do the show just fine."

"I bet you do," Gerry said. She got up. "Don't worry. I'll take care of everything. I promise. I *promise*." She smiled and unlocked the door.

Then she looked back at Silky and she was no longer
smiling. Her face was scared, like a little kid.

"What is it?" Silky said, scared now, too.

"Libra," Gerry said. "Oh, wow. I feel just like someone
punched me in the stomach. I feel like . . . I suddenly have an
addict in the family. Silky, you have no idea how fond I've
gotten of that man. Now I've got to tell him he's got some
terrible disease. Oh, wow." Her eyes were full of tears.

How could Gerry like him so much? Silky couldn't stand
him. Oh, well, to each his own.

She was really beginning to like the feeling the shot gave
her. She didn't like that her heart was pounding and her
hands were shaking and her mouth had gotten dry, but she
liked feeling on top of everything, as if she could cope with
anything that happened now. She didn't love Dick any more;
he was just another guy she'd once known. She loved the
show, weak as it was, and she loved the songs. She loved her
audience, every one of those dear people who'd paid all that
money to come to see her and applaud for her and laugh at
the phony *schticks* she'd rehearsed so hard until they seemed
spontaneous. She loved singing, and she loved her voice. No
one in the business sounded like her when she really let go.
She prayed to God to make her hate this powerful, carefree
feeling, to give her the courage to remember it and recreate
it when she hadn't had the shot. She'd even go back to the
misery if she could only stay off the speed. It was so easy to
have the speed . . . she could have it all the time, free, with
Libra's blessing. *Help me, Jesus,* she prayed. *Help me do it
on my own. Help me hate Mr. Libra.*

She'd almost forgotten why she'd always hated Mr. Libra,
but she knew she'd remember in the morning. She had to
remember, now.

CHAPTER

EIGHTEEN

THE next three days were the most frantic Gerry had ever spent in her life. The opening was put off for forty-eight hours so Silky could pull herself together. Gerry called Lizzie Libra in New York, who knew everyone or could find them, and got the name of a good Boston doctor for Silky. The doctor said Silky was suffering from malnutrition, nerves, and deep depression, gave her some vitamin shots (with nothing else in them), some sleeping pills (which Silky threw down the toilet), a bland, high-energy diet to follow, and a complete physical examination, including a chest X ray (since her mother had died of TB). Lizzie wanted to send for her analyst, Dr. Picker, but no one approved of that idea at all so he didn't come.

Then Gerry confronted Libra, alone. "I feel I ought to tell you this," she said. "If I don't tell you, I don't know who else will. That Ingrid the doctor, or whatever she is, has been filling you up with shots that aren't vitamins. They're some kind of amphetamine; methedrine, I think."

Libra stared at her for a moment, then he laughed. "You're even more paranoid than I am, sweetie."

"No, no, I mean it! Silky knew. Ingrid gave her one and she felt the effects."

"She felt nothing," Libra said. "The kid's hysterical. You're a college graduate—are you going to listen to some *misha gos* from a slum bunny?"

"Who's to know better about drugs than a slum bunny, as you keep calling her? And don't try to flatter me to change the subject by reminding me I'm a college graduate. You can learn a lot about drugs in college these days. Mr. Libra, you've got to listen to me. Go get that stuff analyzed at a lab. Please! That woman may be killing you."

"I'll tell you who'll get killed," Libra said pleasantly. "You will. By me, if you don't get your ass back to work this instant and stop bothering me."

"Why do you always get so hopped up, then?" Gerry said, beginning to get angry at his denseness. "You always run to the gym right after you get your shot because you can't sit still. You never eat. You hardly ever sleep. I know how often you make me call the drugstore to renew your sleeping pills. I see your hand shake when you're writing something. And you're paranoid, you know it, you say so yourself. That's the methedrine."

"It's the vitamins that give me the energy," Libra said. "The vitamins and my implacable wish to get ahead in this world. Which you obviously don't have or you wouldn't be standing here deliberately trying to lose your job."

"Are you saying you're going to fire me?"

"I just might if you don't shut up."

"You mean you'd fire me on grounds of attempted blackmail? You know I'd never tell anybody but you."

"No," he said, "not blackmail. On the grounds of insanity."

"I give up," Gerry said. "I just give up. You think you're so smart, smarter than anybody else in the world. And all this time you're being victimized by a *concentration camp matron!*" She turned and walked out of the room. She wasn't sorry for him any more, she was just furious; furious at him because he liked being high so much that he wouldn't even let himself suspect he wasn't high on miracle vitamins because then he'd have to give them up. And she was even more furious at Ingrid. She'd like to smash all that woman's little vials and stamp on them and then smash the bitch in the face.

"Gerry!" Libra called after her.

She came back, hoping he was going to change his mind, almost ready to cry from relief.

"If Silky hates Ingrid that much I'll keep her away," he

said. "I know Silky put you up to this. That doctor you hired just sent me his bill. I don't have to pay two doctors for Silky."

"Thank God! And you'll send Ingrid home?"

"Who said anything about home? Ingrid's staying here with me. *I* find her valuable, even if you two don't appreciate her."

Poor old junkie, Gerry thought. *But at least Silky's safe.* She knew that with Libra you could never win an entire battle, and she ought to be glad she won at least part of one. Maybe he was so miserable he needed the drugs. Who knew what went on in that man's mind?

Silky had no aftereffects from Ingrid's shot, except some mild stomach cramps, and Gerry spent nearly every waking moment with her, which seemed to reassure Silky very much. Dick went out of his way to be gentle, and on opening night he sent Silky a huge floral arrangement and a nice telegram telling her he was proud of her. There was an even bigger floral arrangement from Libra, a small one from Gerry, telegrams from Lizzie, Hatcher Wilson and his new bride, the composers, the author, the King James Version (Gerry wondered if Libra had sent it), and some people whom Silky didn't seem to know. There was even a telegram from the Satins, saying they were proud of their very own star, which Gerry was sure Libra had ordered them to send. Silky's Auntie Grace and several members of her family came down to the opening, and Silky put them all up at the hotel, in double rooms, two to a room—a far cry from her poor days in the Chelsea.

Since Elaine had returned from Las Vegas, Gerry called Mad Daddy at the television station to tell him where she had disappeared to, and he telephoned her every afternoon in her room after he had finished taping his own show. They missed each other. They had become very close after that first day they spent together—in fact, inseparable. Their friendship and understanding had turned into a romance almost immediately, and into an affair as well. He was a champion necker, as she had known he would be, but she was rather surprised to find that he was a champion lover. She didn't know now why she'd thought he would be childish or innocent in bed.

Mad Daddy was depressed and almost shocked when Elaine came back to him with no more talk of divorce. He had really been counting on it this time. He was the one who brought the subject up with Gerry; she didn't feel it was any of her business, although she was more disappointed than she wanted to admit to herself when Elaine came back. On the phone, she told Mad Daddy about Libra and Silky and Ingrid's mysterious shots.

"I knew he'd never believe me," she told Mad Daddy. "Imagine trying to convince someone he's a drug addict."

"I know," he said. "I've been trying to convince Elaine she's an alcoholic, but she won't listen to me either. You can never convince these people. Gerry, why can't we go to our desert island?"

"Maybe we will," she said.

"Why can't we just run away together? Why can't people do what they want to do?"

"For one thing, we won't live long on bananas."

"Come home soon. I miss you. I love you a lot."

"I love you a lot, too," she said. Somehow, qualifying it made "love" sound less trite. They'd all been in love before. It was a shame, but no one who was a grown-up came to anyone else newly minted and pure at heart. Still, she loved him in a different way than she'd loved anyone else. He made her feel happy all the time. No doubts, no inner questioning, no games to play. He was happiness, everything good. She wanted to keep anything bad from ever happening to him. If he divorced Elaine, fine—if he didn't, fine, too. She wasn't going to hurry him because he was hers now in every way except living together. It was too soon to ask for more. She had never been so calm and secure in her life.

Silky was brilliant on opening night, and the complicated scenery moved without a hitch. There were seven curtain calls. The reviews were pretty bad for the show, and unanimously raves for Silky. The New York opening was put ahead for three weeks so the author could revise the show and the composers could add two new songs. Libra already had a recording contract for the score, and although everyone was frantic and overworked there was an air of optimism about the whole company. The show would improve, and they knew Silky could hold it and make it run. Gerry felt a surge of pride at being involved in this whole exciting business.

She was in a state near euphoria. Over a month before, right after she'd begun to go with Mad Daddy, Dick had taken her to lunch and presented her with a gold unicorn pin with a diamond-studded horn, from David Webb. "You're the maiden who charms the unicorn," he told her. He didn't know anything about Mad Daddy, so Gerry assumed he meant himself.

"The unicorn is a mythical beast," she said.

"So am I."

She almost laughed in his face. There he was, his famous kiss-off pin in his hand, trying to get rid of her and keep her tied to him in memory, all at the same time. She didn't know how Dick could be so dumb and crass as to give her a kiss-off pin when she knew all about that phenomenon. At first she was tempted to give it back, but then she took it and put it into her bureau drawer and forgot about it. Bonnie came down to Boston for opening night, more to chase the stage manager than to see the show, as Bonnie had next to no interest in the theater or anything else that didn't involve herself. In a moment of bliss, that she'd been in since she started going with Mad Daddy, Gerry told Bonnie to take the unicorn pin out of the drawer and keep it, since she'd always wanted it anyway.

"I knew I'd get one one way or the other," Bonnie said cheerfully.

When the show got to New York everyone was feeling the effects of the hard work and strain, but Silky had gained five pounds and looked well. She'd had a bad scare and was really trying to take care of herself now. Gerry wished there was a man for Silky, but she knew that once Silky was a Broadway star there would be parties and admirers and she'd have a choice. She hoped Silky would pick better this time around.

Opening night in New York, there were even more flowers, more telegrams, people rushing around, the four Satins recruited, wreathed in saccharine smiles, the B.P.'s and many of their friends, all the inveterate first-nighters, a healthy sprinkling of celebrities. The word was out that the show was nothing much but that there was going to be a bright new star. The columns had been full of Silky Morgan for weeks. Policemen on horseback guarded the sawhorses that kept the first-night civilians at bay, and long black limousines lined the curb. Flashbulbs popped, a klieg light split the sky. Libra had arranged everything—it was an autograph-hunter's dream.

The first five minutes after the curtain went up Silky seemed a little frightened and unsure. But as soon as she had her first song she was the same old Silky—confident, emotional, soaring, a bright bird you couldn't shoot down with a firing squad of machine guns. When the show was over, the

audience gave her a standing ovation. The audience was as
intoxicated by the knowledge that they were in on the emer-
gence of a star as they were by Silky's charisma. She stood
there on the stage, taking bows, looking small and skinny and
young, tears pouring down her face. The audience loved the
tears—they couldn't have expected more from a Miss America. Gerry didn't like the tears at all. She knew Silky too well.

There was a party afterwards upstairs at Sardi's while they
waited for the reviews. Silky came in with Libra and Lizzie
and Dick (Dick had an elegant-looking blonde in tow and
maneuvered her into all his photographs, then spent most of
the evening table-hopping and ignoring her).

Mad Daddy had come with Elaine. Gerry realized suddenly that if she'd needed a date for the opening, instead of
hovering around backstage to be of moral support to Silky,
she would not have known whom to ask. It was ridiculous;
she was loved, cherished, and she had no one. But what no
one else might have understood was that she didn't feel
alone. She knew Mad Daddy was with her. She wondered
how many people sitting at those tables with the people they
were married to, or the people they were being seen with
because it was good for them, had other people somewhere
else they were with in spirit right this minute.

There was a buffet with food, but Gerry didn't feel like
eating, so she wandered around saying hello to people she
knew and then went to the bar and had the drink she felt she
really deserved. It was hard to believe the show had finally
opened. She would believe it when she saw the reviews.
Elaine Fellin was sitting with Lizzie Libra, hoarding her own
private bottle of champagne. Mad Daddy spent a polite
amount of time with her and then came looking for Gerry.

"We look so great together," he said. "Do you think
anybody's noticing how great we look together?"

"I notice it all the time," she said. "Wow, I really missed
you when I was away."

"Me too. You don't have to worry any more, do you?"

"No."

"That's good. I hated it. Hey, I have something for you."

He took something out of his pocket, polished it off on his
dinner jacket, looked around furtively and put it on Gerry's
middle finger. It was the new Mad Daddy Secret Code Ring,
about to go on the market in a few days. She had always
worn rings on her middle finger when she was a kid.

"That's the original," he said. "It's worth a hundred thousand dollars, give or take ninety-eight cents. Now you're officially my girl."

"I'll never take it off."

"You can take it off when I give you the real one."

"I thought that was the real one."

"I mean a real ring, silly," he said. "You know, a rock. I asked Elaine for a divorce today. I told her it was crazy going on the way we were, miserable all the time."

"What did she say?"

"She said okay but I'd have to pay for it. She wants a lot but I don't care; I figure I owe it to her. It's my bail money."

"You didn't tell her about me, did you?"

"Of course not. And I have an appointment to see my attorney tomorrow, and I'm going to move to a hotel. I thought maybe next to the office—then you could run in and see me a lot, like you were going to the water cooler."

"That would be wonderful! I'll have Mr. Libra arrange it. He has pull at the hotel."

"Will he get me a water cooler?"

"*I'll* get you a water cooler."

"And then when I'm free," he said, "will you marry me?"

So this was the way it happened! The knight on the white charger, everything she'd dreamed of since she was a little girl, the proposal . . . Here he was . . . standing in the middle of a crowded opening-night party, whispering so no one would hear, standing discreetly away from her so his wife at a far-away table would not see them. And she loved him so much she couldn't bear it. Well, if this was the way life turned out, then let it be this way. She felt dizzy with happiness and she knew she was blushing.

"Do you mean it?" she said.

"Of course I mean it. Will you?"

"You bet I will!"

"Oh, wow," he said. The way he looked, stunned with happiness, she could believe this was the first time it had really happened to him. Maybe, no matter how often you'd been through it, there was a real first time for two people, a time that could never have been duplicated if they had not found each other.

The reviews came in then, and they were better than Gerry had expected: mixed—one critic even liked the show, the others said it was weak but fun, and everyone loved Silky. This morning Silky Morgan was a star. It was a wonderful engagement present. Gerry and Mad Daddy held hands under the newspaper.

"I'll meet you later, okay?" he whispered.

"Okay."

"I'll call you at home in about an hour."

"Okay."

He squeezed her hand and went back to his table. Elaine was screaming at some woman, standing up with her hands on the edge of the table for support. Poor Elaine. Poor Mad Daddy . . . no, not any more. Poor everybody who was alone or trapped with someone they didn't love or respect. Silky was surrounded by well-wishers. She looked happy but tired. As usual, Libra hadn't spent a moment with Lizzie all evening. All the lonely people . . . as the song went.

Gerry wished she could talk to Libra alone so she could tell him the news and share her happiness with him. He was her family. And she wanted to tell Bonnie, who was her family too. She couldn't possibly call her parents back home and tell them; they'd be stone cold furious. But they didn't really seem like her family any more—as she'd told Libra long ago, her parents were just two people who would come to her wedding. She looked around the room. This was her world now, people she was familiar with and worked with, some she liked and some she didn't, some she only recognized by sight, some she knew down to the bottom of their hearts. She could pick and choose in this world, and she *had* chosen. This time, she knew, she had chosen right.

CHAPTER

NINETEEN

THAT September the Gilda Look swept the country. Elaine
Fellin wore it and looked very good in it. Lizzie Libra wore
it, hated it, and looked dumpy and twice as old as she'd
looked the year before. Little Penny Potter started all the
Beautiful People wearing it; she hadn't even been born when
it came around the first time and she thought it was great
camp. Gerry Thompson refused to wear it at all. But everyone else was wearing it, and the framed oil painting of Sylvia
Polydor above Sam Leo Libra's fireplace looked as if it had
just been painted and hung there on purpose. Sylvia Polydor
was queen of the shoulder pads—she had never stopped
wearing the Gilda Look.

Bonnie Parker was hired to wear the Gilda Look for the
editorial pages of *Vogue*, along with her old friend Fred, a
happy reunion for them both. Bonnie was now a much bigger
model than Fred, but Fred was not jealous because she knew
she was quitting soon to get pregnant. Besides, Bonnie did
not come out too well in those pictures—for some reason the
Gilda Look, with its auburn wig and huge shoulders made
her look oddly like (as one *Vogue* editor laughingly remarked) a drag queen. They used only one picture of Bonnie
in that layout instead of the six full pages they had planned,
and afterwards they kept her in more conservative clothes.
Bonnie cried for days when they yanked her pictures, but she

'was soon cheered by the news that Sam Leo Libra had arranged a screen test for her, and she would soon be flying to Hollywood. She'd always wanted to go to Hollywood and meet stars, and she counted the days.

Bonnie/Vincent was now nearly twenty years old. Lately, he had been moody and depressed, his moods going up and down more rapidly than he could control them. He was not crying merely for the pictures of himself as Bonnie that had not been used. He was crying because he had begun to notice some disturbing physical changes in himself.

For one thing, he now had to shave his moustache every other day. Shaving gave him bumps and irritated his tender skin, but he was working so often that he did not have time to go into seclusion and grow his moustache long enough to have it waxed. It was hard to cover the bumps with make-up, and he was actually afraid someone would notice it and his photos would have to be air-brushed. He knew there were other models with facial hair, but they were all real girls and they did not have to worry. Their pictures were automatically retouched and their hairy identity was a secret of the trade. He couldn't afford to take chances. He worried about it all the time.

The other thing that frightened him was that he had grown two inches in the past two months since he had begun modeling. He knew that Verushka was over six feet tall, but he had no idea how tall he was going to grow. He was now five feet eleven. At first he had not known that he was growing; he had simply noticed that his legs, always a problem, looked skinnier than ever. He always wore two pairs of tights to make them softer looking and less like a boy's sticks, but he wished desperately that the photographers would take him out of mini-skirts and put him into floor-length gowns and trouser suits before anyone else noticed. Then he realized that his legs were getting skinnier because he was growing and not gaining any weight; he was skinnier all over. Every night he pulled at his semblance of breasts, trying to make them grow, and he wondered if he should start taking hormones—perhaps birth-control pills. Sweets made him break out, so he began eating a loaf of bread a day in addition to his regular food, trying to gain weight.

One of the boys he dated was a married medical student whose wife was putting him through med school. This boy told him that he was probably a case of delayed maturity, that some boys didn't grow up until they were twenty-three or -four.

"You mean I'm going to turn into a *man?*"

"I hope not," his lover said.

"But you said ... ?"

"Well, you're growing, and you said you shave now. You didn't shave before."

"I'm not going to get big, butch shoulders, am I?" Vincent asked in horror.

"You've got a pretty good pair of shoulders already, for a girl."

Later that night Vincent spent the better part of an hour in front of a full-length mirror. He certainly did have a big pair of shoulders for a girl—no wonder the Gilda Look had looked so horrible on him! Oh, Jesus, Mary, and Joseph ... ! He started to cry and watched his Adam's apple working convulsively in the relentless mirror. What kind of a man would he turn out to be? He would be a freak then, for sure. He'd never look like a truck driver; he'd just look like another of the thousands of little nippy queens running around the streets. His career would be over. He would never be a movie star. He would kill himself.

He began almost living on Ups to keep away the depression, and the Ups killed his appetite so he found it torture to eat enough to keep his weight. He was as nervous as a cat. He kept wondering when Gerry was going to notice. She'd have to notice soon—he was living right under her nose. But Gerry was so happy and absorbed with Mad Daddy these days that she hardly noticed Vincent at all, except to give him cheerful hugs and kisses whenever she saw him. Maybe love was blind to everyone, not just to the love object. Vincent prayed so.

But one day Gerry noticed. She had just finished hugging Vincent and she drew back. "Bonnie ... you've grown!"

"No I haven't."

"You certainly have. You're a head taller than I am."

"I always was."

"The top of my head used to fit just under your chin. Now you're way up there like Alice in Wonderland. Have you measured yourself lately?"

"No."

"Then how come you let down all your pants? And your wrists are hanging out of your sleeves. Bonnie, for God's sake, you can tell *me.* Are you *growing?*"

Vincent burst into tears and ran and locked himself in the bathroom.

When Gerry finally persuaded him to come out he confessed all of it to her, even the shaving. "And I'm so scared I'm going to turn into a big man," he sobbed.

"Well, not overnight you're not," Gerry said. As always, she was calm, already thinking of a solution. "Maybe you should start smoking and drinking lots of coffee, or is that just an old wives' tale? I don't know, they used to threaten me that I wouldn't grow if I smoked and drank coffee . . . no, maybe that's when you're only ten years old. How tall are your parents?"

"Shorter than me."

"Oh dear, the new young generation is so damn *healthy*. I'll get some wax for your moustache and we'll rip it right out by the roots." Vincent winced. "Never mind, it'll be worth it. You'll take a week off and tell them you have the flu, and you'll sit in the apartment and grow your moustache for me. We'll do it right before your screen test. And we have to get you some new clothes. Thank God you don't have hair on your chest. Some men never get that. The shoulders, though, are going to be a problem. You're growing a nice little pair of those."

"What's nice about them?"

"I'll get one of those beauty books and see how a girl with big shoulders and skinny legs should dress. They always tell you how to mimimize your flaws. I think maybe you should start wearing little falsies, Bonnie. Then you'll just look like a big, *zaftig* girl. Try one of my bras with two make-up sponges in the cups. I think that'll be more natural."

When Mad Daddy came to pick Gerry up she had Vincent in the bra with the sponges and a poor-boy sweater and skirt. They'd told Mad Daddy about Vincent, finally, and he never really could get used to it; he always looked as if he were going to burst out laughing. Vincent would have hated him for it, but Mad Daddy was so sexy and likable that he really couldn't get mad—it was like getting mad at a seven-year-old kid . . . a kid Vincent would really have loved to ball; too bad he was straight.

"You look very sexy," Mad Daddy remarked pleasantly. How could anyone say that and sound so uninterested?

"Do you notice anything different?" Gerry asked.

Mad Daddy shrugged. "He's growing a bust?"

"He's growing, period," Gerry said. "Can you tell?"

"Elaine did that after I married her," Mad Daddy said. "She grew and grew. I had to get her a whole new wardrobe."

"See?" Gerry said. "Girls grow too."

"How old was she then?" Vincent asked.

"Sixteen."

"Well, I'm nearly twenty. Ain't that a *mess?*"

"Isn't," Gerry corrected automatically. *"Isn't* that a mess."

"You look kind of like Elaine from the back," Mad Daddy told him.

"That's not all bad," Vincent said.

"That's a good idea," Gerry said, thinking. "You should let your hair grow. Then people would notice your hair and face more. Twiggy is out anyway. Elaine has big shoulders, but with all that hair spilling around them, nobody notices."

"By the time my shoulders finish growing my hair will cover them, right?"

"Right."

"If they ever finish growing," Vincent said morosely.

"Can't we go eat now?" Mad Daddy asked.

When Gerry and Daddy left, Vincent experimented with his collection of blond falls. He wondered how long it took to make a movie. Wouldn't it be a mess if he made one movie and became a big star and then nobody ever hired him again because he'd turned into a wrestler? Gerry's bra was too tight around the back and it hurt. He took it off. He'd go out tomorrow and buy a Jezzie—that'd push up what he had. He pushed his breast skin up with his fingers. They did look like tits, they *did*. He was scared to take hormones, even though a lot of the queens he used to hang around with took them. He didn't want to be a freak. Those things the queens got weren't tits, they were just membranes. Tumors, cancers. He didn't want two tumors growing out of him.

He washed his tear-stained face and painted carefully, putting on six pairs of upper eyelashes and a pair of lowers. He painted in a beauty spot beside his mouth and one of them on the opposite cheek. He pinned on two of the falls and two little side curls. Then he put on the bra again, even though it hurt, and put in the two make-up sponges. It certainly looked real. He put on his favorite pants suit and noticed with pleasure how much better it looked with a little shape up top. Oh, Bonnie, you are flawless! You are a flawless beauty!

He had no place to go, so he'd go to a gay bar and wreck

them. He hadn't been to one for a couple of weeks, and he didn't want to be forgotten. Everyone would rush over to him when he came in, as they always did, and make a big fuss over him because now he was their star. He'd never looked better, no matter what anyone said. He pouted at himself in the mirror and blew his image a kiss. Oh, what a flawless beauty! Look at that nose, look at those huge violet eyes! He ran his hands down his body and over the cups of the bra. Didn't those sponges feel *real!* Just like a girl's tits—not that he'd ever felt any except Gerry's on the sly. He tossed his head and the hair of the falls swayed and rippled over his shoulders. God, he was beautiful! It turned him on, seeing himself so lovely in the mirror, even though he knew it had taken him two hours to achieve this masterpiece. He was really getting hot. Look at those sensual lips! His cock began to hurt where he'd gaffed, and he realized he was getting a hard on. Now he'd have to pull it before he went out.

Vincent jerked off in front of the mirror, staring passionately at Bonnie's exquisite face. Another man never made him as hot as just looking at himself and knowing he was lovely. The only other thing that really made him hot was being the center of attention and knowing everyone thought he was beautiful and wanted him. He was so lucky he had been born beautiful! Just before he came, he kissed Bonnie's voluptuous mouth in the mirror.

Then he washed and dried himself neatly and tucked the love-hate object back out of trouble. He'd never go have it cut off like some of those crazy queens did. Just yesterday he'd heard on the grapevine that one of the queens who was saving up for the sex change had committed suicide. That came as no surprise. Whatever happened, even if he (God forbid) turned into a big man, he was fond of what he had. It was his identity, his toy, his solace. See, what if he'd had it cut off last year, when he was just entering his heyday as Bonnie, and then he started growing these shoulders and that moustache. He'd really be in trouble then! *If I have to be a man*, Vincent thought, *I'll be a real man*. But taking a last look at Bonnie Parker in the mirror before he went out of the apartment, the possibility that he might turn into an unmistakable man seemed very far away indeed.

ᘿᘾᘿᘾᘿᘾᘿᘾᘿᘾᘿᘾᘿᘾᘿᘾᘿᘾᘿᘾᘿᘾᘿᘾᘾᘿᘾᘿᘾᘾᘿᘾᘿ

CHAPTER

TWENTY

ᘿᘾᘿᘾᘿᘾᘿᘾᘿᘾᘿᘾᘿᘾᘿᘾᘿᘾᘿᘾᘿᘾᘿᘾᘾᘿᘾᘿᘾᘾᘿᘾᘿ

ON a fine, late September morning, Barrie Grover was dozing through her boring history class when her friend Michelle passed her a note. It was a newspaper clipping, actually, a gossip column about celebrities, and it said that TV star Mad Daddy and his wife Elaine were acting silly and going splitsville. It was the first the girls had heard that he even had a wife. Michelle had circled the item in red pencil and written in the margin: "Maybe you're *next*?????"

Barrie Grover nearly went into shock. It was all she could do to contain herself until the class was over. Then she pushed her way through the kids into the hall and grabbed Michelle.

"My God! He's getting divorced!"

"I wonder what she's like," Michelle said.

"I wonder if he's got somebody else," Barrie said.

"You'd better hurry up and meet him now," Michelle said.

"What about you?"

"I don't want to marry him, for heaven's sake. He's old enough to be my father."

"You never used to mind that."

"Oh, I was just a kid then."

"Imagine being Mrs. Mad Daddy," Barrie mused, transported.

"Will you invite us over to your house?"

"Sure I will. You and that *kid* you're going to be married to." They both giggled at the fantasy of Barrie married to Mad Daddy and playing hostess to the former Mad Daddy Fan Club of Kew Gardens. The bell rang for their next class and Barrie decided to cut it. She put her books into her locker and sneaked out of the building. It was a clear, beautiful day, the air crystal clear, the sun shining, but not too hot. The leaves on the trees were just beginning to fade at the edges. She walked a block to the Pancake House, where the kids usually hung out, and went in. It was almost empty, being the middle of a class, and too early for lunch. She sat in a booth at the back, put a quarter into the miniature jukebox beside the table, and selected two happy songs. The waitress was setting tables and ignored her, as usual. She didn't mind because she was too excited to eat anything anyway, and she wanted to think about this new extraordinary development.

Mad Daddy had a wife, and he was getting a divorce! It made him seem more like a real person now. She was just dying to know what his wife looked like, how old she was, was she funny too. Or maybe she was a good laugher. Barrie drifted into a fantasy of actually meeting him, of telling him who she was, and of him saying of course he knew, because he had read and appreciated all her notes and letters. Then he would really look at her, as if noticing her for the first time, and he would ask her if she would like to go for a cup of coffee. They would sit there and talk and talk. They would gaze into each other's eyes. They would realize that they really understood each other like no one had understood either of them before. He would fall in love with her because she was loyal, sensitive and true. They would get married. They would never be separated again. She would sit there at each and every one of his shows, right in the front row. Everyone would know that he was dedicating the show to her.

She had to stop living in fantasies and figure how to make them come true. The first thing would be to get a ticket to be in the audience at his show, and get a seat in the first row, and try to make him notice her. No, that wouldn't work. The kids always mobbed him, and they had all those nasty guards that kept you away from him. The only way to meet him would be to find him after a show, when the guards weren't around and get to speak to him. She knew that if she could only speak to him and tell him who she was that they could be friends.

During her next class she would write him a letter. She started composing it in her head. She would tell him more of her secret thoughts, how she had been maturing and changing, what she had discovered about life, and he would think she was astonishingly bright and perceptive for a kid who had just turned fifteen. Maybe she would send him her picture. Then when he saw her he would recognize her without her having to tell him.

She looked at the clock above the counter and realized she was too late for the next class, too. Where did the time go? The Pancake House started filling up with kids, the ones who had spending money and couldn't stand to eat the school lunches.

"Is anybody sitting here?"

They were all strangers, and they wanted her booth. She nodded shyly and slipped out of the booth, letting the noisy couples crowd in. All those older kids going steady, holding hands over their hamburgers, saying dumb things, proud of themselves because they had someone to be in love with and that gave them status. She hated them. She was above it all. She was going to meet Mad Daddy, a man who was old enough to get married, not just fool around being engaged to be engaged, and she would never have to be a lonely, ignored outcast again.

CHAPTER

TWENTY-ONE

MAD DADDY, registered under his real name of Moishe Fellin, had moved into the Plaza Hotel, in a suite down the hall from the office-residence of Sam Leo Libra. He loved the Plaza; it was big and elegant and old-fashioned, and there were no kids running around the lobby to jump out from behind the potted palms at him. He had thought his apartment was elegant, but this was really *it*. What a long way from the Lower East Side! Sometimes he could hardly believe it. And the best thing of all, the thing he could believe least of all, was that he was in love with the most wonderful girl in the world, and Elaine the ogre was finally going out of his life forever.

He supposed it was a rotten thing to do to their kid, but he had always felt himself totally inadequate as a father, and Elaine would probably marry someone much better at it than he had been. He just couldn't think of himself as a father, an authority figure. When he was with his daughter he felt like another kid. He made her giggle, and they played together, but he couldn't stand to discipline her, and he hadn't the faintest idea of how to teach her anything. He wondered if Gerry would want to have kids. He didn't want to have any more. He had kids he hadn't seen in years, and he was sure their mothers had told them he was the dirtiest of rats. No, he and Gerry wouldn't have any kids. They would just be

together and love each other for the rest of their lives. The
world was a bad and dangerous place, and kids grew up to be
killed in wars. He had no special desire to perpetuate his
name and his image. His show was his name and his image.
It was all the creativity he needed.

The lawyer said he and Gerry couldn't live together until
all the financial terms of the divorce had been arranged, but
they were together nearly all the time anyway. They simply
kept separate residences. He saw her a dozen times a day
when she ran down the hall to visit him on the sly, and after
the show was taped he would go to the office to pick her up.
He pretended he had come in to talk to Libra, because he was
just down the hall, and he didn't want Lizzie to catch on and
tell Elaine. Lizzie was hardly ever there anyway. So then he'd
give Gerry the high sign and she'd grin at him and then if
Libra was there and Lizzie was not, Libra would give them a
drink and have one with them and look very pleased about
the whole thing, as if he was their matchmaker. And then
Libra would send them on their way with his blessing and
they'd have the whole wonderful evening together.

Sometimes they would go to Gerry's apartment and cook
dinner together and make love and watch television, and
sometimes they would go to a late movie (Mad Daddy with
big sunglasses on and a beret pulled down over his face like a
foreign movie director), and a couple of times he rented a
car and they drove out to Coney Island and bought hot dogs
at Nathan's and had a private picnic on the beach because
the season was over and there was nobody there but them
until the cops came and chased them away. And once they
went to Chinatown and wandered around and ate Chinese
food and bought each other presents and went into a funny
apothecary shop where they bought dried-up things wrapped
in paper that were supposed to be brewed into medicines.
And then they went home to Gerry's and brewed up all the
funny dried-up things and smelled them and tasted them and
threw them away. And once they went to the Planetarium
because neither of them had ever been there, sneaking in after
the show had started and leaving early so no one would
recognize him. And a couple of times they took a cab to the
Cloisters, where Gerry had never been, and wandered around
pretending they were living in medieval times, telling each
other stories. He always went home to the hotel, alone,
because the lawyer said he had to, and many times it was so

late it really seemed ridiculous, but rules were rules and Elaine was asking for almost more money than he could pay. He didn't care, really; he'd pay her anything she wanted, but the lawyer and Libra kept telling him he was crazy not to try to lower the alimony. What difference did it make? It was his money, not theirs, and Elaine was his soon-to-be ex-wife, not theirs, and his kid was going to go to private school and camp when she was old enough and have all the pretty dresses and bicycles she wanted.

Life was like a happy dream. The best thing was that he no longer had that rather embarrassing urge for fourteen-year-old girls. Mad Daddy had always felt it was kind of unseemly to want to be with all those little Lolitas because, after all, what could you really talk to them about? People would think he was mentally retarded if they knew. The thing that had always made him feel guilty about it was not that he wanted to go to bed with them, because they always made the first pass somehow, but that he enjoyed their actual company so much. He could communicate with them. People were always talking about the generation gap, but his gap was with his own generation. Gerry was all the best things of a grown-up and a little girl. She was intelligent, understanding, beautiful, funny, sexy, and she never put him down. He felt as if they'd known each other all their lives, and at the same time every day brought new surprises. He wrote little private jokes into the show for her. When he did, they watched it together at midnight, something he'd never been interested in doing before. But now he wanted to see if she liked it, and he was much more interested in the show because she was. Gerry was never unaware that it was he, Mad Daddy the man, who was with her, who was the one she loved. She didn't squeal and sigh over his television image. She knew that was just him doing his work. It made him feel as if he had gone sane for the first time in years.

He measured her ring finger and went to an expensive Fifth Avenue jeweler Elaine had often patronized. The owner started bringing out big rocks, thinking it was for Elaine, and Mad Daddy suddenly realized that he thought big rocks were vulgar and ugly. He said no, no he wanted something dainty and romantic. Big rocks didn't suit Gerry, because she was little and romantic too. So finally Mad Daddy designed something himself: a circle of forget-me-nots in blue enamel on gold, with a tiny little diamond in the center of each one. It

looked like a wedding ring but she could wear it for her
engagement ring and then he'd get her a real old-fashioned
gold band for a wedding ring, the kind real live wives were
supposed to wear. In the Jewish religion it said that a
wedding ring was supposed to be an endless circle of gold to
symbolize an endless marriage, but none of Mad Daddy's
wives had ever wanted an old-fashioned wedding ring, and he
wondered if that was why none of his marriages had ever
lasted. They had been jinxed from the start because he got
the wrong ring. That was what he deserved for flouting the
rule. Gerry wasn't Jewish, but it didn't matter because none
of his other wives had been either. He was totally unreligious
himself. It was just that he was superstitious about some
things.

They decided to have an engagement party in his suite,
and they invited Libra, Silky Morgan, and Bonnie the Boy. A
divorce took so long, but at least they could be officially
engaged, even if secretly. Mad Daddy realized that, except
for Libra, he really didn't have any friends. Even if he was
divorced and could have the biggest, loudest engagement
party in the world, there was no one he liked enough to invite.
He didn't much want his sister and brother-in-law. Ruth
would just criticize everything as usual, starting with Gerry.
So they just asked Gerry's friends, and she didn't seem to
have any friends either. Mad Daddy was rather pleased that
she didn't have a lot of friends. It meant they both needed
each other more. He wanted her to need him a lot. He would
take care of her.

Libra sent over the biggest bottle of champagne in the
world, on a little contraption with wheels and a handle to
push it with, and Gerry ordered a cake. Mad Daddy got
millions of blue and white flowers and put them in vases all
around the living room, and he hung balloons from the
chandelier. He arranged it so Gerry came over first, so he
could give her the ring, and when he gave it to her she cried,
and then he knew he was right to have designed that ring
because it was perfect.

Then Libra came, with a carnation in his buttonhole, and
they had champagne and cake and played all the new hit
records on Mad Daddy's new hi-fi, and then Bonnie the Boy
came in for just one second because he was really very shy,
and when Bonnie the Boy saw Gerry's ring he cried because
he knew he would never get married, and Mad Daddy began

to feel awfully sorry for him and wondered why he used to feel like laughing whenever he saw him because the poor kid really wasn't funny at all. Then Silky Morgan came in for a minute, between her matinee and evening performances of *Mavis!*, bringing a beautiful china breakfast set for two from Tiffany's, with little blue forget-me-nots painted on it because Libra must have told her about the ring.

And then Lizzie Libra came poking her nose around the door, saying: "Okay, I can smell a party a mile off, and why wasn't I invited?"

"Because you'd open your big mouth, is why," Libra told her.

"Don't be silly," Lizzie said. "You really don't even *know* me, Sam, after all these years, not that I'd expect you to, since you never see me." Lizzie had brought some embroidered hand towels that she said were guest towels and not to be used, and which Mad Daddy recognized as the same guest towels Elaine had given her for Christmas the year before because someone had sent them to *them* and Elaine didn't like them. Gerry pretended to like them very much, and Lizzie kept looking anxious and asking her if she was sure she really liked them; and Mad Daddy couldn't understand why Lizzie was so worried since they were obviously hideous and Lizzie was so cheap.

Then they all had more champagne and Bonnie the Boy said to Gerry that he was really embarrassed because he didn't know you were supposed to bring presents. Gerry told him you weren't. And Silky Morgan left, and Libra said he wished he could take the four of them to dinner but he was sure Mad Daddy and Gerry would rather be alone anyway, which was true. So Libra said he would take Lizzie to dinner at 21, and Lizzie said: "What do you know—sentimentality finally got to the old bastard."

After everybody was gone except Mad Daddy and Gerry, he sent down for pizza and they had it for dinner with the champagne, and then they made love and Gerry said it felt funny doing it with an engagement ring on and Mad Daddy said wait till you do it with a wedding ring on—it's actually kind of dirty.

They figured out that if all went well with the lawyers they could get married on Valentine's Day, and if they couldn't then they would get married on the first day of spring. Gerry asked him if he wanted to wear a wedding ring and he said

no, because he'd have to take it off for his television show
and he thought it was bad luck ever to take a wedding ring
off so he'd rather not have one. And she said she didn't like
them on men anyway.

They decided they would live in a penthouse because
they'd both always wanted to live in a penthouse if they had
to live in New York at all, and Mad Daddy wondered how
he was going to be able to afford one, but he didn't say
anything because he knew everything would work out. Everything had always worked out.

They'd missed his show on TV, which didn't seem to
bother either of them, so they watched the late movie in bed
and then they had to get up and get dressed so he could take
her home because of the lawyers. He really hated that. It was
so ridiculous. He wished they could elope that minute, to Salt
Lake City, where they had Mormons with plural wives.
Gerry didn't want him to take her home and said she could
get a taxi, but he said he certainly wasn't going to let her go
home alone on her engagement night. When the cab got to
her front door, he didn't even get out to take her upstairs
because he knew if he did he could never stand to leave.

He felt terribly depressed when he went back to the hotel
alone. Libra had left a big pile of fan mail on the living-room
table, which they'd started sending over from the studio so
Mad Daddy could spend more time in his suite. He looked
through a few letters but they always scared him, as if those
people were right there in the room, in his life, where they
had no business to be. One kid had sent a picture of herself—
he guessed it was a she—with the long hair the kids had
sometimes you couldn't tell, and his or her name was Barrie.
He tossed the photograph into the out box with the rest of
the fan mail so that his secretary at the studio could answer it.
The secretary would send everyone who included a home
address an autographed photo of Mad Daddy, wallet size,
with the autograph signed by her. Libra didn't approve of
autographs signed by duplicating machine. Libra also didn't
approve of stars signing their own autographs because he said
you never knew when some nut was going to forge your
signature on a check.

Mad Daddy got back into bed and telephoned Gerry,
waking her up, to say good night. They talked for forty-five
minutes. They both agreed how lucky they were that they
were never bored with each other, and he blew a lot of kisses

into the phone, and after they hung up he felt sadder and
lonelier than ever. He'd picked up the morning papers before
he went upstairs and before he went to sleep alone he read
the columns and saw that he had been enjoying himself very
much at a party he'd never attended at a restaurant he never
frequented, given by some people he didn't know.

CHAPTER
TWENTY-TWO

IN THE YEARS she was struggling to get where she was now, Silky Morgan had never thought specifically about what she expected fame to bring her. But now that her show was the first hit of the fall season and everybody said it would run as long as she cared to stay in it, she had recorded the cast album, two of the songs from it were climbing on the charts, her allowance had been raised to a hundred dollars a week, she had charge accounts at Bonwit's, Bendel's, and Bergdorf's, Gerry called up every morning at eleven to read her the list of interviews and appointments that had been set up for the day, her name appeared almost daily in the columns, she was recognized in the street, she received fan mail from lunatics and a few sensible-sounding fans, and there was talk of a piece being done on her for *Life* Magazine—now she realized she was indeed famous, and for the first time she began to wonder what it was she had expected from fame and where it had all gone wrong.

She had finally persuaded Mr. Libra to let her take an apartment of her own (he insisted on a sublet) and Gerry helped her find a lovely three-room modern apartment on the East Side with a terrace, air conditioning, a uniformed doorman, a wall oven, a dishwasher, and a full wall of mirror in the bedroom facing the king-sized bed which had a purple velvet bedspread and wall-to-wall white fur rug. The apart-

ment belonged to a faggot interior decorator. The living
room was done in white with glass tables, glass objects, and
unframed modern paintings; a room to receive the public;
but the bedroom was probably pure tenant, and certainly
pure Silky. There was a hi-fi, with an extra speaker in the
bedroom, and a large supply of the newest records, supple-
mented by Silky's own collection, there was a color television
set between the wall-to-wall mirror and the bed, with remote
control, the living-room bar had been fully supplied by Mr.
Libra as a house-warming present, and she had a one-year
lease on this perfect playpen, with no one in the world to
share it with.

Hatcher and his bride were on tour, the Satins hated her,
and she felt strangely reluctant to have her family move in
and make of this romantic haven a crash pad before she had
a chance to find someone to fall in love with. It was her own
place at last, she had worked like heck for it, and now she
was stuck here alone day and night like Eve in the Garden of
Eden without Adam.

She stocked her refrigerator and freezer with the best
steaks and lots of vegetables and ice cream, taking perfect
care of her health and weighing herself every day on the
doctor-type scale her landlord had installed for himself in the
tortoise-shell-wallpapered bathroom. Her many perfumes,
colognes, and beauty aids lined the glass and brass hanging
shelf. Every night and twice on Thursday and Saturday she
did the show, trying to keep it as fresh every time as it had
been the first time, and then she went right home in a taxi
and treated herself to a glass of champagne on her terrace,
watching the lights of the city, before performing her nightly
beauty routine and getting into the too-large king-sized bed
to watch television until she fell asleep. The reporters who
took her to Sardi's for lunch or came to her apartment to
interview her asked her what she did in her spare time, and
she said she read (which she still did) and saw friends (which
was a lie) and wrote poetry (because Mr. Libra had told her
to say that). She said she performed her own kind of medita-
tion (another Libra fantasy) and did not add that it consisted
of her half hour on the terrace at night with her lonely glass
of champagne. She said she would like to get married someday and have children, but that right now she felt she was too
involved in her new career to give the proper time to a
relationship. She said she dated, but refused to divulge any
names, and yes, most of them were black boys, although she

didn't have anything against going out with a white boy. In truth, she didn't go out with anybody, and she wouldn't have minded if he was green with purple spots.

Once in a while Mr. Libra supplied her with a date—Shadrach Bascombe, the boxer, who was his client and soon to be a movie star—and a few young men about town Mr. Libra knew who wanted to have their names in the papers, but with the exception of Shadrach it was more like a business meeting than a date and she never saw them again. Shack Up, which was what everyone called Shadrach, dragged her off to bed almost immediately, and she went because he was attractive and she was lonely, but he was dumb and conceited and she didn't care if she ever saw him again. He told her she was a lousy lay and he was going to cure her. He saw her twice again and didn't cure her. She didn't even feel like pretending. She thought of Hatcher Wilson from time to time and decided she had been a fool not to like him more when she could have had him. She hardly ever thought of Dick Devere, and when she did she was glad she was out of that disaster forever.

She did a few television talk shows, saying the lines Mr. Libra had written for her, avoiding anything controversial, being cute and funny and innocent and sincere. Sometimes it occurred to her that she could sit right there with a million and a half people watching her and say some dirty word or unforgivable things and it would ruin her career forever in one second. It was a terrifying thought. She wondered if the other people on the shows with her thought the same thing about themselves. They were all very nice to each other in the Green Room before the show, because they were nervous and trapped together as if on a lifeboat, but when the show was over they never even bothered to say good-bye. Once in a while she saw guest celebrities exchanging telephone numbers, but they were always saying that they and their wife or husband should get together with the other person and his or her wife or husband, and none of it was ever romantic, just suburban. What a laugh and a fake fame was! You lived in your own plastic bubble, you smiled and pretended to be charming and happy, and it was all a lie. No one could get into anyone else's plastic bubble with a blowtorch. No one even wanted to.

She wondered what would happen if once—just once—she were to tell a sympathetic reporter that she was lonely and miserable and forgotten. He'd print it, of course, because

that would be interesting. She'd get a lot more crazy fan
letters from losers who were just as lonely and miserable and
forgotten as she was. And she wouldn't have the courage to
meet any of them on the street corner they designated in
their badly spelled, pencil-scrawled missives on lined school-
room paper, with the stamps that looked as if they'd steamed
them off a bill that had missed the canceling machine.

Her phone number, of course, was listed under the name
of the tenant she'd sublet from, and her own name was
unlisted for the sake of safety. She didn't want to hear any
two a.m. breathing at the other end of the phone.

She went to publicity parties occasionally, if they were
given at night after the show; usually with Mr. Libra and a
few other people, or sometimes with one of his arranged
escorts. There would be a lot of stars at these parties, and
everyone seemed to have friends except her. The stars tried
hard to be just folks and carefully ignored her, not wanting
to be square and say congratulations or act impressed—or
maybe they weren't impressed, because they were stars too
and they must know by now what a fake it was. The other
stars talked to each other about their children or golf or their
new diets, and sometimes about show business or politics, but
mostly about the dull things all their fans talked about back
home in the suburbs, where most of these stars were from
anyway. She enjoyed recognizing people she'd heard of, and
when Mr. Libra introduced her to a star she'd admired she
was impressed and tongue-tied. They probably thought she
was either stupid or a snob.

No one in her show bothered much with her. She arrived
at the theater in time to hole up in her dressing room and do
her face, the hairdresser would flit around with her wigs, the
wardrobe woman would make tea with honey for her, and
they would exchange banalities because Silky didn't want the
woman to mother her. Then she would be onstage for almost
all the show, and when she wasn't onstage she would be
rushing into another costume and another wig. Then it would
be over, and she would be too wound up to feel tired and too
tired to try to find someone to shock by asking them if they'd
like to go out to eat. The doorman downstairs didn't let
strangers into her dressing room, and she had hardly any
friends. The people she'd grown up with didn't have the price
of even a balcony seat. When strangers did get in, because
they were a friend of a friend, Silky would be glad to see
them and very self-conscious, not knowing how close she

should get, whether they wanted her to go out with them or keep her distance. She always seemed to do the wrong thing, because they usually looked embarrassed too. If they did ask her to go out drinking with them after the show, she said she was too tired or had a date or something, and then as soon as they had gone away she was so sorry she could have killed herself. She knew she was acting this way because she was depressed, and she knew she was depressed because she didn't have a man—and she knew she would never get a man if she didn't get out at night. She was ruining her life but she was too afraid of disappointing people to be anything but elusive.

There was a boy in the chorus she'd begun to notice because he was the prettiest thing she'd ever seen. He was about six feet tall, with the face of an angel and the body of a middleweight fighter. He had a nimbus of curly black hair that looked as soft as chinchilla, huge murky green eyes, and skin that looked like a good suntan but was what he'd been born with. He looked to be a mixture of two races and four nationalities, the best of each. His name (his own?) was Bobby La Fontaine. He was a dancer. She thought he might be gay, but if he was he was the man. He always smiled at her with his perfect white teeth (definitely his own) and she always smiled back gratefully, but they never spoke. Then, after the show had been running for two months, he started asking her how she was, and she asked him how he was. He was her only friend, if that could be called a friend.

Then one evening he knocked on her dressing-room door.

"It's my birthday," he said. "Do you want to come to my party after the show?"

"I'd love to. Congratulations."

"Okay," he said, edging out.

She wanted to keep him for a minute. "How old are you?"

"Nineteen."

So was she. She smiled at him. "Me too."

"I know."

"See you later."

She had forgotten to ask him where the party was, but the wardrobe woman found out for her—it was in a dressing room shared by only two people because Bobby La Fontaine dressed in the chorus boys' room, which smelled like a pigpen. Silky went there with her stage make-up still on, frightened, wishing she had said she wouldn't go. But everyone seemed glad to see her, getting her drinks, offering her cake, trying to give her their chair. That embarrassed her too, because she knew they were being nice because she was the star. None of them really knew her.

Bobby La Fontaine was in the corner, talking to two pretty white girls. He excused himself to them and came right over. "I'm glad you could come."

"Thank you."

"My mother sent me a birthday cake she'd baked, so I thought I might as well throw a party."

"That's nice."

"So meanwhile I had to buy about fifty dollars' worth of booze." He laughed. "I hope you don't mind paper cups."

"Of course not."

He sat on the edge of the dressing table next to her chair. "I didn't think you'd come. I'm honored."

"Why wouldn't I come?"

"Well, you're the star and I'm just a chorus boy. Why should you bother?"

"That's an awful thing to say."

"I didn't mean you're a snob, I just mean I'm honored."

"I wish you'd stop saying honored."

He grinned at her. "To tell you the truth, I've wanted to get to talk to you ever since the first day I saw you. But you always run away."

"I'm shy," Silky blurted out. She drank her whiskey and water. The birthday boy waved at one of his dancer friends who came running over with a refill. He introduced them and then gave his friend a look that said "Go away and leave us alone." The friend went back to the group. The dressing room was crowded with people, hot and noisy. The little air conditioner in the window wasn't doing enough for that mob, especially all those sweaty dancers. Silky noticed with pleasure that close as he was to her, Bobby didn't smell at all, except faintly of a nice, light masculine cologne.

"I kind of knew you were shy," he said, leaning over her so she could hear him above the noise. He had a soft, sexy voice. "You're always so aloof, like a duchess, but you remind me of a scared little girl."

"Don't be so smart—we're the same age. In fact, I'm six months older."

"I don't care how old you are. To me you're about six."

They looked at each other, smiling, and Silky hoped he wasn't gay because she liked him and he certainly was beautiful. He had a strong New York accent that she unaccountably found very sexy.

"Do you live with anybody?" he asked.

"No. Do you?"

"Not me. I like to have my little room where I can throw my clothes on the floor and throw the furniture around if I get drunk. I love chicks, but I couldn't live with one—I'd have to be too neat."

"Unless you found a girl as messy as you are."

"That would be a disaster." He laughed happily. "Do you like to dance?"

"Sure."

"Well, a couple of us are going to a discothèque after here. Will you come? I want you to be my date."

She was tired, but she didn't care. "Okay, I'd love to."

"As soon as all the booze is gone, which should take ten minutes, we can sneak away."

She thought it would be groovy to dance with a real dancer, and that she would probably not be good enough because he probably went out with girls who danced professionally. She didn't want him to be disappointed in her. He thought she was a star, and he didn't know she was just as inadequate as anybody else, maybe more.

"Let me go talk to some of my guests and I'll be back." He peered into her paper cup, saw that it was still nearly full, and jumped up. She saw that he knew everybody and that everybody liked him. He was running around the little dressing room, kissing girls, hugging guys, being congratulated, making jokes. He sent a couple of guys over to talk to Silky and she made lame conversation with them, feeling hot and itchy and self-conscious. She realized that except for Dick, who'd been more of a lover than a date, she'd been out on less dates in her life than any other girl she knew. What did she know about men? It had always been work, ambition, work, then love and suffering, then the string of Mr. Libra's dates who weren't dates at all. She might as well be six years old, like Bobby said. She had two more drinks and played a word game with herself.

Life ... Laugh. Life is a laugh. Date ... Late. Too late to date. Date ... Fake. Sex ... Wrecks. Men ... Them. Games ... Pain. Bed ... Get Ahead. Did he just like her because he thought she could help his career? Suddenly she wasn't hot any more, she felt chilled and depressed. Why else would he like her anyway? He didn't even know her. She was just the star of this show ... no, she was *the star*, and he was *just* a boy who danced in the chorus. But who else was she going to meet in her secluded little life?

The crowd was beginning to thin out and Bobby La Fontaine, whom she no longer liked, came bouncing back to her like a happy lamb-haired angel.

"Let's go," he said, and pulled her to her feet.

Silky let herself be led to a cab, climbed in with him and two other couples who were high and giggly, after the boys had argued with the taxi driver who didn't want to take six. They went to a discothèque that had just opened, which Silky had never heard of: beautifully air conditioned, dark, with slides of beautiful girls thrown on the walls and loud music, most of it American songs translated into French.

The tables were tiny cubes, with everyone packed together. In the back room there was every game you could think of to play except a slot machine. Everyone who entered looked like a model, male and female. There didn't seem to be even one ugly tourist who'd gotten in by accident. Bobby seemed to know all the waiters.

"I've been here every night since it opened," he told her, "which is about two weeks. I love it. Aren't the people beautiful? I love beautiful people."

Which should make me last about five minutes, Silky thought, still depressed. No one seemed to notice her or recognize her, which made her feel better, until their waiter, a beautiful blond faggot of about nineteen, came with their drinks, and said to her: "Oh, Miss Morgan, I loved your show and I love you."

"Thank you," she said, and smiled at him.

The other kids from the show were already on the dance floor, which was packed but not too much to dance. Black lights flickered, making it hard to tell who could dance and who couldn't.

"I love to drink," Bobby told her. "I don't like pot, and I only take LSD occasionally, but I love to drink. I'm old-fashioned. Most of the dancers don't drink because they think it's bad for them, but even with a hangover I can go on. Dancing is the best thing to cure a hangover."

"I guess you don't plan to be a dancer forever anyway," Silky said, hoping to trap him into revealing his ambition and get it over with right away.

"Oh sure I do, until I'm too old. Then I'll open a ballet school. I have absolutely no desire to be an actor or a movie star."

"Oh? Why not?"

He looked at her. "Why? Did it make you any happier?"

"Sure it did."

"Well, you have talent. That's different. I don't have talent in that direction, so what would be the point of it? People have asked me to model, but I'm not that interested. I like to *move*. Let's dance."

They got up then and danced on the crowded floor, and Silky could see that he really did love to dance; he had forgotten she was there. He was a wonderful dancer, and she saw people looking at him. He didn't notice them, either. Some of the people who were watching Bobby dance smiled at her, not because she was Silky Morgan, the star, but because she was a girl out on a date with a boy who was the best dancer in the room. She liked that. They must be thinking that he really liked her if he wanted to take her out dancing when he knew she wasn't good enough to keep up with him. Maybe he really did like her a little. After all, why shouldn't he? She was nice, refined now, she'd educated herself, she could talk if she wasn't scared, she looked okay. She hadn't planned to come here so she wasn't dressed for it, but she didn't look frumpy or out of place.

Finally when she was exhausted, Bobby decided he wanted to sit down. They had another drink and fanned each other with the menus, and he kept looking at her and smiling at her. The other couples they had come with didn't bother to make much conversation because it was so noisy, and Silky began to feel more secure and glad she had decided to come. She should get out more. It was a great cure for depression. She saw girls without dates and she realized that other people didn't sit home their whole lives waiting for the window washer to pop in through the window. They just got a friend and went out. No one looked at anyone funny for being out without a date. There seemed to be lots of good-looking guys alone too, looking for girls. No one was nervous about it or uptight; they just looked relaxed and glad to be there with the good music and the pretty people. She wondered why Bobby came there every night—because he liked to dance or because he met a different girl every night? What difference did it make? He was here with her and he liked her tonight and she was having a good time.

At three in the morning the six of them went for something to eat, and then it was four and everybody had to go to bed because there were lessons and appointments tomorrow

and a show to do at night. The other two couples split and
Bobby dropped her off at her apartment in a cab. She had a
good excuse not to ask him up because it was late, but the
truth was that she didn't want him telling everybody in the
chorus tomorrow that he'd had the star on their first date.
She kissed him good night and said Happy Birthday to make
it a friendly kiss not a sexy one, and then her doorman was
there behind them and she ran to the elevator. She omitted
her usual glass of champagne on the terrace and cleaned her
face and went right to bed. She was unaccountably happy.
She kept seeing his face. He was so beautiful! How could a
man be so beautiful? Every time she saw him she had
forgotten how beautiful he was, and seeing him again was
like a shock. It was like seeing a sunset. *I wonder if I could
marry a man just because he was the most beautiful thing I'd
ever seen* ... She drifted off to sleep, curled up in the fetal
position with her knuckles in her mouth.

That evening she saw him just before their first number
together and he said hello brightly, as if she was no more and
no less a friend than yesterday. She liked that he was playing
it cool. She wondered if he would come to her dressing room
after the show, but he didn't, and then she was disappointed
and oddly hurt. She spent longer than usual taking off her
stage make-up, just hoping he would come by, but when she
finally realized that she was the last one in the theater she got
up to go, realizing for the first time how hurt she really was.
He hadn't even stopped by to say good night! What an evil
little rat!

She stepped out the stage door into the alley and there he
was, standing in the shadows behind the garbage cans. He
came out of the shadows lithely, as if he were a shadow
himself, walked close beside her without touching her, and
said softly: "Hello. Where do you want to go?"

She was happy and confused. He had waited for her all
that time so no one would know they were dating. "Why
don't you come to my apartment?" she blurted out without
thinking. "I have a terrace and I'll make some eggs."

"Groovy, baby."

In the cab she couldn't think of a thing to say, but he filled
in the silence by telling her how some of the boys in the
chorus had been stuffing their jeans with socks until tonight,
when the stage manager caught them and made them take
all the socks out right between the acts. He laughed about it
and wondered if the audience had noticed. Silky noticed that

he had no need to stuff his jeans with anything. When they got to her apartment she was stiff and self-conscious in front of the doorman because she had never invited a man up before, and because she was unmarried and famous, and because the doorman was white and had all the snob of a honky peasant and she wondered if he thought she was a tramp. She even wondered for one frantic moment if the doorman would stop Bobby. But the doorman only gave a half salute and said "Good evening," and Bobby said "Good evening" right back in a confident, friendly way, and then they were safe in the elevator, which was self-service.

When she opened the door to her apartment and put all the lights on, Bobby ran around like a puppy in a field. "Oh, this is a groovy pad!" he said softly. "Oh, wow!" He ran out on the terrace, spread his arms out, and yelped into the night with joy. "New York!" he screamed. "New Yorrrrrk!" She popped the cork on a cold split of champagne she had in the refrigerator and brought it and two glasses out to the terrace on a silver tray with a linen napkin on it.

He poured the champagne, gave her hers first, clicked their glasses, and they drank, looking into each other's eyes. Oh, wasn't he beautiful! She was glad he was the first man she had ever invited to her apartment . . . and then with a small shock she remembered Shack-Up Bascombe: he had been there three times and she had forgotten all about it! She had put Shack-Up and his brutish ways completely out of her mind. Well, the heck with him. She probably didn't exist for him any more either. Bobby La Fontaine was the first man who had ever been up to her apartment; that was the way it was going to be.

There was only one glass for each of them in the split so Silky got another and they drank it, leaning on the terrace railing and looking down at the lights. The lights had never seemed so beautiful before, as if she had ordered them along with the apartment to impress people.

"Right there's my room," Bobby said, pointing.

"Where?"

"There."

She certainly couldn't see anything but the whole, vast city. She wondered if he was ever lonely.

"You must be lonely here alone," he said, as if reading her mind.

"Not often. I mean, I'm alone, but I'm not lonely often."

"You shouldn't have to be alone," he said. "Being alone in

a beautiful place is much worse than being alone in a dump."

"I know."

"You have everything, don't you?" he said. "I bet everybody just wants to know you because they can get something from you. Most of them because you're a star, and some of them, the smarter ones, because you're the kind of woman who gives too much of herself."

"What makes you think that?"

"I know it. I hope you don't think I'm here just because I want something from you. I would have been glad to take you to my room. I don't need anything from anybody."

"I'm sure you don't," she said.

He grinned. "That's a lie. I need affection."

"Who doesn't?"

"You'd be surprised."

No, she wouldn't be surprised. She'd known too many people who didn't need or want affection. All of them holding themselves back, holding other people away. She shivered and Bobby put his arms around her and began kissing her.

He was very gentle and very sexy. She pulled back once and looked at him, and he had his eyes closed as if he was in a trance. She thought he probably thought she was very sexy, too. He didn't know where the bedroom was so she took him there. After all, they both knew what they were going to do and they weren't going to do it out on the terrace, were they?

She didn't know much about men but she knew there was something extraordinary about this boy. For one thing, he was better in bed than Dick, who she had thought was the greatest lover in the world, but more important, he was gentle and tender and cuddly afterward, as if it was not over at all but simply a different phase of it. His body felt marvelous, lots of muscles but very soft over them, super-cuddly, and wasn't he beautiful! He kissed her hands and kept looking at her, and Silky took a last desperate grab at reality and realized she had lost it—she was in love with him.

She looked at the bedside clock and realized it was half past one. She had a matinee the next day. She decided not to think about it.

"Could I have some orange juice or something?" he said.

"You must be starving! I promised you eggs." She jumped out of bed, threw on her bathrobe, and ran into the kitchen. He put some records on the hi-fi and poured more champagne for them while she made scrambled eggs with cheese

and bacon—he refused toast because he didn't want to gain
weight—and coffee.

"Where do you want to eat it?"

"In bed, where else?" he said.

They ate the eggs and drank the champagne and decided
not to drink the coffee after all because it would keep them
awake, and they listened to the records and held hands and
kissed, without saying anything. Silky couldn't think of anything to say, but she didn't feel uncomfortable and she hoped
he wasn't bored. She wasn't bored, just content. She felt as if
she had been running uphill for a long time and now she had
finally come to a peaceful place where she could rest.

"Can I sleep here tonight?" he asked.

"Of course."

"Where do you want me to sleep?"

"In the bed, of course."

She set the alarm and turned off the hi-fi, and he put the
dishes into the sink. He didn't seem to notice the dishwasher
she was so proud of. She put the chain on the door and
turned out all the lights. "Do you want a toothbrush?" she
asked.

"Do you have one for me?"

"It just happens, I do."

She had an extra one, unopened in its box, and she gave it
to him. She liked seeing it in the glass next to hers. They
slept in each other's arms. She had done it with her first boy
when she was fourteen, but she had never slept in any man's
arms before, and it was the safest place in the world.

In the morning she made breakfast, which it turned out
was only the coffee from the night before heated up because
they both disliked breakfast, and while she was dressing she
began to worry about how they could walk into the theater
together. She ought to be proud of him, but she didn't want
anybody to know about them and think the wrong thing . . .
that he'd scored with the star, that she'd do it with anybody
in the show or all of them . . . any wrong and vicious thing.
He was dressed before she was and took her in his arms to
kiss her good-bye.

"I have to stop off at my place for a minute," he said. "I'll
see you at the theater."

She knew it was a lie and she loved him for it. Her heart
went out to him with tenderness. How could she have been
so mean not to want anyone to know she'd made love with
him? What was wrong with him, anyway? Who wouldn't

" ant to make love with him, and who wouldn't be proud of it?

After he left she called her service for messages from the night before and that morning because she hadn't answered the phone. Then she wasted a little time so he could get to the theater before her, and finally she left. She knew she looked different when she walked into the theater; glowing, radiant, happy. She didn't care. It was about time she had something in life.

On matinee days Silky usually had something sent in from a restaurant so she could take a nap between shows, so she did, but she wasn't hungry and she wished Bobby was there to share it with her. She forced herself to eat—she wasn't going to repeat that Dick Devere incident!—and then she lay down and closed her eyes but she couldn't sleep. She thought about Bobby and imagined his face. She didn't think anything special about him; he was more like a presence that filled her entire mind so she couldn't think about anything else. She was happy, and worried that he might not like her as much as she liked him. Maybe he was cuddly and tender with everybody because *he* needed tenderness. She was relieved when it was time to get up.

There were times during their numbers together when they passed each other on the stage, and they both looked at each other and tried not to smile. She saw the smile beginning on his face and being held back. She did the show better than usual and she was pleased with herself. The audience applauded and yelled at her like they always did, and she was glad but she didn't feel as desperately grateful as she always did. They loved her and she loved them, but they were like a family, not her lover. Her lover was waiting.

She began to worry that he wouldn't be there in the alley and her hands were shaking as she removed her make-up, but she forced herself to time it exactly as she always did so she wouldn't be there before he got outside. If he wasn't there, what would she do? She would go to the bar down the street where the dancers always hung out after the show. She would walk right in as if she had a right to join the other kids in the show, and somebody would ask her to join their table and she'd sit right down and have a drink and look around until she saw him. She'd say hello and he'd have to talk to her. She would die of humiliation. The wardrobe woman knew by now to respect her silence, so at least she didn't have to make conversation, and she watched the clock on her dressing table until she was sure Bobby had to have left the theater and then she said good night and went outside. She was so nervous she had to go to the bathroom.

He was there, in the shadows, where he had been the night before. He walked beside her again, close but without touching, and said: "Hi."

"Hi."

"Where do you want to go?"

"Home," she said. "Where do you want to go?"

"Where do you think?"

They held hands as soon as they were in the taxi and started kissing as soon as the taxi was out of the theater district. When they got home they had champagne together on the terrace and looked at the lights and kissed, and then they went to bed, happy because the next day was Sunday and they had the whole day together. At least she *hoped* they had the whole day together. Maybe he went to a gym or something on Sundays! She wasn't going to worry about it, but she couldn't help worrying about it anyway.

The next afternoon he said he had to do some errands and Silky felt deserted and frightened. He promised to come back at six o'clock. She washed her hair, and washed her underwear because she couldn't stand to make a maid do those personal things even though she had a cleaning woman who came in three times a week (who went with the apartment).

At five thirty she started getting nervous and turned on the television, but she couldn't watch it, so she made herself a drink—a Scotch and soda—and lit a cigarette even though she never smoked. She puffed at it without inhaling and gulped the drink, knowing she was a fool to be so frightened but not able to do anything about it. She'd known the boy—how long? Three dates? What was wrong with her? When the hand of the clock hit six she felt like somebody on Death Row waiting to go to the gas chamber.

She had records on, and she made another drink, feeling herself getting high already. When he came back she was going to ask him to move in. How could she do that? He would be insulted. He didn't want to be trapped, to go steady. She wanted to scream and bang her fists against the wall.

At five after six the bell rang and she ran to the door. It was Bobby. He had some clothes over his arm, wrapped in plastic cleaner's bags.

"I just thought I'd bring some stuff for tomorrow," he said casually. "I have an audition. Can I use your closet?"

She ran to the closet and pulled her clothes aside so he could have space. He had brought a jacket and two pairs of pants and two shirts. That was a lot for one audition. Maybe he didn't know what kind of clothes he would have to wear. He had also brought a bottle of after-shave lotion, which he had in his pocket, and his razor. He put them in the bathroom beside her things. She gave him a white terry-cloth bathrobe she'd bought when she was going with Dick because it was like Dick's, one size fits all, and he grinned at her.

They had a drink together and then he took her to a movie, a Western, which he loved and she hated. They groped each other shamelessly all through the film, in the safe darkness of the balcony, and fed each other popcorn. Then they went to a Chinese restaurant that had take-out and bought a lot of food, which he paid for, and went back to the apartment.

He asked if he could use her phone and she walked out of the room in case it was personal, but she was listening as hard as she could from the bedroom. He called his service and then he called someone whom he talked to as if it was someone he didn't like very much but was putting on. She didn't know if it was male or female. She also couldn't tell if he was making a date with this person because he talked mostly in yes and no when they got to that part of the conversation and he knew darn well she was listening. She walked back in the living room when she heard him hang up, and he took her in his arms right away as if he was relieved to see her.

They fooled around in the king-sized bed for hours and hours, ate dinner there out of the paper cartons, which she had heated up, and watched a rerun of some awful ball game on television. Bobby loved playing with the remote-control buttons much more than he liked watching the program. He was like a kid with a toy. They hardly talked at all, but she felt secure and content. She really knew hardly anything about him, she realized, and perhaps she should try now to find out.

"We don't know much about each other," she said.

"Everything I want to know about you I'm going to find out," he said. "I never listen when girls talk, anyway. They just jabber on and on and lie. Girls don't know how to talk to men. I realize now that it's not what people *say* that matters, it's what they *do*."

"Do I lie?"

"You don't say anything that matters. You're too scared to. I'm going to find out all about you . . . just give me time."

"I'll give you all the time you want," she said.

"You'll find out about me, too. You'll learn to trust me. That's what I want."

"I want you to trust me, too," she said.

"Okay." They shook hands.

"And when I trust you," she said, "then what?"

He looked into her eyes. "Then I'll never lie to you."

The next day around noon he went off in the clean jacket and one of the clean pair of pants and Silky went off to an interview at Sardi's where she smiled and laughed a lot and carefully restrained herself from saying that she had a boyfriend or was in love. She felt wildly frivolous and could hardly keep her mind on the same dull questions and her same rehearsed answers, but she did her best and felt very tired when the interview was over. She went home and took a nap, ate a steak, and went to the theater. Monday night was usually the worst night of the week, but tonight it was a good audience and the house was full again, which made the cast very up. After the show she met Bobby in the alley.

"I had a hard time getting rid of my friends," he said. "They wanted to go down the street."

"Do you want to go?"

"I didn't know how you felt."

"I don't care."

He took her to the bar, then, and they sat at a table for two. His friends kept coming over and greeting him, and they were all nice to her. Bobby kept holding her hand and pressing her knee, and Silky began to feel less self-conscious about being seen as his girl in front of all the kids from the show and soon she didn't mind at all. He dragged his chair over so he could sit next to her, and after a couple of drinks they were all over each other and then they went home.

"Well," she said, "I guess they know."

"Do you care?"

"Do you?"

"I only mind if you mind."

"I'm proud of it," she said.

When he was undressing he took off a pair of gold and sapphire cuff links that she hadn't seen him put on in the morning. He saw her looking at them and showed them to her.

"Cartier's," he said. "Eighteen-carat gold. I just got them back."

"Where were they?"

He grinned. "Pawned. Sometimes I get drunk and buy drinks for everybody in the place and then the next day I have to pawn something just to get carfare."

"You mustn't do that."

"I'm going to try not to—now."

"I mean . . . I don't want to tell you what to do . . . but . . ."

"No, you're right. I have a woman now. It's different."

"Who's your woman?"

"Who do you think?"

During the next few days he kept going to get more clothes either "from the cleaner" or "for an appointment," and soon he had a whole closet of his own and Silky doubled her things up in the other one. He brought shaving cream and deodorant and underwear and socks and a vibrator, which he used for various things the manufacturer had probably not intended it for. He bought whiskey when they finished what Silky had in stock, and she bought the food. She was paying the rent, of course, because he was officially living in his room, where he paid the rent. At the end of two weeks she realized they really were living together without either of them having mentioned it.

She wondered what had happened to her ambition for marriage and respectability. It didn't seem to matter right now. She knew that when they really fell in love they would know it without making speeches, just as they had begun to live together without a formal decision, and she also knew that someday they would get married, and that when it happened it would be a quiet, natural decision, just like every decision they had ever made since the moment they met.

Then, just when everything was going along beautifully, Mr. Libra reared his ugly head. He made Gerry call and tell Silky to come to the office. She went, carefully dressed as befitted a young star, complete to a little pillbox hat, and walked into the Plaza suite trying not to look frightened. She didn't like being summoned, but she supposed he had a screen test for her or something. She wished that she could stop being frightened of this man and stop hating him, but just when she thought she could stand him he antagonized her again. Like why didn't he just talk to her on the phone this morning, instead of having Gerry summon her and make it all so formal?

"What is that thing you have on your head?" Libra greeted her. "Who do you think you are—Jackie Kennedy?"

"What's wrong with it?"

"It's corny."

Silky took the hat off and placed it carefully on her lap. She was sitting on the couch, looking at Mr. Libra with big eyes, clenching her teeth, trying to look pleasant.

"I want you to look like a lady, but you don't have to go too far," he said. "Coffee?"

"No thank you."

He deliberately poured a cup for himself. He had sent Gerry out of the room. "All right," he said. "What's the story? Do you just want to get laid or are you in love with him?"

"Who?" she said. So that was it!

"Bobby La Fontaine, chorus boy and professional hustler. I know everything you do, you know. I don't just supervise your contracts. Tell me your little story now."

"There's nothing to tell." Her palms were wet; there were big damp blotches on the hat she was holding.

"He's been living in your apartment for two weeks, that's chapter one. What's chapter two?"

"I don't know what you're talking about," Silky said.

"You might as well admit he's living with you because I know it already. I made a few phone calls when I found out and I know a lot more about that boy than you do, Silky. Are you in love with him?"

She wished she could tell him it was none of his f . . ., none of his business. "Yes," she said.

"And he's in love with you?"

"I don't know."

"Do you know that he's given up his room?"

That was a shock. She didn't answer. Her heart was soaring.

"I gather from your silence that you didn't," Mr. Libra went on. "Do you know what he did in his spare time before he met you? Aside from dance in a chorus, I mean."

She shook her head. Given up his room . . . that meant he

wanted to stay with her. She wondered why he hadn't told her: pride, she imagined.

Mr. Libra stood up. He seemed nervous. "I'll tell you what he did in his spare time," he said. "He was a hustler. Men, women, anything the traffic would allow. I have a list of names and dates, which I can show you if you don't believe me. He was very well provided for by these people. You may have wondered how he had so much money to spend when he made only ninety dollars a week."

"He pawned things," Silky said.

"Such things as a pair of gold and sapphire cuff links from Cartier's, given him by a very old, very wealthy, and very fruity producer ... ? Oh, I see you've seen the cuff links. Would you like me to list the rest of his jewelry?"

"I never noticed his jewelry," Silky said. "Can I go now?"

"Sit down! You can go when I'm through with you. You may also have noticed the labels in his clothes. Or perhaps you're not interested in his clothes. I think not. What I want to know is, is this an indulgence on your part because you're lonely and you think you deserve a treat, or are you foolish enough to want to marry him?"

"I don't believe he's a hustler," Silky said. "And if he is, I don't care."

"You know he is. You may not care, but you know I wouldn't lie to you. I didn't pick you out of the gutter and educate you and teach you how to behave like a lady so that you could turn around and behave like a fool. I'm not telling you you're a tramp or a tart. Everyone's entitled to find sex where they can. If you want to pick up a little hustler and play with him for a week or two, and you're discreet about it, then that's your business. But I know you too well for that. You're not playing. You never play. I wish you did play. I wish you had more guts."

"You can't tell me who to fall in love with," Silky said.

"I can tell you who *not* to fall in love with. I can tell you not to fall in love with a hustler who's going with you because of what he can get out of you, because you're a star, because you're rich, because it's comfortable for him, because people who marry stars end up getting good jobs in show business and becoming stars themselves just because of the publicity. I'm not saying he doesn't care for you—he's given up his other lovers and he evidently thinks this gamble is worth it. You're not entirely unlovable. If he was a nice boy, he would probably fall in love with you because of what and who you are as a woman. But Bobby La Fontaine is not a nice person."

He paused, looking at her to see if it was sinking in. She looked back at him with as little expression showing on her face as possible, wanting to claw his eyes out. How *dare* he make phone calls about her? He had probably hired a detective. She wouldn't put any low thing past old ape-face Libra, not even that. She was too angry to worry right now about whether or not the information was a lie. It didn't matter! She loved Bobby and he loved her, and she was entitled to some happiness. She'd been unhappy for so long. This wasn't going to change anything, no matter what else old ape-face Libra pulled out of his hat besides shit.

Libra sighed. "You've seen them at ringside tables at the night clubs where you sang, the old, lonely stars with their young men. You might have thought they were pathetic and ridiculous. Famous, aging, pathetically drunk and drugged old stars, clawing at their purchased young men. And the young men, with eyes like snakes, all feelings dead, nothing left but a hard-on that they can't even get often any more, but it doesn't matter because the poor old star who keeps them doesn't care about sex any more either. You never thought in a million years that you would end up like that. But you have, just in a few months. You're a young girl— you have your life ahead of you, you're beautiful, you're going to be even more famous than you are now. Don't become a satire. It's not worth it. You're too good for that, Silky. Leave that to the old bats who went wrong. I won't let you go wrong. I'll protect you. Don't settle for a Bobby La Fontaine."

Somehow his sweetness angered her even more than his presumption. He had always been able to play her like a fish. He'd get her worked up, then scared, then she'd snivel and cry ... What *right* had he to run her private life? He'd never allowed her even a free thought!

"I'm not saying I'm not grateful to you for all you've done for me, Mr. Libra," Silky said quietly. "But if I'm a satire it's because you made me one. You tried to change me from the inside out. You changed my thoughts, even the dreams I had at night. You made me act like a puppet. You still do. Every word I say is something you wrote down for me. You tried to destroy my *soul*. You can't do that. I won't let anybody do that. I'll act like anything you want when I'm working or being interviewed, but when I'm on my own time I want to have my own life. Otherwise none of it is worth it, not even being a star."

"I can destroy you," he said. "I made you and I can destroy you."

"How?"

"If people find out . . ."

"People will *love* it!" Silky cried. "They love to hear about scandal! I'll be a bigger star than ever and you know it."

"I can drop you."

"It's all right. Other agents and managers will have me."

"I can let you destroy yourself. You're evidently better at it than I could ever be."

"All I want is a chance to destroy myself," Silky said, smiling. "Let me do it my own way and enjoy it."

Libra shook his head sadly. "You've changed and I'm sorry for you. I'm sorry for all your friends who trust you."

"Uh *uh*," Silky said. "I haven't changed. I'm just doing something *human* for the first time in my life."

"Do you know what a hustler *is?*" he asked, sounding almost pathetic.

"I certainly do. I've been around enough of them in my life."

"Forewarned is forearmed," he said. "You can go now."

"Thank you. Good-bye." She got up, went to the mirror, and put the pillbox hat firmly on top of her head. She could see Mr. Libra looking at her and he looked strange. She walked to the door.

"Silky . . ."

"Yes?"

"If you *get* in trouble . . . call me. Day or night."

"Thank you, sir."

She went running down the hall, leaping with joy, and ran down the stairs instead of taking the elevator. She had beaten him! She had won! It was worth everything to see that strange look on his face when he was watching her in the mirror. She really was a grown-up now. She had beaten Mr. Libra.

And if Bobby was a hustler and only wanted her for what she could do for him? Her heart pounded. She began to feel afraid. But she would know . . . She would watch everything he did and she would know. She wouldn't even mention this little talk to Bobby. It would only make him mad. But she would be watching. And meanwhile, she would be happy. Bobby made her happy, and before she had been unhappy, and that was all that mattered. She deserved some happiness. She had too many wounds that had to heal. Bobby would make them heal, and then she would have scar tissue and be strong again, and then she would think about it. Meanwhile she would be happy. She loved him. She loved him enough to stand up to Mr. Libra, and that was a present Bobby had given her without even knowing it. Everything would be all right.

CHAPTER

TWENTY-THREE

JUST before Thanksgiving Lizzie Libra decided to quit her analyst. The main reason was that she no longer had anything to talk to him about. Her sex life had dwindled alarmingly. In fact, it might be described as nonexistent. She sat at home at night watching television, waiting for Sam to come home. One evening, watching her favorite grab bag of stars, she realized that she had slept with each and every one of the men on the panel at one time or another; it was like old home week ... no, it was like her past passing before her eyes as she drowned. She might as well face it: she was old.

There was no point to run to Dr. Picker to ask him to explain her exploits when there were no longer any exploits. To tell the truth, she was a little ashamed to admit to the old letch that nobody wanted her any more. Besides, she had gone into analysis in the first place to try to come to grips with her infidelities, and since there were no more infidelities then she was no longer unfaithful, therefore she must be cured. Dr. Picker always said there was a reason for everything. Maybe the reason she had no more lovers was not that she was old after all, but that she was cured.

She informed him, and he was angry. He threatened her. Lizzie looked around his office, at the expensive Oriental rugs, at the authentic objects of pre-Columbian art (Did all analysts furnish their offices at an analyst's wholesale showroom, or did they just all have the same taste?) and she began to resent the money she had spent. It was really the money Sam had spent, but it was one and the same. Dr. Picker probably had put a down payment on a painting, and that was why he was so bugged at her. She had the temerity to say this to him, and then he really got angry and told her there was a long waiting list of people who were really sick.

"So I'm not really sick?"

"You can get better."

"But I'm not incapacitated? I'm not suicidal?"

"No one ever said you were."

"All I am is impetuous, earthy, and unfaithful to my husband."

"There's a lot more . . ."

Lizzie Libra took an ax and gave her doctor forty whacks . . .

"I no longer feel the urge to cheat. So I think I can handle my marriage from now on."

"Perhaps you are cured," he said dubiously. "Stranger things have happened."

"I *came* here to be cured. Why do you think it's strange if you've succeeded?"

"It's such a short time."

"What short time?"

"You will remember, this is not Freudian analysis. We have not even gotten to the deep root of our problem."

She wished he would stop being so chummy. It was never "our" problem, it was her problem. She thought of one of Franco's new dresses that she could buy with the money she was spending on this old voyeur. It had big puffed sleeves and a peplum and a tiny little waist. She looked surreptitiously at the clock on Dr. Picker's desk.

"You wish to leave now?" he asked.

"We might as well drag it out since it's my last session."

"I have no desire to drag it out. I can use the time to work on my book."

"Am I in it?"

He smiled.

"If I'm in it I want my money back," Lizzie said. "I didn't give you the rights to my life."

"You are not in it."

"Oh? I'm not interesting enough?"

"Mrs. Libra, you are in trouble and you should stay and have more treatment."

"I think you should use my time for the window-jumpers,"
Lizzie said. She took out her compact and powdered her
nose. Franco's new vermilion lipstick that went with the
Gilda Look made her lips peel. She didn't like it. "I just
have nothing to talk to you about any more.'"

"That is because we are getting at the real root of our
problem."

"What *is* that root?"

"That is for us to investigate."

"I'd rather investigate my peaceful old age," Lizzie said.
She knew it was a lie; she would go down kicking and
screaming before she would give in to a peaceful old age, but
she wanted to say something that sounded well-adjusted. He
seemed mollified.

"Perhaps you are not so frantic," he said. "You seem
calmer. I see great progress. Would you like to take a
sabbatical?"

"Yes," Lizzie said, just to get rid of him. "I think some
time off to digest what I've learned would be good for me."

Dr. Picker looked at the appointment book on his desk.
Then he picked up the phone. "Tell Hudson she can have
Libra's appointment times for the next few weeks," he told
the nurse outside.

Lizzie resented being called "Libra." It was like being a
stock on the market. She looked at the creep's prison pallor
and wondered if he had ever seen the light of day. How
could he, sitting in here in this air-conditioned womb from
eight in the morning till eight at night? When had he ever
seen real people with real problems? Everything was out of a
textbook for him. He ought to go to one of Sam's parties.
That would teach him a thing or two. She decided to invite
him to the next one. Did he really like her? Had he ever
really liked her? Did she even exist for him? She felt sad. She
didn't like saying good-bye to anyone.

"Perhaps you are having second thoughts, Mrs. Libra?"
The doctor stood up and extended his hand firmly, as if to
punish her. "You have made a decision. If you have second
thoughts you can phone me. Good-bye."

His hand was dry, reptilian. He should get out in the air
more. They shook hands and Lizzie dawdled to the door
because there was still five minutes left of her time and she
resented having to pay for it if she didn't use it. He was
going to cheat her of her five minutes if it was the last thing
he did. Those analysts learned the Power Play at analys

chool, along with Punishment, Voyeurism, and Answer a
Question with a Question. Why couldn't he have learned to
peak proper English without an accent? He'd been here for
ears. Maybe they learned the accent at analyst school too,
o they would sound more authentic.

She went directly from Dr. Picker to the Oak Bar, where
he had three martinis which she signed for and two more
martinis which a tall, handsome young man bought for her.
He said he was a model. She thought he looked a little too
old and soft to be a model, almost flabby, but she phoned
upstairs and found that Sam was at the gym and Gerry had
gone home for the day. She looked at her watch, smiled at
he young man, and took him upstairs with her.

They had a pleasant twenty minutes in the bedroom and
then he said he had an appointment and she was glad to see
im go because it had been foolhardy to bring him here when
Sam could come home unexpectedly. She realized she had
rather liked her romp with the young man, even though he
was much too flabby through the middle to be a model
(perhaps he was an out-of-work model?) and she realized
that she was going to enjoy her sex life a great deal more
now that she didn't have to report every detail of it to Dr.
Picker. She no longer had the creepy feeling that there were
always three people in the bed. The young man said he would
call her, and she thought maybe he would and maybe he
wouldn't, but it didn't matter either way. She felt pleased
with herself. He left, and she douched, saying good-bye to
im with his babies, took a shower, washing him off with
perfumed soap, put on her prettiest negligee and went into
the living room where she mixed herself a fresh batch of
martinis. Even if he had lied about his age (he had volun-
tered his age, so he must have been lying), he had wanted
er—a woman old enough to be his mother! Well, ten years
der than he was anyway. She wasn't through yet!

When Sam came back from the gym, all clean and damp,
izzie greeted him with pleasure. He was such a dear old
iend, and she loved him more than any man on earth. She
ad remade her bed and she knew he would never find out
ecause he never went near it anyway. She wondered how he
uld live without a sex life.

"I have to take Sylvia Polydor to dinner," Sam told her.
"he's passing through on her way to Europe. I guess I'll take
r to Pavillon."

"Can I come?"

"You know she hates other women. We're just going to talk business. I'll be home early. Did anybody call me?"

"I let the service get them," Lizzie said.

"Why don't you order something in the room—you look tired."

You bet I'm tired, Lizzie thought. *I have a right to be tired.* "I guess I will," she said.

He took his calls from the service and went into the bedroom to change his clothes. She heard the shower running, then she heard him making some calls. He had forgotten she existed.

When he had left she called Room Service and ordered a non-fattening dinner: broiled liver, plain spinach, melon, and tea. She weighed herself and was pleased to see that she sweated off a pound and a half with the male model, or perhaps it was just that liquor dehydrated you. She missed Elaine, who was in Reno getting laid by a millionaire rancher and putting in her residence time for her divorce. Elaine called her almost every night, drunk of course, but not incoherent. The millionaire rancher was a big drinker too, so they had a lot in common.

She didn't feel like watching television this early, so she ate dinner in front of the windows that looked out over the city and thought about things. She was a women who had everything: people probably envied her. She knew everybody, she had adventures, she had all the money anyone could want, she had a beautiful hotel apartment, a famous husband, limousine with chauffeur at her disposal, the latest clothes, masseuse, a standing appointment at one of the best beauty salons in town, unlimited charge accounts everywhere, good friends, a young face, a still trim (almost) body. Her husband trusted her. They never fought seriously about anything. He needed her. They were content. She began to cry.

Did Sylvia Polydor have everything too? Did people envy her? Was she going to Europe alone?

When the telephone rang Lizzie wasn't going to answer it but then she thought it might be Sam wanting her to meet him somewhere for an after-dinner drink, so she blew her nose and picked up the receiver.

"Yes?"

"Is Mrs. Libra there?"

"This is she."

"This is Jared."

"Who?" Who the hell was that?

"Jared. From Las Vegas. The King Cactus Bar."

She remembered. That bartender who looked like Paul Newman. "Oh my God," Lizzie said.

"I don't know whether I should be flattered or hang up," he said. He was making his voice even lower and sexier on purpose.

"Where are you?" she said.

"I'm in the lobby. Can I see you?"

"Are you crazy?" she said. "What if my husband was sitting here, you dunce?"

"Is he?"

"No."

"Well then, can I come up?"

"I'll meet you in the Oak Bar." *No,* she thought, *they'll think I'm working split shifts.* "No, make it Trader Vic's."

"I'll be waiting," he said. He hung up.

What a nerve! Lizzie thought. She washed her face and put on new make-up, white under the eyes to cover the circles, false eyelashes, because she'd cried them loose, and a young, pink lipstick—the hell with Franco and his vermilion skin remover. She wondered if the kid had come all the way to New York on his motorcycle.

She tried on three different dresses until she was satisfied. The Gilda Look was not her, but she couldn't be unfashionable. No, it was not her at all. She finally settled for a last year's Courreges—the kid probably wouldn't know the difference. She brushed her hair out loose and pulled it back with a little Alice-in-Wonderland hair band. From far she looked nineteen. She took her sable coat, which had just come back from storage, and a key. She dropped everything on the floor then and ran into the bedroom to spray herself with perfume. She was just going to have a drink with the kid and that was all. But she might as well make a good impression on people who saw them together—people shouldn't think he was out with his mother. She took the coat and the key and her purse and went downstairs.

Jared the ex-bartender was waiting at a table by the wall in Trader Vic's. In the half-dark he looked so much like Paul Newman it was scary. The waiters kept looking at him as if they were not sure. When Lizzie entered the room they all looked at her, first with curiosity and then appreciatively when they saw her sit down at was-he-wasn't-he Paul Newman's table.

Jared smiled and took her hand. "I'm glad to see you."

"So you came to New York."

"I told you I would."

"Did you ride your motorcycle here?"

"No, I sold it to buy a plane ticket." He squeezed her hand. "What are you going to drink?"

"A Navy Grog." Might as well get stoned.

He motioned to the waiter. "Two."

"Well," Lizzie said.

"Are you glad to see me?"

She smiled. "Why are you in New York?"

"To see you. To seek my fortune."

"Oh?"

"I told you I was coming."

"Yes, you did."

"I hope you're not in the middle of a romance," Jared said.

"I have no romances. Only mistakes."

"Don't say that." He was squeezing her hand so hard he was hurting her, and Lizzie loosened his grip and took her hand away. The drinks came and he raised his glass in a toast, looking at her with those blue, blue eyes. She didn't hate him as much as she wanted to. He hadn't done anything really, just bang her, which was not exactly his unsolicited idea, and *she* was the one who had run out on *him*.

"Why did you run away?" he said.

"Me?"

"Yes. You. I waited for you."

"I decided to go home."

He looked down into his drink. "You thought I wasn't good enough for you."

"I never said that."

"You don't have to say it. You're a sophisticated woman and I was just a bartender you picked up one day to play with and throw away." He looked up and blasted her with those blue eyes. "Isn't that so?"

"Why did you look me up, then?" Lizzie asked, her hands shaking.

"I'm a glutton for punishment."

She laughed.

"I'm going to be somebody," he said. "You wait and see. I'm going to make it here in New York. You'll see. You'll want me."

"You don't have to yell," Lizzie said, although he was no yelling.

"I got in this afternoon, dumped my bags at a friend's house, and came right over to find you," he said. "I want you."

"You can borrow me," she said. "But you can't have me."

"Then I'll borrow you." He started feeling her knee under the table with his knee, and then he reached down and grabbed her knee with his hand. "Can I borrow you, Lizzie Libra?"

"I happen to be free for this entire evening," she said.

He paid for the drinks and took her off to his friend's apartment, a rather nice one-and-a-half with a big window and a double bed on the floor. Lizzie was so stoned at the idea that from nothing, absolutely nothing, she'd had two men in one day, and beauties at that, that she rather enjoyed it this time. He was nicer to her than he'd been in Vegas, more sentimental, and she thought the kid might actually have a crush on her. She watched him appreciatively as he walked around the room afterwards and she thought he would really be a catch if only he was somebody. Maybe he could act after all. But she wasn't going to help him, no matter what he thought.

He gave her his phone number on a slip of paper. She folded it and slipped it into her wallet under the bills. "Let's go out and have a drink," he said. "I don't want to drink my friend's liquor."

"Girl or boy?" Lizzie asked.

"What difference does it make if it's just a friend?" he said.

Because it was just the right time to be seen she took him on a tour of a few of her favorite watering places. She nodded gaily at the people she knew and steered Jared quickly away without introducing him as if he really was Paul Newman and she wanted to protect him from the public. She was delighted to notice a few mouths drop open at the sight of them. Everyone just thought that she was with him for business, although they knew Paul Newman was not Sam Leo Libra's client, but then when she and Jared began holding hands and whispering and looking very cuddly-cuddly in the corner they really stared. This wasn't any potential client of Sam Leo Libra's—this was a personal catch of his wife's!

She felt euphoric. She let him jabber on about his ambitions now that he was in New York, and she tried to keep from smirking because it looked to everyone who was watching as if Paul Newman had found a woman to whom he could talk a blue streak. She saw one of the columnists looking at her and almost purred. Then just as the columnist started making his way toward them, she dragged Jared out of the bar on the pretext that it was one of her husband's friends. She didn't want to blow her act.

As they left she saw a couple she knew. She introduced Jared to them. "And you know Paul, of course . . ."

He stood there looking nonplussed, and before he could give it away Lizzie pushed him into a cab. The couple stood there on the sidewalk looking after them: the husband as if he'd never realized before that Lizzie Libra was a sexy woman, and the wife consumed with envy.

"What did you do that for?" Jared asked, angry.

"Oh, don't be silly. I was just kidding."

"I hate that," he said. "I want to be me."

"You *are* you, of course," Lizzie purred, rubbing her face against his. She could see the driver looking at them through the rear-view mirror, and he seemed in shock.

The driver turned around. "Hey, ain't you . . . ?"

"No," Jared said.

"Wow, I certainly thought you was him."

"That's the way the cookie crumbles," Lizzie said brightly.

It was time for Sam to be long since home, so Lizzie told Jared to take her to the hotel. She knew everybody would be talking about her tomorrow and she felt warm and serene. Sam would hear about it right away, of course, but he knew too much about publicity to believe a word of it. He'd been making up lies for the columns for years. He would think it was a great laugh.

"When will I see you?" Jared asked.

"Tomorrow?"

"Right."

"*I'd* better call *you*," she said.

"Can you get me an appointment to meet your husband?"

"My husband?"

"I'll need a personal manager."

"I'll be your personal manager," Lizzie said firmly, and smiled at him.

"But I'll need a publicist . . ."

"I'll be your publicist."

"Do you know how?" he asked dubiously.

"Do I know how? Just you wait and see."

"Well, maybe I should meet your husband . . ."

"Is that why you wanted to see me?" She threw the knife in and waited for him to pull it out.

"No, no, of course not! You know that, Lizzie!" He was bleeding to death and she wanted to laugh.

"Well, then, everything's going to be all right," she said.

Their cab pulled up in front of the Plaza. He stepped out and helped her out. She gave him a nice little kiss so everyone could see. "I'll see you tomorrow," he said.

Lizzie Libra sailed into the hotel like a super-star. Everyone bowed and scraped as she passed. When she got upstairs Sam was in his bed asleep. He had taken a couple of sleeping pills. Lizzie helped herself to two of them, removed her make-up while they were working, and crawled into her own bed. She was so glad she'd given Dr. Picker the bar rag. She hadn't been this happy since the old days.

CHAPTER

TWENTY-FOUR

AS THE jolly Yuletide season approached, Bonnie Parker and a queen named Garbo were wandering down Third Avenue doing some Christmas shopping when they were approached by a cute boy. He said hello, so they said hello. The cute boy then pulled out a badge identifying him as a plainclothes policeman and arrested them on the charge of impersonating women. Luckily, Bonnie was wearing Mad Daddy's raincoat, which he had lent to Gerry one night when it stormed and which Bonnie had mopped from the apartment, and it had a label in it from a men's store. She was also wearing boy's jeans. Therefore it was decided at the station house (where they were unceremoniously hauled, as Vincent/Bonnie later gleefully told Gerry, "along with all these rapists, muggers, Negroes, and other criminal types!") that Vincent Abruzzi was not impersonating a woman after all, and just happened to have an unfortunate feminine appearance. As for his make-up, make-up was not illegal. He was let go, but poor Garbo had to raise bail. Neither Vincent nor Gerry told Mr. Libra, of course.

Gerry Thompson decided after some deliberation that she would not go home for Christmas, so she did her shopping early and mailed all the Christmas packages home by December fifteenth. She was busy planning her wedding to Mad Daddy. They decided it would be small and intimate, in a

judge's chambers, to be followed by a wild party at P. J.
Clarke's, which they would take over completely for the
occasion. They thought a Third Avenue bar was just the right
combination of informality and sophistication, although Mad
Daddy rather leaned toward the zoo. (Gerry vetoed the
zoo—Valentine's Day would be too cold, and besides, who
could get a permit?)

Sam Leo Libra was too fastidious to let anyone but himself
do his Christmas shopping. He bought a white fox jacket with
shoulder pads for Lizzie, because that was what she wanted,
silver money clips with his own initials for each of the
clients—except Sylvia Polydor, who got a silver goblet with
his initials on it, to add to her collection—and a Gucci bag
and wallet for Gerry. He had Gerry send out his usual five
hundred Christmas cards, this year bearing a message of
peace.

Although Bonnie Parker had not yet taken her screen test,
Libra was negotiating for Dick Devere to direct her first film
in a package deal, whatever it turned out to be. Libra was
surprised and rather baffled when Dick flatly refused to
direct Bonnie in *any* film, but after the success on Broadway
of *Mavis!*, Dick could write his own ticket and there was
nothing Libra could do. Dick Devere accepted a sophisticated
tragi-comedy, and planned to leave for the Coast directly
after the first of the year. He was going to spend Christmas
in the Bahamas, where he had rented a bungalow on a
deserted patch of beach.

The King James Version appeared on the Ed Sullivan
Show, doing two numbers from their hit album of the Songs
of Solomon, and received 2451 letters of praise, 1552 letters
of condemnation, and a fifty-dollar check for "their church"
from a confused viewer.

Shadrach Bascombe started costume fittings for his first
film, in which he played a former boxer who was now a spy,
and Libra engaged a ghost writer to pen Bascombe's
memoirs, highly expurgated.

Lizzie Libra's analyst, Dr. Picker, left for two weeks in
Acapulco, where the in-analysts were going this year, and
included Lizzie in his Christmas-card list so she would
remember to come back.

Lizzie was seriously considering returning to her doctor
because of the unfortunate turn of events with Jared-Paul
Newman. The joke had been a great success and had made
all the columns, but Jared, for some crazy reason, had been

very annoyed. He had decided that being passed off as Paul Newman was going to be the death of his embryonic career as an actor, and he had walked out of Lizzie's life forever with some very harsh words. Lizzie telephoned him repeatedly, but he refused to have anything more to do with her. She was not upset, only confused. She felt lonely after he was gone, and thought it would be nice to have someone to talk to, so she phoned Dr. Picker's office, found he was away for the Christmas holidays, and made an appointment for the first week in January.

Silky Morgan wheedled money out of Mr. Libra from her account for Christmas and bought Bobby La Fontaine a mink-lined raincoat. She would have bought him a mink coat, but he wouldn't wear it. She sent her family gifts costing ten dollars apiece, because they hadn't been very nice to her lately, she decided.

Bobby La Fontaine, who'd given up his former clients, took a set of diamond studs he was particularly fond of and had them set into a dainty little bracelet for Silky. He'd managed to set aside a bit of money because Silky was paying all their living bills, but as it turned out he didn't have to pay for the work on the bracelet after all because the jeweler liked him.

Mad Daddy wrote out his first of many future checks to Elaine, a down payment on her attorney's fee. He was glad it was only one ex-wife now, plus child support, of course, for the others. He bought Gerry a huge Christmas tree that was too tall for her apartment and had to be cut off above the trunk so it looked silly, but neither of them minded, and they spent an entire night trimming it with every bauble and toy they could find in the Village. They even strung popcorn on it, the way Gerry remembered from her childhood, although Bonnie the Boy ate the popcorn almost as fast as they could pop it. That kid really could eat! No wonder he was growing. Mad Daddy could hardly wait until he was married to Gerry and they had an apartment of their own so they didn't have to have these strange people hanging around. He was counting the weeks.

The B.P.'s were invited on a yacht belonging to a middle-aged millionaire couple, which was cruising the Greek islands for the Christmas holidays. Penny Potter was delighted that Mr. Nelson was also invited, for that meant he could do her hair every day after she went swimming. She was only sorry that her mother couldn't come too, but her parents always

went to Palm Beach this time of the year to escape the
holiday festivities because her father was not well.

A young man Franco knew inherited a good deal of
money and took Franco and two other young men to Lake
Tahoe for sun and gambling. While there, Franco ran into
Elaine Fellin and went to bed with her, as a change from the
three young men he was traveling with, who were becoming
boring. He was furious when Elaine asked him afterwards for
a free dress, but he spent several amusing evenings telling the
story.

Sylvia Polydor spent Christmas in Beverly Hills, doing
what she always did, going to the same parties, seeing the
same people, and doing a half-hour documentary of her life
and career which Sam had arranged for television.

Arnie Gurney spent the holidays performing in a New
York night club, and Christmas Eve he and his wife gave a
small, intimate party for fifty people in their apartment,
which they kept all year because he had to have some place
to vote from.

The Satins went home for Christmas and had a housewarm-
ing party for the new homes they had bought for their
families.

Ingrid the Lady Barber packed up her hypodermic needles
and went to Switzerland for a minor face lift around the
eyes, sending a silent assistant to give her patients their shots
so they would not suffer confusing withdrawal symptoms.

Sam Leo Libra decided not to give a cocktail party this
year because so many of his clients and friends were out of
town, so he and Lizzie attended several parties given by other
people instead, and he decided it was high time he did this all
the time because he saved so much money.

All in all, it was a nice Christmas for everyone, even for
Vincent /Bonnie, who managed to forget the trauma of his
arrest when he went home to his mother for Christmas
dinner and the new husband of one of his high-school girl
friends made a pass at him. Vincent gave the initialed silver
money clip Mr. Libra had given him to his father, because it
was a shame to let anything so expensive go to waste.

CHAPTER
TWENTY-FIVE

IT SNOWED for days that January. The city was almost a white wonderland. Cars were parked along the curbs under mounds of snow, and there was virtually no traffic. Vincent Abruzzi hopped a bus, which he hated to do because people always stared at him, and was a mass of nerves by the time he reached the Plaza Hotel where Mr. Libra had summoned him. He hadn't worked at all for nearly three weeks and had gotten back into his habit of sleeping late, so having to be here at ten in the morning made him feel sick. There was eyeliner in the corners of his eyes and eyelash glue stuck on his long lashes from the night before (he'd been romping with his friends until half past eight that morning and had just had time to get out of drag and put on something neuter and suitable for his appointment). His thrift-shop fox coat, an exact copy of Lizzie Libra's, smelled funny when it rained or snowed, and his hair was all matted down from the falls he'd pinned on it the night before. He looked the worst. He was wearing an oversized pair of dime-store sunglasses, so covered with fingerprints and make-up that he could hardly see, but he could see enough in the mirrors in the hotel corridor to make him sorry he'd looked. He turned up the collar of his coat to hide the stubble that was already growing in on his upper lip even though he'd shaved the night before, and he wished he was home safe in the dark apartment.

At the door to the suite Gerry gave him an anguished look and ushered him in to Mr. Libra. There was coffee and Danish on the table and Vincent looked at it hungrily. He was starved. He hoped he didn't smell from all the liquor he'd been drinking.

"Coffee?" Mr. Libra said.

"Yes, please."

Vincent poured himself a cup of coffee, half cream, with three spoons of sugar, and took a Danish. He gobbled it down and felt a little better. Gerry left the room.

"Cigarette?" said Mr. Libra.

"No thank you."

Libra took a folder from the desk and opened it. It was full of contact sheets from Vincent's last two photo sessions for *Vogue*. "Look at these," Libra said.

Vincent looked. He'd known the photographer hated him, the nelly little closet queen. Look at those terrible shots! They made him look just like a boy—an ugly girl at best.

"Impossible," Libra said. "These pictures are impossible."

"They're pretty bad," Vincent admitted. "That photographer was the worst."

"Not the photographer," Libra said. "Not the photographer. You, Bonnie. Take off that coat."

Vincent took off his coat.

"God in heaven, you look like the halfback for the Green Bay Packers. I'm afraid Bonnie Parker, model of the year, is going to have to go into a convent. I'm sorry."

"What do you mean?" Vincent squeaked. Whenever he got excited, or upset, like now, his voice slid around the upper registers just as if he was an adolescent and it was changing.

Libra took Vincent's contract out of the desk drawer. He held it out so Vincent could see it, and then slowly, deliberately, he tore it in half. "No screen test, I'm afraid," he said. "You don't actually have to *go* into a convent; I'm just going to put it in the columns that you did. I think that would be nice since you're Catholic."

"What do you mean, convent?" Vincent screamed.

"A beautiful, touching send-off," Libra mused. "I'll send them an old picture, you don't have to worry. I can't call you Bonnie any more ... What's your real name?" He looked at the contract. "Oh, yes, Vincent." He sighed. "I had great hopes for you, Vincent, great plans. You were like a but-

terfly, one short season and then faded. But it was all worth
it, wasn't it? You had fun? You made a lot of money. I saved
it for you, so you won't have to want for anything until you
decide what you want to do in life."

"I want to be a model!" Vincent screamed. "I want to be a
movie star! You *said* I could be a movie star."

"Wrong. I said Bonnie Parker could be a movie star. You,
probably, could be a lifeguard. Why don't you try Miami?
It's in season now. Do you like the sun?"

Vincent stared at him. He couldn't believe it, it was like a
nightmare. Maybe he was asleep and he would wake up. He
knew he shouldn't have drunk so much last night.

Libra reached into the desk drawer again and took out a
little box wrapped in blue paper. He handed it to Vincent.
Vincent took it, stunned, and ripped off the paper. Inside was
a box from Tiffany's, holding a solid-gold fountain pen.

Libra gave a wry smile. "A Bar Mitzvah present," he said.
"Today you are a man."

Vincent threw the pen on the floor and stamped on it. "I'm
not a man!" he screamed.

Libra picked up the pen gingerly with his handkerchief. He
put it into Vincent's hand and closed Vincent's fingers around
it. "Take it. Maybe some day you'll want to write your
memoirs. If you do, I'll be glad to handle you for that. You
could make quite a bundle. Magazine serialization, publica-
tion, paperback rights, maybe even a film. Think about it,
Vincent."

He wasn't going to cry in front of this bastard, he wasn't.
He gritted his teeth and forced back the tears. "Where's my
money?"

Libra handed him a bankbook. "You'll find you made quite
a lot," he said. "Maybe you'll want to get married someday.
Don't throw it all away. There will be other days, other
careers. Keep in touch." He held out his hand. "Good luck."

Vincent wouldn't shake the pig's hand if his life depended
on it. He picked up his fox coat and ran out of the suite. He
ran down the stairs and out to the street, the tears coming
freely now, sobbing great gulps of the frosty air that hurt his
lungs. He ran for blocks, slipping on the snow and falling
once or twice. He didn't even know where he was going and
he didn't care. He knew people were looking at him and he
didn't care about that either. He ran all the way to the
apartment, locked and bolted the door, pulled the curtains
closed, and fell on the floor, crying until he was exhausted.

Dimly he heard the phone ringing and thought it must be Gerry, but he didn't answer it and finally it stopped ringing.

Maybe an hour later, maybe more, he got up and went to the mirror. He had never seen anything so awful. His eyes were red and swollen, the tears had streaked his make-up, his sprouting moustache looked like a black and red rash. Why did he have to have a dark moustache when he was so blond? A halfback, Mr. Libra had called him. Oh God, what was he going to do now?

He could never face his friends—they were all jealous and now they would be so glad they had a chance to laugh at him. He could never hold his head up in a gay bar again. No one he knew would believe that story about going into a convent. They would all know he was fired, finished, wiped out, rejected. He felt as if he was walking through water. He made his way into the bathroom, reached into the dirty-clothes hamper, and took out one of his bottles of sleeping pills. Then he took another from a drawer, another from the back of the closet, and another from his shoebag. There were enough pills here to kill an elephant. He found a quart of orange juice in the refrigerator and took it and the pills to the couch.

The first few pills made him feel more relaxed and not so depressed, so he piled his favorite records on the turntable and listened to them while he took the rest of the pills. His tongue felt fuzzy, his lips numb, and his feet like lead. His finger tips were cold and numb, too. He decided to write a farewell note, so he took a sheet of paper and a pen from the desk and wrote:

"Dear Mother: I am sorry. I love you. This bankbook is for you."

He laid the bankbook on top of the note on the desk and sighed. He didn't feel well. His whole body felt weighted down; his eyelids felt as if they had weights on them too. He put the sofa pillows on the floor and lay down on them, listening to the music. Dimly, he heard the phone ring, then stop, then ring again. He'd forgotten to sign the note. Was that because he didn't know what name to sign? It didn't matter; they would know who wrote it when they found him. How sad that he had to die without ever having found anyone to love. But he wasn't really dying. Bonnie Parker was dead, and there had never really been a Vincent Abruzzi. What was dying was this unwanted freak of a body that was of no use to anyone now. He wondered who would get all his clothes. They were too big for Gerry. Maybe she could have them altered. It would be a shame to let all those beautiful clothes go to waste . . .

They'd be sorry . . .

They'd remember beautiful Bonnie and some of them would cry . . .

If he had lived, what would have become of him . . . ?

He'd never hear that record again . . .

Someone was putting a dagger down his throat with a balloon at the end of it. He thought his stomach was about to burst from the pain. He couldn't swallow, but he wanted to swallow or else he would throw up. God, his stomach hurt. Who was holding him down? It felt like a two-ton octopus had hold of him. He was hot and cold and his face and body were bathed in sweat. The room was full of a blinding white light that he could see through his closed eyelids. Then the pain turned into a sore numbness and everything went mercifully black again.

He was strapped into a bed with sides and Gerry was holding his hand. His other hand was strapped down because his arm was attached to a board and there was a needle in his arm. The needle was attached to a tube that led to a bottle above the bed. The room was painted greenish-white and it was dim. Gerry's face kept swimming away.

"Oh, Bonnie," she said. "Oh, Bonnie. How could you do a thing like that? Don't you know we all love you? You are a stupid turd. Do you know it cost me fifteen dollars for the locksmith to break down the door and replace the lock? You're lucky you're not in Bellevue."

"Where am I?"

"You're in a private hospital. I came home early because I was worried about you. You're lucky you're not dead."

"My stomach hurts."

"I don't wonder. They had to use a stomach pump on you. Where did you ever get all those pills?"

"I want to die," Vincent said. He began to cry. Crying made his stomach hurt even more, and the pain in his stomach only made him cry harder. "I want to die."

"You can't die—it's against the law. So you're not a model, so what?" She wiped his tears gently with a tissue from the metal table beside the bed. "Don't cry, Bonnie. Everything will be all right. You're still beautiful. So you're

ot a beautiful girl. You never were a girl in the first place.
But you *are* a beautiful boy. Everything is going to be all
ight, Bonnie."

"Stop calling me Bonnie."

"Vincent. You're getting better already. Listen to me,
Vincent. Are you listening?"

Vincent nodded. He squeezed Gerry's hand. "Don't go
way."

"I'm not going away."

"I hate that Libra."

"It's not his fault. Blame nature. Everything is going to be
ll right, Vincent. When you get home in a couple of days
'm going to have weights and bar bells ready for you.
You're going to use them, every day. You're going to develop
hose beautiful muscles. I'm getting you a membership in a
ealth club. You're going to swim, and jog, and do exercises,
nd sit under the sunlamp. You'll even meet numbers there,
ou'll see. You're going to be a beautiful man, Vincent.
You're not going to look like a nelly fruit. Vincent is going to
e just as beautiful a man as Bonnie was a girl. You'll start
ll over again."

Vincent looked at her. She looked serious and enthusiastic.
Maybe she really meant it . . . maybe she really believed it
. . maybe it could come true. "You think so?"

"I know it."

He tried a little smile. "If I get to be a man, will you
narry me?"

"No, but I'll make you a movie star."

"As a *man?*"

"Why not? Do you think you'll be the first fruit who ever
ecame a sex symbol? You're going to be about six feet two,
with those gorgeous shoulders and your new muscles; and
hat blond hair and those violet eyes will be wonderful with a
an. Libra still owes you a screen test, you know. If Bonnie
oesn't take it, maybe Vincent can."

"You're just saying that to make me feel better."

"Why would I do that? So you'd kill yourself again when
ou find out I'm lying? No, I mean it, Vincent. You get well
nd do what I tell you, and if Mr. Libra won't handle you, *I*
will."

Vincent felt a great wave of peace wash over him. He
losed his eyes. "I want to sleep now. Don't go away."

"I'll be right here."

"Gerry?"

"What?"

"What will you call me when I'm a movie star?"

"Vincent ... not Vincent Abruzzi. Vincent ... Stone! Vincent Stone. How does that sound?"

"I like it," Vincent said. He felt himself drifting off into peaceful, healthy sleep. Gerry's hand felt so tiny in his ... God, girls had tiny hands. "I have money," he murmured.

"I know. That will pay for the new Vincent."

Vincent Stone ... sex symbol. Vincent Stone ... movie star. Bonnie Parker in the convent and Vincent Stone in Hollywood ... Gerry's hand was so tiny, so delicate, but at that moment Vincent knew with love and gratitude that it was the strongest hand in the world.

When he woke later it was night, and she was still there beside him. "Where's my mother?"

"We didn't tell her."

"That's good. Gerry?"

"What?"

"Is it true? What you said before? I didn't dream it?"

"You didn't dream it," Gerry said. She kissed him on the forehead. "You hurry up and get well so you can get out of here. You're going to be a star, Vincent Stone."

CHAPTER

TWENTY-SIX

AT THE END of January Silky's show was bought by the movies, and she would star in it. Libra reminded her smugly that it had been a real coup for him, making them take her, but she did not really believe it had been that difficult. She was becoming more confident of herself. Love had made her confident. Besides, she had seen the photos of herself in most of the magazines, and she knew she was photogenic. She was beginning to wise up to Libra's tricks to keep her scared of him, and her hatred had softened to dislike and vague disgust. What was the point of hating him when he was crazy? You should feel pity for crazy people.

The thing that bothered her was that when the show closed, probably during the slow period in the summer, she would have to go to California, and what would happen to Bobby? Would he come too? Would they break up? She knew it was useless to worry about something that far away—besides, they might not need her till next fall or winter—and people often broke up long before a separation period they were both so worried about, but still it bothered her. She didn't want to discuss it. He hinted about it, though. He would say things like "Oh, Big Sur is beautiful," or "California might be a good place for me," and then she would hold her breath and wait for him to decide everything for her. She didn't want to be just another star who went to Hollywood

with her lover in tow; she wanted to go there as a married
woman with her husband. They could get a house with a
swimming pool and set up housekeeping. She didn't want to be
in gossip columns, the subject of those nasty guessing games—
"When will Silky Morgan and constant companion Bobby
La Fontaine tie the knot????"—she wanted to be married.

Bobby had mentioned casually that he'd given his apartment to a friend, and had brought all the rest of his things to
her apartment, mostly books and records. He'd left the furniture and phonograph for the friend. Knowing him, he'd sold
them to the friend. There was no reason for him to marry
her, but there was no reason for him not to either. Neither of
them saw anyone else unless they were together. They never
lied to each other. They loved each other. *Why* couldn't they
get married? Maybe he was waiting for her to ask him. But
she didn't dare.

Then one morning they got up and she said, "What do you
want to do today?" and he said, half kidding, "Why don't we
get married?"

"All right!" she said, and jumped out of bed. "We'll go to
City Hall and get a wedding license."

He looked surprised. "Today?"

"Why not?"

"Well ... I have to cash a check."

"It's two dollars!"

"Don't you want a ring?" he said.

"You get the ring when we get married, not when we get
the license. We have to have blood tests and everything. We
couldn't get married for a couple of days."

"Don't you want a big wedding?"

"No," Silky said. "I want you. Let's elope."

He looked pleased. "I hate big weddings. We could get
married Saturday after the show, and then we'd have Sunday
and Monday for the honeymoon. We could go to Connecticut."

She felt oddly disappointed. What she'd really wanted, she
realized, *was* a big wedding, or at least one with all her
family present, and a few friends. Eloping was like playing a
game. It didn't seem real. She wanted to buy a white dress
and a veil, or at least a little hat, and have a bouquet, and a
wedding cake with a bride and groom on top, and champagne. And music! She didn't want a judge or justice of the
peace she'd never met before and would never see again to

be the only person present at what was the most important and sacred moment in her life.

"Maybe we should ask a few people and have a party," she said.

"Oh, now I don't want to start all that. Libra will find out and he'll turn it into a circus. I just want to elope. When we get married it's our business and not everybody else's. I don't want to go through all that shit. I'm marrying the girl I love, I'm not marrying a star."

"It wouldn't be like that."

"It would. Believe me."

He gave her a look so tender and sweet that she couldn't argue with him. Besides, she was not used to disagreeing with anybody. She was too afraid they would get angry with her. But Bobby had given her an idea. So when he went into the bathroom she telephoned a columnist she knew rather well and said: "Listen ... don't tell anybody because it's a big secret, but I'm going to get married. We're going to get the license today. Don't tell a soul, okay? I'm just telling you because you're my friend and I'm so excited I had to tell somebody."

She put on her favorite wig and took great care with her make-up and the choice of a dress because now she knew there would be photographers at the marriage-license bureau. When Bobby wanted to wear jeans and a sweater she told him mildly that maybe it would be nice if he wore a suit and tie, because, after all, a girl didn't get a wedding license every day. She made sure he had enough money, because it might not be two dollars, it might be five or more with inflation, and she didn't want to have to hand him the money in front of the photographers. She felt a little evil and rotten doing this to him, but after all, a girl *didn't* get married every day, and when Libra saw the pictures in the papers tomorrow he would make sure they had a nice wedding, because, after all, she was his star ...

As she'd expected, the columnist had sent a photographer, and there were some there anyway who evidently just hung around waiting to see if anybody interesting turned up, or maybe he'd leaked the news, so there were four in all for some reason, and Bobby looked annoyed except when they took his picture, and then he looked darling because he was in show business too and he couldn't afford to look ugly in the papers. He didn't seem to suspect a thing.

The surprise was Libra's reaction. (She'd stopped thinking

of him as Mr. Libra somewhere along the last few weeks, but
when he called her, furious, he was Mr. Libra all over
again.)

"Get your ass to my office this instant," he said in a cold,
hard voice.

"I don't want you to speak to me like that, Mr. Libra," she
whispered.

"You get down here and bring that fiancé of yours with
you." He said "fiancé" as if he was saying "gigolo," which was
certainly what he meant.

"Yes, sir."

"What did he say?" Bobby asked.

"He wants to see us. He's mad."

"What right has he got to be mad? He doesn't own you."

"I don't know why he's mad. But we'd better go over
there."

"Well, I'm not going over there," Bobby said. "Screw
him."

"Oh, please," Silky said. "I'm scared to go alone."

"What are you scared of?"

"I don't know."

"What can he do to you?"

She thought about it. Bobby was right. What *could* Mr.
Libra do? Keep her money? So what. How much did it cost
to get married? She had expected that when he saw the
photos and read that they had the license he would just
accept it and arrange a nice wedding for them, because Mr.
Libra liked to arrange everyone's life, but it hadn't occurred
to her that he would be angry like this and even try to stop
them. She'd been so excited about getting married at last that
it had just never occurred to her that everyone else wouldn't
be delighted too.

"I guess he can't do anything," she said, finally.

"Damn right he can't. Come on, I'll go with you. Just
remember—he works for you, you don't work for him."

"I don't, do I?" Silky said, surprised. "*I* can fire *him!*"

Still, it was the children against the grown-ups, and they
both knew it. It didn't make any sense, but there it was.
Bobby was defiant and Silky was sick from nervousness, just
because they were going to Mr. Libra's office, he wasn't
coming to their apartment, and he had made them come
because he always knew how to take advantage.

When they went up in the elevator, Bobby held Silky's
hand, and she glanced at him for reassurance and noticed

with horror that he was wearing a sweater and jeans again
and his awful Army jacket, and he looked like a hippie,
especially with all that hair ... and oh, Lord, he was wearing
that gold Peace thing on a chain around his neck! Mr. Libra
would pick on that, too. But Bobby was so clean. He was the
cleanest boy she'd ever seen. Mr. Libra should like that,
anyway.

"Smile," Bobby told her, smiling.

They rang the bell to the suite and Gerry opened the door
and threw her arms around Silky's neck with a little squeal.
"Congratulations! Oh, no, you're not supposed to say that to
the girl." She kissed Bobby on the cheek. "Congratulations,
Bobby. Oh, Silky, I'm so delighted!"

"Where is .. uh?" Silky whispered.

"He'll be out in a minute."

"He's mad, huh?"

"Furious. Don't worry. Let him scream, he'll feel better.
When's the wedding?"

"We ..." Silky began, and then Mr. Libra was standing
behind Gerry, dressed in black as if in mourning.

"Out," Mr. Libra said to Gerry in a voice of ice.

Gerry winked and disappeared. Silky and Bobby stood
there with fixed smiles. Mr. Libra's face had such a look of
cold rage that Silky began hating him all over again. With
the hate came the old fear, and she didn't even know why.
That man just always scared her, that's all.

"Take off your coats and sit down." When he said "coats"
he looked at Bobby's Army jacket and everything else he had
on, and that look was enough. He might as well have said
"rags." Silky took off her two-hundred-dollar leather coat with
the little fur collar and handed it to Bobby to hang up.
Bobby put it over the back of a chair. They sat side by side
on the couch. Mr. Libra paced in front of them like a father
deciding if he should take his kids to the woodshed.

"This is ridiculous," Mr. Libra said. "You can't get married."

"Oh?" Bobby said.

"You know that, don't you?" Mr. Libra went on. "You two
can't get married. The joke is over. I'm sending out a
retraction next week. You've changed your minds."

"I haven't changed my mind!" Silky burst out. "I can
marry anybody any time I want to, any time I want to, and
you can't stop me. I'm over twen ..." She stopped, realizing
she wasn't.

"But you're not," Mr. Libra said. "You're only nineteen."

"Eighteen is legal age for girls in this state," Bobby said.

"Indeed? And for boys, I believe, it is twenty-one. How old are you? Nineteen? You see, you're a minor, and I have a very good attorney." Mr. Libra clasped his hands under his chin and smiled.

"I don't understand," Bobby said. "Why should you care?"

Mr. Libra kept smiling that smug, infuriating smile. *Oh, Lord,* Silky thought, *why did he have to ask that!*

"I think *she* knows," Mr. Libra said.

Silky didn't answer or even look at either of them. She realized that Mr. Libra wanted to start a fight between her and Bobby.

"You're not *married,* are you?" Bobby said to her pleasantly.

"No, of course not. *You* aren't, are you?"

"No." They smiled at each other.

"You see?" Silky said.

Mr. Libra walked to his desk and took a folder off the top of it. He walked a few steps toward them with the folder in his hands. Then he opened it and began to read. "May 4 to August 14, last year, 200 East 57th Street, c/o Antonini, August 14 to August 20, parked yellow 1960 Plymouth, August 21 to September 15, 5 Fifth Avenue, c/o Mrs. Bruns . . ."

"What is *that?*" Bobby said angrily.

"A list of your former residences."

"A car?" Silky said. "You lived in a parked car?"

"Just slept there," Bobby said. "I was out of money."

"Better you should ask about Mr. Antonini and Mrs. Bruns," Mr. Libra said. "Shall I continue to read the list? It's quite long. You never seem to keep your friends for very long. Do they find you too expensive?"

"Let's go," Bobby said. He stood up.

Silky shook her head. "I don't know who these people are, Mr. Libra," she said, "but I think you wasted your money hiring a detective to get you that list. I know all about that and I couldn't care less. A man is entitled to have friends and just because you made a list of them doesn't make them any more than friends no matter what you think." Bobby sat down, looking expressionless, which she knew was his way of trying not to look surprised. She went on, feeling braver.

"I'm sure you have a list of my lovers before I met Bobby, and if you don't I'm sure you can hire a detective to get one."

"What lovers?" Mr. Libra and Bobby said almost in unison.

Silky smiled. "Oh . . . my lovers. Quite a few of them had their pictures taken with me in the papers." What a lie! She didn't know if Mr. Libra believed all those publicity dates had been her lovers or not. "In fact, Mr. Libra, you fixed me up with them. So you might say you were pimping."

"You little . . . !"

"Slut," Silky supplied sweetly.

"I'd like to see you two live on just your allowance," Mr. Libra said. "I'd like to see how long it takes before *he* starts seeing his old friends again. If you get married I will see that you go back on your old allowance."

"Then I'll just write my memoirs for the newspapers," Silky said. "They pay a lot. Especially from a new star. And they'd love to know about all my lovers back home in Philadelphia when I was just fourteen years old. I could get a hundred thousand dollars for that."

"You are living in a fantasy world!" Mr. Libra screamed.

"No," Bobby said, "you are. We aren't Romeo and Juliet. We're adults. And you aren't even a very good liar, sir. You wouldn't expose Silky to any bad publicity if your life depended on it—and it does, in a way. Thirty per cent of her income isn't bad, is it? And it'll be even better next year, won't it? I can get married with my mother's consent, and no state in this country will set that marriage aside no matter how many lawyers you hire. And Silky's of age."

Libra ran to the desk and grabbed a sheet of paper. "Your contract," he said, holding it up, but so quickly that Silky couldn't see whether it was or not. He ripped the paper in half.

Silky shrugged. She was sure he had at least a dozen copies in his safe. People only tore up contracts in the movies. She felt tired. She wanted to go home. Nobody said anything. Bobby took her hand and smiled at her. She smiled back. He looked nice in a sweater and she was sorry she was ashamed of him in the elevator. He was more of a man than old Hitler ape-face Libra would ever be. Libra buzzed for Gerry. She came out of the bedroom.

"Do we have any champagne?" he asked.

"Yes, Mr. Libra."

"And get four glasses and your steno pad. We have to make out the guest list for this wedding. I'll hire the Terrace Room."

It seemed so long ago that Silky had made her little plot for Libra to give them a fancy wedding. How a half an hour of hatred could change everything! "We won't have a circus," she said. "Bobby and I will make the list."

"I'm paying for it, and I'll make the list," Libra said. Gerry opened the champagne with a loud pop.

"Just our families," Silky said. "And a few friends."

"And columnists," Libra said.

"Just the ones who were nice to me," Silky said.

"Some stars . . ."

"No! Just people we know."

"Let the bride be the star," Bobby said. "It's her wedding."

"I think that's a lovely idea," Gerry said. She handed each of them a glass of champagne.

"No Terrace Room," Silky said. "I'm getting married in a church."

"The Terrace Room is for the reception, stupid," Libra said.

"Then we can have an orchestra," Silky said.

Libra nodded. He raised his glass. "To the lovebirds."

Bobby glared at him. He wasn't going to drink to the occasion, even though it had turned out to be theirs. Silky put her hand on his arm. "Please, honey?"

"I'm not going to drink with a lunatic," Bobby said. "Whose wedding is this, anyway?"

"Yours," Libra said innocently. "Yours. I'm just helping make it nice."

"Oh, let him," Gerry said. "He hasn't got any children."

"You're all lunatics," Bobby said. But he raised his glass and took a sip of the cold champagne.

Silky drank hers all down with relief and kissed him. Sometimes, like now, she was really glad that Bobby had the soul of a hustler. At least she would get the beautiful wedding she'd always dreamed about. And as for the rest of their lives together, they could do as they pleased.

They set the date for Valentine's Day, about three weeks away. The day was Gerry's idea, because Mad Daddy's divorce still hadn't come through and she felt if she couldn't use Valentine's Day for her wedding at least her friend could. Silky decided with surprise that she and Gerry really were good friends, maybe even best friends. After all, who else did she like?

The next days were frantically busy. There was a church to be found—not so easy because neither she nor Bobby were members of any congregation—and invitations to be printed and sent out, a wedding dress to be chosen, flowers, the food ... Silky insisted on hovering over Mr. Libra throughout all the plans so he would not make her wedding too vulgar. She didn't trust him. Since he wanted to pay for it he seemed to feel it was *his* wedding, more of a publicity party than a wedding at all. He insisted that Franco design her wedding dress, and then Silky had to fight with Franco because she wanted a sweet, old-fashioned kind of wedding gown and he wanted to make something crazy. She won. Nelson was to do her hair, and *he* wanted to stick a bird on her head, so there was another fight. No stranger to fights, Silky finally had her way with Nelson too. She wasn't going to look like any freak just so he could get publicity out of the pictures. She even had to fight with Mr. Libra over the music the orchestra would play at the reception. She didn't want them to play any of her songs, just classical favorites, but Mr. Libra won this fight and said she couldn't tell the orchestra every single song to play or not to play because there were too many songs to choose and people had to be able to dance to some of them.

She didn't want to have bridesmaids because they would have to be the Satins and that would be a farce. Luckily, they found a minister who said he would marry them in the little chapel outside the main room of the church, so all she needed was someone to give her away, and she decided that would be her older brother Arthur. Old ape-face Libra actually looked disappointed—he had thought she was going to ask *him!* What did he think she was, an orphan with no family at all? She bought Arthur a groovy tux, and he would wear a little flower in his lapel, maybe lily-of-the-valley if there were any that early.

She ordered a great big three-tier white wedding cake, with a bride and groom on top, and told the baker that the bride and groom *weren't* going to be white. There would be champagne and canapes, and then a big dinner with roast beef, and cherries jubilee, flaming. And she would have a bouquet to toss after the reception when she and Bobby rushed away. She went to Bendel's and bought a little suit to rush away in, because she wouldn't be caught dead in one of Franco's jobs with the shoulder pads and peplum.

Where were they going to rush to? The theater to do their evening performance? The idea seemed sacrilegious. Silky pleaded with the producers of her show, who had been invited to the wedding, and they agreed to give her a week's vacation as a wedding present, so they were going to go to a ski lodge in Vermont. Neither she nor Bobby could ski, but snow and quiet and a roaring fire in a big room seemed very romantic, and it wasn't very expensive, so he could manage to pay for their honeymoon himself, which was what they both wanted. A friend of his was lending them a car to drive up in. Mr. Libra gave them a matched set of Vuitton luggage—six pieces—for a wedding present.

She went with Bobby to pick out a wedding ring, and they decided on a plain platinum band because it looked nice with the little diamond bracelet he'd given her for Christmas, which she never took off. She got him a matching ring.

There were so many things to do and so little time to do them in, with their shows every night and two matinees. Lizzie Libra even made her go to register her silver and china patterns at Tiffany's so that people could give her wedding presents, which Silky thought was ridiculous because nobody in her family had any money except what she and the girls gave them, and everybody they knew gave cash for a wedding gift anyway. Besides, she was living in a sublet, and then they would be renting in California, so who wanted a lot of dishes and silverware to lug around all over the country? Still, Lizzie insisted, saying that was what a bride did.

"What do you want, paper plates?" Lizzie said. "Are you going to register your china pattern at Hallmark?"

The invitations went out, really a formality, because Silky had already telephoned her family and told them all the details. She knew they would be impressed with the engraved invitations. She arranged for their transportation and hotel rooms for them to get dressed in, and sent her Auntie Grace a check so she could buy anything she wanted to wear. She knew that would make the twins mad, because they bought Auntie Grace more fancy clothes than she wanted, but it was *her* wedding and Auntie Grace was the closest thing to a mother she had.

Bobby was patient with all the plans and the shopping and

actually seemed to enjoy it. He always enjoyed nice things, and everything at their wedding was going to be very nice, in perfect taste. Silky decided one thing no one would ever be able to say at her wedding was that here was an ex-slum bunny getting married.

The night before the wedding the kids from the show chipped in to give Silky and Bobby a party at her understudy's apartment. She noticed with surprise that it was really kind of a dump, and she realized that actresses didn't make much money unless they were stars like she was. Silky had never been to the homes of any of the kids in the cast, and the party gave her a warm feeling. It was funny how when you had a man everybody got very nice to you and wanted you around. She decided that after she and Bobby were married she would give little dinner parties for people at their apartment. She'd never invited any of the kids up there before.

And then it was her wedding day. She and Bobby woke up and looked at each other and at the sun streaming in from the terrace into the living room and realized it was their wedding day, and it made them both feel strange and shy. It was like opening in another show. She was almost sorry they hadn't eloped, after all. She put on her robe and went out onto the terrace alone. The air was cold and crisp and there was some snow along the edges of the tops of small buildings far below.

"This is my last day as a single woman," she said to the world. She wondered if Bobby minded that it was his last day as a bachelor. It was much harder for men to get married. They had so much to give up. But she would make it up to him. She would make him happy. She would never let him regret what he had done for her.

The wedding was beautiful, like a dream. Silky cried a little, Auntie Grace cried a lot, and even the Satins looked touched. Then they all rushed over to the Plaza in rented limousines and they had the most perfect reception Silky could ever have imagined. Even though there were more strangers there than she would have liked, it didn't matter. Everybody was all dressed up, and they ate and drank and danced, and nobody got drunk and made a scene ... it was lovely. Really, it was like a wedding in the movies. She never would have imagined, when she was a kid going to see movies where rich people got married, that someday she would be having a wedding that was much like that but ten thousand times better. It was *her* party, the first real party she'd ever had in her life. It made up for all the birthday parties she'd never had. It almost made up for everything. Everybody liked each other, and everybody liked her, and she liked all of them, even old ape-face Libra there, unwillingly dancing with his wife. Bobby would never treat her the way Libra treated Lizzie, not even when they were old. But looking at Bobby's beautiful face it was hard to imagine that either of them would ever grow old. It seemed now in this magic time that they would both stay young and beautiful forever.

At the end of the reception, just before Silky and Bobby rushed away, Silky threw her bouquet to Gerry. "You're next!" Gerry pulled out one of the white carnations and put it into Mad Daddy's lapel. They both looked so sweet together. Honey was looking mad because she had hoped Silky would throw *her* the bouquet for luck. Fat chance. That one needed more than a bouquet for luck.

When Silky and Bobby returned from their honeymoon, Mr. Libra told them he'd gotten an offer for Bobby to be the lead dancer in a television special, with billing. Their marriage had gotten a lot of publicity and people were calling to offer him jobs.

"It always happens that way," Libra said.

Didn't it always! When something wonderful happened and you were really happy it seemed as if everything good started happening for you after that. Silky knew that there was no stopping them now.

CHAPTER

TWENTY-SEVEN

DAMN telethons anyway, Gerry thought. Here it was March, still freezing cold, and everyone would have to sit in that hot, overcrowded room in their winter clothes, waiting for hours to go in front of the cameras for one minute, bored, miserable, and not even getting paid. The worst was that Mad Daddy hated telethons so much, and she had to go with him to hold his hand and keep him happy when she didn't feel exactly happy about the whole thing herself. He was dawdling in the bathroom, combing his hair, changing his tie three times, doing anything to be as late as possible.

"Libra acts like the great man of charity," Mad Daddy had told her, "but the real reason he makes all of us do so many benefits is it's free publicity. He couldn't care less about the cause."

"Hurry up," she called. "I want you there early, before the crowd."

He came out of the bathroom, tieless again. "Do I have to go?"

"You know you do. You promised, and they announced that you'd be on. You can't back out now."

"They'll never miss me," he murmured miserably.

"You know they will."

"There'll be that mob outside . . ."

"We have the limousine. There'll be cops. I'll hold your hand. Come on, don't be silly. Let's get it over with."

"I'm glad you're with me," he said. "Even though you *are* little."

"I love you," Gerry said.

"I love you, too."

The person who was probably happiest about the telethon that night was Barrie Grover, president of the now-defunct Mad Daddy Fan Club of Kew Gardens, its only surviving member. When she'd seen on TV that Mad Daddy was going to be on the telethon she decided she would go, and meet him at last. She knew it was going to be on all night, so she told her mother she was going to sleep overnight at Donna's house so they could study together, and then she put on two sweaters under her winter coat in case she had to stand outside the stage door all night. She took her schoolbooks so her mother wouldn't suspect anything, and dropped them off at Donna's.

"If she calls, say I'm in the bathroom or something," she told Donna.

"You're crazy," Donna said. "There'll be two million people there and you'll never see him."

"I'll see him. He knows me."

"Sure he does."

"He *does!*"

"You really going to wait there all night?"

"Maybe he'll be on early."

"Well, if he is," Donna said, "be careful coming home. You'd better take a cab."

"I haven't any money. Do you?"

"Are you kidding? I bought false eyelashes this week and I have to use my lunch money for bus fare. You should have asked your mother for money."

"For what?"

Donna shrugged. "Well, just be careful. You shouldn't run around by yourself in the middle of the night."

"I'll be all right," Barrie said. But she was scared. Love was stronger than fright, and she knew she had to go, but she was scared. She just wouldn't think about that dark, lonely walk from the bus stop. Maybe she wouldn't have to come back till morning, and then she could go straight to school.

"Will you bring my books to class tomorrow?"

"Yeah, okay."

"Don't forget."

"I won't. Good luck." Donna grinned. "Maybe he'll ask you out for a drink."

"Ohhh, wouldn't that be great?"

"Here, listen, let me fix your eye make-up."

Donna was a great expert on make-up by now, and she skillfully put eye liner and shadow on Barrie's eyes, making them look twice as big. Barrie could hardly recognize herself. She really was pretty. Maybe Mad Daddy *would* ask her out for a drink. Stranger things had happened!

"Here, use some of my perfume," Donna said. "Why do you have to wear all those sweaters? You look fat."

"I do? Oh, then can I leave one at your house? You can bring it with the books."

She did look better without the bulky sweater; she looked cute. Donna combed and teased her hair for her and sprayed it lightly because Barrie hated a lot of spray. They both observed the results in the mirror.

"You look older," Donna said. "You should fix yourself up like that all the time."

"For what?"

"For school, you ding-a-ling. Then you'd meet somebody."

"There isn't anybody in school I want to meet," Barrie said. Donna walked her to the door and she went out into the street.

It was dark, but there were cars going along the block and she walked carefully near the curb, not close enough to the dark shadows between the houses so someone could jump out at her, and not close enough to the street so anyone in a car could get the idea she wanted to be picked up. A car honked at her and she heard the raucous laughter of boys. She felt cold. She hated those boys she didn't know, who didn't know her but made rude remarks, but she wasn't really afraid of them. What she was really afraid of was some unknown grown man who might drag her into an alley. The sound of her boot heels clicking along the sidewalk sounded very loud and too feminine, too enticing. She tried not to walk too fast, so her footsteps would not sound afraid. She wondered if anyone lurking there could smell her perfume. She was sorry she'd let Donna put it on. She knew that in her purse was the little knife she'd bought to protect herself with, but she also knew that she'd never have the courage to use it. She looked straight ahead, and finally she saw the bus stop and breathed a huge sigh of relief. Some maids were waiting there—she could tell they were maids by the way they were dressed and the tired way they stood. She was glad to see them. Supper was over in all the houses, and the dishes were washed. Many lights were out, and she could see the blue light coming from all those TV sets. The telethon would start in half an hour. She climbed on the bus to Manhattan, feeling a great surge of joy. Mad Daddy! Oh, she loved him so!

The stage door to the television studio was at the end of a wide alley between two big buildings. The alley was crowded with people waiting to look at the stars who were coming in and going out. A few police held them back so there was a narrow place for the performers to enter the stage door. Limousines and cabs pulled up to the curb, and every time someone got out the crowd would make a rush to see who it was. If it was someone very famous they would ooh and ah, and if it was someone they didn't recognize they would ask each other who it was until someone knew, and then they would rush forward again, but not so enthusiastically. There were kids with autograph books, but what surprised Barrie was that there were so many adults. Sleazy-looking adults with dead, stupid faces. Some of the fans seemed to know all the stars, and called out to them by their first names when they went by. She stationed herself at the edge of the crowd until she saw a little space to dart through so she could get closer, then waited again, then darted again. Because she was so small it was easy to get under people's arms by ducking and weaving, and to squeeze by them before they could stop her. Most of the people seemed friendly and curious and just plain stupid, but she was surprised by the vicious ones, who didn't seem to know what they were waiting for but were determined that no one should get anything they didn't get first. She even saw some well-dressed middle-aged women in fur coats, who had probably been attracted by the fuss and had stayed when they saw what it was all about. She noticed with pleasure that there were no really pretty girls who Mad Daddy might single out to like. They were all standard kids, like her friends.

Barrie had no interest in any of the stars except Mad Daddy. She noticed idly that the King James Version, carrying instruments, were coming in, their hair as long as girls' hair. Michelle would be thrilled; the lead singer was her new crush from afar, but her feeling for him was nothing like her feeling for Mad Daddy had been. Michelle just liked him and bought their records. The kids in the mob started to scream when the group pushed their way through, and the cop who was trying to hold back the crowd near the group had a mean look on his face. Barrie wondered idly if the cops would decide to start hitting people on the head with their nightsticks. She stood there very quietly, making no noise, tensing her muscles so no one could push her away from her good place. She was right in front of the opening for the stars, and no one who entered or left could get by without her seeing him.

Where was Mad Daddy? Maybe he wasn't coming after all. Maybe he'd come early, before she got there. Maybe he was going to come really late, near the end. It wasn't cold any more because of the big crowd, all sending off heat from their bodies. Some of the people smelled bad. There was a smell she absolutely hated, of old cocktails drunk at dinner, and cigarettes smoked all day. She breathed into her glove.

Some of the people in the crowd left and new people squeezed in. It was like a dirty river, always moving, pushing its trash up against her. Her feet began to feel numb, but she couldn't hop up and down because there wasn't room. People really were disgusting, she decided. She could imagine all those stomachs digesting all that food, all those mouths with decaying teeth, all those female organs hidden under girdles and pants, dirty holes yearning for sex and never getting it because their owners were so old and ugly. Why didn't those women go home to their ugly husbands? Maybe they had no one to go home to. Ugh . . . pigs.

Someone stuck a sharp elbow in her shoulder. She smelled dusty cloth from someone's winter coat. Up high in the sky she could see the clean stars, twinkling far away. She held her head up and tried to breathe clean air from the heavens. She pushed her sleeve up and looked at her watch. It was midnight. She'd been there forever. Those stupid pig faces looked so happy, just because they could look at famous people who didn't know or care that they were alive. Mad Daddy would be glad to see her. He would smile when he recognized her from the picture she'd sent him and remembered all those nice, sensitive letters she'd sent him and all those thoughtful presents she'd made.

"I'm Barrie," she would say.

"Barrie!" And he would reach out to shake her hand and pull her from the crowd. "Where have you been all this time?

Why didn't you ever come to see me before? Do you mean
you've been standing out here in the cold all night just to see
me? Oh, you must be cold and tired. Why don't you come
into my nice warm car and I'll buy you a nice cup of hot
chocolate? Unless, of course, you'd prefer a drink? You look
old enough to drink. I thought you were just a little girl when
you wrote me."

"I was then," Barrie would say. "But I've grown up."

Grown up? She'd aged ten years standing here in this icky
mob. Where was he? Where was he? Where was he? One
o'clock. She was so tired and aggravated she thought she
would die.

Two o'clock. Her feet really were numb. But she'd stay
here the rest of her life if she had to, just to meet Mad
Daddy. He was everything that was good and beautiful and
funny in this world. He made everything worthwhile—all the
loneliness, the strange depressions she seemed to be falling
into more and more lately, the dreams, the nightmares she
had at night. She felt more sense of purpose standing here
waiting for him than she ever did at school or with her
family and friends, doing what was supposed to be real life.
Tonight was her destiny: she could feel it. After tonight
everything would be different. Nothing would be boring
again. Everything would be good.

Even though Gerry stayed right by him every minute,
except of course when he was onstage, Mad Daddy felt
himself being overcome by the same claustrophobic, paranoid
feeling that always got him when he was subjected to a
crowd. When he was on the stage for those five minutes
before the cameras, and the large live audience held back by
darkness and propriety, he felt free, and he enjoyed himself
as he always did, clowning around, doing silly things, not
minding at all that he wasn't getting paid for this, because
performing really was something he would have done for free
all the time if he had no other choice. Funny how an
audience out front of a stage was a friend, but that same
audience let loose in the street became an enemy. They had
their role to play—audience; just as he did—performer. But
when the show was over they took on their new role—
hunters—and he became the hunted. As soon as he got
offstage and Gerry kissed him and handed him his overcoat
he began to sweat.

"Are you sure the car is right out front?"

"I checked. It's right at the curb," she said.

"I'm ready for a drink."

"There's something in the car," she said, grinning. Gerry always knew how to plan ahead for emergencies.

"I wish I had something now."

"Come on to the car. You'll have something in two seconds."

She didn't really understand—no one could, except him. It was like those people who became uncontrollably paranoid when they had to go up in a plane. You could quote statistics to them, how a plane was safer than a car or even crossing the street, but their bodies wouldn't listen; their legs became rubber, their guts turned to water, their hearts pounded—he could imagine what it was like because crowds affected him that way when the crowds knew who he was, and nothing could talk him out of it. He'd never dreamed, long ago, when he wanted to become somebody, that being somebody could be so terrifying.

His palms were wet and he felt dizzy. His skin had become so sensitive in these last few moments that a mere touch felt as if he was being scraped raw. There were cannibals out there, and they were going to rip off his extremities and gnaw on them. The cop at the door opened it and Gerry went out first, Mad Daddy clinging to a piece of her coat like a four-year-old. The crowd started to squeal and it sounded like the roar of an insane animal. He thought he was going to throw up from fright. In a moment they were separated, and although he could see her right in front of him he could no longer touch her, and his panic and loneliness overwhelmed him.

Dimly he saw all those nymphets, those girls he used to be so attracted to, and his panic combined with a sense of guilt and revulsion. Now that he loved Gerry and belonged to her, and she to him, those little girls seemed nauseating, obscene. *He* was obscene. How could he have mauled those delicate little limbs, kissed those children's mouths? He must have been crazy! They seemed completely sexless to him now, and those sexless, horny children were jumping up and down, trying to touch him, actually trying to touch him in the most embarrassing places, *wanting it!* They were assaulting him. He wanted to scream at all of them to go home.

They were screaming at *him*, screaming his name, all those

maddened little foxes. He walked on doggedly, making
for the sanctuary of his limousine, and prayed, prayed,
prayed . . .

A squeal came from the direction of the stage door, then
more squeals. "MAD DADD-EEE!" It was him! He was coming
out!

Barrie strained on tiptoe to get her first glimpse of him as
the mob pushed against her back. The cops pushed at the
crowd, the crowd pushed back; they were like the rocking
waves of a river. She saw him then, walking quickly toward
her. The reality of him was a shock. She had never seen him
in color before. His face, ruddy with the television make-up,
seemed to glow. He was solid flesh, a person, a real person,
her love. "Mad Daddy!"

The edge of the crowd had broken through now, raggedly,
and Barrie ducked and weaved through the people until she
was right in front of Mad Daddy. She was so close she could
reach right out and touch him.

"Mad Daddy!" she cried.

He looked right at her . . . no, right through her. His eyes
were flat and scared and full of hate, like a snake's eyes. She
knew he didn't know in the chaos who it was so close calling
to him.

"Mad Daddy!" Barrie said. "It's Barrie. *Barrie!*"

She needed something to hold him there a moment so he
would remember. An autograph . . . she reached into her
purse for her pen and pad.

He hit at her with the side of his arm and his elbow. He
shoved her away from him. His look said so completely that
he didn't want her, he didn't know her, that she meant less
than nothing to him, that it hurt more than his shove. He
smashed at her as if she were a bug; his unseeing eyes were
draining all the life juices out of her. "Don't you touch me!"
he snarled.

Her hand, searching for her pen, closed on her little
knife.

There was a great sigh from the crowd, like the sigh of a
dying monster. Barrie tried to focus her eyes and saw that
Mad Daddy was lying on the ground right there in front of
her with blood coming out of his chest. A red-haired girl was
kneeling beside him, holding his head and looking terrified.
Some girls in the crowd had begun to cry. People pushed at

her, shoved her, impersonally, not caring, just trying to see. "What happened?" people were asking. "What happened?"

Barrie turned to someone next to her. "What happened?" No one bothered to answer. "What *happened?*"

Mad Daddy's eyes were closed and he looked gray under the ruddy make-up. The red-haired girl on the ground started to cry without making any noise. The cops had their hands on their guns, and then one of them walked slowly over to where Mad Daddy was lying on the ground and put a coat over him, over his face and head, so he didn't look like Mad Daddy any more, he just looked like a lump on the ground that could have been anybody.

The crowd let out another great sigh, and some of the women and girls started to cry. Barrie realized she had something clutched in her hand, hidden there in the folds of her coat, and she let her numb fingers open and the knife fell to the ground. There was blood on her coat and on her glove. She didn't know how it had gotten there.

People were crowding around, defying the cops, trying to see that lifeless lump on the ground under the coat, and in the confusion Barrie managed to squeeze closer to the stage door. She would just stand here and wait until her own darling Mad Daddy came out.

CHAPTER

TWENTY-EIGHT

THEY kept staying with her: Libra, Lizzie, Silky, Vincen
... Vincent followed her like a dog. They were afraid sh
might kill herself. She wasn't going to kill herself—that wa
the farthest thing from her mind, for what good would anoth
er death do? But she had to be alone to think. Silky's docto
(not Ingrid) gave her pills; tranquillizers for the daytim
and sleeping pills for the nights. She preferre
drinking, and while Vincent watched her, playing upbea
records and trying to think of something to say, Gerr
methodically and pleasurelessly drank down a half bottle o
straight Scotch every night, finished the last of her third pac
of cigarettes for the day, and took her pill. She was docil
like an inmate. Why did they treat her like an inmate? It wa
that kid who was the inmate, the teen-ager Barrie somethin;
who had been caught two days after the ... after it ha;
pened (what had taken them so long?) and was away now i
some institution, it said in the newspapers, under psychiatr
care.

Elaine had come back for the funeral, dressed in blac
with a huge picture hat like that strange woman who pu
flowers on Valentino's grave every year, and Elaine had crie
and carried on as if the loss was hers. Gerry had sat ther
numb, drugged, drunk, looking calm and stolid for the worl

to see. There were his sister and brother-in-law. Funny to see his family for the first time that way ... She wanted to tear he box open but that wouldn't bring him back.

The public had fed on him and finally killed him. It was so ironic that he, the sweetest of men, had died saying something unthinkingly hurtful that was so entirely unlike him. Ironic too that someone they had never heard of should appear from nowhere and change all their lives. If that was what being a public idol meant, then Gerry wanted no part of it any more. No more sickness, no more sick love for strangers she had helped create, no more animals living vicariously off people they could never understand. She hated her job, she hated New York, and she had to get away.

She would go to a desert island, one of those islands she and Mad Daddy had dreamed of. She would stay alone, and pretend she was with him, until time made it easier to live by herself without the fantasy. She had to tell Libra she was leaving; it was only fair. Two days after the funeral she packed and told Vincent she was going home to her parents. She picked a deserted island from an ad in a magazine and made a plane reservation by phone. Then she went to the office to say good-bye to Libra and lie a little.

"Don't," he said. "Please don't." She saw pain in his eyes and it was strange because she had never thought he cared about anybody. "Don't go to your parents. Stay here and work. Work is the best cure. We're moving to our new offices soon. Look, see how nice the building is? You can see it from the window. You'll have your own office. You can decorate it any way you want to and I'll pay for it. You don't have to work at all while you're decorating it. Keeping busy is the only cure, believe me."

"I'm going," she said. "I just wanted to say good-bye and thank you for everything you've done for me."

"Don't."

"Well, good-bye," she said.

"Look," he said, "if you have to go, I have this nice little house at Malibu where Lizzie and I used to spend weekends when we lived in California. It's open, and there's a live-in housekeeper. You might as well use it since it's going to waste anyway. It's all alone on the beach, the neighbors won't bother you. I'll get you the plane ticket. Go there for a couple of weeks and lie on the beach in the sun. It's nice in California this time of year. You need a vacation anyway, you've been here a year."

A year? Was it a year? Just a little over a year since she'd
come to New York, and so many things had happened. Time
got condensed in this business. She thought about the house. It
would be nicer than a hotel, nobody to bother her. Besides,
she didn't have much money saved, and even on a deserted
island it wouldn't last long.

"Stay in the house as long as you like," Libra said.
"There's a phone, you can keep in touch."

"No, thank you anyway," she said. "You'll call me every
day about business, and I'm quitting. I can't stay in your
house free and not talk to you about business. It wouldn't be
fair."

"Fair? What's fair? Shut up." Libra reached for the phone.
"You can leave tonight. Go home and pack."

"I am packed."

"Then you'll leave this afternoon. I'll send you to the
airport in my limousine with Lizzie for company. You take a
cab from the airport and there's a car at the house with the
keys in it. The housekeeper shops, so you won't starve. There
are books and records at the house, a color TV set, and a
small projection room with a whole library of films."

"Just a simple little bungalow?" Gerry said, smiling in spite
of herself.

Vincent came along to the airport with her and Lizzie. He
had let his eyebrows grow in and was wearing his hair
combed like a boy. Without make-up, in a turtleneck sweater
and jeans, he looked like a very pretty faggot, but not like a
girl any more. Lizzie almost didn't recognize him. When
Vincent carried her bags to the baggage scale, Lizzie said to
Gerry: "Has he ever done it with a girl?"

"Oh, no."

"Hmmm," Lizzie said, looking at Vincent's broad shoulders
from the back, and smacked her lips.

They kissed her good-bye and Lizzie cried. "I'll take care
of the apartment," Vincent promised. "Do you have your
pills?"

"Yes." She also had a bottle of Scotch in her airplane bag.
"Take care of *yourself,* and lift your weights every day.
Don't forget to go to the gym and swim every morning.
Write to me; don't phone, it costs too much."

"I love you," Vincent murmured, and tears spilled out of
his eyes. They all knew she was never coming back, even
though she hadn't said anything. Gerry kissed him again.

"There's a whole wine cellar," Lizzie said. "Under the sink
the bar. Feel free."

"Thank you. Good-bye. Good-bye."

Buckled into her seat in the first-class cabin of the plane,
Gerry realized it was the first time she had been alone since it
happened. She wondered if the plane would crash. She really
didn't care, except it would be a shame for all the other
people. They wanted to go on. She didn't care one way or
the other; she just *would* go on because that was what you
did, that was all. She drank the free Scotches they gave her,
and the free wine and champagne, washed down with a
tranquillizer (one every four hours, the label said) and she
fell asleep. When she woke up she was in California with a
hangover.

The house was lovely and small, set high on the dunes
above Malibu Beach, with a little garden in front that was
sunny all day long, and its own private strip of beach. There
were houses on either side, but nobody bothered her. The
housekeeper, evidently briefed by Libra, kept to herself,
requesting only a list of the week's menus, which Gerry forgot
to give her, so the housekeeper planned and cooked all the
meals at her own discretion and did the shopping before
Gerry woke up in the morning. Gerry chose Libra's bedroom
for herself because it looked out at the sea. It had a king-
sized bed with blue sheets, and the colors of the room were
blue and green, like the sea, with a vase of fresh flowers from
the garden in a crystal vase on the dresser. In the mornings
when she woke, the housekeeper brought her breakfast on a
tray, and afterwards Gerry would take the morning
papers, also brought by the housekeeper, and read them on
the front porch in the sun. She lay in the sun for hours, with
a bottle of wine by her side, stupefied with the heat and the
quiet and the excellent wine (Libra always had the best of
taste) and wrote crazy poems in her head. At first the poems
were full of violence and hate.

There was a wood-paneled den (the one with the color
TV) with a typewriter and paper in it, so she began to write
her poems. They were terrible, but they made her feel better.
She wrote every afternoon, half drunk, then took a nap,
showered, and ate dinner in front of the television set. She
watched anything. The housekeeper showed her how to operate the projection machine for the films, but at first Gerry was
too numb to bother. But finally, out of curiosity and boredom, she began to show films for herself, all the good ones

she had missed during the years she was away in Europe. Sh
kept Scotch and ice by her side, and sometimes if she liked
film she showed it over three or four nights in a row. Ther
was something strangely satisfying about seeing the sam
characters up there on the screen, doing the same predictabl
things. It was like having people in the house with her. Sh
found a Zak Maynard film among the collection and wa
surprised that her professional curiosity was still with her
She showed it twice. He wasn't such a bad actor after al
She wondered if Silky would be good in the film version o
Mavis!

Silky wrote to her occasionally, although she was a terribl
letter writer and could never think of anything to say. Sh
wrote whatever news there was in New York, but Gerry wa
more interested in hearing from Silky than in the news
which seemed far away and unreal. Silky's husband, Bobby
had been a hit in his first solo dance appearance on the T
special, and was going to do a summer replacement series a
lead dancer, with billing. Some variety show. Silky wa
thrilled.

Vincent wrote too, almost every day. His news was entire
ly different: it was as if he and Silky inhabited different planet:
He couldn't care less what went on in New York or sho
business.

"Marcia the Sex Change had to go to the hospital becaus
her silicone started to slip," he wrote. "When she got ther
they made her take off her wig with the hundred and fift
falls, and she's all bald underneath, just an old bald mar
They didn't know whether to put her in the ward with th
women or the men. She said she had to go with the wome
because she had it lopped off. So there she was, with all thos
women, an old bald man, six feet four, with sliding tits. Wha
a *mess!*"

Vincent was afraid to go to the bars with his new look, fc
fear the queens would laugh at him, so his whole life wa
spent on the telephone keeping up with his world. He lifte
his weights, had gained fifteen pounds, grown another incl
and was becoming quite a good swimmer. "Guess what?" h
wrote. "I met this really nice boy at the gym. He's straigh
He says he hates nelly fruits and drag queens. He likes me.
didn't tell him I used to be Bonnie Parker. He would hav
died. He took me out twice this week, to straight restauran
for dinner, and nobody laughed or stared at us or anythin
I'm letting my hair grow long like a hippie, and I'm growin

a moustache. It's funny how when I didn't want a moustache it came in too fast, but now that I want one it's coming in too slow. A *girl* flirted with me at the supermarket this morning! Poor sick freak!"

Girls were beginning to look at him. Wow! Girls would look at anything, Gerry decided, but she was still pleased. Maybe Vincent had a movie career ahead of him after all, maybe even in another year. Teen-agers liked effeminate-looking boys, they weren't such a threat.

She noticed (on Libra's doctor's scale in the bathroom) that she was gaining weight from drinking so much, so she cut down to a few drinks a day and told the housekeeper not to cook anything rich. It was pleasant to be cared for, waited on, coddled. She wrote a postcard to her parents, telling them she was taking a vacation in Malibu (they never *had* known about her and Mad Daddy because she was keeping the news from them until after his divorce). She wrote brief letters to Silky and Vincent and Libra and Lizzie. She wrote more poems, not so angry now, sadder and more fanciful. They were just as terrible as her angry ones, but she kept them all because the growing pile of papers made her feel she was doing something besides vegetate.

She read a few magazines because they were piling up, and finally she began to read some of Libra's books. She liked history the best because she didn't have to relate it to anything in her life. It was another world. Libra had put reruns of all Mad Daddy's old shows on television, so she stopped watching TV early and began to get more sleep. The pills were wonderful. She tried not to think too much. The pills made her so stoned before she fell asleep that one night she wandered into the den and turned on Mad Daddy's midnight show. It made her hysterical and she took a bottle of Scotch and a glass and went wandering off along the beach by herself, drinking and sobbing, until she was lost.

She found herself in front of a house where a party was going on. People were running around the beach and in and out of the lighted house. A man saw her.

"Hey," he said. "Come join the party."

"Why not?"

She looked terrible: no make-up (she never wore any here) and all teary and red-eyed, wearing her nightgown, but she went in anyway. Everyone seemed young and tanned and pretty. They were wearing far-out clothes, and nobody seemed to notice or care that she was wearing a nightgown.

They thought it was just a hippie dress. She got some ice for the Scotch she had brought, found some cigarettes, and sat on the couch, trying to focus her eyes. Some men spoke to her and she smiled, trying not to act too stoned. There was loud music, and people were dancing. Someone asked her to dance and she refused, afraid she would get sick. She got up to find more ice and suddenly there was Dick Devere, on his way from another room, looking very tan and happy.

"Gerry!" He smiled with delight. "I didn't know you were in California. How long have you been here?"

"A little over five weeks, I think."

He put his arm around her. Was this Dick, whom she'd once loved? She hardly knew. "How are you, Gerry?" He didn't wait for her to answer. "I'm so happy. Everything is going so well for me. My film is going to be wonderful. I've been investing in the stock market, and I've made a bundle of money. I have a stock for you to buy, it's great . . ."

She drew away from him. He didn't know anything about what had happened to her, and if he did he wouldn't care. He went on babbling about his stock and how rich he was going to be. "I've bought a house in the Hills, and I have a Japanese houseboy," he went on. "I've always wanted a Japanese houseboy. I'm so happy. This is *my* year!"

"Good," she said absently, but he had already rushed away, leaving her standing there.

"That is a nightgown, isn't it?" someone said. She turned and saw a boy, not a bad-looking boy, just a boy. Some movie actor, she couldn't place him. She nodded. "Why don't you take it off?"

She moved away from him, into another room, which turned out to be the bedroom. The lights were dim in there, and she could see couples lying on the floor, and five people on the large bed. She thought at first they had all passed out; then she realized they were having sex, all of them, in pairs and groups. There was something singularly detached and dreamlike about their actions, not entirely the result of her foggy state—it was they who were out of it, not her. Naked, they looked like strange fish underwater, perhaps octopi. Music came from a speaker on the wall. A uniformed maid came in with food and drinks, passing among the bodies as if there was nothing unusual about it. An arm reached from the tangle on the bed and took a glass from the maid.

She had run away to find a desert island and she had found it; right here, except none of them seemed to know it.

Entwined, making occasional faint slurping and moaning sounds, they were as far away from each other as any shipwrecked person alone. It was odd how little it affected her, when only a year ago she had been shocked to discover Lizzie Libra going off into a bedroom at a party with Zak Maynard. But that had been people she knew . . . that had at least been two people who knew the other was alive.

The boy from the living room came up to her and kissed her on the ear. She recoiled, but he had his arm around her. She let him kiss her mouth, wondering if she would like it. It had been so long since she had felt a human touch, and she was so lonely . . . She felt nauseous and pulled away from him. He had little eyes, like a pig. He was nothing; just a body, a body that could die any minute. This room was more filled with death than the nightmare of her mind had been these past weeks, and these people were alive!

"Hey!" he said. He was drunk, or drugged, or both, and he was holding her nightgown. She heard it rip as she ran from him into the lighted living room, but she was still wearing it, it was just torn. He ran after her. "Hey!"

"You ripped my dress," Gerry said.

"Nightgown."

"It's a dress. Go away."

Another boy came up to her, trying to grab her, and she ran away from them into the bathroom. Three men were in there, standing in front of the large marble sink, fully dressed. They were so occupied with what they were doing that they didn't notice her. All three had their pants open and their penises out on the edge of the sink, measuring themselves and marking off the length with an eyebrow pencil. One man was short and he had to stand on his toes to get his equipment on the sink. The second man she recognized instinctively from his reflection in the mirror as another of those faceless super-beauties who roam the Sunset Strip waiting to be discovered as an overnight movie star. The third man was Dick Devere.

"I win," Dick said. "By nearly an inch, and it's not even fully hard yet." He began stroking himself.

"Let me do that," the would-be star said, and got down on his knees in front of Dick and took it in his mouth. Dick looked down and watched in bliss, his legs spread apart and his arms folded over his chest like the Jolly Green Giant.

Gerry stared at them, feeling that it was all totally unreal. The scene was like something from a dirty fresco in Pompeii—

this couldn't be the man she had loved, the super-romantic who broke so many girls' hearts ... But it was, it was Dick Devere. And all she felt was a little bit sick and a little bit sorry for him because now she suspected that no matter how much he had made those girls suffer, he was going to suffer even more for the rest of his life. She fled.

She ran out of the house, and when she was safely away she wandered the rest of the way home walking in the cold surf. The sounds and music faded away behind her. The other houses were quiet and dark, the way houses should be. The black sky over the ocean was filled with stars and a few lovely night clouds. Oh, Mad Daddy, Mad Daddy, where were you? Were you a star up there? She prayed to believe it was so. She would pick a star and it would be him, watching over her forever.

When she saw her house in the distance she was glad to see it. It seemed like *her* house now, a peaceful haven. It wasn't lonely or frightening any more. The star shone serenely overhead. When she got to the house she wanted to write another poem, about the star, but she was too dizzy, so she fell into bed and was asleep instantly.

"What day is it?" she asked the housekeeper the next morning.

"May twenty-third."

"*May?*" She'd been there longer than she'd thought. She tried to think of something to say to the housekeeper, to keep her there for a moment more. "How do you like working for Mr. Libra?"

"It's a job. Is the egg all right? Too soft?"

"No, it's fine. How long have you worked for him?"

"Since my husband died."

"When was that?"

"Oh, six years ago next December."

It was hard to think of conversation after so long, and the woman evidently wasn't eager to talk. "I guess it's boring here all alone," Gerry said.

"No. I have friends."

"I don't know much about him," Gerry said.

"Who?"

"Mr. Libra."

The housekeeper smiled. She was a plump middle-aged woman. "I don't know much about him either, and I've known him all my life."

"You have?"

"Oh, didn't you know? I'm his sister."

"His sister?" She sounded so dumb, just repeating everything.

"Sam takes care of his family," the housekeeper said. Gerry couldn't decide if the woman sounded bitter or proud.

"He takes care of me, too," Gerry said. "That was nice of him, wasn't it?"

"Who knows what's nice and what's guilt?"

"I'm not his girl friend, if that's what you're thinking."

"Who said girl friend? People can feel guilty about some people and be nice to other people to make up for it." The woman shrugged.

"Who does he feel guilty about?"

"Don't ask me. I don't run around in his circles. Believe me, I wouldn't live in New York if you paid me. I lived a beautiful life for twenty-two years with the same man, I have two married daughters, I don't hang around with show people. Who knows what he does in New York?"

Who, indeed? Gerry thought.

The housekeeper took the breakfast tray. "Why don't you take the car and go for a ride? It's not good for a young girl to stay cooped up here day after day. Go ahead, I don't need it. It's not good to sit and think all the time; it makes you morbid. Go sightsee a little. California is beautiful." She left the room, humming: a woman who had done her good deed for the day by dispensing advice, and therefore had made the world a little bit brighter. *I bet he would pay her not to live in New York,* Gerry thought. *He does!*

She dressed and took Libra's car, which she had never driven, and drove down the Pacific Coast Highway, looking for the supermarket the housekeeper (no, it was Libra's sister, she'd have to start thinking of her as his sister now, but it was impossible: they were so unlike), the *housekeeper* always went to. It must be in the other direction. She found a piece of beach with kids surfing, and she went to sit there, watching them. They looked happy, and they made her feel happy just watching them, even though none of them noticed her. They must think she was an older woman. She bought a hot dog and a Coke and ate them on the beach. What a bore the beach was! Why hadn't she realized it before? She was so tan she looked like Silky. She couldn't *get* any darker, so why roast? She'd never much liked swimming, except to cool off. She wouldn't dream of surfing—you could drown or get a tooth knocked out. *I sound like Libra,* she thought, and

laughed. She realized she missed Libra. She wondered who he
had hired in her place, and if the girl was as good as she was.
She wondered if he missed her.

That night Vincent called, collect.

"I told you not to call," Gerry said.

"It's *collect*. I miss you. What are you doing?"

"Nothing. Resting."

"Is it boring?"

"Sort of."

"Well, it's boring here," Vincent said. "I got the air conditioner fixed because it broke again. We had a hot day. The
man said this is the last time he can fix it and you'd better
get another."

What do I need another for? Gerry thought. *I'm never
coming home.* "What else is new?" she said.

"I got some pictures taken. I'm sending you one. I met this
writer, he's gay, his name is Mr. Emerald, and he says they're
making a movie of one of his books and he wants me to read
for the boy. It's sort of an effeminate boy, like me."

"You're not to read for any effeminate boys!" Gerry said.
"Do you want to blow your whole career before you even
start? I don't want you to come out until you're hatched.
Next year, *next year*, when you've finished growing up, I'm
going to make you a sex symbol. I don't want you identified
with any fruits."

"Well, Gerry, I can't *do* anything without you," Vincent
said, pathetically but not whining. "I don't know what to do
unless you're here to tell me. I need you."

"You just stay there and do what I told you. Tell him you
can't read for the part. Promise me."

"All right. But he says I'd be perfect."

"How many effeminate-boy parts do you think there are in
the movies?" she said, angry. "One? Two? Do you want to
work or not?"

"Of course I want to."

"Then you'll wait. You can play plenty of college boys—
next year. Maybe even this winter. Send me that picture."

"Okay. I'll mail it tomorrow. When are you coming home?
I miss you."

"You'd better say good-bye—this is costing Mr. Libra a lot
of money. Thanks for calling. I'll write to you."

"Good-bye," Vincent said sadly.

"Good-bye. I miss you too, you silly thing. You know I do.
Be good. Send me the picture."

She hung up. The hell with him. She wasn't his mother. She was through with the business. She made herself a big Scotch and soda and went into the projection room. There was an old movie she remembered seeing one night and she wanted to run it again. It would be great as a remake, updated a little. The lead would be perfect for Vincent. A pretty, rather shallow, innocent-looking college boy who turned out to be a psychopathic killer. Who would ever suspect Vincent with his sweet face and soft voice? Perfect offbeat casting ... next year, of course. Not that she would ever get involved in any project like that, or any project at all, for that matter, ever again. She was through.

The next few days passed in a boring haze of sun, naps, her poems (they were worse than terrible! she decided, and really getting juvenile because she seemed to have run out of ideas), and half-hearted dips in the ocean. She felt as though her brain had become baked by the sun. It was hard to think of anything. Libra's books bored her. Magazines bored her. She'd seen all the films in Libra's film library at least twice. It was getting hot in California now, and she took long drugged naps. She was running out of tranquillizers and sleeping pills and decided to try to get along without them. She was becoming a vegetable anyway, with no one but that grouchy woman to talk to. She watched the neighbors on either side, and they seemed very domestic, with children and children's friends, barbecues on their front lawns ... very dull. She asked the housekeeper how to get to the supermarket and discovered there was a shopping center. She drove there.

There was a stationery store, so she stopped in and bought a copy of *Variety*. The newspapers were boring, what with all the fuss about the forthcoming elections and the conventions. It would be good to read about something else for a change. There was also a beauty parlor, so she went in and had her hair trimmed, the sun-bleached ends snipped off.

"Your hair is sick," the man said.

"Sick?"

"Sick from the sun. You must have a conditioning treatment. Your hair is human, too, you mustn't make it sick."

Shades of Mr. Nelson. What had ever happened to Mr. Nelson?

"I've never seen you here before," the man said, slathering some ill-smelling goo on her hair. "Do you live around here?"

Where *did* she live? "I'm visiting," she said.

"Now the heating cap. I've never seen such terrible sick hair. I will make it well."

Now he sounded like Ingrid the Lady Barber-Doctor. What had happened to Ingrid? Probably still giving poor Libra his shots.

"Oh, *Variety*. Are you in show business?"

"No."

"Your husband?"

"This isn't a wedding ring," Gerry said. Her heart turned over and she covered Mad Daddy's forget-me-not ring with her other hand. Still ... where was the sharp pain she had become accustomed to every time she looked at the ring? Gone. A dull ache, which would always be there, but the terrible stabbing pain was gone. She opened *Variety* so the man would go away.

She told him not to bother setting her hair, and just let it dry straight. She thought she looked dowdy. She was getting hopeless. But who was here to see her? After the beauty parlor she went to the liquor store and looked around, but she was tired of Scotch. Scotch was medicine, for pain. She hated the taste. She bought two bottles of champagne.

When she got back to the house the housekeeper said there had been a long-distance call from New York. *Oh God, Vincent again,* Gerry thought. But it wasn't Vincent; it was Silky.

"How *are* you?" Gerry said.

"Fine. How are you?"

"Okay ..."

"I'll tell you why I called," Silky said. "Libra says you're still working for him, even though you say you're not, so I just thought you'd like to know I've quit him."

"When? Why? Where are you going?"

"Oh, all the agencies are after me—I'll decide after I've talked to a few of them. I only quit old Libra today." She sounded much different, surer of herself, even though she still had the same soft voice.

"What happened?"

"Well, you know, Gerry, I'm just sick and tired of the way that man treats me. He's never for one minute treated me as if I'm a human being. Even my wedding ... well, that was nice of him and we're grateful, but it was really like I'm something he owns that he was showing off, something he created. He doesn't think I have any brains at all. He thinks

I'm *dumb*. If I didn't have talent in the first place, I don't care how hard he would have pushed me . . . well, that's water over the bridge. Anyway, Bobby and I have gotten very interested in politics. It's our country after all—we're the people under twenty-five, it's up to us to do something to make it better. That's what I tried to explain to Mr. Libra. I just wanted to endorse McCarthy, that's all. Somebody asked me, because I'm a name, so I said sure. I was going to sing at a rally to raise money. Everybody's doing it for somebody. Well, Libra went crazy. He was so mad he was running around screaming and yelling, like he always does but worse, and he said I don't belong in politics, that a star can't have opinions, that *I'm* too stupid to have opinions, that I have no right . . . all that crap. And all of a sudden I just got fed up with him. I wasn't afraid of him any more. I realized he only makes me unhappy and I can't work with him any more. So I quit."

"Wow."

"What do you think?"

"I'm surprised."

"No, I mean what do you think about what he said?"

"Well . . . I think he was wrong."

"I knew you'd understand," Silky said. "You have no idea how good I feel to be rid of him. When are you coming home?"

"Soon, I think," Gerry lied.

"Good. Call me as soon as you get in and come have lunch at the apartment. I've fixed it up a little and it's cute. I miss you."

"I miss you, too. Thanks for calling me."

They hung up. Gerry lit a cigarette. *Libra really blew it this time*, she thought. *I could have kept Silky. She'd work for me.*

My God, she thought. She stubbed out the cigarette after one puff. For the first time since she'd come to California she felt alive, interested in something. How could Libra have been so stupid? He thought he was the only one who could change people, Geppetto the puppet-maker, and he never realized that life changed people, and that they could also change themselves. He'd been so sure of himself that he'd never even bothered to look at Silky and see that she was changing into a woman; she wasn't his little girl from the gutter any more. She hadn't been that for ages.

I thought it was the life I hated, Gerry thought, *but it wasn't* the *life that dealt me a blow, it was just life. Mad Daddy could just as easily have been hit by a car, God forbid, or had a heart attack. I could have been engaged to an account-ant and he could have been mugged. But if it wasn't for my job I might have been engaged to an accountant, or to nobody, because I never would have met Mad Daddy at all. I wouldn't have not met him and not loved him for anything. I can't blame the business for the bad thing that happened to me . . . but I can thank it for a lot of the good things. I can't stay here and rot another minute. Whatever else is meant for me, I can't let this be my life.*

She went into the kitchen and told the housekeeper to chill one of the bottles of champagne and bring it to her in the bedroom. Waste not, want not. Then she called the airline for a reservation on the midnight flight to New York that would get her there in the morning, and she started to pack.

She had forgotten how lovely New York was on a spring morning. Central Park was getting green, the days would be long again, the air sometimes even smelled good. Vincent (whom she'd called from California before she caught the plane) had actually cleaned the apartment for her return, and even waxed the floors. He had hung a new eleven-by-fourteen photo of himself on the wall with Scotch tape (he wouldn't dream of spending his own money for a frame) and under it he had printed VINCENT STONE. He was halfway to paradise now: never to be mistaken for a girl again, more easily to be taken for a very handsome young man—perhaps not too virile yet, but no more asexual than a lot of other boys she'd seen walking hand in hand with their equally asexual girl friends. No . . . he was more sexual than they were . . . Bonnie's cuddly, animal quality lingered; he would be sexy whoever he was. She watched him while he cooked breakfast, so pleased and gratified by the changes in his appearance that she could hardly take her eyes off him.

"How do I look?" Vincent asked. "What do you think of me?"

"I'm thrilled. I don't know whether to thank nature or me."

"It's both," Vincent said, flexed a bicep, and giggled.

"Don't ever giggle," she said. "Please."

"Haw, haw, haw," Vincent said, very *basso profundo*, and then they both giggled.

Gerry tossed her clothes out of the suitcase onto the bed so they would not be too wrinkled, took a quick shower, and called the office to say she would be in at ten thirty.

She liked the new office building because she had never seen it before, it had no memories, it would be a new start. Everything was very modern and spotless, with the smell of new paint. The glass doors to the reception room had a small astrological sign painted on them, the scales, and above them: LIBRA, in gold letters. It occurred to her that Libra probably wasn't his real name, that he might have invented Sam Leo Libra just as he had invented all his clients. There was so much she still didn't know about the man, even after all this time. She was going to have to try to know him better now. It would be interesting.

Libra came out, in immaculate silky gray, his maroon hair damp and glistening, his skin smelling faintly of a cologne that was like freshly cut grass. He gave her a great smile (oh, beautiful King Kong, foolish, pig-headed genius!) and said: "It's about time."

He showed her the office which was to be hers, unfurnished except for a telephone and a horrid metal desk (*that* would have to be replaced) and took her into his office to talk.

"That nitwit I hired while you were gone is driving me crazy," he said. "You're lucky. But she's too pretty to fire, so I'm keeping her on to do some of the dull secretarial work so you'll have more time for the important things."

Gerry knew him well enough now to know he was leading up to something—he never gave something for nothing. She waited, smiling a pretty thank you.

"Silky's left me," he said.

"I know."

"Oh?"

"She called me last night in California."

"Good," he said. "You're still friends. Coffee?"

"Please."

He poured her a cup of coffee and she noticed that his office was much like his old office had been, with expensive, tasteful accessories, flowers, and the free breakfast assortment on a table. Sylvia Polydor's picture hung over the black leather couch.

"When are you going to see Silky?" he asked.

"Probably this week. I'm to call her."

"You call her now and see her today. I want you to get he
back."

"I don't think I can."

"Of course you can," Libra said. "You're her best frienc
You can get her back on the basis of your friendship. Te
her how hurt you are that she's left the office."

"I can't do that," Gerry said. "I'm sorry she's left, but
think you were wrong to speak to her the way you did. Yo
can't keep hurting people and expect them to keep takin
it."

Libra glared. "And me? What about me? Don't I g
hurt? Am I inhuman? I am *very* hurt at Silky's ingratitud
Without me she'd be nothing. I made her. All those sta
think that when they get big they can turn around and do
all on their own. They don't know how fast they'll com
running back whimpering for advice. She's doing a stup
thing, a stupid thing."

"Nobody likes to be called stupid all the time," Gerry sa
mildly.

"So she took something the wrong way. She's probabl
under the influence of that hustler she married. Next thin
he'll be wanting to be her manager. He'll *ruin* her. You hav
to go to her and explain the facts of life ... sweetly,
course, as you do so well."

"What do you want me to tell her?"

"To come back, because she's your friend and you're h
friend. You know what to do."

"Would you be willing to apologize?" Gerry asked.

"No. But you can apologize for me. That's one of t
things I pay you for."

"All right—I'll try."

"You can do it. Oh, by the way. . . ."

She stopped at the door and turned.

"You'd better start looking for office furniture ar
things," Libra said. "Charge them to me, I take it off r
taxes."

"Thank you." *Thank you for nothing,* she thought, know
ing it was just a bribe. She went into her office and call
Silky, and arranged to see her at one thirty.

Funny, Gerry thought as she went to Silky's apartme
she and Silky probably were each other's best friend, b
neither of them had been to the other's apartment, ever.
this business the people you worked with became your be

friends, and sometimes it was the other way around, but how little they bothered to know about each other's private lives! *When I get Silky back,* she thought ... *No, if I get her back ... we'll have to start to know each other better on* all *levels.*

Silky and Bobby were waiting for her in the apartment, a star-type place with a terrace. They really were a stunning couple, no matter what Libra thought of Bobby, and they seemed to love each other very much.

"Coffee or champagne?" Silky said.

"Whatever you're having."

"Sha, let's have champagne; you're back."

Bobby brought a bottle from the refrigerator, opened and poured it. *He's very fetch-and-carry,* Gerry thought, *but definitely the man in this house.* She didn't know how to begin saying what she had come to say.

"What did Libra say?" Silky asked.

"About you?"

"Yes."

"Well," Gerry said, "he's very sorry and he apologizes."

"You *bet* he's sorry," Bobby said.

"I'm in a funny position," Gerry said. "Libra feels terrible about your falling-out and wants you back, and naturally I feel terrible about losing you, too, because you're my best friend. I think you're absolutely right to object to the way Libra treats you, but on the other hand I think our office is in the best position to help you because we're so good. If you did consider coming back to us I can promise you that I'll be the buffer between you and Libra and see that he never mistreats you again."

Silky shook her head and looked at Bobby.

"I'm going to tell you the facts of life," Bobby said to Gerry. "Do you want to listen?"

"Sure."

"Okay. First of all, if you're Silky's friend, you'll be her friend whether or not she comes back to the office, right?"

"Right."

"Okay. Now, what Silky needs right now is not a friend, she needs a manager. If you're willing to be Silky's manager, then she'll sign with *you,* not with Libra, with you. That means *you,* not Libra, not you fronting for Libra—*you.* You know what to do, you've had enough experience. She trusts you. But she wants a separate contract, with *you.* Her contract with Libra has run out, so you're in the clear."

"I think he'd kill me," Gerry said. She drank her champagne and Bobby poured more.

"This is a tough business, girl," Bobby said. "This isn't a business for friends; it's for business people. Life is tough. You have to have guts or you're nowhere. You can't be a little girl forever, expecting people to be nice because they like you. That isn't business, that's social life. You have to grow up. You have to be tough."

"That's true," Silky said. She held out her empty glass and Bobby filled it.

"I think you can be tough," Bobby said. "You're just too used to doing other people's work for them without taking any credit. If you can be tough enough to handle Silky's career, and do a good job, then sign her yourself. Otherwise she goes to another agency. There's your choice."

I like him, Gerry thought. *He's going to go somewhere and he knows it. I can't lose Silky. I'd be a fool if I did. He's right. I can handle Silky and Vincent, and Bobby too, and then if Libra kills me I can have my own clients and start my own agency. I think I'm going to be sick.*

"What do you say?" Silky said.

"Do you want to sign with me?"

"Yes."

"All right. I'll sign you. To me, not to Libra."

"Great!" Silky said. They shook hands. Gerry stopped feeling sick and began to feel excited.

"Bobby—you don't have a manager yet, do you?" Gerry said.

"Not yet."

"Will you sign with me, too?"

"I'd be glad to."

"All right, it's a deal. But remember—this isn't two against one; I'm handling both your careers separately."

"You're learning," Bobby said approvingly, and they shook hands.

"I'll draw up the contracts this afternoon," Gerry said. "You'll give me the same percentage you formerly gave Mr. Libra."

"You're *really* learning," Bobby said, grinning. "Agreed."

"Agreed, Silky?"

"Absolutely."

They all shook hands again, a little high, and killed the bottle. Gerry made a dinner date with them for the end of the week, and went back to the office to face Libra.

Libra was waiting in his office. He had changed his suit and
his hair was damp. "You look pleased with yourself," he said.
"I take it she's coming back."

"Not exactly. She *is* coming back, but she's signing with
me. I'm sorry, but it's the best I could do. I'm also signing
Bobby La Fontaine."

"For what? I don't want him for my twelfth client."

"He won't be. He'll be my second client. Silky will be my
first."

Libra stood up, enraged. "*Your* client? What do you mean,
your client?"

"She said it was that or nothing. So it's that."

He thought for a minute and then sat down again. "I
suppose you're right. You have a good head. I don't mind;
you can handle her. She's gotten too obnoxious for me to
bother with anyway."

"The other thing is, I want Silky's thirty per cent commission. She's agreed."

"You're dreaming," Libra said.

"No I'm not."

"Then I'm dreaming. You didn't say that."

"I did. Silky's and Bobby's."

"Bobby you can have. He's nothing, he's nobody, you
can operate his career out of your desk drawer. But you
can't take Silky's commission! I've treated you just like a
daughter. I made you what you are today. What were you
before I gave you a chance—a two-bit flack?"

"A publicist," Gerry said calmly. "Thirty per cent."

"Look at everything I've done for you!"

"You're not my father and I'm not your daughter. That
was my salary, not my allowance. I'm handling Silky and
doing all the work, so I want the commission."

"Presents, cars, the use of my house . . ."

"I worked twelve hours a day. Sometimes more. Thirty per
cent."

"Fifteen. The other fifteen is mine for overhead, the use of
the office, the use of my *name*."

"Your name is the last thing Silky wants."

"You see how far you get in this business without my
name. Fifteen per cent."

"Twenty," Gerry said.

Their eyes locked. She felt nothing, no fear, no sickness,
no shaking; just a mild exhilaration at the contest. They were
two business people sitting down to a business conversation.

He wasn't Big Daddy Libra any more and never would be again.

"All right, twenty," Libra said.

"It's a deal," Gerry said, "For *now*."

Libra shook his head. "I've created Frankenstein's monster."

"And by the way," Gerry said, ignoring that, "while I was in California I had an idea for a package we can put together, a remake of a film I saw at your house. I'll check on the rights. There's a boy I want you to see. I think he'd be perfect."

"Who is he?"

"A client of mine. His name is Vincent Stone."

"All right, bring him in and I'll have a look at him. Vincent who?"

"Vincent Stone."

"You can't go picking up clients off the street," Libra said "That's no way to run a business."

"As you told me yourself," Gerry said, "that's how you got started." She smiled prettily at him and went back to her office to type up the contracts.

She buzzed the new secretary to bring in the standard forms, and typed in the changes that signed Silky, Bobby, and Vincent over to her as their publicist-personal manager. She found a rubber stamp in the desk drawer to stamp the squares where they would initial the changes. It looked a lot more professional than the piece of paper Libra had typed up himself the time he had signed Bonnie Parker, and she was pleased. Her first real clients!

She realized, then, that along with everybody else, except Libra who would never change, she had changed. She wasn't just an experienced assistant any more, she was a business person. It wasn't what she'd planned, or dreamed, or even thought life would be, but it wasn't bad, either. This wasn't the end, but the beginning. All this time she'd been working to make other people famous, but it had turned out to be her fame game too.

She found herself smiling. She'd do the office in blue and white, with a couple of kinky antiques from that place Dick had sent her to last year, and there was a Robert Indiana poster that said LOVE on it that would look nice over the couch. She certainly wasn't going to put an oil painting of Silky over it the way Libra had with Sylvia Polydor. That might make him froth at the mouth. But an eleven-by-fourteen photo of Silky framed on the wall would be nice, and one of Bobby, and she was sure Vincent had more of the one he'd hung in their apartment. When he got some money, Vincent would have to get his own apartment. She didn't want gossip. After all, everyone was supposed to think Vincent was a sex symbol, and it wouldn't do for him to be shacked up with his manager. Everyone would think he'd made it in the business because they were lovers, and that certainly wasn't the way *her* clients were going to get ahead.

FAWCETT CREST BOOKS
ON TOP WITH THE BIG BESTSELLERS

THE FAME GAME Rona Jaffe	M1477	95¢
THE KING'S PLEASURE Norah Lofts	M1478	95¢
THE PARABLES OF PEANUTS		
Robert L. Short	M1479	95¢
THE PROMISE Chaim Potok	P1449	$1.25
SIEGE IN THE SUN Dorothy Eden	M1450	95¢
MR. BRIDGE Evan S. Connell, Jr.	M1451	95¢
MRS. BRIDGE Evan S. Connell, Jr.	M1452	95¢
THE DAY OF THE DOLPHIN		
Robert Merle	M1438	95¢
COP! L. H. Whittemore	M1439	95¢
THE DEATH COMMITTEE Noah Gordon	M1444	95¢
SILENT SPRING Rachel Carson	M1455	95¢
ADA Vladimir Nabokov	P1409	$1.25
SUNDAY THE RABBI STAYED HOME		
Harry Kemelman	T1384	75¢
THE LOST QUEEN Norah Lofts	M1398	95¢
THE GODFATHER Mario Puzo	Q1388	$1.50
EXPENSIVE PEOPLE Joyce Carol Oates	M1408	95¢
THE WINTER PEOPLE Phyllis A. Whitney	T1377	75¢
THE VINES OF YARRABEE Dorothy Eden	M1365	95¢
COUPLES John Updike	P1252	$1.25

FAWCETT WORLD LIBRARY
Wherever Paperbacks Are Sold